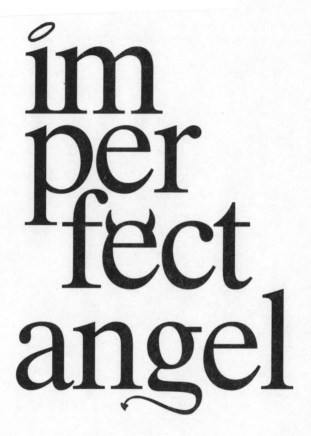

im
per
fect
angel

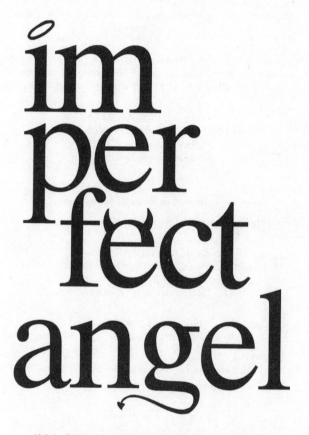

imperfect angel

USA TODAY BESTSELLING AUTHOR

CHRISTI BARTH

Entangled Publishing, LLC
644 Shrewsbury Commons Ave., STE 181
Shrewsbury, PA 17361
rights@entangledpublishing.com

Amara is an imprint of Entangled Publishing, LLC.

Visit our website at www.entangledpublishing.com.

Edited by Heather Howland
Cover illustration and design by Elizabeth Turner Stokes
Stock art by Dana Bogatyreva/Shutterstock
Interior design by Toni Kerr

ISBN 978-1-64937-211-6
Ebook ISBN 978-1-64937-225-3

Manufactured in the United States of America

First Edition October 2022

10 9 8 7 6 5 4 3 2 1

AMARA
an imprint of Entangled Publishing LLC

To my absolutely perfect angel of a husband.

CHAPTER ONE

Maisy Norgate had hoped for *some* presents for her thirtieth birthday, but a surprise inheritance hadn't even been on her Amazon wish list.

Neither was trying to find a parking spot in downtown Buffalo during rush hour.

Or the bonus surprise of a will reading at a lawyer's office.

Not for the first time since finding out she had an uncle she'd never known—followed by the news that he'd just died—curiosity tugged at the corner of Maisy's mind. Her parents had died years ago, leaving a scar on her heart that would never fade. But news of this unknown uncle who'd left her...*something*...gave Maisy hope that she hadn't lost every tangible reminder of her family.

What that reminder might be, she had no clue.

She stared at the unbroken line of parked cars. "Maybe I should've taken the bus."

"That's silly," the voice of her best friend, Liss, scoffed through the car's Bluetooth. "You need the car in case they hand over big boxes of treasure. Or even a diamond necklace. You can't wear diamonds on the *bus*, Maisy. Be sensible."

Maisy snorted. "I'm sure Uncle Harold didn't leave me anything like that."

"Where's your optimism? It *could* be a family heirloom. Why not a diamond necklace? You gotta dream big."

While finding the silver lining was usually Maisy's thing, dreaming big at this point was more along the lines of being able to quit *one* of her jobs. Besides, it felt wrong to be excited about getting anything from a more-or-less stranger.

"I never met the man," she reminded Liss. "Before three days ago, I didn't know I *had* an Uncle Harold. So even if my luck does a one-eighty and my surprise relative was a reclusive gajillionaire, why on earth would he leave his fortune to me?"

"Because you're awesome."

Aww. Maisy smiled as she gunned it into a space that wouldn't fit anything but her teensy aqua Mini Cooper. "You're my best friend. You're required to think that. And here's your requisite 'right back at ya.'"

"Okay, then, because dead uncles trying to make up for missing the past thirty years leave fortunes to their nieces?"

Which was the other confusing part of the whole situation.

Why *would* anyone wait to make contact until after they died? After skipping family holidays and hugs and having someone to remember your stories after it was all over? Her heart squeezed at the thought of those lost years.

No. It made more sense that Harold just hadn't wanted to bother keeping up with relatives. She was probably about to inherit an ugly vase or be tasked with cleaning out a hoarder-level house.

But a beautiful, undiscovered Monet *would* be awesome...

She craned her neck to look up at the brick building. Didn't even need to see the sign—its classic stodginess screamed "lawyer's office." Always fun to spot a stereotype in the wild. "Hey, I'm here, Liss."

"I wish you'd let me come with you."

Yeah, Maisy wished the same thing. She had a knee-jerk squeamishness about all things death-related. Didn't take a therapist to point that back to the manner in which she'd lost her parents, but being an emotional wimp wasn't enough reason to make her friend and roommate skip a lucrative waitressing shift.

"You came with me to the funeral. That was more than enough. Time for me to pull up my big-girl panties and do this all by myself."

"Call me after. Good luck!"

Needing a friend at her first funeral had been justifiable. Needing one to talk to a lawyer? While it absolutely freaked her out, this was what thirty-year-olds did: put on sensible black pants—*not* the patterned leggings she practically lived in—add a high-necked blouse to cover her tattoo, and play it supremely cool with the lawyer.

She did the requisite rearview-mirror check. Pale as a ghost, but that was her redhead complexion, not her nerves. Hair in a French braid completed the solemn mourner/inheritor look. And, yes, fake eyelashes rather than mascara on the off chance that the man did hand her a check for a million dollars and she burst into tears.

The elevator was tiny and ancient, and the gears wheezed with the effort of dragging her up to the fourth floor. The ominous noises did nothing to lighten the mood of a creepy will reading.

The stereotype continued when the elevator door slid open. The interior of Milton Turk, Esquire matched all the law offices on TV shows: dark wood, navy carpet, somber lighting. The receptionist's desk was empty. Too bad. Maisy had hoped to be offered coffee or a very elegant tea.

"Miss Norgate, come in." Turk, like his office, also matched the Hollywood version of an aged lawyer: short, pudgy, balding, bespectacled.

Maisy hesitated, one hand on her crossbody purse, hand-painted with colorful dragonflies. "Is it just me?"

He sniffed. "Yes. This isn't a Southern Gothic reading—no need for a crowd and drama."

Yup. He was just as brusque as when he'd introduced himself at the funeral. Good thing she wasn't *actually* all choked up about dear departed Uncle Harold. Sheesh.

She followed his impatient hand gesture down a short hallway into a bigger, darker room. The blinds were drawn against the afternoon sun. A small, green library-type desk lamp provided the only brightness. An enormous wood-and-leather chair creaked as he settled into it.

"Let's get right to it, shall we?"

Wow. She'd plugged the meter for a whole hour. Between the lack of coffee and his apparent need for speed, maybe she should ask for reimbursement of at least two-fifty.

There wasn't any official, parchment-y paper on his desk. "Where's the will?"

He tapped his monitor. "In here. It's the twenty-first century, Miss Norgate."

Okay, so not how it went on TV. "Darn. I was hoping for a big glob of red sealing wax at the bottom of some truly exquisite calligraphy."

"Sorry to disappoint. There's no need to read you the entire will." Turk opened his desk drawer. "Harold Sasson left you a specific bequest."

That sounded promising. But she didn't want to get excited about, oh, say, a diamond necklace, and then discover it really belonged to someone else.

"Are you sure about that? Me? Maisy Alexa Norgate? Thirty, MFA, type O positive? Because I still think you may have me confused with some *other* Maisy Norgate. If I had an Uncle Harold, I really think I would've known about it."

It'd been a closed-casket funeral. Maisy had no desire to look at a dead body, but she hadn't even been able to peek in and try to find a family resemblance.

His bushy eyebrows drew together into a scowl. "I assure you that I've done my due diligence. I can't explain away the vagaries of your familial relationships. Perhaps you should take it up with his sister. Your mother."

Flatly, Maisy said, "My mother's dead."

Turk looked confused by her curt response. "Didn't you say that Harold's service, two days ago, was your first funeral?"

Her temper pricked. Really? On top of being as warm as an iceberg, *that's* the part he focused on? Milton Turk, Esquire, was about to feel like a *jerk*.

"It *was* the first I've attended." Maisy sat up straighter. Curled her hands over the armrests. "When my parents were buried, I was in the hospital. Missed all the excitement and what I'm told was a stellar buffet."

Turk blinked. Fast. And abruptly cut eye contact with her.

"I do apologize. A lawyer should know better than to make assumptions. As I said, Harold was quite specific that this be handed over to you within three days of his funeral."

The way his hand scrabbled in the drawer, Maisy knew Liss would be disappointed with whatever he presented to her. No big box o' treasure. No briefcase of cash. Certainly no artwork.

Oh well. It'd been a fun fantasy.

He extracted something, then pushed what turned out to be a large key across the blotter onto the polished cherry desk.

Maisy waited for the lawyer to explain. It was far too big to unlock a house, unless that house was the size of Warwick Castle. Her trained artist's eye put it at a solid nine inches long. An antique-style skeleton key. Brass or pewter maybe? The ornate top part contained arrows and an infinity sign surrounded by curlicues. The bottom, where it jutted out to go into a lock, had more cutouts and zigzags than any key she'd ever seen. It'd take a magnifying glass to decipher the script etched along the shaft.

It was absolutely *beautiful*. Old. Exquisite craftsmanship. Possibly symbolic?

When Turk said nothing, she leaned over to see if anything else was coming out of the drawer. Maybe a box that it went to? "What does that open?"

He slammed the drawer shut. "I don't know, but it is yours now."

What? She tapped his monitor, hoping the will was at least pulled up on the screen so he'd get the symbolism of her gesture. "Isn't there a note explaining it?"

"No."

"I don't understand. My supposed Uncle Harold—"

Turk drilled a finger onto his blotter to cut her off. "He's definitely your uncle. You've got to accept that at this point."

It still seemed improbable. "A man who never contacted me, not even after my parents were killed, gave no indication at any point that he knew or cared I existed, made a point of *paying* for the time of a lawyer to draft a will only to leave me a mystery key?"

"I can't attest to most of what you just presumed. But yes, he drafted the will and stipulated that I had to make personal contact with you to hand this over within a set time period."

Why? That was the question doing zoomies around Maisy's skull. "Have you been to his house? Was he a collector? Is this sentimental? Or does it unlock the world's biggest mailbox somewhere?" It *had* to be important. Meaningful?

With a huff to indicate just how much she was trying his patience, Turk said, "Miss Norgate, I have nothing more to share with you. Simply a form you must sign to attest that you are taking possession of the bequest." He got up to pull a page off the stack of folders on the bookcase.

Maisy hesitated. Yes, she always appreciated the thought behind a gift, even if the gift was weird or the wrong size. The gesture mattered more than the actual thing.

But in this case...

The more she thought about it, the angrier she was that the man had the audacity to reach out to her only after he'd died. Well, hurt, too. She'd needed family after her parents passed, and she'd had no one. Her found family, especially Liss, was fantastic, but an uncle would have been amazing.

He'd denied her that.

She glanced at the key, and goose bumps raced up her spine. There was a…pull. Like a ghost was nudging her forward, urging her to pick up the key.

Ridiculous. She and Liss had comfort-binged *Chilling Adventures of Sabrina* over the weekend. Clearly the eight episodes of witches and hellscapes was at least one episode over her limit.

Fine. She reached for the key.

It didn't budge.

Frowning, she had to work to get it off the desk, like when cards get stuck to the table. It was surprisingly heavy. It couldn't possibly unlock anything. You couldn't carry this around in a pocket.

Ouch.

Guess she'd figured out what it unlocked—her skin. Blood oozed from where she'd snagged open her thumb on the sharp edge at the bottom.

Turk slid the signature page under her hand, catching the first drip. Maisy winced. What could be creepier than signing an official document in a smear of her own blood?

Maybe she deserved the cut for being ungrateful. It wasn't a diamond necklace, but it was *something*. From family. The first present from family she'd received in seventeen years. And now she had an excuse to slap on one of the Disney Princess Band-Aids Liss gave as a stocking stuffer last year.

CHAPTER TWO

Wings fully extended, Rhys Boyce burst through Alamere Falls. They made sure to fly low so beachgoers wouldn't panic over the three men that *jumped* down the waterfall. Their wings were fully visible for the instantaneous transition between the falls in Buffalo and here, but as soon as they crossed the waterline, the *Nephilim* were able to make them translucent.

Since it was past midnight, the beach below was empty.

Good.

Alamere Falls was one of only two in California that emptied directly into the ocean. It was fun to fly full out across the moon-dappled waves for a few seconds before turning inland. And then Rhys *pumped* it.

Gideon caught up to him in less than a mile. "What's your rush? The demon infestation's been going for a week. Us putting on the speed won't make any difference. Except we'll be tired before the fighting even starts."

Maybe *he* would be. Not Rhys.

Not that he'd admit, anyway. "Lazy, Gid? Or finally ready to admit that you have to work to keep up with me?"

After a long whistle, Gideon said, "Trash talk *and* speed? Who pissed you off? I mean, I assume it was Zavier, because that's always a solid choice."

They split apart to avoid a cell tower. Then a second, because this section of the California coast was full of them. Freaking tech companies.

But flying low was still safer to stay off of radar. Right now, they could be taken for large birds. Go higher, and an intel officer looking to get ahead might start tracking three things in a flight path way too high up for birds.

Rhys twisted sideways to check on Zavier. His black-and-silver wings melded perfectly with the dark night and the clouds. All Rhys could see was the shine of his fighting leathers and the thick silver chain wrapped around his wrist. He flew in a wavy line. Not because they were being followed or attacked, but because he *always* stayed on the defense.

That's how they'd been trained.

As part of the elite fighting force to protect humanity from creatures of Hell.

And even though they'd quit the Order, that was no reason to abandon the training that'd kept them alive this long. Because they still hunted evil. They were troubleshooters for the supernatural world. Fixers that kept humans safe without ever revealing that demons and angels existed.

"Don't blame Z for my mood. You can be just as much of a pain in the ass as him."

Gideon laughed. Unapologetically. "Right back at ya."

That was the comfort of living and working side by side with someone for a literal lifetime. The insults and honesty could fly without any offense being taken. No matter what was said, Gideon would have his back in tonight's fight, as Rhys would have his.

"Yeah, I'm pissed. You and Z skipped out on the meeting with the reps from the longshoremen's union." The three of them were equal partners in their shipping company. Today, though, his so-called partners had left him alone to face the angry horde.

"We told you we wanted to go for a run. Sunny April day. In Buffalo." Gideon flew a lazy, laughing circle around him. "*Gather *ye rosebuds while ye may.*"

Both of these men were closer to him than brothers, but there were times they worked on his patience with the irritation of sand on an oyster. "You think quoting a seventeenth-century poet will make me stop being pissed at you?"

"I think it was a lighthearted attempt to take the stick out of your ass." Gideon's effort to soften his words by beaming a smile? Yeah, that only worked on the human women who gaped at his blond good looks.

It didn't work on Rhys.

He'd seen that golden hair covered in mud, blood—human and demon—and worse. And he'd had Gid's trademark smile tossed his way right before the man tossed him over his shoulder and off the side of a damned mountain in their combat training.

Rhys didn't fall for Gideon's tricks anymore. Not after eighty-plus years of living and fighting by his side.

He consulted the GPS on his watch. Corrected their angle. "Can't we fight first and talk never?"

Moonlight spilled a corona behind Gideon's blond hair as he shook his head. The illusion of the halo they'd never have as only *half* angels. "I need to know where your head's at if my life's at stake. Which it'll be, if you start swinging that sword without being focused."

"Fair enough."

They flew on for a few minutes in the darkness. Only the soft swoosh of their wings broke the silence. It'd be peaceful—if they weren't on their way to kick some demon ass.

Houses and shopping centers gave way to clusters of office buildings. They were almost to their target. Which suited Rhys just fine.

He needed a good fight. They hadn't been on a mission in three weeks. Which always made him antsy. Snarly. Made him wonder what big trouble was brewing.

This request for their assistance from a company that made

apps couldn't have come at a better time.

Did he care about the chaos the demons had sown in the Everywhere365 app that apparently tracked your family? No. Rhys thought the app was creepy. Why did you need to have twenty-four seven surveillance on your nearest and dearest? But was he thrilled that a savvy witch on the company's development team had recognized that their programming was virus-free but rather infested by demons?

Hell, yes.

Zavier was charging double for the three of them to drop everything and come out same day. So he was happy about this mission, too.

Z didn't need the money. He just liked knowing he'd gotten the edge on someone. Winning an extra twenty dollars at poker with the crew at the docks. Charging a coven—who *knew* better—double for catching an accidentally summoned wolf demon. Both ends of the spectrum gratified him equally.

Gideon was less so. He'd had to cancel a date for tonight. The man had a date for every day of the week, so Rhys had ordered him to suck it up. He knew Gid's objections were mostly for show. They all enjoyed a good battle, and it had been at least a couple of decades since they'd fought monkey demons.

Keeping it fresh...

Zavier came up beside him. "How about we not alert the little shits that we're coming to kill them? Could we get some stealth going? Or did you two want to blow off this doubly lucrative mission and finish this conversation over beers in the Mission District?"

Shit.

Z was right.

He checked his watch. Then he pointed at the multistory pentagonal building, its roof covered in trees and bushes and flowers. The center courtyard was open to the sky.

"That's where we go in. No need to hunt them. Monkeys are

curious. As soon as the demons sense our energy, they'll come find us. Be ready."

"We've been ready since we left Buffalo," Gideon shot back. "*You* be ready."

Rhys gritted his teeth as they landed. Pulled his sword from its scabbard and bent his knees, ready to attack. "You bet. I'm ready to prove my superiority. To assert my Heaven-given powers over a being of Darkness. To stand up for right and defend that which the humans have painstakingly designed."

"Oh, for fuck's sake." Zavier's eyes were mere slits of black as he unwound the heavy chain around his wrist. He swung it wide, arcing it against the concrete to make sparks flash. "Are you ready to fight?"

"Yeah."

So ready.

"On your left!" Gideon yelled.

Rhys leaped into the air, his wings giving him an extra six feet of thrust as he spun left. Sure enough, that took him up and over the hissing monkey that clawed at the space where he'd been.

He slashed down with his sword. The damned thing skittered away, demonically fast. Zavier grunted out a laugh. "At least they can't fly."

"Of course they can't fly. This is real life, not *Wicked*." They'd laughed way too hard in the wrong places at that show. Clearly the production staff of the hit musical had someone with paranormal abilities, because there really *were* green demons. Monkey demons. Human-sized talking goats.

Not flying didn't mean the monkeys couldn't use their tails and climb up the window-washing scaffolding to jump down onto the *Nephilim*. Annoying, frisky little screechers. Dangerous, too. If they landed on your wings and took a bite—which they loved to do—they were hard to get off. You couldn't swing your sword at your own wings without risking a slice.

So this fight to take down the nest had an added layer of difficulty. Rhys had to constantly keep eyes on Gid and Zavier, too, to make sure their wings stayed clear.

They'd started out back-to-back in this courtyard until a monkey leaped from the trees along the roof's edge of the office building and landed right in the center of them.

San Francisco and their green roofs. Good for the environment, sure, but also a good place to harbor demon nests. If there hadn't been a witch on the payroll putting the pieces together, this thing would've gotten out of control in a matter of weeks. Dozens of companies would've been affected.

"What the hell!" Gideon yelled. "I can't tell what their next move will be."

Yeah.

Rhys had noticed it, too. *Nephilim* were trained to be able to anticipate their opponent's moves. Trained in so many fighting styles and martial arts combat techniques from around the world and through the centuries. It usually gave them a serious advantage in battle.

Not tonight, however.

"Chaos demons, remember? That *is* their move." The little fuckers disrupted the frequency. They scrambled energies—from cell phones and apps to nervous systems. Guess they'd had *way* more fun once technology took off.

"It's confusing as fuck," Zavier huffed as he stumbled backward, narrowly avoiding a swipe of extended claws.

Because—hello—monkey *demons*. Their teeth and claws injected venom in their prey.

Usually it was no big deal to limp home from a fight with a cut or five. Tonight, though, a single scratch could be deadly. Their fighting leathers covered most of their body, but their wings were vulnerable—and an enormous, easy target.

This wasn't working.

Which was unacceptable on several levels.

The client needed their app to work again. The *Nephilim* wanted their fee and, more to the point, *didn't* want word to get out around the paranormal world that they'd lost a fight. Especially to a mere animal.

He wouldn't stand for it.

"We're not losing this fight," he ground out between gritted teeth.

"Right now?" Zavier punted a monkey with his steel-toed boot, sending it back up onto the roof. It sprayed an arc of piss as it soared through the air. All three of them scrambled to avoid it. Even if it turned out not to be venomous? It was *gross.* "We kind of are."

The monkeys tightened into a circle in the opposite corner. They chittered at one another. And screeched menacingly across the courtyard at the *Nephilim*, baring their teeth.

Rhys eyed the scaffolding. Normally they tried to disrupt the human environment as little as possible.

Normally, they weren't getting their asses handed to them by creatures who didn't even carry weapons.

He buried the tip of his sword into the wood shavings around a tulip bed. "New plan."

"Thank God." Gideon wiped his forehead with the back of his forearm.

"Do everything wrong."

Zavier gave him another squint of a glare. "That's not a plan."

"You fight chaos *with* chaos." Rhys launched into the air to plant his boots along the top of the scaffolding. He kicked it over. The wooden pieces shattered against the concrete. And the steel framework was no longer an advantage for the monkeys.

"Ignore all our training." Gideon sheathed his sword. Pulled out three throwing stars instead. Skepticism laced his words thicker than the fog would be on the Pacific in a few hours. "Not to mention years of experience."

"Exactly. Be erratic." He felt his mouth stretch into a smiling grimace. This would be epic. "Have fun."

"Aren't you the serious one? Have you been possessed?"

"Not yet." Not at all, if his plan worked. "How about we kill these demons to make sure that doesn't happen?"

Zavier lifted a marble bench overhead. Shook it as though it was headed straight for the cluster of monkeys. When they scattered, Gideon already had his throwing stars in motion, headed to puncture those that went left.

And in a beautiful theater of misdirection, Zavier canted his body forward but sent the bench flying to the right and slightly behind them. It caught three monkeys that had shimmied down the drainpipe from the roof.

Rhys let out a whoop. He knew they'd find a way to win.

They always did.

"Keep it up! Ten more to go!" He ran forward, tucked into a somersault, holding his wing tips, and rolled right through two of them. As he straightened out of it, he grabbed their tails and threw them against the glass of the atrium. Green-and-orange blood dripped down the formerly clean windows, then burst into flames.

Huh.

That'd be a *lot* less cleanup. Most demons weren't helpful enough to self-destruct once killed. This was turning out better than expected.

Which, in his experience, just promised that something shitty was on the horizon.

Rhys flew low over the ocean, looking for a big wave. Nothing better than salt water to wash off all vestiges of demonic energy. "Send the full mission report to Master Caraxis, Z." He aimed himself straight at a ten-footer, grateful for the storm churning up the water.

When he came out the other side, Zavier was already there, waiting with a scowl that there was just enough moonlight between the clouds to make visible. "Paperwork talk already? Can't we just freaking enjoy the rush of the win for an hour?"

"Of course." Rhys still felt it, too. The thrumming in his blood. The urge to find something else to fight, to keep the adrenaline pulsing. "But the last time we fought the monkey demons, there were only two. A nest's a whole different skill set. The others can learn from our strategy."

"Since when do we worry about the *others*?" Zavier spat the word out like a curse.

Not this again. "We're all on the same team, Z. Fight evil. Keep humans safe. Pretty short mission statement." They both arrowed straight up to sluice the water off their wings.

When they were high enough to spot the Golden Gate Bridge in the distance, Zavier grumbled, "We split with the *Right and Holy Seraphic Order of the Nephilim* for a reason."

"We have this same fight every time. Every time for the last twenty-five years." And given the extended life expectancy of *Nephilim*, along with Zavier's determination to hold a grudge, they'd still be having it decades from now. "Give it up, Z. Staying in touch with Caraxis keeps us safe, too. Information flows both ways."

Below them, Gideon was treating the waves like an obstacle course, curving in and out of them like a snake.

He didn't want Zavier to stay in his bad mood. Not after such a great win. "C'mon. Once we're home, we'll do a quick sweep of the city. See if there's any trouble left to be cleaned up tonight."

"Like a dessert course to our battle."

Rhys laughed so hard that he dropped ten feet before catching himself. Zavier was dark. Brooding. Snarly. The fiercest warrior of the three of them, but the man's Achilles' heel was his sweet tooth. His lens on the world was always through how fast it would get him to cake, how close, or how it could be equated to something with frosting.

They flanked Gideon. Pointed at Alamere Falls. Then all three of them flew straight at the ribbon of water crashing over the high cliff...

...and came out seconds later through Niagara Falls. The American Falls, instead of the bigger Horseshoe, so they wouldn't be tempted to just hunker down in their Watchtower behind the falls.

A quick turn over Goat Island had them flying straight downriver. It was three in the morning. No worries about being spotted, especially with their wings being translucent and wearing all black. Gideon tugged on the dark knit cap he always carried to cover his bright hair on a flight. The time in the air was exactly what they needed after the battle.

Although Z would no doubt say that what *he* needed was a stop at the twenty-four-hour donut shop near SUNY.

As if he'd read his mind, Z was there in front of them. "Donuts?"

Laughing, they came together to bump fists.

Which meant they were all touching when power rippled through them. The force sent them hurtling outward.

Gideon came out of his somersault first. "Whoa."

Zavier popped his knives into his palms while he was still free-falling. "What the hell?"

Then it was gone.

It was obvious that they weren't about to be attacked. They were alone in the night sky.

Rhys breathed evenly. Thought hard. "You both felt it?"

Gideon nodded. They'd shifted into a triangular formation, backs to one another as they scanned above and below, hovering in place. "Yeah. Like a wave. Not good or bad—just a surge of pure *power*."

"A *shift* of power," Zavier corrected.

"It's familiar," Gideon said quietly. "I've felt it before, but a long time ago." He raked his hands through his hair. "Damn it, why can't I remember?"

His words made the pieces click into place for Rhys. "It *was* a long time ago. Sixty years, give or take. Right when we started training. That's why it was hard to pinpoint. We just felt the echo of it, since it was meant for another *Nephilim*."

Gideon turned around, realization dawning across his face. "The Key."

Yeah. You could say that the *literal* key to one set of the Gates of Hell being activated counted as a major shift in power.

To make absolutely certain they were thinking the same thing, Rhys spelled it out. "The Key now has a new Gate Keeper."

"That's...wow. A blast from the past." Gideon shook his head. "We haven't talked about the Dungeon in decades."

"Don't call it that," Rhys snapped out automatically. Because their *Nephilim* trainer had always said that in response to Gideon's joking. Things existed in Hell that were bad. Very bad. Not-to-be-diminished-by-joking bad. You always respected the strength of the enemy.

Gideon flung out his arms as they all resumed their flight path. "I wouldn't have to if imagination wasn't in such short supply in the demon realms. Why couldn't anyone come up with a name for Hell's prisons? They've had eons to work on it."

"Guess we'll file demons under lazy slackers," Zavier muttered. He shook out his fist—the one that had been almost crushed by a frost imp who'd gotten the jump on him a month ago. It was healed, of course. Zavier probably still felt the sting to his pride more. "Even though they're sure motivated as fuck when we're fighting them."

"After all the things we've fought and beaten back for the past sixty years?" Gideon scrubbed a hand over his jaw. "It's strange to have an official *Nephilim* task for the *first* time."

Yeah.

The shiny newness had definitely worn off their job at least—what—fifteen Olympics ago? While their bodies only appeared about thirty, their memories were packed full of decades of missions, near-death scares, and confrontations with what always felt like the ultimate evil and yet never turned out to be.

It wasn't like they'd been playing hooky from their duties. They'd never handled a transition themselves—only felt the power surge and heard the accompanying lecture on what to expect when their turn came. Which boiled down to one main point.

If the transition isn't complete within fourteen days, the Gates of Hell open.

"Do we know what, or who, is in the Dungeon these days?"

Rhys bit back another admonishment.

Gideon loved to bait him. Couldn't help himself. He brought the humor to every situation, no matter how dire.

Zavier brought a double dose of danger and a strategic mind.

And Rhys was the one who held them together. Who always looked ahead, who always looked behind. On good days, Gideon accused him of being too serious. On bad days, he got accused of being grumpy.

But it was his job to look for the bad to crop up in every situation, on any given day—to trust almost no one. How could Rhys *not* be serious?

Zavier pointed at the ground. They landed in the green space across the Kensington Expressway from the city's impound lot. No one would notice them there. And, as a bonus, they were practically guaranteed they could scare up something nasty to fight.

Once they were grouped behind some trees, Zavier paced in a tight circle. Tension roiled off his skin like heat off of asphalt in the summer. "There's no updated directory to this wing of Hell's prison. No monthly email listing new prisoners."

"Almost like they don't want us to know, isn't it?" Rhys drawled.

Gideon whipped out his phone and started typing an email. "The information's out there. It'll take a bit to dig up, but we all know the paranormal world likes to gossip more than grandmothers in a quilting club."

That was...random. "Have you ever spent even two minutes in a quilting club?"

"Yeah. Bodyguard duty on an old witch. I posed as her grandson. It was brutal."

"Did you at least get to fight something at the end of it?" Zavier asked, sounding hopeful.

Gideon snorted. "Sort of. She'd pissed off a Japanese witch. Sent an *ittan-momen* to attack her."

Every major culture and religion had their own special versions of evil. It was impossible to remember all of them. And with the advent of the internet, Rhys barely tried. "What's that?"

"A piece of cotton. It gets possessed by an evil spirit and tries to smother the victim."

Rhys blinked. "That's one hell of an attack for a woman in a quilting club."

"It was clever," Gideon admitted with a shrug. "They didn't anticipate her having a bodyguard. I cut it in half with her quilting scissors, and it was all over."

Rhys couldn't help it—he burst into laughter. "Yeah, well, I guarantee that whatever's locked behind those Gates is exponentially worse than a scary piece of cotton."

Zavier flipped his dagger. Repeatedly. "We need to find the new Keeper. Simple."

"If it was simple, they wouldn't require *Nephilim* to safeguard the Keeper through the Transition." Rhys didn't believe anything connected with the denizens of Heaven and Hell was simple. That lack of trust had kept them alive through many surprise attacks. He didn't care if an archangel came down and promised them it'd be a breeze.

He and his friends would stay on alert.

Like always.

"I don't know. Maybe we're just supposed to stand around looking intimidating and hot." Gideon winked. "We're freaking experts at that."

Rhys shot him a withering look. No time for joking. Not when they didn't know what would happen next.

"The clock's already ticking." He closed his eyes. Honed in on the threads of power that thrummed through his veins. Ignored the aching muscles from the monkey-demon fight. Carefully scanned every inch of his body—*there.* "I feel it."

"What?"

"The Keeper." He tapped the back of his left wrist. "It's faint, much fainter than I would've expected. The Keeper's energy. I can follow it like a homing beacon."

"Well, I don't feel it." Gideon's thumbs raced over the keypad on his phone, already trying to tease out information from his network of supernatural informants. "No point in all of us going. Don't want to scare whoever it is."

"Humans scare so easily," Zavier said, annoyance sharpening his tone.

"Not if the last Keeper did his job," Gideon countered. "The guy did have sixty years to prepare to pass on the Key."

"What if he didn't?" Rhys let that sink in. He couldn't risk doing anything but assume the worst. He rubbed at the back of his neck. Wished he could go sink into their hot tub instead of chase a whole new pot of trouble. "There will be at least one demon trying to track the new Keeper. To take away the Key before they accept the calling."

Zavier squinted up at the moon. "It's three in the morning. You'll scare the crap out of 'em if you go now. Bad first impression will make things more impossible for you. Better to wait and go tomorrow."

Gideon nodded. "Start the mission off right."

They looked at one another. Took a collective breath. Rolled their eyes and said the same thing they said at the start of every mission. Tradition and all that. "Or else the world might end."

One of these times, it might happen. Especially this time. The unknown Keeper was a wild card. Hopefully already fully trained and raring to go. Full of all the knowledge Rhys and his friends didn't have.

Evil being what it was—not to mention Murphy's Law— chances were far stronger that this whole Transition would be a shitshow of danger.

CHAPTER THREE

Interacting with humans wasn't difficult for Rhys.

Not as easy as it was for Gideon, who pretty much liked everyone he didn't want to kill. Not as rough as it was for Zavier, who carried around a singular weight that made interacting with, well, anyone who wasn't Gid or Rhys a lot of effort.

Rhys liked a good percentage of humans. He worked with them all day at their company. Threw a Christmas party where everyone drank a little too much. Took 'em all to a Buffalo Bisons game in June. Their employees seemed to like him when they joked around in the break room.

So talking to the new Keeper should be simple.

Only thing was? In his world, things were never simple.

Plus, the new Keeper lived half a block from Forest Lawn Cemetery.

Why?

An educated affinity for the kind of trouble that could jump out of there? Or was the new Keeper oblivious to the paranormal world? Rhys's job would be a hell of a lot harder if he had to guard them against any and everything that skulked out of a grave. A burial ground was a crossroads between the worlds of the living and the dead.

He parked just off of Gates Circle. *Also* a crossroads.

Was it a coincidence that the new Keeper of the Key to the

Gates of Hell's prison also lived on a street with Gates in its name?

There was no such thing as a coincidence. And this situation was about as "coincidental" as a storm burying Buffalo in lake-effect snow a dozen times a year.

He shot off a quick text to Gid. *$50 says this transition'll be a PITA and go south.*

Gideon: *You're a PITA. Have a little faith. Make it $100 so you have something to focus you on not fucking this up, and you're on.*

Rhys looked at the square brick building. Not great but not shitty, either. Didn't tell him much about the inhabitant, but the much stronger tug on his left wrist told him this was the place.

The doorbell had barely stopped pealing when the door opened. A redhead with a messy ponytail smiled at him. The smile was bright and open and packed a wallop of friendliness almost strong enough to distract him from the sports bra and workout shorts that didn't do much to cover the rest of her.

Both halves of him—angel and human—couldn't help but appreciate her delicate frame. The way her breasts were snugged tight and shelved right up for his viewing. The pretty tattoo of pale pink cherry blossoms that climbed up her neck to her hairline. The creamy skin of her midriff, and the sparkle piercing her belly button that was...

It was a set of angel wings.

Yeah, the coincidences were piling up. Which put Rhys on high alert.

"Hi?" Her voice went up at the end in a question but was still friendly.

His first question was already answered. The warm pulse on top of his wrist was pinging constantly like sonar, although still weakly. It didn't feel like enough...but...this *must* be the Keeper?

Wait.

This was the new Keeper? This beautiful, warm woman who

looked like she'd invite him inside even if he told her he was on the run from a robbery? She was too trusting. Too open. Too young. Too...vibrant. And no, he had not been thinking *tempting*.

"Hello. I'm Rhys Boyce."

"Nice to meet you. I'm Maisy Norgate." She stuck out her hand. There were streaks of bright blue paint across the back of it. His hand swallowed hers, but she gave a firm shake. "Is this random introduction day? Did you move in next door?"

The beacon cut off its pings in his wrist as soon as they touched. "Sad to say that I'm not your new neighbor." *I'm here to ask you to please prevent unspeakable horrors from being unleashed.*

"Hmm." She gave him an obvious and unapologetic once-over. "I'm a little sad about that, too. Always smart to keep your enemies close, and hot men tall enough to change lightbulbs without a ladder even closer." Her bubbly giggle ricocheted off the mounted light straight at him. It was...potent.

Rhys stretched up to curl his fingers around the gutter hanging just off the eave. "You should see me in action stringing Christmas lights. I'd finish before your cocoa's cooled enough to sip."

She glanced down at where his shirt had undoubtedly ridden up. He'd worn a basic gray polo. Nothing flashy. Nothing creepy. "That's an intriguing visual, but it's only May. What can you do for me now?"

Rhys let his arm drop. A few answers leaped to mind.

Flirting would be fun. Maybe even a smart way to get her to let down her guard and hand over the Key. But it could take too long. "I'm actually here to ask a favor."

She fisted her hands on her hips, lips pursed. "Well, you're too big to be a Boy Scout. You clearly aren't trying to hawk a giant tin of popcorn. And you're not a Mormon missionary, hoping I'll favor you with an on-the-spot conversion."

"How do you know?"

"They always come in pairs." Maisy lifted her chin. Her eyes—unusual with a ring of green around brown—sparkled with amusement. "Plus, I caught *you* checking me out while I checked *you* out. No point in either of us denying it."

Busted.

"You're obviously handsome," she continued. "You've got that whole knife-sharp-cheekbone thing going on, mixed with all that thick hair. So whatever you *are* selling, I'd be interested in a sample."

Rhys hadn't been on a date in…well, at least half a decade. Not since they'd been caught off guard by that nest of alligator demons. It'd been too close. He'd doubled, no, *tripled* down on strategies and training and security. Dating was a distraction from duty.

Sure, he had needs. Hookups took care of those. Whether at a bar here in town or, better yet, after an assignment ended in a foreign country. Nothing was clearer about not being available for a repeat performance than mentioning your flight boarded in an hour.

The new Keeper of the Key was off-limits, though. Both for hookups and anything more. It'd be distracting.

Dangerous.

Thoughtless. Plus, Gideon and Zavier would never let him hear the end of it.

So while he'd very much like to take her up on whatever she was offering, his answer would have to be no.

Hellfire.

He shoved his hands into his pockets. "Not selling anything. And sadly, I'm under a time constraint. No time for any sort of sampling."

"That's a pity."

"Agreed." Did his voice deepen with promises he couldn't keep? Yeah. She just looked like a strawberry mint—sweet and refreshing. Rhys knew he'd spend tonight thinking about the taste he *didn't* get of her.

"So, since you're none of those things, what can I do for you? Car break down? Need a phone? Calf cramp you can't walk off? Or do you just need a good old-fashioned pep talk to start your day?"

Rhys rubbed a hand across the back of his neck.

She was *bubbly*. The woman practically sweated sunshine and rainbows. Even her name—*Maisy*—was ridiculously happy. It wasn't a stretch to assume the previous Keeper hadn't trained her, let alone even clued her in.

Which meant it fell to him.

Well, it'd been a fun two minutes while it lasted.

Still striving for casual and/or nonthreatening, Rhys asked, "Did you recently receive an inheritance?"

Maisy took a small step back and arched one bright red eyebrow. "Are you stalking just me, or do you follow the funerals section in the newspaper like all those apartment hunters in Manhattan?" she asked. "Maybe this is a good time to mention that my roommate's home."

Rhys took a step back to mitigate any perceived threat. "I'm an acquaintance of Harold Sasson." Zavier had dug up the scant info they'd found on the previous Keeper at dawn.

Her eyes narrowed. "I didn't see you at the funeral."

"The news of his passing just reached me today. I thought maybe he'd left you something of great import to both of us. A key?"

Maisy lurched forward, hanging on to the doorframe with both hands like she was leaning out a window. "You know what it unlocks?"

Good. She had it. Rhys relaxed by a whopping 2 percent. "Yes."

"Well, what?"

Her reaction could mean one of two things: she knew what the key unlocked and was testing him, or she knew nothing at all. This was his shot to find out if she'd been trained. If she knew *anything* of what she truly was. "The Gates to one of Hell's worst prisons."

She rolled her eyes. "Right. And then if you turn it the other way, it opens a portal to where Elvis is alive and well and hiding in Brazil. Don't be an ass."

So she had a little bit of an edge herself. Damn it, if he didn't find that as attractive as that belly-button piercing... But she knew nothing. Maybe the world would truly end this time.

"Miss Norgate, I'm telling the truth."

This was where it got tricky. Rhys didn't want to risk flaring his wings as proof. The fewer people who knew *Nephilim* walked among them, the better. It'd become apparent, over the decades, that humans believed in the supernatural. Heck, they yearned to believe. Being told Heaven and Hell were real gave their lives meaning.

But they didn't do well when that belief was proven. It was often too much for their minds to handle. Safer to reveal as little as possible. Until he was sure, without a doubt, that she'd truly been called to be the next Keeper.

No matter how improbable that seemed.

"That I just happen to have an actual key to actual Hell? C'mon." Maisy shook her head so fast that her ponytail smacked her cheek. "First of all, if that were true, wouldn't it be, like, lava hot?"

"No." Good question, though. Maybe?

Perhaps when in close proximity to the Gates? But since the Keeper was a descendent of an earthbound angel, it stood to reason that they could handle the Key without blistering pain.

This would all be a lot easier to handle if they'd *been* at the last Keeper transition instead of just hearing about it afterward.

She jabbed up two fingers. "Secondly, you're talking like Hell is really a place. Isn't it more of an idea? Or, I don't know, an interdimensional spot that isn't a physical reality? Since you don't have bodies anymore when you die?"

Why did humans work so hard to convolute their logic? The truth was so much simpler to accept.

"Believe me, Hell is real. A very real place. You can touch the walls, the floor, the doors, the chairs, and yes, the Gates. Although I wouldn't recommend that last one." Because now Rhys *was* wondering if they were sheathed in flames.

Guess he'd find out soon enough. As would she.

"You don't need to recommend against touching any part of Hell." Impatience sharpened her tone until the words were as finely honed as his favorite obsidian-edged katana. "News flash: I don't intend to ever go there—real or imaginary."

"Except that you might need to. Soon." Another thing he didn't know for certain. "To keep the Gates locked."

"Why would Hell even need a prison? Isn't the whole thing a prison?" Maisy crossed her arms and shot him a smug smirk. Like she thought she'd just delivered the knockout blow to his argument.

Humans.

It took all of Rhys's decades of ruthlessly honed control not to roll his eyes. "That'd take some time to break down. And it looks as if I've interrupted you." Rhys pointed at the paint on her hand and, now that he looked, a smear on her arm as well. In the dim room behind her, he glimpsed an easel. "The short answer? Your Key locks up some of the very worst demons. For the sake of the entire world, they need to stay locked up. That is now your sacred, weighty, and dangerous responsibility."

She blinked slowly. Then again.

It'd be so much easier if he could handpick a more suitable Keeper. He'd offer her money for the Key—a *lot* of money—but it had to be given of free will.

Rhys had no choice but to stick with presenting the most logical solution. The easiest one. Where she gave it to him for safekeeping for the duration of the Transition, until he could pass it to the next Keeper. Humans loved to take the easy way out.

Without another word, Maisy slammed the door in his face. *Hellfire.*

CHAPTER FOUR

Maisy started to tuck a strand of hair behind her ear. Remembered that by this point in the late-afternoon shift she'd acquired a smear of latte foam on one finger and the streak of strawberry syrup on another, and instead looked down to find a wet rag.

Working in a coffee shop/patisserie wasn't much of a step up on the neatness ladder from her old job teaching art at a high school. Aside from sticky sweetness wiping off a lot more easily than acrylic paint.

It was a job, though, so she couldn't complain. At least, she wouldn't *let* herself complain…more than once a week. Life was too short to wallow in badness. Better to focus on the good.

Those complaint days somehow always intersected with payday. The day on which she got a check far smaller than her original tiny teacher's salary. A check that didn't have any insurance or sick time taken out of it, as they were not options here.

But…it was better than working at a big box store. No uniform was a good thing. And Maisy still got to use her two art degrees, a little.

Painting the front windows, doing artsy things on the chalk menu board with the daily specials. The check was padded, too, by the extra hours she put in decorating all the pastries. The owners had hoped her talent would extend to a frosting piping tip. It only took about an hour of practice before she was turning out fancy cupcakes more elaborate than anything in the display case.

It was art...even if it did only last a few hours.

People weren't shelling out money to buy her paintings. She could at least take comfort that they paid extra for her creatively topped cakes and cookies.

Because if you didn't find *some* good in every day, what was the point of getting up? Like...how good it was to ogle the massively hot-yet-strange man that had come to her door and asked about the key. The conversation hadn't gone anywhere, but a daily dose of eye candy was just as nice as her daily square of dark chocolate.

Well, it hadn't gone anywhere *believable*.

It had, however, added another whole layer to the annoyance surrounding her mysterious inheritance.

She didn't believe a word Rhys had said. But...how had he known to come to her door? How had he known about the key—or her uncle? None of that was randomly googleable information.

It was driving her bananas.

The bell on the door jingled just as she was about to head into the back to grab a restock of milk. Maisy crossed her fingers that someone who actually understood the principle behind tipping would enter.

Or someone as hot as that grumpy guy who'd knocked on her door before her shift and gone off on a tangent about Hell being real.

Yes, she'd thought about him three times in two minutes. He'd been just that handsome. So tall. So broad-shouldered. So darned yummy.

"Miss Norgate. This is a surprise."

Her uncle's lawyer? Whom she'd never once seen in the patisserie before? "Hi, Mr. Turk. Kind of far for you to come on a coffee run, isn't it? Don't you have people for that?"

"I have a machine in my office, actually. Little pods that pop right in."

She *knew* it.

He totally could have offered her a drink while she was there. Some people just lacked basic warmth and hospitality. Which maybe explained why he was a lawyer, if you believed all the cliché jokes about the profession.

She slapped on a smile anyway. "Well, if you aren't here for coffee, what can I get you?"

"My, ah, niece just won her track meet. This is her favorite shop, so I came by to get her a treat to celebrate."

Huh. That was super sweet. Maybe she'd misjudged the man. "Do you want me to personalize something for her? It would only take a moment. On the individual *Fraisier* cake—it's our signature slice, with strawberries, vanilla cream, and sponge cake."

"That'd be fine."

One sliver of warmth, and then straight back to brusque. Progress, right? She'd pipe a little medal on the cake. "What's her name?"

"Who?"

Weird. "Your niece?"

"Ah. Sorry. Big family. Ah…Milly."

Maisy blinked back an eye roll as she grabbed a piping bag. The name couldn't be a coincidence. "Is she named after you?"

"Sure." His tone was dismissive. So much for his sliver of warmth. "Say, how are you getting on with your inheritance? Figure out yet what it unlocks?"

"Nope. I have to admit, it is driving me bonkers. I almost wish you hadn't given it to me."

He laced his hands across the taut stretch of his pinstriped shirt over his belly. "Inheritances can be tricky. Just because you receive something doesn't mean you truly want it. Or deserve whatever strings come with it."

Strings? What kind of strings? It was utterly useless. Unless she figured out what it opened. Even then, unless it *actually* unlocked the gates of Hell—ha!—what strings could be an encumbrance?

And considering Turk had been rudely insistent in his office that he knew nothing at all about the key, why was he now mentioning strings? Did he know something?

Or was the encounter with the Hell conspiracist making her leap to wild assumptions?

The pink frosting popped on top of the pale yellow marzipan. Maisy wanted to ask how old the niece was but had a feeling Milton Turk wouldn't remember. So she added a fanciful curlicue but no hearts.

"I did not want this key." She laid down the bag, suddenly too frustrated to trust herself with such precise work. "No, I did not want *anything* from Harold Sasson." Nothing inheritable, anyway.

She would've given anything to have his attention. His love. Him to fill the empty space left behind when her parents died.

One bizarre key didn't make up for any of that.

It merely highlighted—every time Maisy thought about it— how he hadn't bothered to spend a single second with her. It was a manifestation, a reminder, of all the hurt of knowing he chose to leave her alone.

Even if she tossed it into a drawer, she'd still know it was there. She'd know that the man who couldn't be bothered to hug a grieving, lonely child just messed with her by leaving her the mystery key.

"You can't refuse the bequest, Miss Norgate. It is done."

"Well, it feels wrong. Like there's someone out there who was supposed to have gotten this instead of me. Someone who would've appreciated it. Or known what the heck to do with it." It felt good to blurt that out. She finished the piping.

The lawyer moved his head very slightly left and right. Like he was trying to check and see if they were alone but had forgotten that his thick tie limited his mobility. "While you can't refuse it, you also don't have to keep it."

That's what Liss had suggested. After putting up with probably a solid ten minutes of Maisy ranting about how her uncle should have been there for her when he was actually alive. Instead, he'd left her a mystery key. A key without a lock. It was, frankly, a sort of cruel joke.

It was a practical solution, but Maisy had dismissed it after scant consideration. As mad as she was about him staying away her entire life, about the insult of a throwaway weird inheritance? It was important enough to her uncle to pay lawyer's fees to pass it on.

"I sort of do have to keep it." She popped the cake into a box and tied it up with red and white string. "Even though it doesn't mean anything to me, it clearly meant something to Uncle Harold. It would be disrespectful to just toss it in the trash. Especially within a few weeks of his death."

"I'm suggesting nothing of the sort. He was my client. Goodness. But I know someone who would…appreciate the key for its intrinsic value."

"Really?" It'd be impossible to even begin to track down what it might open. Especially not knowing a thing about her uncle. He could've picked it up at a yard sale or on a trip to Scotland in a castle gift shop. Who the heck would want a useless, enormous key? Maybe a local theater company that needed a spooky prop for *Dracula* or *Frankenstein*?

"My, ah, cousin is a locksmith."

Oh. Well. That made much more sense. "He wouldn't mind taking it off my hands?" Maisy was certain her mind would stop chasing in circles trying to figure out what it opened if she didn't have it anymore. Out of sight, out of anxiety-curiosity mode.

"I'm sure he'd be tickled to display it in his shop. Where many people could enjoy its ornate, possibly antique beauty."

While she couldn't appreciate whatever the key was supposed

to do or be, as an artist, Maisy certainly appreciated its old-school loveliness. Like a piece of fine art, it absolutely deserved to be seen and admired.

This was an *elegant* solution.

"Mr. Turk, that is a fantastic suggestion. It gets the weight of it off my head."

He gave a throat-clearing grumble. Fluttered his pudgy hands a little. "I'm afraid I can't say how much it is worth. Without any provenance—"

Geez. It had been a gift to her. Uncle Harold's first and last gift. There was no way she'd charge someone to take it off her hands.

"Oh, no. I wouldn't feel right profiting off a...bequeathment"— was that even a word? —"from a family member. I'll *give* it to your cousin. I'm just relieved that somebody will appreciate it."

"Splendid."

Grateful but still mindful of her job. "That'll be eight dollars for the cake and an additional five for the personalization."

"I'm sure Tilly will deem it worthwhile."

"Tilly?"

"My niece." He dropped a twenty on the counter and snatched up the box. "I'll send my cousin your address so he can come pick it up. No need to inconvenience you with a trip to his shop. Good day, Miss Norgate."

The lawyer hustled out of the shop without waiting for change. Maisy figured the tip would help mitigate the exorbitant fee she'd paid to park at his office. As for him not knowing his own niece's name?

Presumably his lawyering skills were at a much higher level than his people skills.

Maisy was simply happy that she wouldn't have to interact with the stuffy little man again.

And even happier that the key was no longer her problem.

Which was a huge relief. She never wanted to see it again.

Something about it gave her the creeps—and something *else* about it made her fingers itch to hold it.

Nope. She'd stay firmly on the side of good riddance.

Although Maisy wouldn't entirely complain if grumpy hot Hell guy with the Welsh name came back again and she got to tell him to his face that she no longer had it...

Fat chance.

The lawyer showing up at her work was enough of a stretch. No way would the second new person she'd met that week also coincidentally ramble past again.

Besides, while grumpy guy was more than hot enough to flirt with, he was clearly part of some odd cult. Maisy'd never sleep with someone she couldn't trust.

Nope. He was on her permanent "do not do" list. Right up there with running a marathon and singing in public.

CHAPTER FIVE

Rhys looked up from his tablet. Pinched the bridge of his nose. And tried to control his patience with as much practiced ease as he did his translucent blue wings. "Why am I the only one who's said anything in the last five minutes?"

"It was your idea to have this meeting," Zavier replied. "Gideon and I are ready to fight."

"Yeah, I am, too." He looked out the window of their conference room. Across the container yard, sun sparkled on Lake Erie. "*However*, it's the middle of the bright-ass day. Forgive me for wanting to prep fully for a mission where we could be seen by any random person."

Rhys's wings itched to flare in frustration. Not that he'd let that happen.

The way *Nephilim* managed to blend into human society was by keeping their true nature under wraps. Their employees wouldn't be able to *see* his wings if they unfurled—not unless he wanted them to. They'd made sure of that. Everyone who worked at Metafora Enterprises got screened to be sure they didn't have any latent supernatural abilities that would allow them to see their bosses' true forms.

Control, though, was what had kept him alive for so long. Control that was twice as hard to maintain because *Nephilim* were only half angel and half human. An imperfect species within the nine official classes of angels. Absolute control at all times had been drummed into them since day one of their training.

And that meant not letting some little shit record them stabbing a demon with a dagger and then upload it to TikTok.

"It's a single demon. Easier than what you had to handle with the longshoremen yesterday. You're overthinking." Gideon pointed at him with a scowl. "And over-boring us."

Riiiiight. "What was I thinking, taking ten extra minutes to talk through what could go wrong and how to freaking stay alive? Obviously, I'm more of a taskmaster than that Slavic demon we slayed last year who cut off farmers' heads when they rested too long in the fields."

"Lady Midday. She put up a good fight," Zavier reminisced with what was—for him—a smile.

This was *not* beer-drinking, telling-battle-stories time. Rhys would damn well start a battle if they didn't kick into mission mode and pay attention. Going over the plan was what kept them safe. Why did they always force him to be the tough guy?

"Look, this is a pissant request. Things have been too quiet lately. This is only our second mission in three weeks. That usually means something big and bad is on the way. We need to be prepared, even if it is only one demon. It could give us a hint of what might be coming."

"Evil," Zavier said succinctly.

Well, yeah.

That's what they did, after all. Hunted evil.

Saying evil was coming was a lot like saying a boat ride over Niagara Falls would get a bit rough.

Rhys angled his jaw from side to side. Took a beat to not just give into his frustration and call his friend a freaking idiot. "That's exactly the helpful clue I needed. Let me go call 1-800-WHO-EVIL and see who answers."

Gideon gave him a slow clap. "Okay, your excellent sarcasm game bought you ten minutes of my solid attention."

Fuck it. He was done fighting with his friends. Better to go fight the demon. He pushed out of his Aeron chair. "Get in the car. We'll have to drive to where this scumbag's been spotted."

Flying across Buffalo in the late afternoon wouldn't keep them off anyone's radar. Which was a shame, because Rhys itched for a fast, hard flight.

He needed a way to let out his frustration over the new Keeper. Frustration at her annoying perkiness. She'd completely dismissed the facts. She'd dismissed *him*. He was even more frustrated at how badly he'd wanted to kiss her when she pursed her lips...

Rhys fumed while they changed out of their suits and geared up.

While they grabbed the police scanner to be sure there wasn't any hint of them where they were headed.

While he stopped Z from taking the wheel with a single glare.

While he burned rubber leaving the parking lot, then caught air going too fast over the railroad tracks.

Gideon grabbed for the passenger handle. "Popping off the exhaust pipe on those tracks won't get us there any faster. What crawled up your ass?"

Hell.

The woman—the oddly beautiful woman with the annoyingly perky smile—was taking up too much of his brain space. After so long defending humanity, Rhys *knew* better. She was just a human. She shouldn't be a distraction at all.

No matter how much his pride stung at not getting her to comply. Or even listen to him.

No matter how he kept remembering the unusual rings of green and brown in her eyes.

"It's the new Keeper."

"The one who slammed the door in your face?" Gideon hooted with laughter. "Good times."

Gideon wouldn't be laughing when they screwed up the

transition—or, rather, the *Keeper* did. The stakes were too high for his friend to find any reason to laugh. "She's not fit to be a Keeper. She doesn't appreciate what's required."

"Did you tell her?"

Oh, for fuck's sake. No, he sat down and had an in-depth conversation about Taylor Swift's latest boy-toy-dumping song. Did Gideon really think he was *that* off his game?

"I tried." The wind through the sunroof didn't cool Rhys down at all as he thought about the irritating redhead.

"How hard?"

The reasonable question stung like salt water in a knife wound. "Not at all after she slammed the door."

"So, you're a quitter." Gideon folded his arms across his chest.

Z snickered from the back seat.

"Take that back," Rhys said through gritted teeth.

"I will—once you get the job done."

"Is this your new motivational style? Irritating me into action?"

"Nah. This is just for shits and giggles." In a much more sober tone, Gideon continued, "I know you'll get the job done."

"Hey, aren't we near the new Keeper's house?" Zavier asked.

He had a heck of a memory for places. Even ones he hadn't been. Which came in handy when they transported around the world through waterfalls and had to then find their intended targets.

But it wasn't handy right now.

It was irritating.

Rhys parked the car next to the entrance to the city dump. It reeked. Was full of rats. What better place to find a demon? They all climbed out and loaded up with weapons. Yeah, it was only one demon, but you never knew what dirty tricks they had up their sleeves.

"You mean the house of the human who bested the great and glorious Rhys Boyce with a single slam of a door?" Gideon held up his hands as if reading off a theater marquee.

Like he thought it was *funny*.

This official duty that they, all three of them, were currently failing at.

"Fate of the world's at stake. *Aka*, it isn't funny," Rhys snapped.

Gideon smirked. "Oh, but it is. You've slain how many Dukes of Hell?"

"And that Andean snake spirit that got her venom in you in five places..." Zavier snapped his fingers. "Ah, the *Amaru*."

"Don't forget the brother/sister double team of the Romanian Burning Ones. They were nasty."

A rare smile lifted up at least one side of Zavier's mouth. "But a human girl stopped you cold."

See, right there. They weren't appreciating the difficulty of the exchange. Plus, weren't they supposed to be on his side? "Maisy's not a girl. She's a *woman*."

Zavier had just begun scanning the quadrants, but he stopped at Rhys's denial. Slowly turned his head back, owllike, to blink at Rhys. "That's specific."

"A woman with a capital *W*? She must be a knockout." Gideon wriggled his eyebrows. "Clearly I should've been the one to talk with her."

"She's not a knockout. She's almost average." And yet...not.

There was something about her too-bright hair. Her way-too-bright smile. The annoyingly bright and happy way she spoke. Something that made Rhys want to argue with her again. But the next time, he'd make her see that he was right.

"Rhys has a crush on the Keeper. Is that even allowed?"

Z crouched. Angled to look underneath the rusted-out semi across the street. "Should this be an addendum on my report to Caraxis? Are *Nephilim* allowed to get down and dirty with Keepers?"

Like Z had a leg to stand on. He pushed back constantly against the rules. On principle, often, rather than out of any real reason behind the dissent. Because his grudge against the *Nephilim* order was deep. Justified, but another one of those grudges he refused to let go of, even a little.

Rhys stalked away. He'd had enough of their mocking. Over his shoulder, he said, "We can do whatever we want. Isn't that what you keep reminding me?"

But Z grabbed his shoulder. "As much fun as it is to torment you, the clock *is* ticking. Ignoring it—ignoring you—that's not an option."

"I'm well aware." Shouldn't it count that he hadn't stopped thinking about Maisy since she slammed the door in his face?

Not that all those thoughts were about her being Keeper. Many were about the damn attraction he couldn't seem to ignore. Rhys wouldn't admit that to the guys, though.

"Otherwise, the Gates to Hell—"

There was no need to rehash. Bad things would happen. Cataclysmically bad things would happen. Rhys pointed at Z's daggers, already in his hands. "We had this mission that came up. I couldn't skip it to...*finesse* a stubborn human."

"Ah, finesse. One of my particular talents." Gideon clapped his hands with a wide smile. "So we're agreed? *I* should make contact this second time? I can 'finesse' the woman into doing just about anything."

"No," he bit out sharply. And a little too loudly. "I'll go back tonight. Make her see reason. This was my fuckup. I'll fix it. You two can deal with the werewolves that want help scaring off that armadillo shifter pack."

"We're not getting involved in a shifter territory spat."

"Of course not. But you can use your damn finesse to be sure they'll want to hire us again when they've got a real problem."

Zavier spun a dagger in his right hand, then pointed it at a locksmith's truck at the edge of the dump. "You see that?"

The figure looked like a human. In a shirt with a patch that matched the logo on the truck. Except that hanging out the waist of his low-hanging pants were at least a dozen skinny gray tentacles. Like flexible twigs. And the faint, rotten-egg scent of brimstone wafted on the breeze.

Dispatching a demon was the perfect way to end this frustrating-as-fuck conversation. A reminder of what he *could* do. What he was good at. Something totally in his control.

"He's all mine," Rhys growled. Then he took off at a run and leaped into the air across the expressway with two mighty flaps of his wings.

He'd do his duty by keeping humanity safe from demonkind for yet a second time tonight.

Why did that feel so much easier than figuring out how to make Maisy Norgate listen to him?

CHAPTER SIX

W hen it came to a low-key birthday party, what could be better than her own backyard? Full of birdsong, a cool breeze that made Maisy feel cozy in her tie-dye hoodie, and, every so often, a little reggae rhythm from the park a few blocks away.

There.

Maisy nodded to herself. Positive thought of the day was in the books.

The wind chime gave out a metallic tinkle. "Hear that? How peaceful is that? Like we're in a spa, blissing out."

Liss arched one dark, perfectly plucked eyebrow. "A spa? There's a stench from the other side of the fence that must be a rat corpse. It's foul. Those idiot drag racers out on the parkway keep gunning their motorcycles. They've been at it for a solid ten minutes. And if I was in a spa, I sure as hell wouldn't be working."

They were all solid points of rebuttal.

But Maisy didn't want her friend to be miserable. It was exhausting. It was depressing. It was, frankly, no fun. Especially since this was her birthday party, which she'd had to wait several days for.

"Hey. This is the no-complaints zone, remember?" She circled her arms to indicate their tiny patio.

They'd painted the fence a bright green to make up for not

having many plants. Stalked yard sales for the adorable wrought iron café table set and painted it white—so that the inevitable bird poop would be less noticeable.

And they'd lugged over cinderblocks from the mostly demolished garage next door and put a dream vacation goal on each one.

The Eiffel Tower. A lily pad and lavender for Monet's gardens in France for Maisy. The Sydney Opera House for her musical bestie. What was left of the Temple of Apollo at Delphi. Oh, and one that was just a beach and turquoise waves representing Thailand, Tahiti, and the Maldives.

When the school district cut Maisy's art program *and* Liss's music program, they'd had to move out of their snazzy waterfront apartment to this much older, squatter, semi-dismal one instead. Which, yeah, *sucked*. As did the crap jobs they'd had to take.

Wallowing in self-pity was waaaay too easy.

It was also no way to live.

You only got one shot at life. And never knew which day would be the last. Better to enjoy as much of every day as possible.

So they'd set the rule that the patio they'd worked so hard to make cheerful was a no-complaints zone. Same with the kitchen—because it was too easy to get wound up ranting and suddenly dinner was burned.

Liss squeezed Maisy's hand. "Sorry. I had a rotten day. New temp assignment at an oxygen tank distribution company. Well, a welding gas supplier, officially."

Ugh. Maisy couldn't think of any way to make compressed gas fun or exciting as a concept. She made a time-out sign with her hands. "Two-minute complaint exemption so you can vent because that sounds beyond boring. Worse than that life insurance office they sent you to last month."

"Oh, yeah. And the people who work there are about as forward-thinking as the characters in *Mad Men*." Liss put a hand to her throat, like she was choking out the words. "One guy called me 'honey.' My supervisor asked me why I wasn't married and popping out kids. Another said I'd look a lot prettier showing some leg in a skirt when I go back tomorrow."

Sexist jerks. She twiddled a spray of hot pink curling ribbon attached to a gift bag. "Tell me you're not going back there tomorrow."

"Of course not. The temp company was decent when I told them, but they couldn't promise me a new job, of course." Liss shook back her long, dark hair. "Whatever. Rant over. We're in for a long night of thinking of all the wonderful things that you'll do in your thirties. Nothing bad can happen with that."

"You're absolutely right. I think it goes against the laws of nature to get so much as a paper cut while unwrapping birthday presents. And I, of course, promise to treat you with the utmost respect and not comment on your fabulous legs. Especially since your butt looks great in those pants."

Liss sucked in air to laugh but then coughed. Then she wrinkled her nose. "Man, that smell is getting worse."

It really was. Like…rotten eggs. And smoke. It was disgusting. Maisy screeched the chair against the concrete as she stood. "I'll light the citronella candles."

"I'm not sure even those can mask it. We've got to move whatever is rotting out there. Dibs on *not* being the one who goes to investigate it."

There was no official statute to deny a dibs. On top of that, her friend had a horrible day. Liss was also still dressed in her nice office attire. And she'd hung yellow and pink crepe paper streamers along the fence. Maisy had no way to escape being the dead-rat searcher.

"Fine. But we don't have a shovel. What do you expect me to use to get rid of it?"

"I'm not suggesting you give it last rites and a full mass before burial. Just poke it away from our fence."

"With my shoe?" Oh, the horror! "No way." She waited a beat, but Liss wasn't forthcoming with any better suggestions. There were days when being an adult was no fun at all, and she'd had a string of them lately. "I guess I'll scrounge up a long twig in the alley."

When she got right up next to the fence, Maisy heard a loud hissing sound.

That was...unsettling.

Buffalo had snakes, but they'd never seen any around their apartment. And this was loud enough to be a whole nest of them. It was spring. What if it *was* a nest of copperhead babies and a really protective mom?

She backed away from the fence. "You know what? Maybe we should call animal control instead. Get a professional to do the job."

"They'll probably write us a ticket we can't afford if we drag them out here for a dead rat. Stop being so squeamish."

Another long hiss.

Maisy shook her head. Her stomach tightened as though she'd just done fifty sets of sit-ups. Dread roiled across her skin, raising goose bumps. "I really don't think it's a dead anything."

The fence shook.

A hand—a claw?—curled over the top of it. The...appendage?... was green. Scaly. Then a head appeared. It was also covered in green scales.

This thing was *definitely* the source of the stench.

And, if Maisy lived through the next few minutes, it would also definitely be the source of her nightmares for the rest of her freaking life.

This thing had eyes, a nose, and a mouth just like a human. Coming out the top of its head was a...tail? A tentacle? And at the top of that was a set of fanged teeth.

Fanged, gnashing teeth. With a little bit of drool dripping down the tentacle.

Maisy screamed.

Liss screamed.

It pulled itself over the fence, tearing the festive crepe paper. Dropped to the ground, showing itself to look mostly human aside from the green scales. The creature hissed again, then did something worse. It *spoke*.

"Shut up." Its voice was as gnarled and rough as though it'd begun a sixty-pack-a-day habit at birth. "Your screeches are worse than nails down a chalkboard. I'm killing you. Fucking accept it and shut up."

This walking, talking lizard thing dared to *mansplain* how they were supposed to react when confronted with imminent death?

Maisy was still terrified, but this time she screamed just to piss it off.

Then she scrambled backward until her butt collided with the table. It rocked over, spilling the presents to clatter onto the ground. She lost her balance and landed hard on her tailbone, popping open what smelled like honeysuckle lotion.

At least the patio smelled marginally better, but how was she supposed to fight this thing off with nothing at hand besides (probably) snazzy new earrings, lotion, and balloons?

Maisy desperately wanted to see what Liss was doing. Taking her eyes off the creature, though, seemed like a bad idea. "Who are you? Why do you want to kill us?"

It put its hands on its waist. Cocked its head to the side. Canted its hips forward so that she became aware it was both very male and very naked. Ewww. Like a sea cucumber down there.

"Are we really doing this?" He hissed out the final *s* on the word. Closer now, she could see that the tongue was forked. "You want to *talk* first?"

"You bet." Every second of aliveness she could eke out, she would. Stalling would give her time to come up with an idea. Maybe. Or for Liss to call 911. Maybe she already had. Maybe help was on the way.

But what would the Buffalo Police Department do? What could anyone do against this thing? Those scales looked thick enough to be armor.

"Hello. My name's Zygerit." He rotated his wrist as if tipping an imaginary hat. "I'll be your killer today. You'll be my dinner."

"But why?"

"It's stupid to let fresh meat go to waste."

"You think you can seriously still eat me after talking to me?" That wasn't how it was supposed to work. All the crime dramas said to talk to your attacker, make a connection, and then they'd be hesitant to kill you. Shouldn't that make him even more hesitant to chow down?

"Look, this is just another job for me. If someone handed you a cheesecake at the end of whatever you do to earn a buck, wouldn't you eat it?" He chomped together his second set of teeth.

"No." Darn it, Maisy couldn't lie. Not about cheesecake. "I mean yes, I'd eat it. But what I wanted to know was why you want to kill us, not your plans for after the deed is done."

He scratched the side of his scaly head. "Who knows?"

"I kind of hope you know? Death's pretty final to not have a solid reason to be meting it out."

He tipped back his head and sighed. Just like her tenth graders used to do when she announced an assignment for over a holiday break. "I was ordered to. You don't ask questions in Hell. You do what you're told. Plus, it'll be fun. Always good to enjoy your work. Not to mention—but I will—the aforementioned bonus of free dinner."

Aforementioned? Aside from the hissing and the overall appalling thesis, Zygerit was having a normal, well-verbalized conversation with her.

It was beyond surreal except for how real her terror felt... along with her absolute belief that, barring a miracle by the BPD, this thing would kill her and her best friend in a matter of minutes.

And *Hell*? Okay, logic insisted that he was probably a demon. Assuming demons existed. Assuming Hell was a real place, just like the hot stranger had told her...

Well, at least if she was about to die, she'd have the mental image of his broad shoulders and high slashes of cheekbones and almost indigo eyes. Not the worst way to go.

"There must be a way out of this. Something you want. Money?" They didn't have any, but that'd be a problem for five minutes from now. Five extra, blissful minutes of being alive. "I'm a painter. I could do a nice piece of art for your, um, home? Anything you like."

"You paint me something, I'm still going to kill you." He crouched down. His face was mere inches away from Maisy's. Turned out the foul stench of his body wasn't half as bad as his breath. "I won't give you false hope, but I wouldn't mind a nice—"

A couple of things happened in quick succession.

First, Liss slammed the edge of a cinderblock right into Zygerit's eye.

He slumped to the ground. Most of him appeared at least unconscious, except for that creepy second set of teeth that clacked together even more furiously.

Maisy scrambled across the sticky lake of lotion to get away from the green blood—burning?!?—into the cement. Liss grabbed her arm to lift her up.

Second, the hot stranger from the other day who'd claimed Hell was real *leaped* over their seven-foot fence. No hands. Like a superhero. Rhys landed on his feet in a fighting crouch, nose lifted to the air. There was a dagger in each of his hands.

He looked down at Zygerit. Then over at Maisy. After a resigned sigh, he muttered, "I knew you were trouble."

• • •

Rhys's adrenaline had spiked as soon as he caught a whiff of the demon from the alley, but now it plummeted right back to nothing. The unconscious demon posed little threat.

Worse than that? The new Keeper was ignoring him.

Again.

Instead, she hugged her friend. "Liss, you were amazing. I was racking my brain trying to come up with something I could use for a weapon. The cinderblocks didn't even occur to me."

The dark-haired woman in the business attire patted Maisy's shoulder. "Well, to you, they're art. That makes sense. You wouldn't use the *Mona Lisa* to kill something, either."

They both inched closer to look down at the block. Still holding hands. Maisy frowned. "Oh, and it's yours of the Sydney Opera House. Don't worry. I'll paint you a new one."

"Yeah, we should definitely dump that one. No point trying to clean it. Who knows what kinds of germs are in that thing's blood."

"Did you call the police?"

Liss rolled her eyes. Rhys realized he was doing it, too, simultaneously. Many police were well-meaning, but they were still *human*. Incapable of dealing with paranormal problems. "No," he said. "What would they have done?"

Liss scoffed. "That's the same thing I thought!"

Both women laughed. A little bit maniacally. Which was understandable. Being confronted with the irrefutable evidence that Hell and demons existed was much more of a shock than just being told. Most humans would've reacted the same way, but he'd hoped for more from the new Keeper.

Especially since Rhys *had* attempted to tell her. Warn her. It stung that she'd needed proof rather than taking him at his word.

Did they really not *see* him standing there? "Ladies. You've got a problem."

Maisy's chin jerked up. "Not anymore. Liss, ah, dispatched it."

Another hug from her friend. "I destroyed that thing, but thank you."

"Well, you're not a killer. You're a defender."

Ridiculous. Rhys huffed out a breath. "She's certainly not a killer. Seeing as how the demon's not dead."

The two women clutched each other tighter. "What?"

"You have to kill the parasite demon, too. It's the only way to keep the *Aldokriz* demon from regrowing." This was one of the many reasons why *Nephilim* never revealed their world to humans. Nobody had time for all this explanation. Or rationalization. Rhys could've gotten rid of it three times over while they stood there merely talking the situation to death.

"Where's the parasite?"

He pointed at the teeth with a dagger. He'd already re-sheathed the other beneath his sleeve. "There. That's the new demon growing. When it gets big enough, it drops off and is self-sustaining."

Liss shuddered. Wrapped her arms around herself and retreated all the way to the steps at the door. "I didn't think this could be more disturbing...but now it is."

"Would you like to finish it off?" He didn't want to deprive her of the glory. Or of the ability to sleep soundly in the knowledge that she'd single-handedly brought down the demon. Frankly, at this point her *friend* was looking more likely as a new Keeper than Maisy.

"No. Not at all. Not if, you know, you'd be willing?"

"Certainly. No harder than swatting a fly." Rhys sliced off the teeth. He made sure to angle the cut so that none of the poisonous blood spurted toward his shoes. Then he sliced open the abdomen and dropped the teeth into it. "The smell's only going to get worse."

Gagging, Maisy said, "Not possible."

He gave her a pointed look. "This is definitely an area where you're better off trusting me rather than waiting for proof."

"What do we do?"

First sensible question she'd asked. "Got a match?"

Maisy walked over to the little grill. It was big enough to maybe hold one steak and a potato. She lifted the lid and retrieved a lighter. "Do you need a trash can?"

He noticed the ooze of the blood puddle. Killing the creature was one thing. Cleaning up after it was something else. "No, but do you have salt? A big container?"

The back door clapped shut as Liss went into the building.

Finally. Alone with the Keeper.

Rhys assessed her appearance. Her face was stark white, even for a redhead. The pineapples on her leggings looked like they were in a stiff breeze, so clearly she was trembling. But Maisy was still standing. Not in hysterics. She didn't appear scared of him despite the fact he'd used his daggers right in front of her.

Still didn't at all prove that she had what it took to do the job. However, Rhys couldn't deny that she was the Keeper. The energy beacon in his wrist had stopped pinging as soon as he'd first touched her.

But he knew he'd failed in *his* job. She deserved to know, too. Inclining his head, Rhys said, "I'm sorry. I should've been here to protect you."

Her hands dropped from hugging herself to fist at her sides. "You…wait…you knew this was going to happen?"

"I didn't *know*. I also didn't know if *you* knew." Although he'd been close to certain of her naïveté of all things paranormal, not entirely sure what to anticipate, what with the weak signal from her. Maisy wasn't at *all* what he'd expected in a new Keeper.

"You thought I *knew* a scaly talking creature was going to try and kill me?" She didn't try to finesse the sarcasm in her tone. No, it was all out there, as obvious as a pit stain on a white shirt.

An *Aldokriz* demon wasn't a likely first assassin to be sent. Fairly low-level. Sort of the bumbling, one-track-mind killer that couldn't have stood up to a Keeper with any knowledge or training.

Well, the corpse on the ground proved that. A human had managed to incapacitate him on the first try. No spells. No weapons. No clue.

"Not him, specifically." Rhys extended a hand as if offering her an idea. "I thought—hoped—you might've known you were in danger."

"Believing that Hell is real and that you know about my inheritance, maybe. But not this!" she nearly shrieked, pointing at the body.

"Again, my apologies." None of them had foreseen the forces of Hell getting their act together so quickly.

Although, why *had* they sent such a basic demon to do the job? Was it because they knew the previous Keeper hadn't passed on his knowledge or training?

Did they know that because they'd killed him? If so, that was a much bigger problem.

Liss came back out with the familiar blue container of salt. "Here." She stayed on the step, hanging on to the railing to lean out and hand it to him. Looked like delayed shock had finally kicked in for her. Once Rhys took the salt, she hastily put her hand back on the latch as if ready to slide back inside if a leaf so much as rustled wrong.

"Will you help?" he asked Maisy.

She looked down at the blood. Grimaced. Then back at him. "Why?"

Because it was her duty. Her calling.

And her training had to damn well start somewhere.

Rhys bit back all of those answers. This was a hell of a lot to take in after being seconds away from being murdered. He'd cut her some slack.

For tonight.

Not easy making corpse disposal sound like a can't-miss opportunity, though.

After a single, awkward pat on Maisy's shoulder, he said, "It'll be good for you to be a part of making this disappear. You'll feel safer."

"I think the phrase 'feeling safe' is permanently wiped from my vocabulary after tonight, but sure, I'll help."

Rhys immediately handed over the container. "Sprinkle the salt in a circle around the demon and all the blood. You don't need a lot, just a solid line with no break. Otherwise your entire patio will go up in flames."

"Let's not destroy anything else," Liss pleaded. "The presents are already enough for me to replace."

"I'm an art teacher, for crying out loud. I can draw a circle. Not a face in it, but I can manage a circle." She finished and handed Liss back the salt. "Now what?"

He had to give it to her. It was the most perfectly shaped protection circle he'd ever seen. "The blood's flammable. Light something, toss it on the body, and everything in the circle will go up in flames."

"That sounds a lot like our patio—and our house—will, indeed, burn down."

"Nope. The salt will contain it." Rhys encircled her forearm with his hand. Squeezed it gently. This was his moment to connect with the woman. "You *have* to start trusting me. And if you trust nothing else I say, trust that I will do everything in my considerable power to keep you safe. I won't put you in danger. Just follow my instruction."

She jerked from his grasp. "You had me right up until that last line. I don't blindly do what I'm told. Free will and all. Plus, there's every chance you *don't* know what's best for me. Since you almost missed protecting me from this attack." Maisy tilted her head and narrowed her eyes. "What were you doing skulking around in our alley tonight, anyway?"

The mouth on her.

The lack of gratitude.

Gideon would be doubled over in laughter if he'd had earbud

comms in. "I rang the doorbell. Knocked. When you didn't answer, I came to the back to see if you were outside. Spring in Buffalo gets stir-crazy people on their patios as soon as the snow melts."

Which was at least 70 percent true.

If she hadn't been on the patio, Rhys had planned to fly up and look in the windows. Break in, if necessary. Z and Gid were right—he couldn't risk another night going by without making her listen to him.

"If I follow your instructions now, will you tell me what's going on?" She jabbed her index finger right in front of his face. "The whole, unvarnished truth, no matter how unbelievable?"

God, yes. "I should like nothing more. Will you listen with an open mind? No matter how unbelievable?"

Maisy crossed her arms. Leaned back a bit to look him in the eye. "I need answers."

"Then I won't hold back." Who knew that killing an *Aldokriz* demon in front of the woman was what it'd take to get her on board?

She pulled a wad of yellow tissue paper out of a gift bag. Twisted it into a facsimile of a torch, then looked back over her shoulder at her friend. Liss bit her lip and shrugged. "You'd better be right, Rhys."

"I almost always am."

She'd put the lighter to the end of the paper by then. So even though her forehead furrowed as she mouthed *almost?* Maisy had no choice but to toss the rapidly burning torch onto the body.

And then she curled her hand around Rhys's, hanging on tightly...

...and he gave in to instinct and squeezed right back.

The demon burst into flame with a loud whoosh. The pool of blood sizzled like hot oil in a pan. The flames rose to the standing height of the demon, and then it all vanished, leaving only a faint streak of white smoke hovering in the air.

"Wow," Liss breathed softly.

"Scarily effective. I wish that worked on spilled lattes. I wouldn't have to mop nearly so much at work," Maisy joked, but her death grip on his hand didn't relax one iota.

With as much patience as he could muster, Rhys asked, "May I come inside now?"

"If you help me carry these presents, then yes. Knowing a trick or two doesn't get you out of pitching in."

"Of course not." It was almost cute how she imagined she was ordering him around.

Almost…

He hoped he didn't scare that strength of spirit out of her with the explanation of all things Hell related. Hoped she was still willing to joke around him. Or even *be* around him.

What if telling her the truth made her kick him out? What if transitioning the new Keeper was the first mission he ever failed?

Shit.

Now Rhys was nervous about what'd happen next, too.

CHAPTER SEVEN

Maisy looked across the room to where the hot stranger sat in their forest green wing chair. Well, she should probably stop calling him a stranger now that they'd shared such a...unique experience.

At least, she *hoped* it would be unique.

Rhys looked completely calm. His broad shoulders and pecs pushed against a blue oxford shirt, unbuttoned at the collar. Navy Dockers and polished loafers gave him an air of a mid-level manager, albeit a runway model version of one.

Except for the leather jacket he'd draped over the back of the chair. That lent him a dangerous edge. As did the daggers that must be hidden somewhere beneath the ordinary attire.

She'd thought her belly-button piercing was a big step. Personal daggers, well, that was a whole different level.

"Would you like something to drink?" Liss offered. "Because I'm breaking out the rum. Probably lots of it."

"I'd prefer that you not. Well, not Maisy."

That was ballsy. And needed to be shut down immediately. "My house, my choice of consumption. You don't get a say, no matter how many scary things you kill for us." It wasn't in her nature to be wholly stern and bitchy. So she softened the rebuke with a clenched-teeth smile. "But since you're a guest, you are, of course, welcome to have a drink."

"No, I mean that first, I'd like you to hear me out while you're sober. So there's no question later of doubting the information."

"Oh. Sure." She swallowed hard, past the lump of anxiety in her throat. What the heck was he going to lay on them?

On the other hand, they'd just been attacked by a demon, so why was it a leap *at all* to assume that Rhys was about to blow their minds?

He tapped a long finger to his lips, then pointed it at Liss. "It's also your choice if she's a part of this conversation."

"Uh, darn straight she is. Right, Liss?"

Her friend's gaze slanted sideways. She tucked her legs beneath her, then pulled down the fleece blanket to wrap around herself. "If that's what you want."

Yes. It was obvious Liss was reaching her limit for the day, but no way was Maisy doing this alone. She'd make it up to her later.

"So who are you, really? Why did you try and get me to hand over my inheritance? Why'd you come back tonight? How do you know about demons?" Maisy planted her hands on her knees to lean forward. "What the hell is going on?"

"My name really is Rhys Boyce. And I'm sorry in advance for having to open your eyes to this whole other world. I wish your uncle had prepared you—"

Oh, for crying out loud. Enough with the mysterious uncle she'd just inherited. "My Uncle Harold never spoke to me. Not once. I didn't even know he existed until a lawyer called me a week ago. So preparing me for whatever you're about to say is waaaay down the list of things I wish he'd done better."

Yup. That nerve was still raw.

Rhys's dark eyebrow winged upward. It gave him a sexy, professorial vibe. That she intended to totally ignore. "Ah. Well. Let's start with the basics." He triple tapped the armrests with his palms. "Heaven. Hell. Angels. Demons. Do you believe in them?"

"Generally speaking, for the first two. Not so much the latter, until ten minutes ago."

"It's all very real, Maisy. The paranormal world you've heard about in myths and legends and sermons exists."

Anyone could claim anything. "How do you know?"

"Because I'm a *Nephilim*. Half angel, half human." He sighed, rubbed at his forehead. Then Rhys stood up. "Might as well get this over with. It'll put an end to any doubt."

And then his wings appeared.

Big, beautiful blue wings. They unfurled from his back, the same indigo as his eyes at the top and doing an ombre thing to become ice blue at the tip. This close, she could see the individual layers of feathers. Fully extended, his wings had to span at least ten feet.

They were legitimately breathtaking...in that Maisy suddenly realized she'd been holding her breath in utter wonder. The artist in her appreciated the colors and textures. The human in her appreciated the revelation.

And her woman parts were certain that his wings were the most arousing thing she'd ever seen.

"May I touch them?"

The very tops of his wings curled down a little. As if disappointed in her request. He sighed. "Why is that always the first question from humans?"

"Because we want to understand? Because they're magnificent to look at, and we want to know if they feel just as good?"

He winked. "They do." While she was recovering a heartbeat from the devastating shock and impact of that sexy wink, he nodded. "Go ahead."

Maisy glanced over at Liss, but she shook her head and just circled her knees with her arms. Stepping right to his side, Maisy stroked her fingertips up the curve of a wing. They didn't feel like the feathers shed by crows.

They didn't feel like anything she'd ever touched before. Velvety but also almost...liquid? They moved under her touch, rippled at it like water.

If the sight of Rhys's wings was arousing? The feel of them was practically *orgasmic*.

Hastily, awkwardly, Maisy pulled her hand away and sat back down. She needed the distance of the coffee table and the length of the couch between them. Heck, to guarantee that she wouldn't jump him to touch his wings again, she should probably retreat to her bedroom and have Rhys text her everything he wanted to explain.

As Rhys re-furled his wings, they faded back into invisibility. "Hell is...not entirely what you think. Humans have distilled its legend to a small portion. It's not a giant mosh pit of sinners writhing in flames. It has its own prisons."

"Like the nine circles of Dante's *Inferno*?" Liss asked.

Good. Maybe she was coming out of her shock and ready to fully participate in this mind-blowing lecture.

"Not really." Rhys paused, then waved a hand as if erasing the words. "But you might as well start there. Each prison has a set of Gates, securing it. There are two Gate Keepers with a Key to each set of the Gates of Hell—one for good, and one on the other side."

The other side? Was this a politically correct thing? Or something worse? "Is this like Voldemort? You can't say the name of evil or Lucifer will manifest in front of you?"

One side of his mouth almost, *almost* pulled up into a mini quirk. Was it possible the grumpy, sexy, gorgeous half angel possessed a sense of humor?

"Not at all. I was attempting to not overly frighten you with repeated mentions of evil."

After decapitating the second head from a demon in front of them. Yeah. The *word* evil was much more frightening. Men! Guess half angels still were human enough to have that male-condescension thing down cold.

To which she responded with a half-lidded icy stare of disdain. "You've already said Hell a handful of times. Pretty sure we're at peak frightened right now. Don't bother to sugarcoat anything."

He nodded once. "The good Keeper for the Gates that contain Hell's absolute worst prisoners *was* your Uncle Harold."

What would be considered "the absolute worst" in *Hell*? She didn't want to even know about Hell's minimum-security, country club–type unit.

"Um...so what exactly is in there?"

Rhys's gaze skittered to the side. "We're still trying to track down specifics on the inmates it contains. The three we've confirmed are Balor, Ala, and Pazuzu—demons responsible for blight, disaster, and pestilence from all religions."

Hmmm. He'd said "we." Was that all of Heaven? All the *Nephilim*? Was he part of an elite, SEAL team–esque squad that tracked Gate Keepers?

Maisy had about a million questions. To her surprise, though, Liss beat her to the punch.

"Is keeping them all in one place a good idea? Shouldn't they be separated, like gang members in a regular prison?" Her knees lowered as she leaned forward to jab a finger into the sofa arm for emphasis. "Can't they scheme and plot an escape if they're together?"

"If you have ideas on how to modernize and improve Hell, I'd be happy to point you toward an appropriate representative." Then Rhys snapped his fingers once. Rolled his eyes to the ceiling. "Oh, wait. Nobody down there cares what humans think."

"Rude," Liss said with a sniff. Maisy agreed.

He spread his arms wide, palms up. Opened his eyes into the same look of absolute innocence her freshmen had worn when she caught them using her art supplies to graffiti the janitor's closet. "I was told not to sugarcoat it. Did that demon tonight give you any respect?"

"No," she muttered.

"The way you view animals—without the power to speak, simplistic—is how many of those *with* powers view humans."

What an ugly thing to say. It pissed Maisy off almost as much as being threatened with death had all of ten minutes ago. "That's bigoted."

A single harsh laugh burst from his throat. "Right. Because you humans are entirely without prejudice?"

"Touché." But Maisy wasn't inclined to let Rhys continue, let alone continue to be in their apartment, if he viewed her as little better than an animal. "Do you share those views?"

"No." His response was swift. Hesitation-free. "My job is to protect humans. I respect them. Not having powers merely means that…you're down a sense. Similar to being blind. Still capable. Still interesting and dynamic and worthy."

That was an *excellent* answer.

And then her brain leaped out of the conversation to skip ahead to put the pieces together. Rhys asking about her inheritance. An overly large, ornate key. That used to belong to a Gate Keeper…

Holy crap.

No. It couldn't be.

Too jittery with possibilities she wanted to ignore, Maisy paced to the arched opening to the dining room. Space was good. Space was necessary. Because she felt like she might fly apart at any second.

"So you've got all these mystical, powerful beings, and they're locked behind a set of gates that really closes with a single key? *My* key? And you're telling me that nobody's figured out a way to pick a freaking lock in all these centuries?"

Was she yelling by the end? Yes. And it bled a little of the tension from her system.

Rhys didn't look the least bit perturbed by her outburst. "The Key turns an actual lock, but it's the tool that activates a great power sync of both Heaven and Hell. The Keeper for Heaven is a human but a descendent of an earthbound angel. The Keeper for Hell is a child of Lucifer."

No. Nope. No way. Maisy had loved her parents but knew full well they weren't *angels*. Plus? She wanted absolutely nothing to do with anything Hell-related.

"Sheesh. How many kinds of angels are there?" Liss asked.

"Officially, nine classifications, but really more like a dozen."

Biology was never a fun topic. It always reminded Maisy of dissection days in high school. Although compared to Rhys finishing off the *Aldokriz* demon, a little poking at a cow's eyeball wasn't so bad anymore.

And—oh, hey—no way did she share DNA with *any* kind of angel.

"I don't need the whole genus and phylum breakdown." Frustration and overwhelm sharpened her tone. She immediately regretted it. Rhys was answering her questions. Trying to talk her through facts that were as basic to him as the fifty states and seven continents were to her. "Just—it's a two-step process? Power and the physical key?"

"Precisely. It could be picked, but the Gates still wouldn't open unless the Keepers unlocked them." Rhys steepled his long fingers. "Most of the time."

That sounded ominous. This time her voice was barely a squeak. "What happens the rest of the time?"

"It's a two-part system. A Key and a Keeper. While it is far from obvious"—there was a nearly imperceptible pause as his eyes raked up and down her body—"I have to officially inform you that you, Maisy Norgate, are poised to become the next Keeper."

Hearing him state it officially? Like he was pronouncing her a pageant winner? That was hilarious.

Okay, slightly less than hilarious, what with the assassination attempt by a demon, but c'mon. She was an art teacher. Strike that—a laid-off art teacher working two jobs to keep it together until an opening became available in another district that actually valued the arts.

She sank onto the radiator cover. "Well, that's clearly a mistake."

"Given your complete lack of awareness of this matter, I share your opinion. But our opinions don't count. Sasson left you the Key. You are of his bloodline. Not directly, which is odd. The duty passes from parent to child. Your being his niece is...unexpected."

Rhys had this old-fashioned, proper way of speaking half the time. The other half, he sounded completely normal. Guess an angel *would* be more proper.

It was like having a nineteenth-century romance hero talk to her. When his words weren't pissing her off (half the time), they were melting her knees...and other parts...to jelly (the other half of the time).

"So go back and trace another branch on the old family tree. Aren't we all related if you go back enough generations?"

"Yes. The Keeper's line is descended from an earthbound angel. However small, there must be...residue in you."

Liss scrunched up her face. "Eww. You make it sound like generations-old dandruff is lingering in Maisy."

Maisy chose to ignore that unwelcome commentary. "Find a more likely candidate. Somebody more successful. More brave. More mature. More...everything."

"The choice is not up to me. The Keeper left the Key to *you*."

"Yeah, well, that's what comes of thirty years of pent-up guilt at not reaching out to his niece. A deathbed Hail Mary of a present to try and make things right. It doesn't." She stared down at the floorboards. They were a bit crackly and uneven with multiple thick coats of stain. Which is how Maisy felt right now. Very uneven and with fault lines of emotion cracking open. "I can't do anything with that Key. It reminds me that dear departed Uncle Harold didn't think I was worth literally a moment of his time."

"Oh, Maisy." Liss came over to give her a solid hug.

Rhys gave them a few beats, then cleared his throat. "When

a Keeper dies, there is a period of transition. At first, everything remains in stasis until the Key is transferred to the next Keeper. Blood reactivates its power."

"Of *course* it takes blood," Liss said with a groan and a hair toss. She balanced on the edge of the radiator, too. "Every story in the world about power has a sacrifice and pain and blood. How cliché."

"Those stories exist because of facts. Of eons of deeds. Clichés are based on repetition, on history, even if you now know them only as fanciful stories."

"I can stop you right there." Because Maisy hadn't even played with a Ouija board as a teen. No secret attempts at love spells. "I haven't engaged in any blood rituals. I wouldn't even know where to begin."

"There's no ritual. A drop of blood will do it."

Uh-oh. Maisy scraped her nail against the spot on her thumb that was barely tender. "You're sure that one *teensy* drop would be enough to kick things off?"

Liss's mouth gaped open. "What did you do?"

"Nothing." Not on purpose. "I sliced my thumb on a sharp edge of it. There was just a little blood. It smeared across my signature verifying I'd received the Key. Messy and embarrassing. It'd closed up by the time I got back down to my car. I didn't give it a second thought until now."

"I felt the power surge. When you reactivated the Key. There's no question." Rhys rubbed his wrist. "I felt you. Here. Pulsing."

Well, that was unfair. Why didn't she get any sexy pulsing from *him*?

"I didn't feel anything. Aside from a sharp sting." Wouldn't she know if she'd suddenly become this powerful thing? "I don't have power. All I did with that assassin demon was keep it talking, hoping that help would miraculously arrive. Being chatty is not a power."

"You wouldn't feel the power. Not yet. Once the Key's

activated, a clock starts ticking."

Also ominous. "Ticking off toward what?"

"Your blood activating the Key is proof that the job falls to you, should you choose to accept it." Rhys said it in his formal, doom-and-gloom voice.

Maisy sure missed the flirty voice he'd used at her front door at their first meeting. "Hang on. I have a choice?"

"Not until you hear me out. It must be an informed choice."

"Fine." But Maisy already knew which way she'd vote. A life without any attacking demons, please. Even if it meant a life without ever seeing those remarkable wings again.

"Your, ah, counterpart—the evil Keeper, Volac—will repeatedly send members of his legion of nineteen angels of Hell and his demons to stop you. If your uncle had trained you, this wouldn't be an issue. The transition is usually simple, but since you don't appear to have any Keeper skills, we should prepare for anything." When Maisy *and* Liss gaped at him, Rhys shrugged. "Again, you said no sugarcoating."

Liss wrapped her hair around her hand. Her eyes were more than a little wild. "That's why we had that incident in the backyard? Is there a price on Maisy's head? Are all of Hell's gunslingers coming for her?"

"Some. Not all."

Well. That was a short and to-the-point answer.

Rhys widened his stance. Crossed his arms over his broad chest. It was a perfect example of a power pose. Wow, he was stunning. "Not only will evil angels and demons try to kill her, but good angels may also test her."

"What sort of tests?" Maisy asked cautiously.

"To measure your worthiness to be Keeper. They'll look almost identical to trying to kill you."

Worthiness? If she was worthy, wouldn't Uncle Harold have sought her out at some point over the last three decades? Trained her? Warned her? *Something?*

"Seeing as how there's no chance I'm worthy, it feels like there will be a grand total of one test, I'll get killed, and that'll be that." No grading on a curve. Life or death was more of a pass/fail thing.

Liss rushed over to confront Rhys, her stilettos clicking furiously against the wood. She had to lift her chin once she stood toe to toe, but that didn't appear to intimidate her in the least. "Do we need to go on the run? Make a counteroffer? There's got to be a way to make them stand down. You know so much. Tell us the solution."

"There's nowhere to run. Hell and Heaven see everything."

"Just like Santa Claus," Maisy said solemnly. Because it really seemed as if the situation called for a bad joke.

That's what this whole conversation felt like, after all.

Rhys looked over the top of Liss's head at her. "You're vulnerable during the transition. Until you fully assume your role as Keeper. The Key can't be taken from you—unless you're dead. It must be a choice to give it up. If you do so, the Gates open."

"*That's* your definition of a choice? A choice is five different toppings for hot dogs. Six Frappuccino flavors. Demons escaping to torment the world unless I figure out how to be this ultra-good Keeper is sort of a no-brainer."

He waggled his hand side to side. "More that you're neither all good nor all bad. Humans on the whole are balanced, but Keepers swing more to the side of good, as the descendents of the earthbound angel. It isn't just your shared blood that made your uncle pass you the Key. By doing so, he trusted you to keep humanity safe. *You* can keep the Gates locked."

"By being good?"

"By being *you*." Rhys smirked. "You can still speed. Still jaywalk. Still offer to share a dessert on a date knowing full well you'll end up eating the whole thing with no regrets."

The nerve! "How long have you been watching me?"

"Just an educated guess." He rubbed a hand over a jaw showing more than a hint of dark stubble. "Being a Keeper, once the transition has passed, is generally an uneventful job. We think. But what you're doing is immeasurably important."

Then Maisy remembered the absolutely beautiful thing Rhys didn't know. The thing that meant she didn't have to decide at all. "It's a moot point."

"Why?"

"I already gave the key away."

His arm swung out as if to hit something. At the last second, Rhys just gripped the edge of the mantel. And his knuckles turned white.

His lips turned white at the edges, too, as he compressed them into a straight line. "That complicates things."

"I'd say it solves everything." She'd been so flustered by the near-death escape—and so fascinated and distracted by the wings and his story—that it had taken this long for her to remember that this was no longer her problem. "Clearly tonight's demon just hadn't gotten the memo that I gave it away. Can you help spread the word in your, um, community? That there's a *new* new Keeper?"

"No. The Key belongs to you until the transition ends. It is attuned to you and your blood alone. If you don't have it, you can't perform the ritual. Then the Gate unlocks. Demons spill out. Chaos reigns."

Was that... Were his wings showing again? Two blue shadows had appeared in arcs above his shoulders. The cords in his neck stood out like rebar.

Maisy certainly hadn't *intended* to start the ball rolling on inviting literal Hell on Earth. She interlaced her hands. "It was driving me nuts not knowing what it opened. Or locked. Plus, every time I looked at it, the whole Uncle Harold thing bothered me all over again. His lawyer gave me the perfect solution."

After snorting, Rhys said, "A lawyer? Doubtful."

"He knew someone who would appreciate it. For its craftsmanship. So I gave it to him. A locksmith. Perfect, right?"

Rhys went very still. Maisy thought he'd been standing still before, but now she saw the difference. Saw him overtaken with an otherworldly stillness. "A locksmith? Tell me you're joking."

"If I was, it'd be a crappy attempt. What's funny about a locksmith?"

"Too coincidental. It has to be an agent of Hell."

He must have been too pissed off to follow her story. "Oh, are you making a lawyer joke? No, the lawyer just hooked me up with an interested party. I *gave* it to the locksmith," she said with exaggerated slowness.

The stillness evaporated as Rhys whipped out his phone and scrolled through it. He crossed the room in two long strides and showed her a picture. "Did you give it to him?"

Maisy's stomach roiled. "That's…that's a dead body. With a knife sticking out of its chest. Why would you show me that?"

"Why do you have photos of corpses on your phone?" Liss asked.

"It's a dead *demon*. They don't all have green scales and extra mouths. I killed it. To protect humanity." He enlarged the photo so she could see the face. "Well?"

Well, that was weird. At least with it blown up, she couldn't see the chest wound anymore. "That's him. That's who has the Key."

"Doubtful." Rhys's thumbs moved in a blur as he shot off a text. "That's who *last* had the Key. And now we've got to hustle to somehow find it."

"Or else?"

His eyes flashed with…well, Maisy couldn't tell if it was anger or concern or both. None of which boded well for her. "Or else you don't get the chance to choose. Or else whoever has it now holds on to it until transition ends. Or gives it to an agent of Hell. Either way? Demons on Earth in twelve days."

Death. Destruction. Demons.

Which would be all her fault. So, no pressure, then.

CHAPTER EIGHT

Rhys was a rule follower.

It wasn't due to his angel half making him extra "good." Gid and Z weren't anywhere close to as relentless about following rules.

Rhys found them useful. Rules helped organize life. They streamlined decision-making. They brought a sense of fairness and equity to a situation.

So he'd played by the rules with this new Keeper. As much as Maisy looked and seemed unsuitable for the role? For any role in life besides free-spirited wanderer or maybe ice cream vendor? He respected that there were rules to follow.

That his opinion didn't matter.

The former Keeper had chosen *her*. He must've had his reasons.

Therefore, Rhys had bent over backward to be fair. Yeah, he'd had a sequoia-sized stick up his ass the whole time. He'd gone into lecture mode—which was uncomfortable as fuck, explaining his ordinary world to her—and laid out all sides for her optimal understanding.

Until she copped to having given the Key away.

Then he'd wanted to grab her and shake her. Heaven, Hell, and everything in between depended on the Keeper being in place. If those Gates opened...

Well, it'd literally be Hell on Earth.

He finished his text to Z and Gideon, updating them on the clusterfuck this mission had now become. After pocketing his phone, Rhys walked the perimeter of the living room. The Keeper guzzled a Dr Pepper, watching him.

The brickwork looked solid. Only points of attack would be through doors and windows. For an old building, it had a surprising number of them. He remembered the square shape of it and wondered if it used to be a factory that needed lots of natural light.

The locks on the front door were good. Three of them. Not as good as at his place, though.

"We have two weeks. Less, actually." Repeating would drive home the immediacy of the problem. Hopefully. Rhys took Maisy's hand. He was momentarily thrown off by the juxtaposition of its softness and the calluses along the sides of her index and middle fingers. What were they from? Why did he care? He assessed the healing red line across the pad of her thumb. "The countdown started when you cut your thumb on the Key."

Her striking eyes widened. "There's got to be a catch. It's too enormous a thing to happen in that timeline. Only two weeks to find the Key and then fully become the Keeper?"

"Yes."

Why was he still holding her hand?

Maisy just looked so...shell-shocked. The existence of demons and angels was a lot for humans to absorb. Getting almost killed and discovering her role as Keeper was too much to expect her to just roll with.

Suddenly, Rhys felt bad about heaping it all on her. This had started out as just another mission. Which he'd long ago accepted always being a matter of life and death.

She hadn't signed on for that, though.

He regretted being the one to lay out the information that

made her pulse flutter wildly beneath his fingers. Regretted causing her to nervously bite at her upper lip. Regretted upending her life.

But not guilty.

Because that was his *job*.

Rhys dropped her hand.

Maisy walked to the fireplace. Reached up to touch an urn painted in an exquisite sweep of yellows and reds—like a harnessed sunrise. Votive candles were on either side of it. Clearly, whoever's remains were in there wasn't that thoughtless idiot Harold Sasson but someone she'd cared about deeply. "And if we don't find it, then horrible demons will be released and it'll all be my fault?"

"Yes."

Maisy blinked twice, slowly. "I'd like to request an extension. Like with jury duty."

Rhys swallowed his laugh. This wasn't the time for jokes. He had to make her understand the constraints, the absolutes, the utter seriousness. "It doesn't work that way. The countdown began two days ago. We *have* to find the Key. And I've got to keep you safe until then."

She nodded vigorously, making her hood slip off all that bright hair. "I'm on board with staying safe. Are you, ah, good enough to handle whatever might come at me?"

"Yes. The forces of Hell will assume that we've made contact. That fact alone should scare many off."

Liss snickered. "You've got a rep with Hell?"

Damn straight. "It is the duty of the *Nephilim* to protect a Keeper during transition. This has occurred since humanity began."

"You're not... I mean, as an artist, I've got to say you're, ah, well-preserved." Maisy squinted at him. "Have you truly been around since the dawn of time?"

"No," he ground out. Did he look older than Noah? Was

she trying to annoy him more? Or did it come as naturally as breathing to her?

Liss attempted to masquerade a laugh as a cough. When it didn't work, she went back to the sofa, turned her back on them, and made a big deal out of resettling all the cushions in varying shades of orange.

"No offense intended. You still look"—Maisy waved her hand up and down, indicating his entire body—"great no matter how old you are."

"I'm eighty-seven. Old enough to know more about finding mystical tools and dodging demons than you. Can we get back to business?"

"Oh." She walked stiffly to the chair and resettled herself. *Also* clutching a cushion, this one a pale yellow. "Sure."

The woman got sidetracked easily. Maybe because she wanted to keep sidestepping the reality, the danger. Hammering away about the gravity of it didn't seem to be getting through to Maisy. Rhys tried a different tack.

"The *Nephilim* protect humans. Think of us as the elite bodyguards you never knew you had. We work in teams. Myself, Gideon, and Zavier are a team known for getting the job done. For slaying demons with the least possible collateral damage."

Liss raised her arm, waggling her fingers. "Uh, collateral damage?"

"Injuries to innocent humans."

She pursed her bright red lips before speaking again. "You're saying you're a badass."

"Yes." If Rhys *did* have a business card? That's what he'd want on it.

"Okay, you're hired," Maisy announced with a grand flailing of her hand and arm. "Except for my not really being able to pay much. Certainly nowhere close to what I'm sure you charge, what with being a badass with major Hell cred."

He couldn't wait to tell the guys that description. They'd get a kick out of it. "That's not how it works."

"Would you take payment in kind?" She twisted a lock of hair around one finger. Her gaze darted around the room. Up high on the walls. At the numerous paintings? "I could paint you something."

Those were all *hers*?

They were washes of color. Beauty. The sun breaking across Niagara Falls. A turquoise door edged in flowers. No people, though.

...and now *she'd* distracted *him*.

"No, I mean, my payment is the surety of the Gates remaining locked. Nothing more is needed."

"Really? Not the greatest business model." Maisy leaned over the arm of the chair. Stretched to rub her thumb and finger against the fabric of his jacket. "Your clothes are too spiffy to be from a thrift store."

"We have businesses. Aside from our calling as *Nephilim*." Of all the things that had to happen right now? Giving an accounting of how he padded his bank account was way down the list. "Pack a bag. You're coming with me."

"Where?"

"I can keep you safer at our house. Where I live with Gideon and Zavier."

A half smile lifted one side of her mouth. "No. I think decidedly *not*."

Every sentence he uttered, the woman either argued against or sidestepped the topic. The two conversations he'd had with her thus far were the most maddening in at least a decade. Including the encounter two years ago with a *Sphinx* demon that only spoke in riddles.

But, again, rule follower. One of the good guys. Abduction, even for the sake of protection, wasn't an option open to him. So Rhys had to waste precious time convincing her of the logic of his command.

His request.

Suggestion.

"I'm not insulting your abode. It's merely a fact." He rattled the ill-fitting, old panes with barely a shove. "The glass they use on the president's limo? That can withstand a grenade blast? That's on all our windows." Irrefutable logic. Especially for a woman still shell-shocked from her brush with death at *this* location.

Except, Maisy didn't look convinced.

She looked…well, the same way Gideon had when he got sprayed by a skunk after tripping over his own wings. It had happened more than eighty years ago, but it was seared into Rhys's memory. One of his *favorite* memories, actually.

Tossing the pillow to the floor, Maisy bounded out of the chair. She relocated to sit right next to her friend. "No. First of all, no woman is going to agree to run off with a man she just met."

They weren't *eloping*. How was he not a better choice for her than whatever came after the *Aldokriz* demon? "I'm not just a man. *Nephilim*, remember? Don't the wings give me credibility as a force for good?"

She barreled right on. "Secondly, I'm not leaving Liss. If I did, she could still be in danger here."

Liss gave Rhys a strong side-eye. "Agreed. We appreciate the assist with the whole demon thing tonight, but we're not that naive." But then she turned to her friend. "There has to be another way, though. Maisy, I want you to be safe."

"Ditto. Believe me, ditto." Maisy crossed her arms. She crossed her ankles on the coffee table, displaying those ridiculous rainbow-painted sneakers. "And thirdly, I don't want to leave my home."

Did she really not see the logic? Rhys felt sure a snail could follow it. "This isn't a cardboard box, but it also isn't the most defensible stronghold."

"We're on the second floor. Right there, the danger's diminished."

"You think?" He flared his wings again just a little. Enough to remind her that there were more things in Heaven and Hell than merely had two arms and two legs.

Did he usually show his wings to humans at *all*, let alone three times in an hour? No. But this woman was endlessly frustrating.

"I want my bed with the afghan my mom knitted. My art supplies. I want the comfort of familiar things while all these extraordinarily unfamiliar things are being lobbed at me."

Ah. *That* was understandable.

Also indefensible. "You're not being strategic."

"Tough. I'm being me." Her bicolor eyes blazed. "I may not be the Keeper you want, but I'm the Keeper you've got."

Damn it. She was stubborn and argumentative. Strong-willed. The sort of woman that intrigued him for a few nights of fun and games. The *worst* sort of person to protect.

But Rhys had quite a few decades on her of being stubborn.

"I can't promise that danger will come. Honestly? I don't know what will happen. What with you not being the Keeper I expected." And yes, he enjoyed throwing her own words back at her. "But you want to be safe, keep Liss safe. Bottom line? I can't promise you will be here. Is it worth risking *both* your lives to be able to know what shelf the mustard's on in your fridge?"

Rhys turned his attention to Liss with the last two sentences. He saw her as the weak link, the more scared of the two of them. Figured a good, focused scare might creep her out enough to push her over the edge.

Her gaze skittered away almost immediately. "You know, Maisy, they make WITSEC people go to secure locations. It does seem smart. And he is, well, an angel. What could be safer? Plus, we know it'll be over in two weeks."

An avalanche moved slower than the words tumbling from her mouth. Probably did the trick, though. The stubborn jut to Maisy's jaw softened.

He could bend a little bit more. It wasn't his style. But it felt like everything in dealing with Maisy was different.

"Here's the compromise I'll offer," he said. "Stay here tonight. Volac won't know yet that the *Aldokriz* demon failed. Gather up as much as you want—both of you—to take to our stronghold tomorrow." It left Rhys with no other option. "I'll sleep here."

Liss and Maisy exchanged a look. A long, wordless look. Somehow, in that mystical way of women, they were coming to an agreement. "We don't have a spare bedroom."

If that was their only argument left? He'd won. "I'll sleep on the couch." It was covered in a nubbly fabric that would irritate the fuck out of him. It had two extra wide cushions but was more of an oversize loveseat than a full couch. It'd be torture.

The next Keeper's transition? He'd *definitely* let Gideon take point.

Maisy looked up at him. Then she bounced up onto her toes and still had to look up to maintain eye contact. "You're too... How tall *are* you?"

"I'm six feet, three inches. Useful when fighting. My height has no bearing, however, on my ability to sleep on your couch. You need protection twenty-four seven. Period." Rhys paused. "If you feel bad enough about how cramped I'll be, then perhaps you should just agree to come with me now."

"I don't feel that bad," she sassed back. "We'll bring you some blankets."

"And a pillow?"

Liss waved one at him as she stood. "There are *six* pillows on this couch."

"They all have fringe. Can you sleep with fringe glued to your face?"

"Wow." Maisy crossed her arms. Cranked enough side-eye that she should've toppled over. "Eighty-seven, and you're still this high maintenance?"

Okay. She was still peeved about leaving and taking it out on him. Thing was? Rhys was also still pissed about her not being trained and therefore being quadruple the work *and* danger for him.

Better that they both stopped talking and retreated to separate rooms.

He drew on his years of training and still barely managed to give the women a reassuring nod. "I'll be on guard. Nothing will get past me. If there's anything out of the ordinary, I'll hear it."

"*You're* out of the ordinary," Maisy muttered as she left the room.

Well, she wasn't wrong.

Three hours later, the apartment was dark. Rhys had waited for full dark, then flown to the roof to make sure there weren't any surprises up there. He'd also used his time on the roof to bring Z and Gid fully up to speed on what a pain in the ass the new Keeper was turning out to be.

They'd laughed at him.

The night *should* be uneventful. Hell wouldn't wonder if the *Aldokriz* demon had failed until tomorrow at the earliest, but Rhys didn't assume. Didn't take chances.

He had Zavier run checks on the upstairs and downstairs neighbors. Did a perimeter sweep. Ate a good half dozen of the oatmeal cookies the women had shared while officially, if stiffly, thanking him for killing the demon.

But now he was stuck on the worst couch ever. He'd tried letting his legs hang off the arm, but his foot fell asleep. Sadly, the rest of him did *not*. Maybe the floor would be better. They'd slept on the rocky ground during the Korean War. And on plenty of missions. Even once on the Great Wall of China—

What was that?

Was Maisy watching a show? Her light had gone out thirty

minutes ago. It sounded like choked laughter, or...no, choked-off sobs.

Hell.

The woman was crying.

Rhys would fend off attackers. He'd figure out how to find the missing Key. He'd help with the ritual—once they figured out what it was—to complete the full transition to Keeper.

Comforting her was not on his list of duties.

She had a friend literally on the other side of the bedroom wall she could turn to for that. Or, if she omitted the specifics, she could call or text any of her friends.

Rhys wasn't a friend.

He was a bodyguard. A fierce, half-angelic warrior. A savvy businessman. A badass with major Hell cred, to use Liss's words. Not the guy to hand out hugs and ice cream after a bad day.

He grabbed for one of the annoying fringed pillows and jammed it against his ear.

She had to toughen up.

Welcome to the paranormal world. Things could be scary. Dangerous. Crying over it wouldn't remove the danger. Maisy would have to learn to accept this new reality.

But...she wasn't stopping. Another five minutes ticked by. Those tiny, muffled sobs just kept coming.

They were unceasing.

The woman needed sleep. She wouldn't be any use to him tomorrow unrested.

Damn it.

Rhys rolled off the couch. Padded down the hall in his bare feet. No sound from Liss's room. How was she sleeping through all this? He rapped the backs of his knuckles twice against Maisy's door. After an overly loud sniffle, she invited him in.

"What's wrong? Are we being attacked?" Maisy sat in the middle of the bed with the sheet clutched to her chin.

"You tell me. You're the one wailing like a banshee in here."

"So we're safe?"

Would he have fucking *knocked* if demons were attacking? "If you weren't safe, I'd already be dead. It would've been noisy."

"Then why are you half naked?"

It was bad enough sleeping on the couch. He certainly wouldn't do it dressed for a meeting. Shoes, socks, belt, shirt—all ditched. Not that it had helped him get anywhere close to sleep. "Do *you* sleep in your clothes?"

"Oh. No." She lowered the sheet slowly back to her waist, revealing a tank top. There were wet blotches from tears at its top seam. Blotches that adhered it to her breast like a second skin. "Sorry. We should've thought of that."

"Because you've got a closet full of ex-boyfriends' reject pj's? No, thanks." Rhys eased around the foot of the bed to get a better glimpse of her in the moonlight filtering through the cracked curtains. Her hair stuck out everywhere, as though she'd been tossing and turning while sobbing. Twin trails of tears bisected her cheeks.

"Want a robe? Red terrycloth?" She managed a watery half smile. "You could probably fit one arm in it before your back popped out the seams."

"I'm fine. Unless this bothers you?" Rhys waved a hand at his chest. Figured he could try teasing the tears away. "That's why you're crying? The perfection of my abs is too much for your brain to contemplate?"

She sniffled again. Then she reached out and *flicked* him, just below his nipple. "Don't mock me for being human."

"I would never. I was teasing you for being a woman confronted with a vastly superior male specimen."

Maisy flicked him again. Those small fingers popped with some power. "I'm not sure that's any better."

Strike two. Rhys had been trained in every style of combat from every country from the beginning of time. He'd been trained in mystical histories, in battle strategies. In field medicine.

He'd received *zero* training in Comforting 101.

It was tempting to throw up his hands and walk right back out, but he was in charge of the Keeper for the next two weeks. And Rhys Boyce never left a mission unfinished.

He sat on the edge of the bed. "Honestly? I was trying to shock you out of your head so you'd stop crying."

"Some people offer hugs."

So on top of being too naive and too young, this Keeper obviously had no ability to judge character. What on God's green earth made the woman think he was a *hugger*?

Rhys propped his ankle across his knee. "You want a hug from a stranger you don't even trust?"

"Well, yes."

"Well, good luck getting it delivered from Grubhub, because you aren't getting one from me."

After tapping her finger against her lips, Maisy said, "You're talking normally now. Like any other man."

"Yeah. This is how I talk."

"No. Before you were all tutorial and *Downton Abbey* about it. Stiff."

"Not the worst thing to accuse a man of being," he said drily.

She bounced on the bed. A smile stretched across her face. "You made a joke!"

"It happens."

"You've got to clue me in. Did you take off your other personality along with your shirt? You're a completely different person."

Now he knew what she meant.

Yeah, he'd been a pretentious prick when they first met, and again tonight, but there was a reason. Maisy deserved to know it. Because no doubt he'd accidentally pull this Jekyll-and-Hyde switch again at some point in their search for the Key.

"I take my work very seriously. It has very serious consequences. Life-and-death consequences. Both to you and to others. War.

Strife. Unless you're secretly a fighter jet pilot, I assume that you've never been faced with such grave consequences for your actions. I was just trying to impart that to you."

A sob caught in the back of her throat. Tears slowly rolled down her face.

Hellfire. Weren't women supposed to like honesty? His intent was to make her feel better. How'd it backfire so massively?

"What'd I say?"

"Everything." She hitched in a ragged breath. Then another. "You got everything across. Which is why I'm crying. Why I've *been* crying. I'm terrified."

"I'm glued to your side now. Nothing gets past me. You don't need to be scared of dying." It was a slight exaggeration. Reassurance, though, seemed the obvious, necessary remedy right now.

Was he going to have to hug her after all, to get her to calm down?

"Not of dying. Well, of course that's terrifying, but I'm crying because it's too much to take in. How can the fate of the world rest on my shoulders?"

Rhys was genuinely confused. He'd explained it. "Because your uncle chose you as his successor."

"Not the logistics of it. Which, yes, weird enough that a few drops of blood and DNA kicked this whole thing into gear." Maisy thudded her fist against her chest. "*I'm* nothing special. I dabbled at being an artist, but I'm not good enough, not special enough to *be* one. I can't even draw—well, there are basics I can't do. I was a good teacher but not good enough to convince the school board that my lessons had lasting impact on my students. Not enough to keep them from cutting the program and laying me off."

Rhys remembered the news coverage. "That's all about budget numbers. Not your ability. Cutbacks. Bottom lines."

"I'm certainly not wholly good as a person. I cheated on my

calculus final in eleventh grade." She wrapped the sheet around her fists. Looked down at them. "I ghosted a guy last year who had a horribly small penis."

"Sounds justifiable." There were enough men in the world that she shouldn't have to settle.

Her head snapped up. "Don't you see? I'm not *worthy*. I don't want to let the world down. I don't want people to suffer, to die horrible deaths, because I wasn't good enough or strong enough to prevent it."

His leg thudded back to the floor.

Rhys had traveled the world, encountered every imaginable evil, many times over. He'd seen good people, so-so, and toxic sucking horror shows of people. After all these decades, nobody surprised him. Not anymore. Everyone fit neatly into a category.

Until tonight.

Maisy *stunned* him.

She didn't feel worthy? That's what had her crying her eyes out?

So many of the humans he'd encountered were too selfish or prideful to ever worry about being worthy if this had fallen in their laps. Maisy just might be different after all.

No training. No innate skills or strength that would mark her as Keeper, but she had a tremendous heart.

She wasn't worried for herself. No, it was all concern for others. That wasn't the mark of simply a good person.

It made her *extraordinary*.

Rhys moved closer. Lined up his thigh against her hip. "I'm going to tell you something. You have to swear never to repeat it, though. Especially not to my partners, Zavier and Gideon."

Maisy nodded, sniffling.

"I'm not worthy, either."

Her eyes went wide. "You're an angel."

"Half angel," he corrected. "I carry around these Heaven-given wings. Powers. Doesn't stop me from being petty and enjoying a win at cards. Snaking the last cookie away from Gid. I hold grudges. I exact revenge. I won't share the remote."

"Shocked your wings haven't molted right off for that transgression."

Good. If she was snarking at him, she wasn't crying. "The secret to doing the right thing? It's not being a good person. It's not being the *right* person. It's commitment. Following through on your intent. Not letting anything dissuade you."

Sniffing and squinting suspiciously, Maisy said, "That sounds too simple."

"It's not simple at all. Some days. Others, it comes naturally. Either way, you just keep going."

"Or I could stay in bed and *commit* to having a good cry."

"Aww, Maisy, don't do that." Rhys wiped away her tears with the side of his thumb. A shock pinged through him at that small touch. Almost like the energy ping he'd felt in his wrist when her power activated. "It won't fix anything."

"What will? I swear I'm paralyzed at the thought of how many things I could do wrong."

Extraordinary times called for extraordinary measures. Guess he'd have to fake being a hugger.

Just for tonight.

Just to fix this. Since it was partially his fault.

"Come here." Rhys snaked an arm low around her hips. Put the other over her shoulder to pull her flush against him. At first, she was rigid. Once he started stroking her head, though, she absolutely melted against him.

He felt every individual inch of her body where it touched his.

The thin tank top didn't prevent him from noting the soft globes of her breasts against his bare chest. The firm jut of her nipples. The warm softness of her arms as they encircled his ribs. Her hair smelled of lemons and lavender. It felt like satin ribbons streaming under his hand.

Rhys wasn't aware of her as the Keeper. As the mystical

power conduit he was charged to keep safe.

Rhys was overwhelmingly aware of Maisy as a woman.

As the woman he *wanted*.

How much time had passed while they embraced? No clue. Rhys just knew it was too long to only touch her and not have more. So on the next pass of his hand, he gathered all that silk and tugged to tilt her head back.

Maisy's eyes flew open, blinking at him.

Then he kissed her. And her eyelids immediately fluttered shut at the press of his lips against hers.

That inherent softness she radiated extended to her mouth. It was like sinking into a down pillow, slicked with honey. Maisy molded her lips to his, giving back every bit that he gave her.

Rhys was giving a *lot*.

He kept one hand on her head to tilt it for optimal access. With his other, he dragged her up onto his lap in one swift yank. Maisy's butt landed right on top of his stiff cock. Her lips parted as she gasped. Rhys seized the moment to infiltrate her mouth with his tongue. She welcomed it, twining in a dance with his. Both fighting for control, but neither one a loser.

God, but the woman could kiss. Not just with her mouth. Her entire body rubbed against his. Her hands stroked up and down his back, leaving goose bumps in their wake.

Goose bumps?

Yeah, it was still spring in freaking Buffalo, but a hardened warrior didn't get goose bumps. Not from the cold. Definitely not from a random kiss with a—as she kept hammering home— mostly stranger.

This was a bad idea.

The woman annoyed the crap out of him.

If this building was suddenly on fire and he told her to jump, Maisy would argue with him. Come up with six different reasons why she didn't need to, or needed to grab something first, or that he didn't have the right to order her around even if it was for the express purpose of saving her damn life.

This was a fucking bad mistake. It would complicate everything about the next two weeks.

Rhys wrenched his mouth off of Maisy's. She let out a moan. No way to tell if it was from his kiss or from being *denied* the kiss.

Using both hands, he grabbed her waist and set her back against her pillows. Abruptly, he stood.

Her eyes popped open. They were wide again, but not in astonishment or arousal. No, if he had to choose a word for her expression, he'd call the big eyes, deep frown, and her mouth slashed into almost a grimace...*horrified*.

It was probably a perfect reflection of his own expression.

"Sorry. Try to get some sleep."

And he retreated back to the living room.

Even though *Nephilim* never retreated from anyone or anything.

These next twelve days were going to be torture.

CHAPTER NINE

M aisy didn't want to look at Rhys.

She also didn't want to be caught *not* looking at him a normal amount. Didn't want to give him the satisfaction of knowing how his kiss had...

Unsettled her.

Aroused her beyond all telling.

Confused the living hell out of her.

Oh, crap. One more complication. She *casually* looked up— way up—at him. "Can I still say Hell?"

"Yeah?"

"That sounded like a question. Doesn't help. My question is, can I still say, ah, 'that hurts like Hell' when I stub my toe? Or will that suddenly manifest creatures from Hell as soon as I say the word? Now that I know it's real?"

"You just said Hell three times." Rhys waved an arm at the wide expanse of Lake Erie in front of them. "You see anything fiery or scaly trying to attack us?"

"No."

"There's your answer." He kept walking across the parking lot at a brisk enough clip that Maisy and Liss had to almost trot to keep up with his super long legs. Even though he was weighed down with her suitcase in one hand and Liss's tote bag slung over his shoulder.

Why'd he have to be such a jerk? Good thing she was wearing sunglasses, because she was giving him a full-on glare.

"Shouldn't he be nicer to you?" Liss murmured. "I mean, this job as Keeper sure sounds important. Rhys is treating you like an annoying stray cat he's stuck taking to a shelter."

Maisy had been about to say that he made her feel like a piece of gum stuck to the bottom of his loafer. "He should be nicer on principle. Out of basic courtesy." Especially now that Maisy had firsthand knowledge that he *could* be nice. It'd been downright sweet of him to check on her last night.

But she didn't need that sort of sweetness from him if it turned into the sourness she was getting this morning. *He'd* kissed *her*. This wasn't her fault. She certainly hadn't asked him to do so. Rhys was everything she didn't like in a man:

1. Too tall. It put a crick in her neck to look all the way up that towering trunk of lean muscle.

2. Too much of a know-it-all. Sure, she was basically at kindergarten level with all this paranormal stuff. As a teacher herself, though, Maisy knew you didn't educate people by talking down or being dismissive or exasperated.

3. Too handsome. Maisy dated good-looking guys. Men like Rhys, who turned heads with their drop-dead gorgeousness? They always turned out to be too full of themselves. Too cocky. Too self-centered.

Rhys paused outside the glass main entrance doors. Metafora Enterprises was etched in a swoop across an ancient oared ship with wide sails. "Don't talk to our employees. I don't want to have to make up a reason why you're here."

"Make up a reason? You couldn't possibly be interviewing us?"

"Dressed like that?" He sneered as he gave Maisy's outfit a once-over. "Doubtful."

She hadn't rolled in mud, for crying out loud. She'd even eschewed several of her favorite bright leggings for the far more subdued black-and-white Greek key design. Paired them with a white cami and a black sweater.

"I dressed to move." Maisy stuck out her leg and waggled her well-worn black Converse. "In case something else attacked, I wanted to be able to run."

"Ditto." Liss wore head-to-toe workout gear. Including silver reflective stripes down the legs and arms.

"You'll never outrun a creature with Hell's power. Don't even try. You *can* outsmart them. Be strategic. Running will just get you clawed in half from behind."

Maisy figured that was at least marginally better than getting clawed in half from the front. "Can't you make us invisible, like your wings, if you don't want anyone to see us?"

"Not a wizard. The wings are part of me. You're not." Rhys opened the door and ushered them inside. "Elevator on the left."

They passed a reception desk to a short hallway that held exactly one door that must've led to the rest of the large building, and an elevator on each side. Rhys flashed a key card, and the doors opened. Once in, he breathed on a scanner.

"I thought you guys did shipping. What's with the top-of-the-line security?"

"The other elevator's for our staff. This one's only accessible by Gideon, Zavier, and myself. Plenty of shapeshifters out there, so we use biometric screening. If I stepped off this elevator, you'd be locked in."

Unfreakingbelievable. "I thought we were going to your house? I didn't agree to be locked up in a basement!"

"I'm avoiding a thirty-minute car ride. And the need to flash your passport."

"You live in Canada?"

Oddly, Rhys shifted his feet. Looked away. "Not...exactly."

It was a yes-or-no question. Was this how the next two weeks would play out? With him parsing out information on a need-to-know basis like the FBI, without caring that she *did* need to know, well, everything?

They rode in stony silence for another three seconds. When the doors opened, Maisy rushed out but only made it two steps.

Her way was barred by two more impossibly handsome, overly tall men. One blond and one brunette. They both wore business attire but still looked menacing with arms crossed and stony expressions. Behind them was nothing but utter darkness.

"Let them by," Rhys ordered.

The blond man oh-so-slowly pivoted to face Rhys. "I'm not sure we should even let you by. What's with bringing humans down here without our permission?"

"I texted. That's how you knew to play non-welcoming committee."

The other man spoke in a voice as deep and dark as the void behind him. "We've never let anyone else in."

"Sure we have. Leo. Braunfels."

"They're *Nephilim*."

Rhys scrubbed a hand across his mouth. "Did you not read my texts? Hell's already sent their first assault against the Keeper. And since her friend was there for the whole thing, she deserves a modicum of protection as well. Our big secret? Angels and demons walk the earth? They're already very much in the know."

"It's on your head if it all goes to shit."

"Thanks for the team spirit." He pushed past the men, jerking his head for the women to follow.

As Rhys surged forward, the lights clicked on. And curiosity put (metaphorical) wings on her heels.

At first glance, this sub-structure was as big as the entire building above. The walls were the same rough rock as what Maisy had seen along the cliffsides at Niagara Falls. Shelves were mounted on the left side of the room, holding more variations on guns than she even knew were possible. Clear drawers below held smaller pistols, plus rows of knives and throwing stars and things she couldn't identify at all.

Glass doors on the right carved off a big workroom set up

to resemble a science lab. It had a long island complete with a Bunsen burner and test-tube stands. Along the wall behind it was a sink, a two-burner stove, and myriad glass-fronted cabinets filled with bowls, goblets, vials, and what Maisy absolutely had to describe as an honest-to-goodness cauldron. Looking out of place amidst all the sleek glass and chrome was a tall wooden apothecary cabinet.

Another room looked like a superhero's closet, filled with holsters and Kevlar vests, leather armor, breastplates, and an array of kicking-ass clothes.

Straight ahead, a looooong way down, was a target-practice area. Spears, arrows, and guns were in cases next to it.

The whole place was equal parts intimidating and impressive.

Suddenly, Maisy felt much, much safer with Rhys by her side. Clearly, the man was far more qualified to be a bodyguard than she'd even imagined.

"You're saying you've got all of this stuff and then some at your house?"

"Yes." He beelined to the knife drawers.

"Fighting great evil requires great tools." The blond man stuck out a hand to shake. "I won't apologize for our caution, but I will make up for it. I'm Gideon Durand. Out of the three of us, I'm the most handsome, most charming, and most knowledgeable."

Maisy shook it, more than a little amused. After Rhys's constant grumpiness, Gideon's flirty charisma was as refreshing as a gin and tonic. "What does that leave for the others to excel at?"

The unnamed third *Nephilim* grabbed a leather pouch that looked identical to what cooking show contestants used to carry their knives. He thrust it at Rhys. "Are we really doing this? Spouting off our resumes?"

"Forgive him. He's flunked our HR training six times." Gideon rolled his eyes toward the women, then back to his friend. "We're breaking the ice here, Z. Go on."

"Zavier Carranza." He did not bother to offer his hand. "I'm the deadliest."

That simple statement of fact sent chills down Maisy's spine.

"I'm sticking with him," Liss announced. "Liss Jemison."

"You're not the Keeper."

"Well, no, but it would make the Keeper very unhappy if anything happened to me. So unhappy that she'd be unable to fulfill her duties." Liss batted her eyes at Zavier.

It appeared to affect him not at all, which was shocking. Maisy was the awkward, nerdy, bohemian friend. Liss was the stunning pinup-girl, vivacious, manslayer friend. No man was unaffected when her dark eyes flashed.

That's when Maisy reminded herself that these weren't just men. All three were half angels. Her brain had processed that more overnight. Accepted it. But she didn't think it'd ever stop being shockingly awesome.

Rhys strapped a knife holster around one ankle. He put a pistol on the other. Then he rolled up his sleeves to add knives to his arms. "Gid, get the ladies some protection amulets while I load up on weapons."

And then he pulled a *sword* off the wall. Not a sleek fencing sword like she'd seen used by her college's team. No, this was an Excalibur-level thing with a jewel-studded hilt and engraving on the blade.

The artist in her wanted to touch it. Museum caliber, it was the sort of archaic weapon she'd sketched so many times as she copied the works of the Old Masters. Her fifth-grade teacher claimed it was the best way to learn. Maisy had spent five summers in a row doing so. Not anymore. Not now that she couldn't paint—

It didn't matter.

"Seriously, where would you put more weapons? You're going to clink when you walk."

"The fate of the world is at hand. That's a situation that calls for *every* kind of weapon."

"But a sword? People don't walk around Buffalo carrying swords."

"Can't assume that we'll stay in Buffalo. Evil doesn't stick to one set of GPS coordinates."

Ooh, he *infuriated* her. The way he pushed back against absolutely everything she said. "C'mon. You can't carry a sword on a plane."

"Nope."

Admittedly, watching Rhys so effortlessly handle the weapons was...well...unutterably sexy. If he'd been an action hero in a movie, she would've been rooting for him.

But this was her life, not a movie. Admiring the smooth play of his pecs beneath his dress shirt was fun. The deep relief she felt at how well prepared he seemed to protect her was calming.

His curt responses, however, kind of made her want to root for the bad guys to kick his ass. As long as they then vanished without also attacking her.

Rhys looked up. He must've caught the roiling exasperation in her eyes, because he held up his hands in question to his friends. "Can I take them to the Watchtower?"

Gideon shrugged. "No point holding anything back now."

"Note that I asked your permission first."

"Note that you're being an ass," Zavier shot back.

"Come along, Red." Without waiting to see if she followed, he crossed the wide room to a blank section of wall.

Yeah, she didn't have a clue. "What's this?"

"Another biometric scanner." He hinged forward to puff on a crag of rock...

...and then a doorway-sized section of rock just *opened*. A series of lights flicked on to illuminate a cavern containing a massive underground waterfall.

"That's remarkable."

"Two hundred and forty-seven feet of it. *That's* how we travel with a sword without setting off security."

There weren't any stairs up or down. No bridge across to the waterfall. "I'm going to need you to elaborate."

"Waterfalls are portals for *Nephilim*. Enter one, and you can exit through any other in the world seconds later. It's how we'll get to the Watchtower." He flared his wings. Just a little, so the arches of them appeared just above his shoulders like a blue shadow.

"Do you get wet?"

"*That's* your question?"

"Yep." Because she was almost wordless at this point. Additional pieces of this new world just kept being thrown at her. Every time Maisy gathered herself for freaking five seconds and managed to process what he'd told her? The next shoe dropped.

Magical keys. Snarky demons. Dissolving demons. More weapons than she'd seen in all the action movies she'd ever watched put together. *Nephilim*. Magical waterfall transport systems. How much more was there left to discover? The thing was…it was all *fascinating*. With the immediate threat of near death vanquished, it was like watching a really great book unfold.

One with a thoroughly unsympathetic hero.

"No." After a brief pause, Rhys, shockingly, divulged a teensy bit more detail. "We don't touch the water—the portal immediately opens for us."

Maisy felt Liss crowd in next to her. They listened to the thunder of the falls for a minute, the roar echoing off the walls of the enclosed cavern. Liss squeezed her hand, and Maisy was beyond grateful to have her there, sharing this moment.

"Can anything come through that waterfall and attack us?"

Excellent question. Maisy wished she'd thought of it herself.

"Yes and no. Other *Nephilim* can enter, but they wouldn't attack you."

"Because there's a code? Because I'm giving off a secret Keeper aura?" Maisy was tempted to sniff her arm, see if there was a perfume-y scent. Although when she thought of what the

Key might smell like, all she came up with was the tang of her blood, rust, and brimstone.

Ugh.

Better double down on her deodorant, just in case.

"Because you're with us." Zavier took the tote from Rhys. "We are feared and respected." His shoulders moved up and down under his black tweed sport coat. "And disliked, but that won't make you any less safe."

Liss jumped right on that. "*Why* are you disliked?"

"Long story."

"Seeing as how we just met you, it feels like a story we should hear. Are you bad at sharing? Bad-tempered? Bad at returning texts in a timely manner?"

"Me, personally? All of the above." Then he stalked away, evidently done with sharing for the time being.

Rhys had two settings: lecture mode and terseness. Zavier seemed to just have the one—curt, brusque, dismissive. Guess that actually made him the trifecta of abruptness. Or maybe they didn't like protecting her.

She faced the wall of scary/impressive tools. Reached out to touch the...stock? Handle? Butt? Crap. She touched the part of the gun you curved your hand around. And tried to ignore how much she really, really didn't want to ever use it.

"Okay, what weapons do I get?"

Rhys didn't slap her hand away. Good thing, or she'd have kneed him in the balls, but he did gently nudge it back to her side. "None."

"Why not?"

"Can't risk you accidentally killing yourself due to lack of proper training—for which we've no time."

So snotty. The way he made it sound like it was *Maisy's* failing. Which she refused to accept. Had her uncle seen fit to clue her even remotely in, she would've prepared. Somehow. Maisy Norgate didn't fail tests. And she didn't go down without a fight.

"I'm not asking to be the vanguard of all things mystical. Don't I need to be able to protect myself?"

He had the audacity to smirk. "That'd be ideal, but you can't, currently, so you've got us instead. Mostly me."

"Why? Did you draw the short straw?"

"It is our duty and our honor to safely guide the Keeper through transition," Rhys intoned like he was reading it off a teleprompter.

The only thing worse than snotty, know-it-all Rhys was snotty, professorial know-it-all Rhys in lecture mode.

"Cut the crap. It's obvious you're not loving this. Or is it just me you've got an issue with?"

Gideon chortled. "You stepped in it this time, Rhys. Is this where I remind you that I offered to take point originally?"

Rhys twisted around partway. Just with the top half of his body, in a superhero move that totally called for the swoosh of a cape. And his eyes slitted to an icy glare. "Bring the protection charms." Then he grabbed Maisy's waist and...flew.

She was flying.

With an angel.

Before she could swallow or scream, he flew them right through the waterfall to land in a room that looked identical to the one they'd just left. Well, it was double in size. More weapons on a much longer wall.

When Rhys let her go, she turned to look back at the waterfall. But it wasn't there.

Instead, she saw a wall...of water straight in front of her. Gushing across the entire length and then some. After all her years as a Buffalo resident, it was a familiar bluish green. It made no sense, but—

She swung back around to face him. "Is that Niagara Falls?"

"Yes."

"You live *behind* Niagara Falls? How is that even possible?"

Liss and Zavier landed next to her. Liss's face was ghost white.

Maisy was suddenly tempted to ask if ghosts were real, too, but it was probably best to stick to one shocker at a time.

Rhys led her along the non-wall. She couldn't hear the falls or feel the spray. Some invisible barrier prevented anything more than the jaw-dropping view.

"There are Watchtowers all around the world. *Nephilim* maintain them to guard humanity. Secret strongholds behind the most powerful waterfalls on each continent."

Guess he hadn't been a condescending jerk about "not exactly" living in Canada after all.

The beauty and magic of it was dizzying. And yet something to postpone really thinking about until later. Being with all three *Nephilim* was Maisy's best chance to get more answers. She deliberately turned her back on the breathtaking waterwall and fisted her hands at her hips. "Do you bring all the Keepers here?"

Rhys didn't answer. No smirk. No eye roll. Simply a shift of his gaze sideways, to his friends in the lab space.

What the heck? Since when did he not have an answer for everything?

Finally, Zavier muttered, "No."

And in a brightly cheerful tone, Gideon volunteered, "We've never done this before." He walked to the laboratory section, then clanged a long-handled spoon on the edge of the sink to punctuate the shocking reveal.

"What?" Liss shrieked. Which took a load off of Maisy. She'd *wanted* to shriek but would've regretted it as not befitting her status as Keeper. Keeper-To-Be. Whatever.

In a slow, grim tone, she said, "So you don't *actually* know what to do to keep me alive?"

"Way to make her feel safe, Gid," Rhys spat out sarcastically. "Well done."

"Honesty is better than lies almost all the time. Except where battles are concerned. Then it's expected to lie like the Devil and be sneaky as shit." He came out to lean through the doorway, both hands grazing the top of the frame. It accentuated his height, the overall tautness of his chest and abs, and the way the pants fitted to his hips and thighs that told her they were *not* off the rack and that *Nephilim* had freaking amazing bodies. "We know how to keep you safe. Better than anyone else—that's for damn sure." Again, Gideon sounded both chipper and cocky. Absolute opposite of her gloomy bodyguard.

Rhys tipped his head to the ceiling. Closed his eyes. Then he pressed the heels of both hands onto his orbital socket. "That's why I'm so uncomfortable. We don't entirely know what we're doing. We expected that *you'd* know what to do to transition to the Keeper."

"Well, I'm right there with you." Was it weird that it made her feel a bit better that they were *both* blindly feeling their way?

"The issues complicating this whole thing are twofold." He held up a finger. "We've been doing this a long time as a team. We've got our rhythms, research, and strategies down. You, however, are an unknown. You bring the unexpected, which always complicates things."

"Getting off of autopilot is probably good for you?" Maisy suggested. Everyone knew it didn't optimize brain health to stay in a rut. Not even one that worked for you.

Without so much as acknowledging her suggestion, he continued. "Secondly, Gideon's correct. We've never handled a Keeper's transition before. It was touched on in our training, but that was sixty years ago."

"So crack open the books again. Call up your trainer. Use Google." Liss threw up her hands. "You've got a biometric scanner in your elevator. Clearly, you've embraced technology."

Deep laughter rolled out of Zavier. And wow, seeing his expression crack from surly flatness highlighted that beneath all the obvious muscles was an actual person. "Us, sure. Master Caraxis? Not so much. We're on it. Just might take a bit to get the info we need."

"Time, I hear, is not on our side," Maisy said in a prim, know-it-all tone that hopefully set Rhys's teeth on edge. He deserved it after all those *fate of the world* references.

Sure enough, a vein satisfyingly pulsed at his temple before he ground out, "We don't need the reminder. We'll give you protection amulets. Cover bodyguard and protectee guidelines, along with a few basics on what to expect from our world."

Maisy edged into the lab space—also much bigger than at the armory. It smelled terrific from whatever Gideon had ground up. Coconut was the predominant scent. Who knew smelling like a day at the beach could keep away demons? "As long as you wrap it up in an hour."

"Why?"

"I've got a shift at the patisserie this afternoon. And we've got an order of gift baskets to make. For orders that have already been taken."

Rhys's perfectly handsome face went completely blank. "You…you plan to keep up with your two jobs?"

"Of course," Liss said without looking away from the waterfall. "If the world *doesn't* end, she'll still need those paychecks."

Zavier stepped toward her, phone at the ready. "I'll give you money. Just need your account. I can put ten thousand in right now—will that cover you, to start?"

That was…astounding. No. Maisy had to be misinterpreting his offer. "Dollars? Or are you talking about some angel currency like feathers or…nectar?"

He snorted. "Funny. American dollars. So you can quit your jobs. Focus on finding the Key."

"That's not going to happen." Maisy was pissed he'd even suggested it. She'd give him a chance to fix it, though. "Look, I don't know you, and you don't know me. Maybe you don't realize it, but what you just said is offensive."

"Sorry. I wasn't trying to lowball you. Is fifteen thousand less offensive?"

From behind, she heard Liss suck in a breath. Yeah, the two of them didn't deal in sums of money like that. It was astonishing that he'd offer it so casually.

And that Rhys and Gideon looked equally as casual about what had transpired.

"I won't take *any* of your money." Did they really not see? "The amount isn't offensive. It's that you think I'm the kind of person who would up and quit with no notice. What kind of selfish, irresponsible person would just ghost a job?"

Bitter laughter spilled out of all of the men. "So many," Zavier said.

Gideon nodded. "People *are* selfish. That's a big part of what makes it so easy for Hell to do its work."

Rhys looked at her with bemusement brightening his face. "You'd really rather toil at jobs that are beneath you than take our money—which has no strings—just to be a good person?"

"Yes."

He toed out a stool from beneath the island and pushed it over to her. Was that a symbol of a truce? "Like I said before— you're quite unexpected, but this isn't open for discussion."

Zavier didn't scowl, but his expression was utterly flat. "You'd be potentially endangering every customer that walked in the door. Liss can go to work, but you're a beacon to those demons who have a bounty on your head."

"My job is to protect *you*." Rhys had the grace to not bark the order at her, but his calm explanation didn't make it easier to swallow. Maisy was used to making her own decisions. Despite agreeing that she absolutely didn't want to put anyone else in harm's way. "Can't do that if I'm also trying to save a bunch of other humans who wanted a sugar rush."

Lifting his head from whatever he was doing with their protection amulets, Gideon grinned. "No reason you can't do the gift baskets, though. Right here. We can help. Wouldn't want to let down all the women in desperate need of de-stressing lotion."

Rhys and Zavier both *snarled* at him. Liss hiccup-swallowed a laugh. And Maisy smiled broadly. It was a good compromise, made better by the mental image of these angelic warriors struggling with cellophane and bows.

Maybe the next two weeks wouldn't be so bad after all.

Except for the whole a-demon-could-try-and-kill-her-at-any-moment thing.

CHAPTER TEN

Rhys leaned against the car as he finished inputting their space number into the app. The April sun felt great. Not as great as sun in Mallorca, where he'd trained so many decades ago, but a nice enough luxury for Buffalo.

"So you won't take our money to quit your job, but you *will* let me pay for sky-high downtown parking?"

Maisy already stood under the shade of the stone lintel over the entryway to the brick building. Guess a redhead couldn't drink up the warmth with the same vigor as him. She pointed at him. "You drove." Then she pointed at his white Land Rover. "Your car. That makes parking *your* job."

"You're splitting hairs there." Rhys pocketed the phone, opened the lobby door, then slipped in first.

Chivalry went out the window on bodyguard duty. He had to make sure there wasn't a nasty-ass demon on the other side of the door before he let her through it. After seeing nothing but a marble floor and Art Deco inlay on the elevators, he beckoned her inside.

She continued as if the pause for the security assessment hadn't even happened. "I'm out-logic-ing you. Don't be a sore loser about it."

They were arguing. Just like they'd done nonstop since the moment they met.

Except for those moments when they'd kissed.

Which made Rhys want to kiss her again to shut her up. Especially now, in this slow elevator so cramped he couldn't have extended his wings if he'd wanted to. So cramped that he stood close enough to smell Maisy's perfume—something light and sweet that made him think of kissing her on a hillside covered with wildflowers.

The obvious distraction from the need to kiss her was to concentrate on his mission. "Remember, don't disclose anything you've learned from us. You got a letter from your uncle, explaining the meaning behind the key. Now you want it back. We get the address of the locksmith's shop. Period."

"I know, Professor Boyce. The letter was my idea, remember?" Maisy echoed his words with a mocking lilt to her tone.

Was he lecturing again? Yeah. Did he expect her to pay attention? Yeah. "Do you want a gold star?" he snapped.

"No, but I could certainly do with a cookie. Ooh, or the adult version—a glass of champagne. Or prosecco. I'm not picky. Although I think you could shell out for the French stuff for the new Keeper."

Why was she so lighthearted, so damned *perky* all the time? The impossibility of her relentlessly upbeat attitude beat against him like an emotional sandblaster. "This isn't a joke. The fate of the world is at hand."

"Oh, for goodness' sake!" Maisy threw up her hands. Would've clocked him in the jaw if not for his excellent defensive reflexes. "I am *aware*. You have made it abundantly clear. If I made a drinking game out of you saying that phrase, I would have been absolutely wasted for the last two days. You're even more repetitive than the little old ladies who ask me every time they come into the patisserie when I'm settling down and having babies. Don't you and your friends ever joke around to cut the tension?"

Her question caught him off guard. As they exited the elevator, he said quietly, "Yes. All the time."

"Then why can't *I* do it, too?"

It was a fair point. "They know the stakes. We've lived it. Taken lives. Battled back from injuries. Seen innocents suffer. Your experience as a human isn't as…"

"Utterly depressing?"

"Bleak." Maisy was right. She'd stop listening completely if he hammered too hard on a single point. "I'm sorry. Most of our experience is with beings who are already a part of our world. Filling you in from scratch, seeing you react—I just don't know what to expect."

Holding up her hand, she ticked points off on her fingers. "Expect that I'll try hard. Expect that I'll screw something up. Expect that I just might surprise you."

She already had. At least a dozen times over. Which made him uncomfortable in ways that had nothing to do with safety. "Then let's get in and out in under five minutes." Rhys pushed open the door to the lawyer's suite.

"Shouldn't be hard. Milton Turk isn't a font of small talk."

No receptionist at the front desk. Maisy tried to lead him down a hallway. He cut her off with a hand planted on the opposite wall. "I go first. Remember the rules of being a protectee?"

"Sorry." Miracle of miracles, the woman *sounded* apologetic. "I didn't think a lawyer's office counted as a danger zone. His office is the last door on the left."

They appeared to be the only ones there, despite it being a workday. That put Rhys on alert because Maisy was wrong—with demons, *anywhere* could be a danger zone. A water demon could swirl up your sink drain and kill you while you washed your face.

He gave a swift knuckle rap to the door, then pushed through without waiting. Standard office. Standard-looking pudgy, glasses-wearing middle-aged man behind the desk. Annoyance, probably at the intrusion, carved a deep furrow between his brows as he stared at Rhys.

That expression morphed when Maisy waved. "Hi, Mr. Turk."

The man dropped the file he was holding. His hands remained frozen in place, as if still trying to grasp the papers, but they also began to tremble. All the color leached out of his ruddy face.

Heart attack coming on?

Rhys didn't think so.

The way the lawyer was target-locked on Maisy's bright smile with near horror told him that she was the *last* person he'd expected to walk through that door.

Considering somebody had put out a demonic hit on her? It wasn't paranoia for Rhys to wonder if Turk had known about it, if not orchestrated it himself. He sure as fuck looked like he'd seen a ghost.

If he stepped in front of Maisy, she'd just push past him. She had no idea that he believed the situation had escalated. Rhys did the next best thing—angled his body sideways to Turk and pulled Maisy in tight against him with an arm around her waist. And hoped she realized his out-of-character movement was for a reason.

After an almost imperceptible catch in her breath, she went along with it. Splayed a hand on his stomach and—oh-so-wisely—said nothing.

"Hi. Thanks for looking out for my girl." Rhys dropped a kiss on the top of her head. Ignored the spike of heat in his belly at the simple touch. "I hated being out of town for her uncle's funeral. Glad you made the whole inheritance thing easy for her."

Turk didn't even look at Rhys while he played the part of the doting boyfriend. Still staring at Maisy, he muttered hoarsely, "What...what are you doing here?"

"Following up on your visit to the bakery." Still chipper as if she'd just downed two espressos, Maisy asked, "Did your niece enjoy the cake?"

"Oh...yes. Fine."

"What was her name again?"

After a too-long pause, Turk said, "Paris."

Maisy's fingers dug into his belly. Clearly, his guess that the name was a lie had been on the ball.

Rhys almost laughed. For a lawyer, he was a terrible liar. He pointed at a collection of framed photos, all with Turk in front of iconic tourist destinations. "You mean like that photo on your bookshelf?"

Maisy tapped a finger to her lips. "Odd, because you told me her name was Milly."

"I've got more than one," he said tersely.

Enough was enough. Rhys could smell the flop sweat coming off the man.

Plan A, which would've gotten them out of there in three minutes, wasn't viable anymore. Time for Plan B, which could get much messier, louder, and last much longer.

"Cut the crap." Rhys pushed Maisy behind him, then surged forward to brace his hands on the desk. "First, you're going to tell us the address of that locksmith. *Then* you'll tell us what you know about the Key. Finish off with a full account of who you work for, and I'll walk out that door without touching you. Hesitate? Lie again? I'll wring the information out of you cell by cell with my bare hands. There won't be anything left but a dry husk of a bruise."

"I can't."

"Wrong answer." Rhys reached across the desk and swiped at the boring, blue, too-wide necktie. It lifted Turk halfway out of his seat.

"Wait," Maisy squeaked. She joined him at the desk. "Look, Mr. Turk, I don't want to hurt you, but I've got a suspicion that Rhys not only wants to, but he'd *relish* it. He's not bluffing. I don't want money. I very much don't want trouble. I just want my uncle's key back."

"You're not worthy!" he bellowed. Spit flew from his mouth.

Maisy flinched back.

And Rhys burned with fury at watching her hurt. He twisted

the tie around his hand, pulling Turk closer. "Watch what you say about her."

"You didn't know what to do with it. If you were fit to keep it, Sasson would've trained you. Would've given it to you himself instead of being careless enough to use me. To trust me."

Admission of guilt. Done.

Now to keep him talking. "Get up," Rhys said unnecessarily, as he already had the man on his tiptoes. He yanked him around the side of the desk. "Maisy, his computer's on. Pull up his contacts and see if you can find the locksmith."

The man twisted and heaved. Not like it made a difference. He didn't have anywhere close to the strength to break free of Rhys. "No! You can't—"

"Don't presume to tell me what I can and can't do." Maisy's fingers were already clicking over the keyboard. Rhys enjoyed her feistiness—when it was aimed at anyone besides him.

"We won't go digging on any of your confidential cases, but I'll bet that's not what you're worried about, is it? We take that Key back, and all Hell will break loose on you, won't it?"

Turk shook. First his head, then his entire body. Such a drama queen.

"Got it," Maisy said.

"Excellent. Let's move on to who you work for."

The shaking increased. A combination of choking and dry heaving kicked in. Rhys thrust him across the room. No need to keep a tight hold on the guy mid-puke.

But when Turk's body hit the door, his face turned orange. Surface-of-Mars orange. Not-human orange.

Hell.

Shit was about to go down.

"Uh, Rhys?" Maisy whispered. "That can't be good, right?" Her hand grabbed for the silver vial around her neck that held the protection amulet.

"Stay in the chair," he ordered. The desk afforded her a bit of protection. "I've got this." Not that he had any idea what *this* was. A flick of the wrist shot daggers into both hands.

Turk's orange head...inflated. Just kept puffing up and out like a balloon until it was three sizes bigger than a standard head.

That was new.

Sure, Gideon had the best mental catalog of all of them when it came to demons, but Rhys was certain he'd never encountered or even heard of one that looked like this.

"He works for *me*." The voice that came out of Turk's mouth sounded enhanced, like a movie monster. Deep, echoing, and very much not the same voice he'd been using before.

The mega-head marked Turk as a demon, but the voice meant he'd now been taken over by his master.

"Okay, we can do intros. I'm Rhys, this is Maisy, and who the hell are you?"

"Volac. Keeper of the Gates of Hell."

Maisy's counterpart. The one who'd undoubtedly sent the *Aldokriz* demon after her. But if all he could do on this plane was *possess* Turk? That scaled back the danger by half. "Great. I hate wasting my time with middlemen."

"This one has proven useless." Volac made Turk slap himself across the face. Hard. "Weak."

"Lawyers. You get what you pay for," Maisy said with a nonchalant shrug.

Her bravery *staggered* Rhys. To watch an apparent human half transform into a demon, then be taken over by something worse, and not even bat an eye?

There was clearly more to this woman than he'd given her credit for.

Plus, the shrug sent her curtain of bright hair rippling over her shoulders. It was...appealing.

Distracting.

The voice boomed again. It was a little hard to take seriously, coming out of something that looked like an inflated marshmallow circus peanut. "I am giving you a warning, Keeper. In the spirit of fair play."

Rhys wasn't buying that for a second. A child of Lucifer? Fair?

Hilarious.

"Fair play?" He casually spun his dagger around one finger. "Didn't you try to have her killed *before* issuing this warning?"

"She survived. So it does not matter."

Maisy tapped on the desk. "I disagree."

"Stop your search for the Key," he commanded. "If you do so, I will leave you unharmed."

She leaned back with a creak of the wooden desk chair. Propped her rainbow Converse on the desk, showing off her yellow-and-pink polka-dotted leggings. "I don't know what year it is down in Hell—does time work differently down there?—but up here on Earth, it is the twenty-first century. No man gets to order a woman around."

Chutzpah. That's what she had. Bold audacity, in any language.

Softly, Rhys murmured, "There's not a significant time difference. It is, however, fairly misogynistic and patriarchal in the Underworld."

"Welcome to the real world, Volac. Women do what they want every bit as much as men. Often, we do a better job of it." Maisy picked up a pen and waggled it, lips pursed thoughtfully. "I do appreciate your offer, though, so in the spirit of fair play, I'll make you one right back. Stay away from me. Call off your dogs. We'll both do what we're meant to do." Without taking her eyes off the lawyer, she reached out to stroke a hand down Rhys's arm. "Or I'll unleash my pet *Nephilim* on you. Let me just say—you wouldn't enjoy the results."

Turk's body began to shake again. "You will do as I say, Keeper! Or else." This time, the voice was so loud, sonorous, that the floor vibrated like they were at an arena rock concert.

Maisy trilled out a high laugh, then dropped her feet back to the ground. "C'mon. I taught high schoolers. That threat doesn't faze me. Strive for some originality. Or else *what*?"

With a wet gurgle, Turk's head exploded in a geyser of black sludge. It waterfalled down his still-standing body.

Shit.

Over the gurgling hiss of the sludge, Rhys said, "He sure called your bluff."

In a shaky voice, Maisy replied, "I guess it's true—lawyers really *are* evil."

A sharp burn on his wrist made Rhys look down. Just under where he'd rolled up the cuffs of his shirt was a drop of the sludge. It wasn't hot, but it was burning through his skin like acid. There were splatters of it all across his shirt. He looked over at Maisy's yellow cotton sweater. It had the same Jackson Pollock treatment.

"Take off your sweater." Then, remembering her recent diatribe on not taking orders from men, he just grabbed the hem and whipped it over her head and tossed it in the corner.

"Hey!" She didn't play the virginal card and try to cover up her bra with her hands, but she did leap up from the chair.

Rhys ripped open his shirt. No time for buttons. The minute it was off, he dug in his pocket for his emergency vial. Then he reconsidered. A teachable moment was worth a little more pain.

Okay, a *lot* more. It burned like a son of a bitch.

He thrust his arm in front of Maisy. "See that?" The red circle was raw. Already oozing blood. The black dot of acid in the middle of it was clearly visible. "Many demons—to be safe, you should assume it's all of them—have acid or venom in their bodily fluids. One could spit at you from across the room, and you'd get burned."

She put her cool fingers on the underside of his arm, supporting it. "It's eating through your skin. How do we stop it?"

He pulled the vial from his pocket. "Pop the top and dump it on. All of it."

For once, she didn't push back or ask twenty questions. Maisy thumbed off the lid and didn't hesitate. She kept pouring it, slowly, to stay right on the wound, even when he let out a single howl of pain.

"The healing can hurt worse than the injury." Rhys sucked in a breath between his teeth. Held it as the last drop fell. "But then it's over." The blackness had washed away.

Gently, she traced a wide circle around his wrist. "Uh, it's still red. And bleeding."

"Yeah, but the acid's gone. That's what matters."

She looked around the office. Files, framed photos, some plaques. What was she looking for? Maisy pulled four tissues from the box on the credenza. Folded them into a thick packet.

She settled them on the gaping wound. "Hold that in place." Then she toed off her sneaker.

"What are you doing?"

"Fixing you. I don't leave a job half done." Maisy rolled off her yellow sock. Brushed aside his hand and tied it around his wrist to keep the absorbent tissues in place. It was a unique field dressing, but it'd do the job.

It was also yet another remarkable display of a cool head under pressure. Not to mention her being a lot gentler than the last time Zavier had packed jungle dirt on a talon slash across his stomach and wrapped it in banana leaves.

"Thanks. I appreciate your help." Because even without the whole exploding demon head, lots of women—and some men, for sure—would get nauseous at the mere sight of his bleeding wound.

"We're even." She pointed her bare toes, tipped in bright red, at her sweater decomposing in the corner. "Thanks for keeping me from getting burned."

"All in a day's work. Speaking of, hang on." Rhys hit speed dial. "Z, we're going to need a full cleanup at the lawyer's office, ASAP. And some clothes. The scene and the Keeper are secure. We'll be waiting."

He headed for the door.

Maisy bounded to cut him off. "Whoa, where do you think you're going?"

"To check the other offices and lock the front door."

She clamped her hand onto his uninjured arm. "Not without me glued to you like a shadow."

Huh. It only took a *second* near-death experience to bring her around to respecting his protection rules. "Look, it should be safe. Volac gave us the big show."

"Thought you said never to assume?" She tossed his own words back in his face. *Again.*

Rhys didn't want her terrified by their ordeal, but made wordless from fear for just a couple of minutes wouldn't be so bad.

In moments, they'd cleared the few other rooms and locked the door. Then Rhys un-pried her fingers. "Unless there are more disembodied spirits waiting to jump into someone, we're alone."

She bit her lip. "Is that a possibility?"

It took Rhys more than a few seconds to answer because he was focused on that juicy bottom lip she'd sunk her teeth into.

Which was what *he* wanted to do.

"Uh, yes. But possession can only occur if you're at least partially a demon, pledged to Hell, or comatose."

"Then you'd better not start in on another one of your lectures about the fate of the world being at hand. I swear I'm escaping into a coma the next time you do." Maisy waggled the silver vial. "What was in this?"

Rhys nipped it from her fingers. The vial had been forged in the sacred fire of a phoenix rebirth more than a thousand years ago. If he lost it, there'd be no replacement. It was one of the few gifts passed down from his angel father.

"Call it a heavenly disinfectant. Salt water, holy water, water from China's Pon Lai fountain, and a ground-up tail feather from a *Caladrius.*"

She pursed her lips. Was the woman just taunting him now?

"Will it do anything to cure a common head cold?"

"No idea. *Nephilim* don't get sick."

"So jealous!" Then Maisy cocked her head to the side. "Can I get one for oh, say, next November and December? I'll be your guinea pig. I get wicked sinus infections."

"Guess you're an imperfect version of that earthbound angel way back in your lineage." Rhys watched her pace a tight circle in the reception area. "Are you okay?"

She flexed her fingers a few times. Shook out her hands. Then her entire arms spaghettied all over. "I'm not oozing blood like you. Just coming down from a big adrenaline rush, I guess. That other Keeper's a real piece of work. He pissed me off."

"Good."

"Really? You're not going to yell at me for snarking at him?"

Rhys took her shoulders. Her smooth, slightly cool, bare shoulders. Because she was only wearing a bright yellow lace bra. Which shouldn't surprise him. Everything about her was bright.

"Maisy, what you did was extraordinary."

"I didn't realize being a sarcastic bitch was extraordinary. Why didn't I get an extra honor cord for that at any of my graduations? Or does it go on my resume under Special Skills?"

It was impossible to tell if she was jittery from the attack and about to crumble…or if this was just her usual pushback to him.

He didn't want her to crumble.

He *absolutely* didn't want her to cry again. So he stroked his hands up and down her arms. Arms that were as smooth as glacial ice. "You stood up to an agent of Hell. An evil child of Lucifer. *Inside* a demon. You weren't cowed. You didn't run. Or scream. Or faint."

Those red lips quirked up at the corners. "Well, it's not the nineteenth century. Very few women swoon anymore, even at the sight of a demon."

How was it that she wouldn't even shut up long enough to take his damn compliments?

"Your conduct was befitting a Keeper. You showed Volac that you're no pushover. You were brave. Strong."

"I mostly faked it. The brave part." She looked up at him from beneath half-veiled lids. "Glad it played well."

Then why was Maisy downplaying it now? Rhys wanted to pick her up and twirl her until she breathlessly laughed and admitted that she'd been great.

That'd be ridiculous, though.

"It was more than I expected." He lifted her chin with the pad of his finger. "*You* were more."

"Thank you."

Now that he'd begun? Turning off the compliments was impossible. Not when every one he gave made her eyes gleam a little more and her smile widen a little more. "You impressed me."

Maisy windshield-wipered her hand across his bare chest. "You're, ah, pretty impressive yourself."

Her touch unlocked the raging desire Rhys had insistently ignored, just below the surface. His fingers dug into her shoulders, lifting her off the ground to meet his lips. Watching Maisy stand beside him, *fight* beside him, albeit with words, was one hell of a turn-on.

It wasn't the win over Volac—sure, Turk's head had exploded, but Maisy and Rhys were in one piece, and Volac had retreated; ergo, *win*—that licked fire along his blood.

It was the *woman*.

Her sass. Her spirit. Her sunny hair and luminous smile that barely faltered even in the face of grave danger.

Warm and pliant, her lips molded to his. They vibrated when little moans escaped from her. And Maisy greedily licked at him, nipped at him, with every bit as much hunger.

She wrapped one leg around his hip. Twined the other ankle around his knee. Scratched her nails against the sides of his skull. Heat bloomed through Rhys with every cant of her hips, with each scrape of the lace cups against his pecs.

He wanted her.

He wanted all of her.

Not to stop her from crying. Not to celebrate coming out the other side of a tangle with a demon.

Rhys wanted *Maisy*. Wanted to taste more of her. See more of her. Be surrounded by her warmth.

Sliding his mouth sideways, he intensified their kiss. Their tongues battled, and God help him if this wasn't the first battle of his life he wouldn't mind losing.

And then his head hit the ceiling.

He'd extended his wings and flown them. Even if only for two vertical feet. *That* was how lost in desire he'd been.

That had never happened before.

It was inexcusable.

Maisy giggled. "I know a certain part of the male anatomy's supposed to pop up. Didn't realize on a *Nephilim* it was also the wings."

"It's not." He landed them. Immediately. Then Rhys grabbed for the cardigan hanging on the coatrack in the corner. "Put this on."

"I'm not cold."

God knew neither was he, now, but he needed her covered up, ASAP. "Gideon and Zavier will be here soon. And Gid's got this thing where he claims once he sees a bra on a woman, he's guaranteed to remove it within an hour."

Maisy put on the sweater. With a scowl. "That's sexist. Borderline harassment."

"Both of those, but also true." What did she do to him? Something to worry about later. Rhys had two priorities right now: not touching her again, and recon. "I know you got the information on the locksmith, but we should still go through all his files."

"For what?" she asked as she followed him back down the hall.

"You'd be surprised how many people are dumb enough that

they'd keep a file entitled 'Lord of Hell' or 'Demon Stuff.'"

"Turk was a middle-aged lawyer. He wouldn't label any file 'stuff.'"

"Don't know until we look." Although Maisy was right. Rhys was just too pissed to come up with something better. Pissed at himself for getting off task. Hell, for *almost* getting off...

"Clearly, he was in deep and knew more. Probably a long-term spy on your uncle. Check his schedule. See what might be knocking soon expecting an appointment."

"What? Don't you mean who?"

"You never know in this town."

At least if another demon did show up, fighting it would give Rhys a way to work off all this pent-up...whatever it was that had him riled and roused.

Distracted.

He'd take a down-and-dirty fight over denying the attraction to a woman he couldn't have any day. If Rhys was lucky enough? An oozing, snarling demon would swagger through that door any second now.

At least he had a goal—something to hope for over the next eleven days. Blood. Dismemberment.

All far better than an accidental slip sideways into a relationship.

CHAPTER ELEVEN

Maisy sat in the back of Rhys's Land Rover. Normally, she'd fight for the shotgun seat, but this thing was filled with three men, each well over six feet. Her knees cramped just looking at their long legs.

Other parts of her wished it was a warmer day so she might see those legs. In shorts. Not just Rhys but Gideon and Zavier, too. Because she needed to know if her attraction to Rhys was a real thing. A this-man-was-off-the-charts-handsome thing? A *Nephilim*-give-off-more-pheromones-than-humans thing?

Maisy needed to discover, with empirical evidence, why she kept kissing him. Why she liked it so much even though the man bothered her to no end the rest of the time.

Except for when he was actually patient. And understanding. And the rare occasions when he let that dry wit roll out.

Not to mention his...well, his bodyguard competence porn. The only reason Maisy had been brave enough to stand there and sass back at a freaking demonic angel—she still didn't understand how those worked—was because she felt safe knowing that Rhys and his muscles and his wings were there to protect her, no matter what.

A tap on her leg jerked her head around.

"You zoned out again. Didn't get much sleep last night?" Liss asked. Little crinkles of concern arrowed out from her dark eyes with their outrageous fake lashes and cat-eye liner.

"Not really." She'd told her friend all about the, ah, encounter with Rhys. Well, she'd led off with the description of Turk blowing up, but Liss had been far more interested in the post–sludge explosion kissing. Maisy didn't want Rhys to think that she'd tossed and turned all night over him. "Stress, you know? End of the world on my shoulders, et cetera."

"They've got a liquor cabinet you wouldn't believe in their Watchtower. Lair." She gave a brisk nod. "Yes, I prefer lair. Anyway, I'll make you a hot white Russian tonight before bed. It's got your never-fail warm milk component, along with Kahlúa and vodka to knock you out so hard you won't even be able to dream."

Maisy rubbed at her temples. "That was the one good part of last night. No nightmares. I guess real life is officially scarier than whatever my subconscious could come up with."

"You need to dream," Zavier said from the row in front of them. He hitched one arm over the back of the seat. "It's how your brain keeps your visual cortex from being rewired."

That sounded like something that shouldn't and couldn't possibly happen if you skipped the usual rounds of stress dreams and *Chris Hemsworth in a hot tub* dreams. "What's that?"

He pointed at his ear, then at his eyes below thick, dark brows. "If you lose one sense, the others become heightened. That's neuroplasticity. The brain rewires the portion not being used. Good news for blind people. Not for people who zonk out for a solid eight. Your visual cortex isn't being used, so your other senses might try to take it over. Dreaming is its defense mechanism—keeps it active to prevent being repurposed."

Repurposed. Rewired. Maisy knew that technically, the brain was similar to a computer, but Zavier's description made her brain sound like the inner workings of a space robot. She blinked away from his unnervingly intense gaze. "I would've been much happier without knowing that," she groused.

He rolled up the cuffs of his black dress shirt. Rhys had told her to dress comfortably for today's expedition. She and Liss had followed instructions, wearing jeans, sneakers, and hoodies. The *Nephilim*? Evidently, comfortable for them just meant discarding coats and ties. All three wore dress shirts and perfectly tailored slacks. "Don't worry—I'm sure you're still dreaming. You've got plenty to see today that'll give your subconscious a reboot, imagination-wise."

Liss harrumphed. "I know that was supposed to be reassuring, but it came out as more of a threat."

"Promise. Threat." He turned to face front. "It's all in the interpretation."

Wow. Liss and Zavier were very much oil and water—if oil and water combusted when mixed. Maisy vaguely remembered something that did that from high school chemistry class, but she'd been too busy drawing on every flat surface to remember the inflammatory substances.

"Do you see the water bottles tucked into the doors?" Gideon asked.

Maisy scrabbled in the compartment. "Yes. Very classy. Thank you."

All the men laughed. "This isn't bottle service in a limo. That's your potion. Drink up." The car slowed to a stop.

"A potion? I don't think so." Liss tossed her hair after tossing Maisy a wide-eyed, *can you believe this* look. "What if I have an allergic reaction? What if it goes horribly wrong? What if it makes my tongue fuzzy? You aren't wizards. Potions aren't your specialty. I don't want some low-level mix-master giving me God knows what to drink."

Yes.

All of that.

100 percent.

But also… Maisy grabbed the seats and leaned forward. "What does the potion *do*?"

Rhys gave a slow, approving nod. At least, she was fairly certain that was approval that firmed his lips. His really talented lips. Hard to tell for sure, since she was so much more familiar with his disapproving scowls.

"At Turk's office, you made a joke about not expecting any more mystical creatures to walk in the door. You were wrong."

"Wrong that it was a joke? Because your sense of humor isn't the most well-developed."

"Wrong that it wasn't likely. Which we could tell you. You'd pretend to listen, but you wouldn't truly *understand*. So, for today, we're making sure that you can."

"The potion's harmless." Gideon's golden eyes crinkled at the corners in reassurance. "All three of us are also taking it. You can pass your bottle to us if it'll make you feel better. As long as you don't leave lipstick on the rim."

"It'll allow you to see past enchantments. Past illusions. You'll see the true form of every being on the streets. We use it. Some creatures we can sense, but not all."

"Does it have side effects?"

"You'll have an uncontrollable urge to sleep with me once you see my wings," Gideon said with a wink. "Otherwise, it'll wear off in an hour. No kick, no hangover, nothing. A few swigs is enough."

Maisy uncapped the bottle before she risked psyching herself out by thinking about it more. After all, if you couldn't trust angels—even *half* angels—who could you trust? Warily, she tipped it onto her tongue.

Omigosh, she could've guzzled the entire thing. "It tastes like strawberry and vanilla ice cream." She gasped.

"Thank Rhys. He made me flavor it for you. Because wormwood's bitter."

Maisy gaped at the back of Rhys's head. Tried to catch his eye in the rearview mirror, but it didn't work. That was thoughtful. Surprisingly thoughtful.

Liss shook her bottle warily. "Isn't wormwood the halluci-nogen in absinthe?"

Zavier snorted. "Do you know your hallucinogens or your booze?"

"I'm well acquainted with laws that infringe on personal freedom. Absinthe was banned here for a century, but they still served it all around the world. I don't like being told what I can or can't do by people or by governments."

"Yes, wormwood is in absinthe." Gideon slammed the door, then opened Liss's and stuck his head in. "No, we aren't getting you high. It's the opposite of hallucinating—you're acquiring the power to see true reality."

Maisy squeezed her friend's hand. "C'mon. Maybe we'll see a unicorn."

"Wrong season." Gideon straightened, his arm resting across the top of the door. "You'd have a better chance come fall."

"Seriously?" Liss sputtered, having taken at least three deep swigs.

Smooth laughter rolled out of him like a satin sheet being unfurled. "God, no. Unicorns aren't real. Alicorns, though…real, but not up here. Too cold. Look to the sky in Provence, you'd have a good chance of seeing a few fly by."

"Less talking, more walking," Rhys ordered as he opened Maisy's door. "Nice day. Lots of people around. You'll be safe with all three of us on guard. And you'll see…well, whatever there is to see."

"When will the potion kick in—ohhhh my." There were Rhys's wings again. Tucked against his back, with just the arches visible above his shoulders. The urge to touch them was just as strong as the first time.

The urge to touch *him* was just as strong as yesterday.

But this wasn't the manta ray exhibit at the aquarium. Maisy told herself to treat it like a…um…lion exhibit—soft and amazing to pet, but with one hell of a growl and extremely dangerous.

Sass was a good antidote to sexiness. Maisy got out of the car without another glance at Rhys. "I think you're overselling this excursion. How many demons can there be in Buffalo? We don't have a crime rate higher than any other comparably sized city."

"That's the Canadian niceness seeping across the border," Gideon said. "It skews the stats."

Maisy made her hands into fists, biting her nails into her flesh. Then she risked a glance at Gideon. His wings were breathtaking. The perfect pairing to his blond good looks. At the top arch, they were a tawny brown, similar to that lion she'd just imagined. From there, they morphed to a deep, ancient gold, then pale yellow, ending in tips of pure cream.

She wanted to touch them.

But she did *not* want to jump him. Or even kiss him. Which meant she could unclench her hands and relax knowing that she wasn't a sexual freak for all *Nephilim*…

…and worry about why she couldn't control herself at all around one in particular.

"Here we go. Market Arcade." Rhys swept his arm to indicate the passersby. "What do you see?"

Maisy's artist brain catalogued the neoclassical structure with its intricate terra cotta facade and soaring glass-and-steel entrance. She noted an elderly woman pulling a folding cart. Two moms holding ginormous coffees with one hand and strollers with the other. A loose gang of man-boys in blue Canisius College sweatshirts with their gold griffin mascots—

"Hey. Are griffins real?"

Rhys tracked her gaze. "Yes. But no, there's no flock hanging out at the college."

"Is that what you call a group of them? A flock?"

"It's what I call a group of most winged things. I don't worry about all those cutesy names."

She bumped him with her elbow. "Like a waddle."

"A what?"

"On the water, a group of penguins is called a raft, but on land, they're called a waddle. Isn't that adorable?"

Rhys tapped the top of his head. Winced. "You just wasted three of my brain cells with that piece of trivia. They're gone. Never to be retrieved."

Men. It didn't shrink their penises by a single millimeter to admit something was cute, but they sure fought it tooth and nail.

"Watch out." Liss circled her arm at the men. "I'll start calling the three of you a waddle."

Zavier bared his teeth. "Go ahead and try. You'll regret it."

Rhys snapped his fingers twice, right in front of Maisy's face. "We're wasting time. The potion wears off, remember? Focus."

Ugh. Talk about a waste of time. It was historic downtown Buffalo. Old. Pretty. Lots of people out enjoying the sunny day. "The wildest thing here is a bunch of frat boys."

"Look harder. At the small details." Rhys jerked his chin at a standard street-musician type: beard, overly skinny jeans, open case at his feet with loose cash. He was playing a saxophone. The music wasn't toe-tapping, but it wasn't *evil*.

She strolled a bit closer. Then Maisy noticed a glimmer of movement along the neck strap. Grateful for the wire-rimmed sunglasses that obfuscated her gaze, she did indeed focus. Let the musician blur away and watched the shadowy motion.

It only took a second to see that there was something moving up and down the strap. In time to the music, even. She swallowed a squeal of surprise. She'd groped a half angel. She could play it cool.

"Is that… It looks like… Well, it looks like a fox? If you shrank a fox down to the size of a mouse."

Rhys nodded approvingly. "That's a Pipe Fox."

"*Kitsune*, in the original Japanese," Zavier corrected.

Gideon flicked him with the side of his translucent wing. "Nobody here speaks Japanese, Z, except for us. Don't be a pretentious pain in the ass. That's Rhys's job."

Maisy watched it flit up and down the strap, then around the musician's neck three times. "How is it so small?"

"It's not an actual fox. It's a shape-shifting spirit familiar."

Aha. She pounced on the, well, *familiar* term. "A familiar? Like a cat to a witch?"

Gideon opened his mouth. Closed it. Opened it again. "Short answer is more or less."

A familiar didn't sound evil. More like a loyal pet. "So that guy playing the sax is…"

"A shaman."

Maisy took heart in Gideon's response. "Like a mystical priest. See? A good guy."

"Nope. Shamans can access good *and* evil spirits. Evil ones are faster and easier to use. He's dangerous. And not just for the way he's butchering that song."

Well, the fox was as cute as could be. And it deserved to be liberated from an evil master. "I like the fox. I kind of want one. Could we rescue it? Or buy it off him?"

"Not a pet," Rhys said tersely. "Small doesn't mean powerless. The Pipe Fox can make illusions, but it can also summon the elements. Lightning. Fire. Wind. Water. It could bring a twelve-foot wave to engulf us right here on the street. Just for shits and giggles."

Maisy changed course with her strolling. She angled to cut across the street. Immediately.

And almost walked right into a bus.

Rhys grabbed her arm, lifting her off her feet. Then he snatched her tight against his chest. It was over in two seconds but shocked the breath out of her. As did the arm banded on her diaphragm.

"Are you all right?" His voice was harsh, but the hand he cupped on her cheek was gentle. Calming.

She sucked in a breath. Then two more right on top of it without exhaling first. "Thanks for saving me. Again."

His thumb made a slow sweep up and down her cheek. "Gives me a reason to get up in the morning."

"Another joke? Wow. I must've come closer to getting bus smushed than I realized."

Zavier stuck his face in hers with an assessing frown. "Do humans not teach their kids to look before crossing the street?"

"I just really wanted to get away from an evil spirit that could drown me five hundred miles away from the nearest ocean."

Rhys set her down but kept a hand at the small of her back. "We can move along."

As they crossed, Liss patted her shoulder. "Evil or good spirit, it's a moot point. Our lease doesn't allow for pets."

Yeah. The *lease* was the problem with the magical element-wielding spirit.

They made it all of halfway down the block before Liss grabbed Maisy's hand. "We're in front of the Performing Arts Center," she murmured. "So please tell me there's a touring production of *Wicked* in town that explains...*that*."

"Elphaba is green." Maisy swallowed hard. "That woman is yellow. Four-days-from-a-liver-transplant yellow."

Not to mention that she was taller than their *Nephilim* by half a foot. With rags dripping off of her in layers like a rotting toga. Oh, and she had claws.

She could be the poster child for evil.

But it was like looking at a double-exposed negative. She could see the demon woman. Maisy could also see, however, superimposed, a perfectly normal-looking little old lady. Shorter than Maisy herself, skin a normal color, wearing a puffy pink cardigan and a cream skirt.

Was that what everyone else saw? A harmless old lady?

How many times in her life had she walked by someone who looked innocuous but was truly evil under a normal facade?

How safe was her city? How safe was she?

Eyes still fixed on the monstrosity, Maisy reached for Rhys.

"Tell me your potion is in overdrive." To her relief, he wrapped her wrist around his arm and covered her hand. And didn't say a thing when her nails dug into his flesh. "Tell me I'm hallucinating."

"Mmm, not if you're seeing the *Busyasta*. Color of cheap beer?" Gideon shot his cuffs. He couldn't have acted less concerned. "Bad dresser?"

"That's an understatement."

"A lethargy demon." Zavier did a half turn, looking up and down the streets. "Yeah. See, St. Michael's Catholic Church is a block over. Delaware Avenue Episcopal is three blocks up and over. Trinity Episcopal, too. No surprise to find a *Busyasta*."

Most of Maisy's general paranormal creature knowledge was centered on vampires, thanks to books and movies. But even though she'd never heard of a lethargy demon before, the whole church thing seemed incongruous. "Why on earth are demons attracted to churches?"

Rhys lifted his chin toward the…thing. "She makes men oversleep and neglect their religious duties. Easier to give them an afternoon nap after a big lunch—they miss the five-o'clock mass."

Okay. Maisy's danger-o-meter dialed down to basically just disgust. "*That's* her whole evil purpose?"

"Yeah."

Liss huffed. "Not so scary." She didn't lessen her white-knuckle grip on Maisy, though.

Gideon took up the lecture. "It is for the people who needed that touchstone of religion. Maybe a potential murderer was coming in, and the right sermon would stay his hand. Maybe a kid is about to go down the wrong path, but confirmation class gets him right in the head. You hear of the butterfly effect?"

"I saw the movie." Mostly for the dreamboat actor who played the hero. Maisy could tell they were waiting for her to prove her knowledge—like a good teacher would. "Travel back in time, change one thing as small as killing a butterfly, come to the present and everything's vastly different."

"Demonic influence is another version of that same theory."

"Oh."

The men got them walking forward again. Maisy didn't try to cross the street away from the demon this time. Not with three *Nephilim* between her and it.

But she was disturbed down to the marrow of her bones as they strolled past.

And she stayed quiet as they turned left at Edward Street and headed toward the massive brick Cyclorama Building.

Suddenly, Rhys stilled. "Really? She thinks she can come to *our* city? That's ballsy."

"Or stupid," Zavier said.

"Or both," Gideon piled on.

Maisy didn't see anything out of the ordinary. "Who's got you all steamed?"

Rhys turned her ninety degrees. "Tour's over. Gid, Z, you got this?"

"With pleasure."

"No. If you want us to see what's truly out here, then let me see." Maisy wrenched free and whipped back around.

That was a mistake.

The *Aldokriz* demon's death had been disgusting. Turk's death had been horrifying. The *Busyasta* demon had chilled her soul.

This, though? This hideousness in front of them? Maisy knew she'd never be able to bleach her brain enough to come close to forgetting the sight.

It was naked. Large, droopy breasts, although covered in hair head to toe. It was topped with a snarling lion's head. The bloodstained hands held thick ropes of snakes. And the so-called normal shape superimposed over it was the sweetest blond tween with her hair in pigtails.

She stopped Liss with a strong hand on her shoulder. "No.

They were right. Don't turn around. Bad enough that one of us should see it. Trust me on this." But Maisy kept staring.

This was the lesson they'd wanted her to learn.

She'd absorb it. The way it stood next to the Girl Scout troop selling cookies. The way none of the kids or moms so much as blinked at its nearness.

Was that what made evil so insidious? That you couldn't always see it creeping up on you until it was too late?

If this was the kind of thing that was allowed to leave Hell and roam the streets...what nightmare was *behind* those prison gates that she was now in charge of keeping locked?

Rhys got shoulder to shoulder with Gideon. "Tell her this is our only warning. Next time we see her, we kill her."

"Does she deserve the warning?"

"It's broad daylight. You can't attack a kid on the street. People see her, not the *Lamastu*. All we can do until dark is threaten her."

"That's not all." Zavier pulled out his wallet and removed a tiny sticker. "I'll hide this tracker on her while we're talking. She doesn't get out of town by tonight? We'll find her and deal with it before the moon's all the way up."

Rhys gave a low whistle and a thumbs-up. "Nice foresight."

"Downtown's always full of crap that we wish we could clean up. Figured our trip would give me the chance to try this out."

Maisy watched them calmly discussing this...this...freaking demon that could do who knows what to people. From the appearance? A lion's head? It seemed a safe assumption that this one would do considerably more damage than the *Busyasta*.

Gideon took the sticker, turned it over. "Is it tech? You can't keep stealing from the military. We need to save our break-ins there for true emergencies."

"Not like they'll stop me," Zavier said with a smug curl to his lip. "And this is a tech-slash-magic hybrid. An experiment."

"If it works, it'll be useful. Good luck." Rhys clapped him on the back. "We'll be in the car." He led the women away.

"Sorry we had to cut this short. Don't need word to spread that there are humans who can see demons. Better for the *Lamastu* not to know that you were aware of her." He slowed his long-legged pace. Gave Maisy an actual smile. Not a smirk. Not a warp-speed quiver of his lips. A full-blown, eye-crinkling smile that transformed his usually stern visage. "You did well, Keeper."

The compliment was appreciated. It warmed Maisy every bit as much as the smile—which meant her heart felt like it was cozied up to a bonfire.

It just wasn't true.

"I didn't do well at all. I am not okay with what you showed us. Please, please tell me that this was an aberration. That there's a demon convention in town. That it's a demon holiday. That seeing three demons in a single block is not normal."

His eyes were full of...pity? "There is no normal."

"Don't get into teacher mode. I don't expect stats. I want you to tell me that my hometown is safe. That there's an explanation, and there isn't usually that much evil lurking." Because Maisy simply couldn't accept it.

Liss nodded emphatically. "What she said."

"I wish I could." Rhys led them back across the street to give the *Busyasta* a wide berth. "But that was the point of today's lesson. Evil is everywhere. Evil just...*is*. The choices you make have to be colored by that knowledge."

No. That was a coloring book she'd throw out before ever opening. "I'd rather seek out and concentrate on the good in the world."

"Knowing there *is* evil makes you more aware of the good," Rhys countered.

How was he arguing in favor of living a gloom and doom–filled life? "No." If she hadn't been walking, Maisy would've stamped her foot. "Do you like ice cream?"

"Uh, yeah. Humans, witches, demons, angels—pretty sure

we're all Team Ice Cream."

Maisy skewered her index finger in the air between them. "What's your favorite flavor?"

"What's your point?"

Liss snorted. "It must be a silly, mash-up flavor if the big alpha *Nephilim* doesn't want to tell us."

Agreed. "I'm getting to the point. Just tell me," Maisy asked again.

"Fine." But the big, alpha half angel jerked his gaze away from her as he admitted, "It's Phish Food. Chocolate ice cream with caramel, marshmallow, and fudge."

Liss reached across Maisy to thwap his arm. "I can't believe you thought we wouldn't know what's in Phish Food. Only one of the best flavors ever. That's insulting."

Well, well. Wasn't that interesting? A man who came off as so obsessively controlled *did* let his hair down enough to enjoy a messy mix of sweetness. Maisy wanted to discover what other layers were hidden under Rhys's regimented veneer.

"My point is, when you enjoy it, you aren't thinking about how much better a flavor it is than vanilla or pineapple sorbet. You don't stack it up mentally on every bite as being superior. You enjoy it because it *is* good. Period."

"I'm not having an ethics discussion about ice cream. Sticking your head in the sand, ignoring the existence of evil, won't make it go away. Won't make you safe."

"It would make me happy," Maisy said softly.

"Maybe." Rhys opened the car door for her. "But that's a luxury we don't all have."

Yeah. The heavy-handed reminder landed on her brain like the Empire State Building. *Choose* to become Keeper. Or ignore the whole situation and have creatures worse than what she'd seen today running rampant over the earth.

Yet another excellent "or else" by Hell.

From now on, the only way to enjoy the good in life, the ice cream-ness of it all, would be to also acknowledge the depths of evil out there.

Maisy wondered if ice cream—and happiness—would always be slightly *less* thanks to this lesson.

She also wondered what soft and melty expression her grumpy *Nephilim* got on his face while eating a container of Phish Food.

It'd be...something...to see what Rhys looked like when his guard was down.

CHAPTER TWELVE

Rhys hefted the last three big cardboard boxes out of his trunk. They'd driven from Buffalo this time, crossed the border officially, and gotten to the Watchtower via an underground cave and tunnel. "How do you fit all this crap in your little car?"

Maisy was pulling bags from the back seat. "I don't. We make multiple trips. With a car this big, I was able to stock up on enough supplies for at least a month. It'll be nice not to go back and forth so much from the warehouse."

He'd been conned.

By a freaking human.

Unbelievable. "You're *using* me for my Land Rover?"

"Unapologetically." There was zero remorse in Maisy's voice. If anything, he was fairly certain there'd been a tinge of amusement. "The faster we assemble these gift baskets, the sooner we can get back to hunting for the Key. Which you keep harping on. I'm just sticking to our agreement."

Gee, was he repeating himself about how the fate of the world was at hand?

Damn straight he was!

Rhys pointed Maisy up the rough stone steps from the garage. "Or you could let me hire someone to do it for you."

"That would be an outrage on two fronts: economically and morally. And I'm not having that particular fight again. I'm keeping this job, at least, as it can be done from your super-safe lair. You've got to accept that being a Keeper is my side hustle," she said firmly.

Good thing the woman was in front of him on the stairs. She couldn't see his jaw literally unhinge so fast that it cracked.

A side hustle?

Keeping millions on this planet safe from untold evil was a side hustle to the woman? Like…like delivering groceries. Or dog walking.

Christ.

He kicked the door to the kitchen shut behind him. Probably vented a little of his frustration in his kick, since the hinges rattled at the force. "Where's your roommate?"

"Liss is working her bartending job. Since you deemed her to be safe when away from me and not at our apartment. So, you know, this whole assembly-line thing would go a lot faster if you helped."

Wordlessly, Rhys hefted his stack of boxes even higher before setting them next to the breakfast table that they never used.

Maisy rolled her hand in a circle. "Yes, I appreciate the schlepping. I'm asking you to *continue* to help. I'll feed you as payment."

Her stubborn need to be fair and responsible just complicated his life. "I can order us food delivered to Metafora. Zip through the falls and pick it up."

"For crying out loud! Is your answer to everything in life to throw money at it?"

At first, Rhys figured that she was bickering with him because, well, that was their go-to method of communication. But then he noticed that Maisy was actually waiting for an answer.

She wanted to understand him? Not just put up with him? Guess that counted as progress. Hopefully, it'd cut down on their snarking.

"I focus on the things only I can do—such as battling a demon marquis who commands thirty legions," he said. "Everything *else*, I throw money at."

"I suppose that's smart time allocation if you can afford it. I can't, but I *can* cook. If your fridge is stocked."

"Of course it is. I know because I lug in all the boxes of supplies. Gideon's an amazing cook."

She stared into the fridge for a few moments. "Greek turkey meatballs with lemon orzo and tzatziki."

"Shhhh." Rhys held a finger to his lips. Tiptoed over to cup a hand around her ear and whisper, "We don't want word to get out to Hell's legions, but it turns out I can be bribed."

To his utter surprise, Maisy didn't laugh. Didn't even smile. Instead? She thwacked him on the arm.

Surprisingly hard.

"See? When you stop assuming everything in the world is horrible and doomed and out to get us, you can be fun. Charming. Why do you have to be so darned serious all the time?"

Oh, she wanted to throw down?

Fine.

He slapped a hand on the doorframe above her head, caging her in with his body. Close enough to feel her chest rise and fall against his with every breath. "Why do you have to assume that everyone is good, everything will work out just fine, and the skies will continually rain daisies and diamonds upon you?"

Usually when Rhys crowded someone, let his temper darken his tone, they quaked. They wouldn't meet his eyes. The dumb ones tried to run away.

Maisy—well, he'd already discovered there was nothing *usual* about her. The woman tossed her hair and glared right back with eyes that were all but shooting green fire at him.

"Do you remember my crappy apartment with its cracked linoleum? I'm in student loan debt up to my ears. No, up to *your* ears, oh very tall one. I *wish* I could afford a simple bouquet of fresh daisies."

That fact just left Rhys more confused. No family. No luck in the career she wanted. No money. No boyfriend.

So what gave her the dogged, persistent, annoyingly unshakable faith in goodness? And why did he find it so appealing?

Rhys stalked away. Because being that close to Maisy made him think about...things...other than the argument at hand.

Made him feel...things...other than the acceptable frustration.

Exasperation.

Infuriation.

Yes. That's what he needed to hold on to. In order to keep his pants from becoming uncomfortably tight. Or not *more* so. Because that had become a problem the instant his rib cage had grazed her breast.

The toe of his polished loafer caught a loose nail in the polished wooden planks. Rhys pushed the tiniest bit of his anger into the floor to seal it in place.

"But you still see the best in every situation," he insisted. "Worse yet, you fight against the truth of what is bad, even when I prove it to you. You turn yourself inside out trying to find an ounce of good in a swimming pool–sized vat full of evil."

"Yeah. That's how I roll."

They were going around in circles. Rhys threw up his arms. "For God's sake, *why*?"

Instead of coming after him to go another round with louder voices, spitting more ire, Maisy bit her lip. Folded her hands at her waist. Quietly, she asked, "Do you truly want to know? Or do you just want to argue about it more?"

They'd hit a good rhythm with the arguing, but Rhys found that he did, actually, want to unlock this mystery. That he wanted to *understand* this woman who caught him off guard and confused him with every other sentence.

"I would like to know."

"Okay. Then help me with dinner, and I'll explain." She opened the pantry door and lifted something bright green and polka-dotted off the hook he swore hadn't been there yesterday.

He'd told her to bring whatever she needed for two weeks. Hadn't batted an eye at the afghan—even though she had to know they'd provide blankets. Or the box of art supplies. But... an apron?

Rhys backed up as fast as if he'd been confronted with a four-headed *Gorgon*. "I'm not wearing an apron."

"Oh, right." She slipped it over her head with a smirk. "You don't care if you spill on those pricey clothes, because you'll just ship them off to the dry cleaners."

"Yes. We take our business clothes to the cleaners. Because we have to do enough of our own laundry when it's covered in supernatural blood and guts after a battle."

"Oh." Her tone was chastened.

Too much. To Rhys, demonic blood spatters were humdrum. Maisy still seemed to get rocked by every new mention of mystical violence. And now he felt guilty for questioning her bringing the apron when she just wanted to protect her clothes.

And how he'd been dismissive of her need to keep both jobs.

Shit.

He didn't want to scare her any more. That message had been delivered. He wanted to get her to open up. So Rhys dialed it all back and made a hard conversational left.

"And because I won't risk you taking a picture of me in an apron and sending it to Gid or Zavier."

That popped teasing sparkle back into the ring of green around her brown eyes. "You're that lacking confidence in your masculinity, *Nephilim*?"

Hardly. His masculinity was still threatening to pop through the seam of his pants and prove itself to Maisy. Huh. At least an apron would cover it... "We live longer than humans. Getting teased about it for the next sixty years is not appealing."

"Get rid of your sport coat, then. And roll your sleeves up. I intend for you to get messy." She pulled ingredients from the fridge and had them assembled in a bowl in no time. "Mix it. With your hands. We'll need sixteen meatballs. Unless your friends are joining us?"

"Gid's got a date. Z's on a mission." Rhys eyed the contents of the bowl. He didn't mind pulling intestines out of a *Trachlerian* demon. All in a day's work. He was not so wild about the slime of ground turkey sticking to his fingers. This had better be one hell of an explanation.

On a chopping board next to him, she went at a cucumber with knife skills that would warm Zavier's heart with pride.

"Your technique's impressive."

"Cooking is just another form of making art. To do it well, you have to know how to wield the tools, just like wielding different brushes or pastels."

He had a sudden flash to the painting over the back door at her apartment.

He'd noticed it because, of course, it was his home. Niagara Falls at sunset, but she'd turned the water gold rather than blue. The mist of the falls joined the golden aura of the sun as though angelic power lit up the sky.

Rhys had a visceral reaction to it—both of overall peace and a *need* to own it. A need to be brightened and soothed by it every day.

At the end of all this, he'd buy it from her. Whatever the price.

"If this meal is half as good as the art on your walls, I'll owe you. Far beyond assembling a few dozen gift baskets."

"Awww, I'm glad you like my paintings. They're mostly a source of, well, frustration to me now."

"Why?"

"I can't physically finish a single painting of my parents. And the landscapes never *feel* finished to me. Never quite perfect enough. Sometimes it feels like half of what pushes me to paint is to keep trying to create that one perfect picture. If I ever did, I don't know if I'd pick up a brush again."

No chance of that happening. Rhys recognized a commitment, a drive in her that was identical to his that kept him going on dangerous missions. For people like them, there was no choice.

"Your talent burns through you. It burns with passion. You won't ever stop."

"I'm also at no risk of achieving perfection." She cocked her head. "What would your perfect painting be?"

He'd seen the world's masterworks in museums. Had seen angelic paintings in the hallways of their *Nephilim* training center. Even enjoyed the range of emotions evoked by the simple line drawings of *The Far Side* cartoons. "I don't know."

"Think about it."

"While I do, what would yours be?" The answer, from an artist, had to mean more, be more revealing, than whatever he said.

Maisy sliced a lemon paper thin. "I don't know."

What a cop-out. And proof that even if they weren't officially bickering, she still found a way to rile him. "Then why hassle me?"

"Because I've tried." She banged a jar of green olives on the counter. Maybe out of frustration but more likely to loosen the lid. Rhys knew enough *not* to offer his lid-opening prowess until it was specifically requested. "For years. What's a representation of perfect happiness? A mother smiling down at a newborn? A sunrise over the ocean? A single, pearlescent golden circle?"

"What about other kinds of perfection?" Rhys held up his fingers, wiggled them as flecks of garlic dripped off. "Perfectly messy? Perfect sadness?"

"I already told you. Happiness and goodness—that's what I'm all about." And she flashed him a smile that almost forced him to squint from its brightness.

"Then we're back to the *why*."

"Why I choose to embrace the good in life?"

"Yes." Was she being deliberately obtuse? Was it something stupid like she had a page-a-day calendar with peppy sayings?

"Because I faced death and walked away. Because I lived through the worst possible thing." Maisy oiled the cast-iron skillet as if she'd said nothing more extraordinary than her preference for crunchy over smooth peanut butter.

"Elaborate." Rhys had rolled two meatballs before he belatedly remembered to tack on a "please."

She looked over at him slyly from beneath half-veiled eyes. "You didn't do a deep-dive bio on your new Keeper?"

"No. We found you. That was enough. Your past doesn't matter."

Maisy gave her head a swift double shake that cascaded her hair over her shoulders. "You're wrong. You can live in the 'now,' but every moment of it is influenced by your past. Same with the future. My past is like a tree ring. Slice one open and you see all the trauma it endured."

And she'd managed to surprise him yet *again*, with that insight. There was definitely more to this Keeper than merely her rainbow sneakers and incessantly annoying optimism. He could see it in her eyes. Beneath the veneer of endless hope and this show of strength was a flicker of grief.

"Did something happen to you?"

"Yes." Her shoulders shifted back a bit. "But that won't stop me. The pain is proof of how strong the joy and the love were. You see, my family was in a car crash. A bad one. Well, a fatal one. Just not for me."

Shit.

He'd been an insensitive jackass, albeit unknowingly, opening this can of worms.

Much slower, Rhys rolled the last meatball. Thinking about her financial straits and realizing she likely had no fallback. Her bravery and the horrific act that had forced it upon her.

He crossed behind her to wash his hands. "How old were you?"

"Thirteen."

Worse and worse. Old enough to truly comprehend the loss. To feel the gaping hole in her life. Rhys racked his brain for something more powerful than platitudes.

Empathy and emotion were not in his usual daily skill set. He fell back on the simple truth. "I am sorry."

"Everyone says that." Maisy deftly browned the meat. "Which is polite, but it doesn't fix anything."

So now he had no kitchen task to do. And no words to plaster over this achingly cracked moment. Rhys had never felt more useless, which was not normal for him.

Even stranger, the one thing he *wanted* to do was hold her, stroke her back in comfort. His instincts were clearly out of whack. That'd be inappropriate. Keeper. *Nephilim.* Clearly delineated lines between protectee and bodyguard. Instead, he backed away to lean against the door, arms crossed.

"Is there anything I could say?"

"No." She wiped the back of her wrist across her forehead. "That's the bitch of it. No do-over. No matter how many times I go over it in my head. Come up with excuses that would've kept us five minutes later to avoid the semi that plowed into our car."

"You were a child. Thrust into a situation that grown-ups can hardly comprehend. But after all these years, you must have accepted that there was nothing you could've done to change the outcome."

"Yes. The truth is, I learned a huge lesson that day, even if it took a while to wrap my brain around." Maisy faced him, wagging the spoon. Steam from the stove had curled the wisps of hair framing her face. Reddened her cheeks, too. Rhys clenched his jaw against the urge to kiss those cheeks. "You can't control what happens. You can only control your reaction to what happens."

It took him a few seconds to unlock his molars. Because he sure as hell was having a reaction to *her.* "I've heard that."

"Yes, well, long before it became a trendy meme, I was living it." She scooped out the meatballs and put the lemons in the pan. How was this woman able to talk about her most crushing memory and continue on with making dinner?

Rhys had a whole new respect for Maisy.

A belief that she, well, at least *might* have what it'd take to be Keeper.

His physical attraction to her? Also grown by leaps and bounds. Despite the conversation topic being her tragically killed parents. Rhys knew he should be freaking ashamed of himself.

That self-loathing in no way diminished his desire to hold her.

"So…your reaction to near death was to embrace life?"

"No, you haven't heard the whole story."

Son of a bitch. What else could've happened? A pet turtle decapitated in the same crash? They were on their way to adopt a baby from China when it happened? "Sure I can't help with anything?"

"Will you drink wine?"

"Yeah."

She started to grab a bottle from the diamond-shaped rack on the counter. Then paused with her hand on it. "Oh, but it isn't cold. We'll have to add ice cubes."

And his respect ticked down a couple of points.

He hadn't lived almost a century to suffer warm wine. Or watered-down wine. "Like hell we will." Rhys swiped it down, set it on the counter. Then he blew on it until frost coated the sides of the bottle.

Maisy dropped the container of feta into the food processor. Good thing it wasn't on. "Omigosh. You're like Superman. Can you shoot lasers out of your eyes, too? Fly around the Earth fast enough to reverse time?"

"No." She appeared frozen, so he emptied the feta container. Had no clue what to do next, though.

"Is there Kryptonite?"

The whole wing reveal hadn't been nearly as shocking to her. Guess someone really liked their superhero movies. "You'd have to establish if the planet Krypton exists first. If you're asking if there is something specifically deadly to angels, yes."

"What is it?"

Hilarious question. "Why would I tell you?"

She finally shuddered in a deep breath and moved. To furiously bat her eyelashes at him. "Because I'm just a lowly human who can't possibly source it. Nor do I have any reason to take out my bodyguard."

Nice try. Rhys tapped the bowl of the processor to refocus her on dinner. If a succubus couldn't flirt info out of him, this woman didn't stand a chance of it.

Even if he did—for some frustrating reason it was impossible to pinpoint—find Maisy far more alluring than any succubus. Including the one who'd brought along two of her compatriots to seduce him in Turkey's antique pool gifted to Cleopatra by Mark Antony.

"Valid points. I'll counter with the fact that you could be captured and tortured to reveal that information. I've also only known you for four days and have no proof of your ability to keep a secret."

A wet cat threw less attitude than Maisy with her immediate spine straighten and pissy hair toss. "How about a little credit? I didn't DM CNN about the half angel who moved into my house."

"Not yet."

Aside from knowing even his long life was too short to drink warm wine? Rhys had learned that trusting people was usually a mistake. Proving themselves once was far from enough to know they could be counted on to keep a lock on his secrets.

"Thanks for that overwhelming show of trust."

A pissed-off protectee had a tendency to act out. Make stupid choices like sneaking—*attempting* to sneak off—in the middle of the night. His REM sleep didn't need any more disruption.

Rhys tossed out a peace offering while he uncorked the bottle. "You want trust? That potion you drank to see the demons? It *does* have side effects."

"Gideon said that it didn't," she shot back. And then, with a sudden warm glow to her bicolor eyes, Maisy asked in breathless hopefulness, "Am I going to sprout mini wings?"

Un-goddamned-believable.

The woman was so blindly optimistic. Anyone else would've interpreted "side effects" to be a bad thing—blinding headaches. Arm scales. Eternal damnation. And they'd be on the right track.

"Gideon correctly stipulated that what you drank would not have a lasting effect. Can't use it often, though. Bad things would happen."

Guarded positivity still radiated from her as strongly as the steam rising from the skillet. "Oh. Well...*how* bad?"

"Bad enough." He'd made his point. No point, however, spooking her any more. Rhys poured the wine. "I can tap into the elements. Some. Not as much as a full-blooded angel. I can't freeze a demon solid. Or burn one up. Just enough power to be frustrated that we don't have more of it. That's the curse of being a *Nephilim*."

"You've got one hundred percent more than me."

It was an interesting comment because Rhys didn't have a damned clue how it was that a powerless *human* always performed the role of Keeper. Master Caraxis had glossed over the topic as not being of immediate import. And they'd been a little busy for the past eight decades fighting the evil that was already on their radar. No time to worry about hypotheticals.

Was there something genetic, even after all these eons, that manifested in the Keepers from the earthbound angel? Would it come out in Maisy at all, since she wasn't the child of the last Keeper? If so, how diluted might it be?

They'd reached out to the master, of course, but his priorities often did not...align with those of Rhys, Gideon, and Zavier. *Aka* he'd get back to them when he was good and ready. No sooner. Even though Caraxis knew about the whole two-week deadline.

So why wasn't he responding? Was something worse, bigger than the freaking Gates opening, going down somewhere in the world?

After flashing a tense smile, Rhys said, "I can't shut the Gates of Hell."

Maisy's smile was so tight you could bounce a quarter off of it. "No guarantee that I can, either."

"So the only time you're not exploding in optimism is when it comes to your own worthiness?"

"No. Of course not." Maisy stirred the orzo slowly, scraping the pan. "Maybe?"

There she went, frustrating him again with an utter lack of logic, but Rhys had learned something over the past three days with Maisy. Blowing up at her would do no good. Aside from feeling good for him.

So in his most reasonable tone, he said, "That makes no sense."

"Life doesn't make sense. Like my parents dying."

Good. They'd circled back to her story. "Why *didn't* you? If it was a bad enough crash to kill both of them, it'd almost be a miracle for you to have survived."

She tapped a finger to the tip of her nose, then pointed it back at him. "Something else that doesn't make sense. I was, well, rescued. Do you want my description of it or the official police report version?"

Fully on alert, Rhys said, "Sounds like I should hear both?"

"Officially, I was asleep. Which made my body limp. My muscles didn't tense and brace, and thus the crash didn't affect me as badly. Then I was pulled out of the car right before it exploded."

"That's not what you remember?"

"That's not what happened at all," she corrected. Slipping off the apron, Maisy gestured to the cushioned alcove behind the table that looked out on the falls. "Let's go sit for this part. Have to kill twenty minutes anyway while it all cooks."

Rhys carried in their glasses. Gave an extra puff of icy air to top them off. "You were old enough to be cognizant of what happened. Why didn't the police believe your story?"

"Because nobody did. Because it isn't believable. But it is true." They settled onto the terra cotta–colored cushions that reminded Rhys of their early days in Greece. "Do you know Sherlock Holmes?"

"Personally? No. Even *Nephilim* don't have the power to converse with fictional characters."

Her laughter rang through the room. Maisy elbowed him. "You actually made another joke. Guess you really want to earn this dinner. Anyway, he's got a famous quote: *Once you eliminate the impossible, whatever remains, no matter how improbable, must be the truth.*"

Rhys flared his wings, made them the slightest bit visible. "I'm used to dealing in what seems impossible. Try me."

"I was wide awake. I saw the truck coming at us. Just like I saw it stop. Everything stopped. The music coming out of the radio, the noise of the car, my mom's voice. I was sketching, and I dropped the marker when I saw the truck and screamed. Only the marker didn't fall to my lap. It hovered on the tips of my fingers."

She paused, clearly waiting for him to be like everyone else and announce that was all impossible.

What must've happened next was obvious to anyone in angelkind, however. Rhys knew exactly what the frozen time indicated, but it'd be wrong to hijack Maisy's story. "I'm still all in for this."

"A man reached through the window. Picked me up. Held me in his arms while time slapped back into focus. I watched the collision happen. A piece of glass flew at me and pierced my calf. Then I blacked out. When I came to, I was lying on the ground, bleeding, near the flaming wreck. Ambulances and police cars were just pulling up."

"What'd he say?"

"The man? That's the strangest part. He told the police that it was, indeed, a miracle. He wasn't supposed to be there. He'd been about to jump off the bridge, end it all. But when he heard the impact, he turned around. Saw my face against the window. Ran to pull me out of the car but couldn't get back to rescue my parents before it exploded."

"That's quite a story. A *real* story," he quickly amended. It was surprising to him, but not for the reason Maisy thought.

Her red lips parted. "You believe me?"

"Oh, yeah. Gideon and Zavier would, too. That was probably your, ah, guardian angel."

She slapped a hand to her chest. "They're real?"

"To a certain extent."

"Then where was he when Zygerit tried to kill me?" Righteous indignation made her voice quaver.

Humans could be so demanding that everything happen all the time. Because they didn't comprehend the scope, the vastness that celestial beings encountered. So he swallowed his knee-jerk annoyance.

Instead, Rhys thought about how terrified Maisy must've been. Back then, in the car, and being confronted with a demon for the first time. How he was insisting that she trust him—even though it seemed to her that "his" system had failed her.

She deserved the truth. From him, if no one else.

And if it freaked her out? Well, good thing the wine was already open.

Rhys wavered his head side to side. "They're not always on the job."

Sure enough, her jaw dropped. "You're telling me my guardian angel was…what? Having a blast at Disney World while my life was almost snuffed out?"

"Not everyone has a guardian angel. And they're not on the job twenty-four seven. Angels are sent to help when the need arises. Like through prayers. In your case, though? My guess is word spread that you were about to be in danger. He *sensed* the goodness in your heart. Knew it had to be saved." It was more proof that perhaps Maisy really was fated to be the Keeper. He pointed his thumb at the ceiling. "Someone's on your side up there. Which bodes well for us."

"Well, whoever the mystery man was, whichever version of the story is true—the fact is that he saved me. Instead of certain death, I escaped with only a three-day hospital stay and a big scar. That's always made me aware of how lucky I am." This time both hands laced across her chest. "How precious a gift life truly is. Because I'll never get to make even one more memory with my parents. Ever. I'd give anything for five more minutes with them."

Cliché. "Not all who escape death are eternal optimists."

Maisy paused, wine halfway to her lips. "It isn't a condition, like chronic neck pain from whiplash. It's a choice. If you look for the bad, that's all you'll see, but if you *look* for the good..."

"You'll miss seeing the mugger coming at you," Rhys snarked. There was such a thing as too trusting. Too oblivious to danger and evil. It'd be stupid to encourage her happy myopia.

But even though he refused to show it, her story *did* affect him.

Who up there was on their side in this quest? And why?

Were there other paranormal beings who realized that there was more to Maisy Norgate than was visible at first glance?

And would she have to be at the brink of death again before they revealed themselves?

CHAPTER THIRTEEN

Maisy leaned back against the mirrored elevator wall. "What day is it?"

Rhys frowned, opened his mouth like he planned to continue yelling at her. Which was what he'd been doing since she informed him an hour ago that she would be leaving his lair for a bit, whether he liked it or not. Fortunately, he thought better of it.

"Thursday." She slapped the heel of her hand to her forehead. "Oh, a day that ends in 'Y.' That must be why we're arguing... *again*."

He got in close. Loomed over her. Did he really think that intimidated her anymore? They were so far past that. "We're arguing because you're stubborn."

"Right back at ya." She poked at his sternum to back him through the opening doors.

After scanning the hallway, Rhys beckoned for her to come out. "Why couldn't you just reschedule this doctor's appointment?"

Men. The entire gender worked so hard to maintain a blind spot to anything even remotely connected to the inner workings of a female body—unless they were legislating against it. "Clearly, you know nothing about gynecologists."

Rhys smirked. "I don't feel like I need to apologize for that."

"Just because you're a man? Men need to know what goes on

with the other fifty percent of the planet."

"No, because I'm a *Nephilim*. I told you we don't get sick."

Oh. Maybe she did owe him a little slack on this subject. Then she remembered the entire armory in their building. "You do battle all the time. What happens when you get stabbed?"

"We deal with it ourselves. Zavier's the best of us at stitching things up. We also have potions. Healers. No need for human doctors."

Lucky. "Well, it takes *months* to get in with an ob-gyn. The whole unschedulable, delay-filled thing about having babies makes it impossible to get an appointment. Preventative medicine is the best medicine. I'm not skipping it." Plus, she'd already psyched herself up for it. That had taken quite a bit of effort that Maisy did not intend to waste.

"Then I'm coming in with you."

She pulled them over in the alcove with the bathrooms and water fountain. This had to be ended before they went in. "As I said back at home *and* in the car, you're allowed to sit in the waiting room. Period."

"The word 'bodyguard' is literal." Rhys squeezed his hands down her arms. Maisy steeled herself not to shiver at his touch. "I protect your actual body. I can't do that from a hallway and three exam rooms away."

Maisy wouldn't want to have this awkward conversation with a new human boyfriend. Friend. Colleague. Whatever label fit.

She even *more* so did not want to have it with her half-angelic bodyguard.

But Maisy knew that communication was better than the opposite. She'd known that forever. And it had been quadruply reinforced while teaching high schoolers. Nine-tenths of their dumb relationship mistakes could be traced back to not communicating.

Nephilim seemed to have the same rules for communicating as the CIA—everything was parsed out on a need-to-know basis.

Which meant she had to be the adult in this relationship…even if she was fifty years and change younger than him.

"Look, we're not talking about it—and I'm fine with that—but we've kissed."

"That is not breaking news," he said drily.

Why did he break out his wry sense of humor at the most inopportune times? "We've *only* kissed. First base. For the record? I'd be, um, open to the idea of getting naked with you for sexy times. I am *not* open to you seeing me naked for the first time under fluorescent lights, in stirrups, with a third person in the room."

His grip on her arms gentled, thumbs slowly stroking up and down. And the stern lines around his eyes smoothed out. "You'll call if anything suspicious happens?"

"I'll scream my head off. I'll out-scream any of her OB patients in their thirtieth hour of labor."

"You can text me, too."

"Rhys. It is a five-minute exam. Plus another five minutes of chitchat."

Two vertical lines appeared between his dark eyebrows. They paired with the long, deep sigh. "Very well. Take this." He twitched his wrist, and a dagger appeared in his hands. It was as thin as a letter opener. Dainty, almost.

A tiny bit of excitement threaded through her at the thought that Rhys trusted her with one of his weapons. But had he not heard the part about her being naked for the exam? "Where am I supposed to put that?"

"Your purse is large enough to hold a baby goat."

"Or, more logically, a sketchbook." She slipped it in. "Thank you."

His big hand cradled the side of her face in an unexpected caress. "Do not be brave, Keeper. Be cautious."

"Are you kidding? The bravest day of the year for a woman is the day she faces a speculum."

Although once she was dressed in a paper-thin blue gown, Maisy felt a distinct lack of bravery.

Sitting on the exam table with the stirrups already splayed just kicked up her pulse. Instead, she wandered to the French doors that led out to the skinny balcony. This was one of the historic, turreted buildings that gave Buffalo its distinctive skyline. Might as well enjoy the view—

There was a person out there. Sitting, legs dangling over the edge of the turret.

And they were on the eleventh floor.

A teen girl, with pink and green mermaid stripes in her black hair. Very similar to a student Maisy once—

What if it *was* Nari? Holy crap, the girl was climbing to her feet. Was she going to jump?

Maisy opened the doors and rushed out. The wind at eleven stories up bit right through her gown. Up and under it, too. Good thing she'd kept her socks on. "Nari?"

The girl's head whipped around. "Miss Norgate? What are you doing here?"

"Really?" She plucked at the single bow keeping her decent. "This isn't a big visual clue for you?"

Her black eyes widened. "Oh. Ohhhh. I'm sorry."

"For what?"

"That you're here."

"I'd say it looks like you need a friendly face right about now, so I'm not sorry." She took two steps closer. "How about you come off that ledge and talk to me?"

"No. I'm jumping."

Not on my watch, Maisy thought. "You can still talk to me first. Catch me up. You must be, what, a senior by now?"

"Yeah. That's the problem. Mom won't let me go to art school."

"Why not?"

"My mom's *Dr.* Hwang." She pointed to the doors behind Maisy. "She's a partner in that practice. You her patient?"

"No. Dr. Bartkowiak," she murmured. Maisy had taken an in-service training in suicide negotiation. It'd been an intense three hours that she hoped to never use. She remembered the bullet points: Keep them talking. Maintain a connection. Don't leave them alone.

But what if she wasn't enough? Wouldn't it be better to run inside and get help?

What if Nari saw that as a final abandonment and jumped the moment Maisy turned away?

Nari nodded. Smiled as if this was an ordinary conversation. As if her chipped blue-painted fingernails weren't digging into the crenelated stone edge of the turret. "Dr. B's nice. I saw her to get birth control."

"Are you pregnant?" There was no time to ease into it. Maisy needed to figure out the problem. "Is that why your mother kiboshed art school?"

"No." Pure teen disappointment at an adult revulsed across her face. "Geez, why would I be dumb enough to ruin my life like that?"

In a tone of practiced patience, Maisy said, "Accidents happen. I won't judge you, no matter what you tell me."

That got a shrug sharp enough to serve a volleyball across a net. "We're Korean. *Tiger Mom* territory. Mom insists I go to a regular college and then become a lawyer."

The profession didn't add up. "Not a doctor?"

"Even the hyper-determined Dr. Hwang couldn't make that happen." Pure impish glee sparkled her dark eyes. And one of her hands let go enough to wipe the wind-tossed hair off her face. "I throw up at the sight of blood."

Handy. If Nari also puked at a Latin declension, she'd be home free from her mom's machinations.

Maisy took another two infinitesimal steps closer. Not that she had a plan. Lunging at the girl had a higher chance of catapulting both of them off the edge than saving her.

"Well, a college degree is useful to have no matter what profession you end up in. Think of it more as a degree to prep you for life."

"But I won't get good enough to become a real artist."

"Sure you can." Oh, she could empathize. Maisy had wanted to go to the Rhode Island School of Design. Live in a drafty New York loft *à* la *Rent*. Sell her paintings to discerning collectors.

She'd also wanted to not have such an astronomical student loan debt that it chased her into menopause.

And she genuinely loved teaching children the power—and the fun—of art.

"I won't," Nari insisted with more than a little of an angsty wail. "Not without the right teachers."

Okay. This sounded like a classic tantrum at not getting her way. It didn't sound like deep depression or some other form of mental illness. Nari's presence on the ledge was a cry to be heard. Preferably by her mother, but probably by anyone willing to pass the message along to Dr. Hwang.

Maisy could handle this. She'd talk her down. Show Nari that she had options. Get her inside, get her hugged by her mother, and it'd be resolved.

Hopefully.

And then, out of a bone-deep sense of utter fairness, she'd have to admit to Rhys that having him in the exam room would, indeed, have been useful...

With another shuffle forward, she raised an index finger. Geez, even that tiny movement created an icy breeze under her gown. "There's a rule, a theory, that says the key to success at anything is practicing it for ten thousand hours. Not that you have to sit at a teacher's elbow for that long. And I shouldn't have to tell someone in your generation that you can learn a lot from the internet."

Tiniest of silver linings? At least when it finally was time for the speculum exam, Maisy would be completely numb down there from the cold.

Nari shook her head. "It doesn't seem like the best path."

Nope. It sure didn't. Welcome to adulthood, kid.

Maisy crossed her arms tight over her chest. "There is no best path. There's only *your* path. The one you make with effort and passion. You can absolutely keep making art—and then maybe selling it."

"Really? Are you?" Nari twisted around to lay a bent leg across the edge. That was progress. At least it wasn't dangling off anymore! "You're not teaching now. Did you become a full-time artist?"

Ouch. Teenagers really excelled at knowing exactly how to verbally stab at a raw vulnerability. "Well, no."

"Then I've got no hope. Which is why I'm jumping. I'm punishing my mom for it, too," she added in a breezy afterthought.

"Nari, if you go through with this, your mom won't just be punished. She'll be devastated and empty and grieving for the rest of her life."

She looked at her Apple Watch. "That'll only be about ten minutes. I planted a pipe bomb in the break room."

With her arms tight to her chest, shouldn't she be able to feel her heart beat? Because it suddenly felt like that pulsing muscle had frozen.

So...*not* just a tantrum.

Suddenly, the wind wasn't the only cold thing whipping at Maisy. Icy fear slashed through her diaphragm and lungs, stealing her breath. It couldn't be true. Nari, sweet, talented Nari, sitting there in a pink sweatshirt with a cartoon panda on it. She couldn't be a killer.

"You what?" Maisy asked cautiously, trying not to screech or overly react.

Nari's eyes narrowed. "It's what she deserves. Dr. Hwang thought she could control my life just like she controls this office, and my dad's life, and my sister's. Well, I'm proving that she can't control me at all."

"There are other doctors, nurses, and pregnant patients in that office. I hear that you're furious at your mother, but you don't have any reason to kill innocent people."

"It'll serve her right."

There were two options. Save Nari—maybe—with an epic lunge and attempt to not just pull her to safety but back inside the window so she didn't just twist away and jump. Or run inside and try to save the whole office. At which point Nari was likely to kill herself.

Maybe Nari was lying about the bomb. For shock value.

Maisy couldn't make that assumption. Which left her with two impossible options to choose between.

"There is a third option." It was a woman's voice. It came from off to the left. Over the edge of the building.

That was the moment Maisy realized that Nari's hair was no longer being batted by the wind. It streamed out, like a fully extended flag, but *stayed* there, frozen, like a flag on the moon. The sound of the wind was gone.

Maisy looked down at the gown's limp press on her thighs. No wind clamping it to her like a second skin. Time and the whole world had stopped again. Just like the car accident all those years ago.

She turned and spotted the woman—no, the *angel*. Maisy thought the *Nephilim* extraordinary, but a full-blown angel was something else entirely.

She glowed, just like angels depicted in everything from medieval to Baroque to Renaissance paintings. Not just backlit with a glow, but light streaming to the sides and in front of her as well.

More vibrant energy than solid flesh. Maisy knew she'd spend the rest of her days trying to capture the radiant beauty of the angel on canvas.

But right now? A heavenly being with untold power could

fix this terrifying situation. Good thing she'd had such vast experience this week talking to demons, the other Gate Keeper, and *Nephilim*. Maisy had zero compunction about speaking her mind.

She marched right to the edge to confront the angel hovering just out of reach. "Hi. I'm Maisy Norgate."

"Elohiala."

"Nice to meet you. How about, instead of a third option for me, you just snap your fingers or flap your wings—whatever mystical thing you do—and save all these people?"

"That is not for me to do."

Funny how that sounded just like Rafi at the bakery, who'd refused to help build to-go boxes, saying it wasn't in his job description. They'd fired his ass for not being a team player.

Maybe this one wasn't a specific guardian angel to Nari—or to any of the people inside—but couldn't she stir herself to do the right thing? Sheesh. "What if I asked as a favor? I probably don't have anything you'd be interested in, but I've got a *Nephilim* in there who could repay you in whatever you'd like."

"This is *your* test, Keeper."

Oh, crap.

Rhys had mentioned the forces of both good and bad would test her. Maisy just hadn't expected anyone else to be involved. That seemed overly harsh. Especially for the team on the side of love and forgiveness.

"Then test *me*. As much as you want. Don't put other lives on the line."

Elohiala shook her head. Lids half drooped over eyes the same yellow as the sun. "It is not a true test without true consequences."

"You set all this up?" She glanced over at the angry, hurting teen who was about to throw away her entire life because she hadn't lived long enough yet to know better. Thought about the friendly nurse who'd proudly shown off her engagement ring as she took Maisy's blood pressure. And Rhys, who might be able to help if he knew that her danger level had escalated to *get the hell out here right now!* "Doesn't that make you an accomplice to murder?"

"We did not engineer what is occurring. We merely took advantage of what was already unfolding."

Okay. That made Maisy feel 2 percent less guilty. Not that it mattered. Her fault, Nari's fault, Elohiala's fault—it still needed to be resolved with, hopefully, no loss of life. "Will you tell me if there is really a bomb?"

"No. Nor can I tell you if Nari will jump. That is her decision. Which brings me back to your third option."

"Hang on." Was it possible she could out-logic an angel? "If you aren't going to help save them, why are you helping me?"

"You are to be Keeper. You must be made aware of all sides, of all possibilities that could result due to your choice."

There was a distinct connotation that this third option wasn't exactly a deus ex machina, *let's all gather round and eat cake* sort of an ending, but Maisy was desperate for any shred of hope. "What's behind door number three?"

Elohiala beckoned her closer, until Maisy was against the rough edge. A ray of light flashed off the white wing to ping off the rusted edge of the fire escape. "By going inside, you risk yourself. If you take the fire escape, once on the street you can get help."

"I'm eleven floors up. It'll take a while to climb down, let alone find someone willing to lend me their phone or assume I'm *not* a crazy person in a hospital gown, screaming about a bomb." This was in no way a significant improvement over the other two ways to go.

"It is the third option."

She looked down. Thought about how stiff each section of ladder would be. On TV, it always looked difficult to pull them down. And, again, not a consideration when life and death were at stake, but she'd be flashing everyone on the street the whole way.

"Would you keep time frozen until I get to the bottom?"

"No. Time has not stopped. I plucked you out of your dimension and we are conversing in one where time is not an issue. Once you have made the decision, you will rejoin your dimension."

Mr. Need-To-Know-Only owed her an explanation about other dimensions when this was all over. "This is an impossible choice. I want to save everybody."

"That is almost never possible."

"You're a lot of help."

The angel shrugged her wings. "That is not for me to do, either."

"Yeah, yeah." The thing was, there weren't three options. There was only one, and Maisy had known it from the start.

Saving Nari would be nice.

Saving herself would be nice.

But she had to save as many people as possible. The greater good. The needs of the many outweighing the needs of the few.

A gust of wind reeled her back a step. Oh, crap. She was back.

Maisy ran to Nari. "Look, you're too talented and too smart to throw your life away on a couple of bad weeks—or months. Don't be an idiot. I'll help you. And I'll be right back." Then she raced to the French doors—which had, of course, slammed shut in the wind—and wrestled them open.

Nari had told her how much time was left before the bomb went off. Not long enough for a bomb squad to get here but long enough for a little angelic intervention.

So she did exactly what she'd promised Rhys at the first sign of trouble. She *screamed*.

"Bomb! Bomb! Everybody out!"

Today's world was such that nobody stopped to ask questions. Exam doors flew open, and everyone raced for the exit.

Except Rhys.

Her *Nephilim* was by her side before she hit the hallway. "Where?"

"Break room." She'd passed it on the way to the scale, and she raced ahead of him. Maisy shut down her fear by remembering that Nari had said it'd go off in ten minutes. It had only been... four, tops? "Don't know where. Can you defuse it?"

"I can do many things with it." They both started opening cupboards. Rifling through, knocking out paper plates and bags of coffee and bowls. "Best plan is to fly it out over Lake Erie."

Maisy realized she had no idea what a pipe bomb looked like. Presumably *not* paper goods or tea bags, though. "Can we call that plan B? I don't want you to risk yourself, but I need proof it exists so the girl who planted it can get help."

"Not punishment?"

"By the time her brain is back in service, the guilt she'll carry for this near miss will be punishment enough." Maisy stopped. Thought like a teenager. Then she spotted the tote bag in the corner with maxipads sticking out the top. Bingo. "Look under there."

With caution and grace, Rhys crouched and lifted the maxipads. Underneath lay a metal cylinder. Well, a pipe, but closed off at both ends. He picked it up gingerly. "I can alter it so that it won't go off. It'll look like it was constructed poorly."

"Don't leave fingerprints!"

"Don't worry." Rhys angled his chin toward the door. "You should go. Just in case."

"For the record, I have faith in you, but I do need to go. I have to help the girl who put it here."

"That is your choice?"

Man, these angels. They gave their words such a heft, like... the fate of the world hinged on each utterance. "Yes."

Rhys gave her an approving nod. "It is a good choice."

She started to lay a hand on his shoulder, but, remembering

he was holding an explosive, just smiled. "Be careful." Then Maisy ran back out into the hallway.

Doors were being slammed against walls. She spotted two doctors in their long white coats methodically clearing each room. Ooh, that was brave of them. "Dr. Hwang."

The woman with jet-black hair in a perfect bun whirled toward her. "You need to leave. Immediately."

"No. Come with me. Your daughter's outside and about to jump. I think you talking to her would help." Maisy frowned. "Tell me if I'm wrong about that."

Delicate hands fluttered, trembled at her chest. "Nari? I knew she was upset, but— Are you certain it is Nari?"

"I was her teacher a few years ago. I'm sure." Maisy paused, peeked out the doors of her exam room. Nari was still out there. There was still hope. "She's, um, pissed about art school. And you should know that she also put a pipe bomb in the break room to hurt you, but I've got my friend working on defusing it. He's a pro—uh, professional security expert."

Yeah, that wouldn't hold up when the cops arrived. Not with the three guys owning a shipping company. Hopefully there was something in his lengthy past to explain his deftness with bombs.

Tears flooded the doctor's eyes, silently streaming down her cheeks. "You go. I'll take care of my daughter."

"No. I made a promise." Maisy dug in her purse for her phone. Called 911. "She needs to see me follow through on it."

"I don't want you to endanger yourself."

"It is my choice." They ought to give her a set of honorary angel wings for the way that just popped out of her mouth. She climbed out the window. Nari gasped at seeing her.

And then time stopped again. Or the dimensions shifted. Or she shifted through them.

Whatever.

Elohiala appeared. Standing on the parapet. She dipped her wings. Was that the same as a nod of…respect? "I did not anticipate your choice, Keeper. This first test of your worthiness and strength went better than expected."

First test?

Oh, Maisy had something to say about that. "I didn't anticipate you'd play so fast and loose with people's lives. You should be ashamed. You know what else? I don't appreciate the testing at all. It's not like I asked for the Key. You should be grateful I'm even willing to show up and make the effort."

"Effort will not be enough to keep the Gates locked. Remember that, the next time you are under duress."

Real motivating.

And then time flipped back on. Dr. Hwang rushed to Nari, hugging her tightly as she dragged her off the ledge. Face tucked into her mother's shoulder, Nari began to sob.

Damn it.

She'd have to psych herself up all over again another day for the Speculum of Terror. Which really ought to count as one of her tests. Or at least prove her bravery.

CHAPTER FOURTEEN

Rhys hefted his backpack over his shoulder. The *kalyva* was kept fully stocked for all *Nephilim* who used the ancient stone building, but he never assumed that people lived up to their promises. Safer that way. So he brought his own knives, candles, supplies—and lots of water.

He sent a quick text to Gideon that they were about to depart. Then he stood at the edge, staring at the back of Niagara. Sensed Maisy stiffening next to him. "You shouldn't feel anything when we go through the waterfall," he reminded her. The last time he'd brought her through had been a surprise. Now that she'd had the time to think about it, the woman was a solid column of nerves.

Maisy blinked a few times. Very fast. "Including the water? I don't want to inhale at the wrong moment."

"Correct." Rhys palmed both of her shoulders. As eager as he was to start this mission, he could tell that the Keeper needed a minute. Who could blame her?

He'd done some fast-talking around medical confidentiality and gotten Dr. Hwang to not disclose either of their names to the police. Being named only as Good Samaritans gave them the ability to slip out unnoticed.

But that was after Maisy had spent more time sitting with Nari and her mother. Time that extended when the girl broke down, overcome at the sight of the evacuated patients on the sidewalk with babies that she'd almost taken out. Maisy refused to leave her side until the ambulance was parked below to take the girl away. *And* promised to bring her art supplies as soon as it was allowed.

The heart on this new Keeper brimmed over with compassion. It humbled him.

But then her nerves kicked in. She'd asked him to stay in the room while she dressed—eyes shut, of course. It took her three tries to put on her sneakers, until he finally turned around and helped with the simple task.

"Do I need a harness, like ziplining, to clip on to you while we fly?" She looked down at the vast cavern. "You said we're going farther after we pass through. My arms are feeling a bit wet-noodleish after this morning. I hope you aren't counting on me to hang on very tightly."

She had all the bravery of a warrior in the heat of the moment. Afterward, though? Maisy let all the fear swamp her.

They didn't have the luxury of time for her to slowly get used to this.

Rhys stroked his thumbs along the soft skin just below the fluttery sleeve of her white tee. "You know my job is to keep you safe. You are *always* my number one priority. Even if I almost failed you earlier."

She blew a raspberry. A very wet one. "Stop saying that. When I *needed* you? You were there. Saved everyone in one fell swoop. I couldn't have managed it. The bomb squad wouldn't have gotten there in time. I did my thing, and you did yours. Teamwork."

Her heart was one thing. Her experience and skills with the supernatural world were another entirely.

Rhys backed away, dropping his hands to feel that his guns and knives were secured. "This next step we take—it's dangerous. So it requires only partial teamwork. You'll need to follow my instructions word for word, without question."

"I can follow instructions. No reason I can't also call out for clarification while doing so, though."

Smart-ass. It'd amuse him, that spirit. Any *other* time. "Maisy." He slapped a hand high up on the rock wall. "We'll be opening a conduit to Hell. No joking. No do-overs. No distractions."

"You've got your *fate of the world is at hand* face on again. I get it. Best behavior, or you'll leave me…where are we going to do this ritual?"

"Lefkada. A small island on the west coast of Greece."

Her eyelids popped wide. "That's not like a casual twenty-mile hop to Canada. That's a whole other continent. There's no celestial border crossing guard on the other end?"

Humans. Did they really think their rules constrained the paranormal realm? "Just a safe space that is shared by all *Nephilim* to work spells."

"How does that work? Do you have a shared calendar? Is it like a meeting room sign-up in Outlook?"

She was babbling. Or stalling. Or both. Rhys grabbed the plastic cup off the shelf and thrust the dregs of the iced mocha at her. "You're nervous, aren't you?"

After a long slurp, Maisy nodded. "Yes. I almost watched someone die today. I almost died myself. I met a full-fledged angel. And now I'm magically blipping halfway across the world through a waterfall. I think I've earned a few tautly strung nerves."

He'd repeated it multiple times over the last few days. Having to say it again didn't annoy Rhys this time. He simply hoped it would calm her. "I'll keep you safe. As long as you follow my instructions."

"Wow. You should just record a voice memo of that. It'd save you the effort. Put it on the home screen of your phone. One press, and it'd play for me."

His patience was wearing thin, even under the circumstances. "I wish you could take the night to settle yourself, but the timing is optimal now. It's almost eleven p.m. in Greece. We want to be finished before midnight."

"Do you turn into an Ionic column if we're still there when the clock strikes?"

Tempting to say yes, just to see if it stopped her endless questions and jokes. "It is a thinning of the veil between worlds. Our spell will be significantly more dangerous if the portal we create is open at midnight."

"Then let's get a move on. Get this over with." Maisy tightened her ponytail. "When we're back, you're buying me a midnight snack. I feel like wings and copious amounts of fries will ground me after all this excitement."

"It's a deal." Rhys waited a beat. Clasped her to his side with one hand. Put on his biggest scowl—the one he used with their tax guy. "As long as you follow all my instructions."

She shot him the finger.

He deserved it. That time.

They launched off the ledge, Maisy's arms a tourniquet around his neck, but she didn't hamper him by wrapping her legs at his waist. When it was time to be serious, the Keeper always came through. Guess he didn't have to worry about her after all.

In a blink, they were through the waterfall. Five minutes later, they landed on the sandy soil of Lefkada. Except Maisy didn't let go. "You're safe now. Ground underfoot."

"I know." Maisy sounded breathless. "That was just... magnificent. I could fly like that all night. With you." She brushed a hand over his feathers as she stepped away from him.

Her caress of his uber-sensitive feathers...it sent a jolt of electricity straight to his cock. He took a look around as he readjusted. There were mossy rocks, the steady tumble of the falls, the soft air of the Mediterranean, and the beautiful woman who surprised him nearly as often as she spoke.

Suddenly, the *last* thing Rhys wanted to do was the damned spell. It was easy to think of other things the two of them could do in the secluded spot.

Many things.

But he'd never stalled on a mission before. Not for injury, not for hunger, and sure as hell not for the lust that was pounding through him as incessantly as those falls.

"Glad you weren't scared."

"Instead of buffalo wings, how about we just go for a long flight over this island once we're done?"

Also tempting. She'd pressed against him like glue...and Rhys had liked it.

A lot. He craved more.

"I'll take you on a flight." He was glad she'd suggested it. There was an intimacy in holding her life in the crook of his arm. In feeling her pulse jackhammer against his skin with each flap of his wings. But what Rhys wanted didn't matter. His only priority was keeping her safe. "Just not tonight. You'll need that food after working magic for the first time. It'll drain you."

"Not literally, right? No vampires?"

"Your energy will be diminished. Your blood level will remain the same." Hopefully she wouldn't notice that he'd sidestepped the question. There *were* vampires, but his skittish, stressed Keeper didn't need to know that tonight. Rhys held her hand as he led her through the unbroken darkness beneath the canopy of trees to the *kalyva*.

Maisy's head swiveled back and forth as she tried to take in her surroundings. "Nothing bad can pop out at us?"

"There's protection around the *kalyva*. Like the barrier between the Watchtower and the falls. The only things coming through are those we invite." He pushed some energy at the stone hut's door. It was charmed to only admit *Nephilim*. "No electricity here. Will you see to the lanterns?" Rhys pressed a lighter into her hand as they entered.

"Sure. Actually, I was thinking..."

That sounded like the opening to a rabbit hole they didn't have time to go down. Rhys opened the curtains to let in a shaft of moonlight. "Should I brace myself?"

"Maybe *I* should be the only one to do the spell. All of it." Maisy lit the lantern on the hook by the door. "Following your instruction, of course. So that you won't be tainted, as an angel, by doing any black magic."

...And she'd surprised him *again* with that selfless offer.

All he ever did was look out for everyone else. Aside from Gid and Z, nobody ever worried about the toll it took on him.

Rhys crossed back to her. Framed her face with his hands. "Thank you. Sincerely."

Her nose crinkled. "Well, I don't want you to molt any of those sexy feathers."

Like he wasn't having a hard enough time avoiding thoughts of sex with her already. Maisy was driving him to distraction. In the best possible way...just not the best way to do a powerful spell.

"But we won't be working black magic. Not magic at all, as you know it. More like a Zoom meeting. The spell is the mystical satellite, opening the portal to Hell." He opened the bureau and pulled out the necessary supplies. Set out the red and black candles, the white ones. The skull, of course. Had to have a representation of death to get through to the underworld.

"Can he hurt us? Once he appears?"

"No. The thaumaturgic triangle will contain him." He held out the chalk. "You're the artist. You should do it. An unbroken circle."

"That's it? Nothing fancy? Some curlicues? Angel wings?"

Setting down the bowl, he muttered, "Remember the whole 'follow my instructions' thing?"

"Right." The circle she inscribed on the cement slab was much more perfect than anything he could've done.

Rhys sprinkled a triangle of salt within the circle. Put the skull and candles each at a point. The four white candles went at the compass points of the circle. "The demon will be held inside the triangle. Still, don't be a jerk. Don't goad him or promise him anything. Demons can be tricksters, talk in circles. In fact, leave the talking to me."

"He doesn't know you, except maybe remembering that you killed him. Why would the locksmith tell you anything?"

"He knows I'm *Nephilim*. That ought to be enough."

Maisy tightened her hoodie's sleeves into a knot at her waist. "Wouldn't that make him a snitch? Snitches get stitches—in prison as much as high school. Hell seems like the ultimate combo of both. Except they probably don't even bother with stitches in Hell."

"Fine. We'll start your way. Charm the big bad demon." If anyone could, it'd be Maisy. Rhys didn't doubt that for a second. "But remember, we've searched his house and his shop. He definitely passed the Key off to someone. This is our only chance to find out whom."

She opened and closed her fingers in a yapping gesture. "Fate of the world, blah blah blah. I promise you, that's sunk in by now."

Rhys placed a bat hair into the bowl. Sprinkled grated mandrake root over it, then a layer of soot. He sliced his own finger. Squeezed the blood on top. "I'm sorry, but we've got to have the blood of all the participants in the summoning."

"I'm tough, *Nephilim*. No worries," she blustered. He barely pricked the surface and only squeezed out a single drop.

Then, surprising himself, he kissed her fingertip. Met her surprised gaze but then had to look away. Back to business. "Here we go. You light the white candles. And stay within the chalk circle, no matter what."

Rhys walked the circle, setting a corresponding Watchtower crystal on each elemental candle to cast the protective circle.

Air, Fire, Water, Earth, Elements pure
Your brother beseeches you keep us secure
Inside this circle, by your might
May we be grounded and protected by Divine light.

He raised his arms and extended his wings. The energy of

the circle crackled out and up to the ceiling. The tips of Maisy's ponytail extended as if she'd rubbed them with a balloon. After lighting the red and black candles, he dripped the wax on top of the bowl and set it inside the triangle.

"Get the name," he whispered.

"Oh, yeah." Maisy pulled a sticky note out of her jeans pocket. Handed it over.

Rhys glanced at it. What a weird name for a demon. This one must've been newly released from Hell to choose something so weak. It'd bring down the level of Maisy's first summoning considerably.

Disappointing.

"On my signal." Clasping her hand in his, he raised them overhead and continued.

We of life call you from death.

Answer our call, aid our quest.

Within this shape, in human form be held fast,

For all the time this circle be cast.

Norman Dooley, we summon you!

No theatrics with lightning or thunderclaps. Just a guy with a potbelly suddenly standing in the triangle, looking back at them with a quizzical tilt to his head. It was the demon Rhys had killed, but that wasn't enough confirmation. "This the guy? The locksmith?"

"Yes." Maisy licked her lips and swallowed so hard he could almost hear her throat working. "Yes, this is the man who took my Key."

Norman's head snapped straight so fast it made his comb-over flap up. "You gave it to me, girly. Don't try to talk your way out of that. You know I couldn't take it from you with a crowbar and a team of demons. Freely given—that's the only way."

"No, you're right. What is it the police say—ignorance of the law isn't an excuse for breaking it? I didn't know the Key was special. But you were gentlemanly and followed the rules. You didn't even try to rough me up for the heck of it."

Maisy was praising the demon for not hurting her? Rhys had to bite back a chuckle at her brilliance.

"That's right. I could have. Other demons would've. Not me. We did a transaction. Fair and square. I treated you right."

Rhys couldn't take much more of this self-aggrandizing. Norman really wanted recognition for not hurting an innocent woman? Demons were shady, just like he'd warned Maisy.

"The thing is, I *thought* I was giving it to a real locksmith who'd appreciate its artistry."

"I *am* a locksmith."

Maisy's lips quirked. Like she was enjoying the negotiation. She sure didn't look scared. "Well, you aren't actively running the shop where I last saw you."

"Whose fault is that?" he snarled.

Rhys raised his hand. "No regrets about it, either. Demons are a scourge upon humanity."

"Don't be a bigot, half-breed. You can't paint all of demonkind with the same brush. Some of us are just grinding it out, not causing any trouble."

Rhys hated stating the obvious. He sauntered over to the edge of the triangle. "We searched your house. We found a dozen *arms* in your refrigerator."

"It's a crime to stock up on snacks?"

Rhys wanted to kill him all over again. Sadly, shipping him back to Hell would have to be good enough.

He glanced at Maisy, hoping she'd wrap this up fast. The Grecian heat in this stone building was no joke. Strands of hair stuck to Maisy's neck. Rhys was sweating in his fighting leathers, but he'd never risk a demon confrontation in shorts and a Hawaiian shirt. Demons meant being prepared for anything to go wrong.

"Norman, this was my mistake." Maisy dipped her head in apology. "I didn't realize it was a cherished heirloom. My uncle deserves better for the thoughtfulness he put into bequeathing it to me. I'm asking you to tell me whom you gave it to. I'd like my inheritance back. Please."

"See? The lady can be polite. You could learn a thing or two from her, half-breed."

A fucking demon was going to lecture him on *manners*? Rhys was tempted to smudge out the triangle and kick Norman's ass all over again. "I don't have to be polite. I'm not the one in Hell. We've got all kinds of freedoms up here—ones you'll never experience again. I have the *freedom* to talk to my contacts and make your stay in Hell a hundred times worse. Quit stalling. Who'd you give it to?"

"I gave it to a witch."

Then a tiny waft of air disrupted the borders of the salt triangle. He didn't know how. He'd shut the door to prevent this very thing from happening. It looked broken by just a few granules. But that was shockingly enough.

Norman reverted to his demon form, gray tentacles immediately popping out over his belt. He bared his fangs.

Worse than that, a fiery shadow-shape coalesced overhead. Flames licked along the amorphous edges as it grew. Heat poured down onto them. Accompanying it was a feeling of absolute dread. Like the amorphous thing *pushed* fear into the oxygen. As it grew, it covered the width of the entire ceiling. At the doorway, it flipped sideways and slid through the crack at the bottom.

Rhys knew it to be pure evil. Which meant it had to be Algul. He raced to the door and threw it open to track his glowing flight out of the canyon.

Every instinct told Rhys to pursue him and send its ass back to Hell before it had a chance to harm a single soul. Or more like the hundreds it would no doubt take down within a week. It was his number one duty as a *Nephilim*.

But...there was Maisy. Splayed flat on the floor, probably to escape the bubble of heat. Norman stood over her. And yeah, he looked like he was craving another arm snack.

Not on his watch.

Right now, the Keeper's safety was his most pressing duty. The demon had his foot on Maisy's shoulder and her hand almost to his mouth. Rhys twitched his favorite dagger out of the arm sheath and hurled it at Norman. Landed right in the middle of his throat.

Shit.

Norman collapsed. Thick streams of gray blood filled the circle.

In one-second hindsight? That'd been the worst way to dispatch the demon. Rhys should've held back, roughed him up, and gotten the name of the witch out of him before killing him again, but he couldn't stand the sight of that creature touching Maisy, scaring her.

The need to protect her drove all thought of battle strategy from his mind. He'd just acted. Explaining that amateur mistake to Gid and Z was going to *suck*.

Rhys rushed to crouch by Maisy. "Are you okay?" He palpated her shoulder, making sure it was still in place.

"Physically? Yes. Otherwise?" She pushed up to crab walk away from the widening pool of blood. "Not so much. What happened to Norman being contained in the triangle?"

"It broke." Rhys scanned the protection circle. *Fuck*. He pointed to where her pink hoodie lay across the chalk line. "You broke it."

She jumped up. Pointed down where her rainbow sneakers were still within its bounds. "I stayed in the circle!"

"You took off your hoodie."

"It's hot in here, in case you hadn't noticed? Greece, remember?"

Habit had him opening his mouth to yell. To snap that the shitstorm that had been unleashed was entirely her fault. That people would die due to her careless action. That keeping her safe was turning out to be the hardest mission of his life, fighting against her freaking sunny "life is a gift and everything is good" nature that blinded her to the intrinsic dangers of their world.

Deliberately, Rhys shut his mouth before saying any of that. Paced to the far corner of the room to think it through.

Because Maisy had to be scared out of her mind. That... didn't sit well with him.

He didn't want to make her feel worse by pointing a finger, but this was a teachable moment. For her to stay alive through this two-week transition, she had to take in every lesson that presented itself.

Making sure *not* to use what she called his lecture tone, Rhys said calmly, "You dropped it over the physical line of the circle. That interrupts its power. At the same time, when you dropped it, it created a puff of air that moved the salt border of the triangle, just enough to break it, too. The double protection double failed."

"Oh." She rolled her shoulder, wincing.

Rhys bounded to her side in a single step—aided by a push of his wings. "Let me look." He gently pushed up her sleeve. A mottled bruise was already darkening her skin. The shoulder joint itself appeared to be aligned correctly, though. "We'll give you a salve that should take most of the ache away. You'll be fine."

Even though she almost wasn't.

With him right next to her, ostensibly protecting her.

That was fucking unacceptable.

Maisy readjusted her shirt. "What was that? The fiery... thing?"

"A hitchhiker. Happens all the time with summonings. He came along with Norman. Stayed hidden until he saw the chance to make a break for it."

"It looked like what I imagine a Hell creature would be. Powerful, even without a form, with all that heat pumping out." She looked out the door into the black sky. In a small voice, she asked, "Is he very bad?"

Oh, yeah. "The demons that usually travel the earth? Think of them as the wine coolers of demons. This one, Algul? He's a shot of one hundred and ninety–proof Everclear." Rhys pulled out his phone. Shot off a text to Zavier, alerting him that there'd been a breach. And, damn it, to inform Master Caraxis that any *Nephilim* in the area should be on alert. Hopefully he'd be caught. If not, once Maisy's transition was done, Rhys would push himself to find it. Algul being on Earth was Maisy's fault but *his* responsibility.

During all this, Maisy picked up her hoodie. Dusted the chalk off of it. Re-cinched it at her waist. "You guys will catch it, right? Algul?"

They'd better. Rhys fisted his hands on his hips. "That'll be the plan. It hasn't escaped from Hell in centuries. Probably spent all that time planning what to do and how to stay off the radar. It'll be a tough hunt. Algul shouldn't have been able to escape."

"Meaning?"

They'd gotten intel back on who and what was behind the Gates that Maisy guarded. Just a few names so far, but Algul had definitely been one of them. It was why Rhys had been able to identify him so quickly.

"It being in the world is proof that *your* Gates, the Gates of Hell's prison, are slipping open wider. They're still locked, but… it's like a chain link holding a gate together. As it loosens, there's space to squeeze out."

Maisy looked down at Norman, her face blank. Then up and back out the door, where nothing was left to be seen of Algul's wake. "Because of the transition? Because I didn't immediately assume the role of Keeper?"

"Yes. The longer this transition lasts?" He rasped a hand over his eleven thirty–p.m. scruff. "It's very bad, very dangerous. That demon is out hunting right now—people *will* die."

Hands flying to cover her mouth, Maisy said, "This is my fault."

Yes—and no.

She shouldn't be burdened with all of the guilt. "I can't quote you the history of every Keeper across the ages, but there's a two-week transition for a reason. The testing is for a reason. There are checks and balances built into the system. Demons escape. We catch them."

"I thought the *Aldokriz* demon scared me. Then I thought Milton Turk scared me when the evil Keeper took control of him. But both of them talked to me, so there was still some semblance of normalcy, humanity. This...Algul?" Maisy gestured to the ceiling. "It wasn't remotely human. And now I can say I've finally tasted true fear. I'm terrified, Rhys."

Anger ground his teeth together. It was not right that she kept suffering. It wasn't right that with him by her side, she was still vulnerable. That she kept stepping up, never shirking from whatever Hell and Heaven threw at her, and still nearly being killed.

"You're not alone."

Her jaw dropped. "*You're* scared of the Algul?"

"Of course. It can unleash death and horror and destruction. I'm scared that we won't stop it. Courage is acknowledging your fear and doing what must be done *despite* it." He took her hands. Kissed the backs of each in turn. "And you, Maisy Norgate, are the most courageous human I've ever encountered."

She gave a shaky laugh. "Well, give it another half century. I'm sure you'll run across someone better."

Rhys drew her outside, away from the stench of death. "You know what scared me the most tonight? You. The thought of Algul's heat blistering your skin. And then more fear pumped through me, churned bile up my throat when I saw that tentacled monster with his hands on you."

"All twelve of them." Her giggle leaned toward manic.

"Indeed. The thought of you being harmed scared me very, very much."

"I'm fine," she insisted.

Rhys slid his hand up her neck. Felt her pulse thrumming so fast it felt like a single, constant beat. He kept sliding up, to cradle the back of her head. "How about you let me make sure of that?"

His mouth slanted across hers. Every bit as much to reassure himself as to calm her. Maisy opened to him immediately. Welcomed him with fast, furious kisses. Her right leg vined around his calf. With a hard pump of his wings, Rhys launched them both into the sky.

A place where they weren't *Nephilim* and Keeper.

A place where they were just two beings who wanted each other. Both to reassure her…and because Rhys didn't know how many chances they had left.

Algul's escape was proof that Rhys might not be enough to keep Maisy safe. Which was more frightening than contemplating the dozens of people Algul would no doubt kill tonight alone.

CHAPTER FIFTEEN

"You do realize this Keeper's smarter than we gave her credit for at the start?" Gideon murmured to Rhys.

Oh, yeah.

The way they'd pigeonholed Maisy might well go down as the worst judgment call of their careers. To say they'd underestimated the Keeper solely due to her, well, annoying-as-fuck perkiness? That was like saying morphine could dull the sting of a hangnail.

But it was never wise to just *hand* Gideon ammunition. Rhys looked over the top of his shades. "In what way?"

"She's learned all our weaknesses. In only a week." Gideon buttoned his tan sport coat. "She *played* us, Rhys. How else do you explain us spending our morning in an old folks' home?"

It was true. She'd charmed Gideon by pointing out that the residents didn't get many visitors, let alone massively tall, handsome ones.

Convinced Zavier that his weapons knowledge would enliven the old soldiers.

And, well, she'd *flirted* with Rhys.

Since he could still almost taste her kisses from last night? It'd worked. Not that he'd admit it to Gid.

"Maisy lets nothing stand in the way of achieving her goal. She's much like us in that respect."

"I'd say more that she steamrolled you."

"She is to be the Keeper. It's our duty to do as she wishes."

The side-eye Gideon gave him at that was sharp enough to cut glass. "You really think she'll be Keeper?"

"I think she'll make it to the Test. None of us can guess what will happen during it. Hell, none of us can find out what comprises the Test."

Gideon looked left and right, then angled closer to Rhys. "About that...think Caraxis is holding out on us on purpose?"

"To what end?"

"To make it a test for *us* as much as for her?"

Rhys stopped in his tracks as, ahead of them, Zavier opened the door for Maisy. "Damn his sneaky old hide. You're probably right."

"Dude, don't say *probably*. It's insulting and inaccurate. I'm *always* right." Gideon spurted ahead to catch up. "Hang on, Maisy. Don't go in yet."

The long floral skirt billowed around her ankles as she spun to face him. "They're on a strict schedule. The window between breakfast *and* stretching *and* crafts and *then* lunch doesn't leave me much time to visit with Mrs. Rathbone."

Rhys still couldn't believe they were visiting her old art teacher. How many people stayed in touch with their teachers a dozen years past graduation?

"This won't take long. I've got a tincture for you. Four drops, under the tongue." Gideon brandished a small bottle.

"What for?"

"It'll let you see magical auras. An early warning system. Not all mystical creatures are evil, but if you do see someone with a muddy, brown aura, get one of us."

"Why not give me the thing that lets me actually see demons? That potion I took the other day."

Ah. Rhys knew she was baiting Gideon. Forcing him to reveal that he hadn't been entirely truthful about the potion. This would be enjoyable to watch.

"Well"—Gideon drew the word out, long and slow—"humans can't have it very often. Side effects of seeing things you're not supposed to see."

Maisy pushed the bottle away. "What side effects?"

Rhys stayed silent. This was Gideon's call. Rhys had asserted that with three of them along there was no need to give Maisy any extra form of protection. But Gid reminded him that nursing homes were basically mosh pits for the paranormal, and Maisy attracted trouble the way a dead body attracted maggots.

Finally, Gideon looked down at his highly polished wing tips. "It'd blind you."

Maisy shot a loaded stink eye at all three men in turn. "And nobody thought to mention this *before* we took it?"

"You were fine with one dose." Gideon batted away her doubts with one hand. "You'd still be mostly okay after a second dose. It's the third in a year that gets tricky, but we want to save that second dose for any emergency that could come up."

Maisy tapped a finger against her lips as if pondering. Which had Rhys bracing. He'd seen that look before from her.

"An emergency, you say. So, not when the evil Keeper took over and exploded a demon in front of me. Not when a full-blown angel dragged me to another dimension. Not when a fiery blob almost seared my hair off. What, pray tell, constitutes *an emergency*?"

The three *Nephilim* exchanged a glance. It was their unspoken equivalent to rock/paper/scissors to see who'd be the one to take the fall for the others. Zavier, who was right next to her, raised one eyebrow. "Something worse?"

"You know what?" She threw her hands up in the air. "I'm not even going to ask. Give me the stupid tincture."

It was nice when his blood brothers were around to take some of Maisy's heat. Even nicer to watch Gideon get smacked down by her.

Feeling as bright as Maisy's hot pink lips, Rhys slipped his hands into his pockets and took point as they entered.

The facility looked nice enough. Colorful, freshly painted artwork on all the walls. But it still had that institutional feeling: low ceilings, linoleum floors rather than carpet—probably easier on the wheelchairs—and an underlying scent combo of burned oatmeal and disinfectant.

Maisy turned her head to address all of them. "Mrs. Rathbone always believed in me. She helped me get the art scholarships that allowed me to go to college. If it wasn't for her, I'd be restocking shelves at Target for a living."

"You work in a coffee shop," Zavier said.

"Not the point. I visit her once a month because she's a lovely woman and because I owe her everything for believing in me. So don't tell her that I'm not teaching right now. Don't mention that I'm not selling my paintings, either."

"We're half angel. We can't lie."

"Really?"

"No." The three men burst into laughter. It had the white-haired patients in the hallway looking up from their parked wheelchairs and smiling.

Maisy sniffed. "You're all obnoxious." When she looked back down the hallway, she stilled. "Almost every third person has an aura."

"*Everyone* has an aura. And to manifest a visible one, you only need to have a smattering of mystical power. Some are probably unaware of it. Others are already being tended to by angels as they near their transition to the other side, and that burnishes their aura."

"Or being healed by a demon." Zavier jerked his chin at a fellow slumped down, napping. A lap robe covered his legs, and a Korean War veteran's cap tilted down on his head.

Maisy squinted. Popped her eyes wide, then squinted again. "I don't see anything. Except...an undulating wave of...blue going into his chest?"

Rhys wanted to make a joke about giving her a cookie for getting the answer right. Except that the guys would never let him hear the end of it.

He spoke softly as an orderly hustled by, whistling and pushing a cleaning cart. "That's a wave of healing energy. *Mandragora* demons can cure disease. I mean, he can't cure how old this guy is, but he's fixing something."

"Why would a demon do that? Feels like I'm stating the obvious here, but aren't they killers?"

"The ones you've met, sure. Hell is a kingdom ruled over by an angel. The population of it's not all evil. Same as how not all humans are good or evil—some just lean one way or the other to a different degree. Someone hired this *mandragora* to do what he could to help."

Zavier snapped his fingers. "Remember what else *mandragora* are good for? They can tell the future."

Rhys gave him a low five. Z for the encyclopedic-knowledge win, as always.

Flattening against the wall—was she trying not to be seen by the demon? That'd never work—Maisy asked, "So he—is it a he?—could tell us where we find the Key in the future?"

Zavier clicked his tongue. "Not that simple."

"Supernatural gifts rarely are." Gideon jumped in. "He can only answer questions by nodding his head. And each petitioner only gets one question. So no, he can't give us the street address of the Key's location. Or tonight's lottery numbers. But he *could* help."

They moved to form a circle around the old man, still dead asleep. The demon winked into view, half translucent. Must've sensed power in the hallway and wanted to play nice. Maisy still wouldn't be able to see him, though.

He was the size of a doll, perched on the handle of the wheelchair. While his overall appearance was that of a tiny human male with combed-over hair, the solid orange eyes gave away his true nature. He waved at the *Nephilim*. Waved doubly hard at Maisy.

How did she bring out the warm and friendly in creatures when she wasn't even interacting with them?

Gideon elbowed her. "He waved at you, Keeper."

She started to lift her hand to wave back but then froze. "In a nice way? Or in a get-away-from-me way, or an I'll-eat-you way?"

"In an *I'm stuck in this nursing home with all the nearly dead and I'm thrilled to see a vivacious, beautiful woman* way."

"He's not a Muppet," Rhys growled. He wasn't loving Gideon heaping the compliments on Maisy. Gideon wielded compliments the way a sushi chef wielded a blade—with flawless expertise. "Don't put words in his mouth."

She flashed one of her usual smiles that could probably thaw at least an acre of the Arctic and waggled her fingers in the general direction of the *mandragora*.

"Go on," Rhys urged with a tap to her forearm. He had to remind himself not to linger on her warm skin. She smelled like a sun-warmed field of lavender in Provence. "One question."

"Hi. I'm Maisy Norgate." She put her hand to her heart. "Thank you for trying to help this man. I'm sure when he wakes up feeling better, he'll appreciate it. He won't be able to thank you, but I'll bet he'd like to."

The *mandragora* stopped the healing flow of energies. He focused all his attention on Maisy.

"A question, Keeper," Rhys prompted her. He circled a hand right above the top of the demon's head to give her a focal point.

She smoothed a hand down her sleek, bouncy ponytail. Her head tilted down, as if she was mulling how best to phrase it. "I'm still learning the ropes about, well, demons and Hell and all that. You're the first one I've met who hasn't tried to kill me, so that's a nice change. With the whole demon aspect, but also being able to heal...I just wonder...does it make you happy?"

Oh, for fuck's sake! Rhys aimed his eye roll over at Zavier.

Who was chuckling.

Zavier never laughed on a mission, unless he was killing something with a ridiculous amount of glee.

Annoyed beyond all measure with the Keeper—as usual—Rhys wiped a hand up his forehead. "Unbelievable. You just wasted a big opportunity. How does that question help us at all?"

Maisy didn't back down at his harsh, exasperated tone. Her chin jerked up, and heat flared into her pale cheeks. "It'll help me understand my role in this whole confusing *other* world of yours. Until two minutes ago, I had no idea there *was* such a thing as a good demon. This is the first one not trying to kill me. I don't want to be an unconscious bigot as I slowly learn the things you've known your whole life. I don't want to take anyone or anything for granted or misjudge it."

"Rhys. Look." Gideon pointed at the *mandragora*. His orange eyes filled with tears. He clapped his hand to his chest. Apparently, he appreciated the personal question, and he slowly nodded. Then three more times, fast, with a big smile. "Maisy, he said yes. Gotta say, he looks happy to me."

"Oh, that's a relief. Good."

Yippee.

Man, the demon wouldn't stop nodding yes. Until he bowed to Maisy in thanks.

His Keeper might be deep in her own existential crisis, but Rhys very much knew how to stay on mission. Time to move along. "Will we find the Key?" he asked tersely.

After a second, the *Mandragora* nodded yes again, but this was only a single nod, with much less enthusiasm, and topped off with a heavy frown.

"What's the frown mean?" Rhys knew he wouldn't answer him. Frustration had spit the words out of his mouth anyway. The demon turned his attention back to the old man, clearly dismissing them.

Gideon kept narrating for Maisy. "It was a yes. It lacked the verve of the yes you got, though."

"I elicit more verve than Tall, Dark, and Grumpy." She flicked her wrist at Rhys. "Sounds like a guarantee of a win for Team Keeper, in any case. I'll take it." Maisy led them down the hall toward a large dining room.

"Don't hold your breath," Zavier muttered.

"Why not? You said he tells the future."

"There could be a twist." Zavier counted off on his fingers. "We find the Key, but you don't pass the test to become Keeper. We find the Key, but one of us gets killed."

Gideon nodded his agreement. "That little demon definitely gave the impression this wasn't a done deal."

"Ugh. You're all so gloomy. A nurse could inject you with thirty ccs of pure joy, and you'd find a way to question its efficacy. And probably break out in a rash." Maisy started down the hall. "C'mon, boys. I'm going to brighten Mrs. Rathbone's day, *despite* your end-of-the-world vibes."

Rhys didn't know how she did it, but as her ponytail bounced in front of him, he believed her.

Believed she'd brighten the day of all the residents. Believed she'd find the Key and keep those Gates locked, despite overwhelming odds and the general shitshow they'd made of the hunt for it thus far.

Maisy made him hopeful.

And happy.

What was he supposed to do with that?

Despite the stroke that had paralyzed one side of Mrs. Rathbone, they always started each visit with a hug.

Until today.

Maisy tried to move in for a hug, but her teacher's left arm shot up and out, fending her off. She practically shoved Maisy into the edge of the piano. "Watchers!"

Odd. Her speech was sometimes slurred, but the *right* words were always in the right order. What was this about? Had she had another stroke? "Mrs. Rathbone, nobody's watching you. It's me, Maisy. I'm here for our visit."

"Watchers," she repeated loudly with surprised eyes and shaking a quavering finger.

"She means us," Rhys said, stepping around the circular table and putting a finger to his lips. "It's another name for *Nephilim*."

Him using that term out in the open had Maisy darting looks left and right. Luckily, all the other patients were gathered at the opposite end of the large room, playing charades. Which, wow, set her to drift on an ice floe before committing her to a place like this in sixty years.

Maisy swiveled her head back and forth between Mrs. Rathbone and Rhys. In a stage whisper, she asked, "How does she know what you are?"

"Good question." He stroked his chin, giving her mentor a once-over.

Which was ridiculous. The woman was in a pink cardigan, with a mohair throw in bright red plaid over her lap and a jaunty red beret on her white curls. There was nothing magical about her. Her aura was barely visible—a pale new-grass green that matched Maisy's. So...*obviously* a human.

Zavier pulled out a chair and straddled it. "Witch, am I right?"

Before Maisy could admonish him for being rude, Mrs. Rathbone bobbed her head. "Oh, my. Do forgive my gawking. You're all quite magnificent in person. You're the first I've ever met."

It was almost possible to hear the gears in Rhys's brain clicking as he recalibrated the situation. After a slight hesitation: "Then we should do this right. I'm Rhys Boyce."

"Gideon Durand."

"Zavier Carranza." They each shook her hand with an almost courtly flourish.

Look at them playing so nicely. As if they weren't also scanning the room for an excuse to hurl a dagger at something.

"You can see...their...you know..." Maisy fanned her hands, sketching the air in the shape of the *Nephilim*'s extra feathered appendages.

"Wings? Yes, dear." Mrs. Rathbone gave the same patient, indulgent smile she'd given freshmen who couldn't identify ROYGBIV on day one of art class. "Can't you?"

"Not for the most part. Same as everyone else in this room."

"I don't understand. Isn't that why you're here with them?" Mrs. Rathbone took her hand. Squeezed tightly. "You're ascending to your role as Keeper?"

Every seemingly normal thing her teacher uttered just sprouted six more questions in Maisy's mind. "I should be able to see their wings all the time when I'm officially the Keeper?"

"Of course."

Interesting. Were there other powers that she'd get? Invisibility would be nice.

But...why on earth was her former teacher talking about this mystical role of the Guardian of Hell's Gates in relation to plain old, perfectly normal Maisy Norgate? Nothing in the previous thirty years of her life pointed towards the possibility, let alone the inevitability of this new job that had been dropped in her lap.

"You *knew* I was slated to inherit the role of Keeper?"

"Yes."

Just as her knees were about to give out as shock noodled all her muscles, Rhys shoved a chair under her. That man noticed everything. "I don't understand *anything*. How is my high school art teacher a witch?"

"There's not a steady paycheck attached to my being a witch. It's more of a calling than a career. And with my powers, I was able to deal with an unruly classroom with more ease than a purely human teacher could." Mrs. Rathbone's cloudy eyes twinkled.

Ooh, that was sneaky.

Maisy *loved* it.

"But how do you know about Keepers and *Nephilim*?" Rhys had given her the strong impression that info was on a need-to-know basis. One that, for example, none of their employees needed to know.

Mrs. Rathbone laughed. Much harder than Maisy felt the question deserved. "Because I'm a witch, dear. I am conversant with all things in the paranormal world. That's like asking how do you know about astronauts and beekeepers and chefs. All just a part of my ordinary world. And, also, because I was close friends with your Uncle Harold."

The breaking news just kept churning out hard-to-absorb updates. "I'm sorry, *whaaaaat*?"

"Oh, yes. I'd give him reports on how you were doing. He positively thirsted for every nugget of information about you."

There was a far simpler fix for that thirst than having a beloved teacher *stalk* her. "Did he consider, I don't know, introducing himself to me? At any point in the last thirty years?"

"He couldn't. It was more important to keep you safe. Cutting himself out of your life meant that nobody could suspect who truly stood to inherit the role of Keeper from him. They all assumed it would be his son. Harold stayed away *because* he loved you so very much."

That was an entirely different take on the matter. The hurt she'd been nursing since learning of his existence just melted away, leaving in its place a dozen more questions. Had her parents known? Were there other seemingly normal people in her life who'd been secretly keeping tabs on her?

And would Maisy be able to find any of this out with Harold now dead?

Wait. "A son? Who was *supposed* to be the Keeper?"

"Well, tradition passes the role to the immediate descendent. Harold, however, wasn't much for following rules."

"Can this...other guy be the Keeper?"

"No, dear. Once you've received the Key, you are locked in, so to speak." She gave Maisy a little wink.

"Ha ha," Maisy deadpanned. "Do you know where my cousin is? Who he is?"

"No. More to the point, I wouldn't waste your time looking for him. If he wasn't good enough for Harold, then he's not a good person."

"That's a *lot* to take in," Maisy mumbled.

"Would you like me to do a little calming spell, dear?"

"No!" All three of the men answered simultaneously before Maisy could open her mouth.

They'd said what she was thinking. She'd just been coming up with a polite way to turn down the kind offer. After hearing the side effects of the demon-visibility potion, she was in no hurry to let anyone work magic on her.

Gideon crossed his arms like he was laying down the law. His expression was uncharacteristically stern. When he dropped his seemingly natural charm, he came off as scary as Zavier, even with the golden-boy good looks. "No offense, but she's under our protection. We can't risk any outside interference."

Laughter shook the elderly woman's shoulders so hard she started coughing. "Because I could be an agent of the Devil. Oh, that's rich. Good for you boys for keeping watch over her, but I could've entranced Maisy hundreds of times over in the years we've spent together."

Gideon held his ground. "Not since she was activated as Keeper. Everything's different now."

Boy, was that a freaking understatement!

Mrs. Rathbone patted her hand. "You'll get more answers when you go to Harold's home. You must go as soon as possible— but be careful. It's being watched."

"I think these guys have stealthiness as part of their considerable arsenal." Maisy had faith that they could sneak her into the Oval Office without the Secret Service being any the wiser. She might not always agree with their methods or their tone, but she didn't doubt that she was safer with these *Nephilim* than with anyone else in the world.

Mrs. R pulled her good hand away to gesture at Rhys. "May I ask a favor, Rhys?"

Those deep indigo eyes crinkled around the edges as he bent to give her a devastatingly warm smile. "Anything for Maisy's favorite teacher."

Aww. He was pulling out all the stops to be kind to her. Maisy *knew* Rhys had it in him. When he pushed aside his constant worry about her becoming Keeper and his *I've seen way more than you in my overly long lifetime* attitude of disenchantment with life, he was a genuinely nice man.

A genuinely good man. Which seemed redundant to say about a half angel.

"Would you sing for me? I've heard stories of the song of the *Nephilim*. It'd be such a treat to hear it myself."

Wait—they were winged, muscled, hot as fuck, and could *sing*? Maisy was pretty sure her panties were on the verge of bursting into flame at the very thought.

Rhys exchanged a look with the other men. "You know it'll affect everyone in the room."

Affect *how*? Maisy hated not comprehending their conversation.

"They're all old, and half are at least half senile. They'd be expecting to drop off into a nap anyway. Charades wears everyone out. I'll convince them it was a dream."

"Then it'd be our honor, Lady Witch, to do so for the woman who helped our Keeper." Rhys brushed past Maisy to play a single chord on the piano. "Anthos Magiko."

The three men stood shoulder to shoulder. A pure, golden

tone like the single pluck of a harp string emitted from Gideon.

But it wasn't just a sound. No, this had a tactile sensation, too. More than that, even. As Zavier and Rhys joined in a few notes later, the music massaged its way through her skin. It stroked every nerve. Every cell, every corpuscle.

The music overwhelmed all of her senses. It sweetened her tongue. The air was suddenly scented like she'd imagine a mountain meadow smelling. And yes, there was even a visual component.

Not only did the wings become fully visible in their ombre glory on all three men, but they *glowed*. Radiant white light luminesced behind them, above them—a whole body halo.

Maisy felt dizzy.

Drunk.

High.

Blissful.

...And more than a little like she'd like to tear off Rhys's coat, his starched shirt, and his Windsor knot tie, and lick him from head to toe.

Was horniness an angelic song side effect? Because the seniors in the room didn't have a wanton, crazed, wild-eyed lust thing in their expressions.

But Maisy *wanted* Rhys Boyce in all his annoying pretentiousness more than she wanted her next breath.

Awkward. The idea was impossible.

The man was old enough to be her grandfather and didn't look like he was anywhere nearing middle age. He'd outlive her. He didn't trust her. They couldn't be more opposite.

And yet she still wondered what it would take to get him to get naked.

CHAPTER SIXTEEN

Zavier stayed, hovering, in the falls when they returned to the Watchtower. "Now that Maisy's home safe, I'll go crack the whip to remind everyone that we still run this company."

Rhys gave a grateful nod. "Thanks."

With every mission, they ended up juggling who spent more face time at their human business. Or, as they thought of it, drew the short straw. Because they all wanted to be out in the field kicking ass. Righting wrongs. *Nephilim* were trained to fight.

Not to sit in meetings and mediate arguments about not removing the used Keurig pods.

Gideon snapped off a salute. "You're a team player, Z."

"Bite me, G." Zavier flipped them off over his shoulder as he flew back through the water.

"He's just jealous about my assignment."

Maisy's eyes popped wide with intrigue. She was much more about personal crises than, say, the bigger picture of demons possibly overrunning the Earth in less than two weeks. "Does Zavier have a *crush* on the witch you're going to meet?"

"A crush?" Laughter boomed out of Gideon. Rhys joined in. Because the mere idea was *hilarious*. "Z doesn't do crushes. Except for how he crushes the heart of every woman that crosses his path. No, he's spoiling for a fight. There's a strong chance I'll have to wade through a series of nasty protective spells before

I get anywhere close to talking to her. Cedella hates *Nephilim*."

"Why?"

"Someone handled things...poorly." Then Gideon shot a significant look at Rhys as they led her to the laboratory.

"Oh. Ohhhh—did you *ghost* a witch?" Then Maisy devolved into giggles. "I'm sorry. It's a cheap shot, but it was just sitting out there, waiting for someone to take it. Might as well be me."

It stung that Maisy thought he'd be so cruel. "No. Cedella was selling fake protection amulets. I reallocated the funds she'd earned from that and exposed her questionable behavior to the head of her coven, Aradia."

"He went in, wings and knives out, demanded her money, and then he gave it all to a women's shelter," Gideon explained.

Her giggles dried up. Admiration smoothed her cheeks into a smile. "You're Robin Hood?"

It felt...good to hear Maisy's approval. Warm. Like the heat of throwing back a shot of tequila. Not that approval from a human should matter.

But strangely, from her, it *did*.

Very much.

He'd discovered that earning one of her genuine smiles was becoming the highlight of his days. And Rhys had no freaking idea what to do about it.

"I'm a problem solver. Cedella was creating a problem of distrust in the community. I fixed it." He leaned on the doorframe while Gideon pulled out the necessary tonic for Maisy to counter the aura-revealing tincture.

She kept her gaze fixed on Rhys, though. And that steady look of approval continued to blanket him in warmth. Warmth he didn't understand.

Warmth he wanted to soak up like a lazy cat in a ray of sun.

Maisy said, "That's quite impressive. Your ability to fix things. Your strong sense of right and wrong. Your commitment to keeping people safe even if you don't really care about them.

You're quite the man. Half man."

Gideon winked as he put four drops under her tongue. "He also cheats at cards."

Suspicions. Unverified. It wasn't like Rhys counted cards in casinos. He fleeced his brothers-in-arms because they weren't as good as him and needed to be taught the lesson. "It's only cheating if you catch me. And you've never caught me."

And...

And...Rhys realized he didn't like seeing Gideon anywhere near Maisy's tongue, even just to dose her.

"Should we raise the rates, due to her being a pain in the ass?" Gideon selected a gun and two more knives to hide about his person. Couldn't be too careful in dealing with a witch. Even one trying to get back in the good graces of the *Nephilim*.

"Why does she want to hire us?"

"No specifics. Just an issue with an Obeah man."

It clicked into his brain. Just a little slower than normal, due to the distraction that was Maisy perched on a stool, swinging a leg in bright orange pants. Gideon was flying to Jamaica. "That's voodoo. Which probably means we'll have to deal with fucking snakes at some point. Yeah, you should up our rate."

"Good." Gideon flew the length of the armory. Maisy rushed over to watch him launch toward the waterfall and then disappear.

Rhys realized he didn't like Maisy staring after Gideon, either. It annoyed him, in fact, more than any other in the long list of annoying actions she'd made since the moment they met. Mostly, he was annoyed at *himself* for feeling so petty. "He won't be back for some time. You might as well stop pining for him to reappear."

"Pining?" The draft from the falls blew her hair into a fiery nimbus.

"You might as well be a nineteenth-century whaling wife on the widow's walk, staring at the ocean, waiting for her man to crest the horizon."

"Wow. That's fanciful in the extreme. Ridiculous, too." She fisted her hands at her hips. "What is wrong with you?"

"I don't know." Because his jealousy was wrong. Uncalled for. *Undeniable*.

"Are you trying to pick a fight?"

"Seems that way."

They were both yelling to be heard over the roar of the falls. "Why?"

"Because it's either fight with you, or—" He broke off.

"Or what?"

"Or this." Rhys grabbed her, laying a hand flat on her back to protect her from the rough stone, and then pushed her against the wall. His other hand bracketed her wrist overhead. His mouth slanted across hers with all the pent-up heat he'd worked so hard to ignore.

And for good measure, he ground his hips against her so she could have no doubt exactly what the "or this" entailed.

To his shock, Maisy kissed him back.

With all the same heat. And want. Even though he'd just argued with her for no real reason.

Rhys was so surprised that he dropped his arms and took two steps back. "What's that?"

"I've wanted to do that since you started singing. Pretty much at your first note. That's when I wanted to lick you. By, oh, five bars in? It almost felt like you *were* licking me."

Well, hell. It wasn't real. Disappointment swamped him. "That's just the effect of angel song."

"No, it's not, or I'd want to lick Gideon and Zavier. They're handsome and bulging with muscles and would show a girl a good time in bed, I've zero doubt." She shook her head. Her green-and-brown eyes narrowed and practically burned with intensity. "But I don't want them. I want *you*." Then Maisy licked her lips. Slowly. "Your singing? Was just the icing on the top of the multilayered cake of goodness that is you."

"So when you complimented me, you weren't drunk on angel song?"

"No. Geez, you're being thickheaded. Did you hear me bending over backward to compliment Gideon or Zavier, who also sang? And frankly, Gideon's tenor is a tad more impressive than your baritone."

Rhys scratched at the back of his neck. "You're trying to prove how much you want me by pointing out that my friend sings better?"

"Well, yes. To prove my feelings for you—and only you—are genuine."

The times he'd previously kissed her had been accidents. Organic reactions to the moment. This, if they acted upon it... this would be a conscious choice.

A complication.

A distraction.

A problem. Humans and *Nephilim* inhabited the same Earth but were part of two different worlds. They had different priorities. Different knowledge. Different lifespans.

None of that changed the balance of how he'd grown to appreciate Maisy's optimism and caring and heart.

And how much he wanted her lithe, beautiful body.

He shook his head. "This is a bad idea. We fight. You don't trust me."

"Are you kidding? Sure, we argue. That makes things interesting. But do I trust you?" She bit her lip, then stepped to the side. "I'll show you how much I trust you."

And Maisy fell backward, into the dark gap between the lip of the Watchtower and Niagara Falls.

Disbelief froze him in place for a breath. Then Rhys plunged after her.

It only took three pumps of his wings to get close enough to catch her in his arms. Maisy wasn't shaking. She wasn't paler than usual. In fact, as he landed them back inside, she was flushed *and* smiling.

Smiling? His heart still hadn't restarted. It felt solid, frozen in his chest. A hard block of nothing, which was what he'd be without Maisy in his life. Rhys couldn't set her down.

Couldn't let go.

His fingers pressed hard into her thighs. Reassurance that she was really there. With him. "Don't *ever* scare me like that again."

Maisy didn't look at all fazed by his rough growl of an order. "I wasn't scared. I trusted you to come after me."

That was enough to kickstart his heart back into action. "Well, *I* was scared. I… Nothing can happen to you. Do you hear me?"

"To me?" Her ruby lips pursed. "Or to the Keeper?"

What a stupid question. "To *you*, Maisy. You and your joyous outlook on life and the way you smile at me like a fucking gift. You. It's got nothing to do with the Key. Or the Keeper, or Heaven or Hell. Just you."

"Then we're all good." And she tightened her arms around his neck, drawing him down into another kiss.

M aisy's elbow had never before been an erogenous zone, but now that it was brushing against the underside of Rhys's wings? The feelings in her left elbow were responsible for goose bumps breaking out from head to toe.

Well, that and the way his tongue danced inside her mouth.

"This won't end with a kiss," he warned.

"It *might* end with a kiss—like a period at the end of the sentence. Which'll be fine, as long as the penultimate word in that sentence is *orgasm*."

One side of his mouth curled up. "You can take the teacher out of the classroom, but you can't—"

"Yeah, yeah. Tease me later."

"You bet I will." Rhys carried her over to the lab. His wings disappeared. "Much later. I just need to have you now, though."

"Fine by me. Great by me." The cold of the island against her ass slammed reality back into her. "Uh, I know you said you don't get sick, but...do *Nephilim* believe in condom usage?"

"Yes. And potions." He whirled around to the apothecary cabinet and yanked open a drawer. It was filled with the familiar blue foil packages. "Your choice."

"Call me overly human, but let's save the potion for another time. I've already got two of them floating around in my system today. If we had a third, who knows what sort of chemical combustion might go down."

"As you wish." In the two steps it took him to get back in front of her, Rhys ripped open the packet with his teeth *and* ripped off his shirt. Literally. Buttons from the Oxford dress shirt pinged against the floor.

Good God but that was sexy. Unexpected, too. Who knew he could be so reckless?

When Rhys first dropped his lecture voice and joked with her, it'd felt like a reveal of a whole different person. Maisy had a feeling she was about to discover yet another side of him.

She couldn't wait.

"We could go to my bedroom. If you want—"

"No. No waiting. No moving." Maisy wriggled out of her denim jacket, then pushed it to the floor. "I don't want you to change your mind."

Grabbing her hand, he placed it right on his dick. The thin gabardine of his trousers did nothing to hide the rock-solid length of him. Nor could her hand cover the entire thing. "Feel that? That's for you. There's no changing my mind."

"Good." Very good. Maisy unbuttoned her pants and began to push them off.

"Wait." Rhys held her wrist before the pants got past her knees. "*You* can change your mind, though. At any time. If the whole sex-with-a-winged-creature thing gets too weird for you. I'll stop. No questions asked."

Well.

That was beyond thoughtful. It made this feel a lot less like a hot hookup and a lot more like something that *mattered*. To Rhys, she *mattered*. After losing her parents and being fired from her job made her feel a lot like an insignificant speck? One that clearly wasn't enough to take on the role of Keeper? Rhys's reaction meant everything to Maisy.

"Will you sprout another set of wings anywhere that I don't already know about?"

"No."

Maisy kicked off one leg of her pants, then paused again. "Are you going to try and tell me what to do?"

Millimeter by millimeter, a teasingly slow smile crept across his face. His indigo eyes hooded. "Only to increase your pleasure."

One good kick sent her pants flying into the main room. "C'mon, then."

He got her sweater off faster than when he'd feared acidic demon blood eating through her clothes. Got her bra off with the deft fingers of only one hand, while the other pushed her hair back to give him room to scrape his teeth down her neck. His dexterity was impressive.

Rhys didn't leave her a lot of room to work, but Maisy managed to get her hands between them to stroke up and down his chest. His chest with muscles that felt sculpted from marble in their taut perfection. Technically, he might be half human, but he absolutely had the body of an angel.

His mouth closed around her breast. Wet heat surrounded her nipple with swirls and sucks and just-sharp-enough pinches of teeth. Maisy gasped. Pleasure flickered up and down her nerves. It spread from her breast to engulf her entire body, pooling in a pulsing ache between her legs.

"Take off your pants," she ordered.

Another flash of white teeth in a lascivious grin. "You do it."

"I want to see if you can rip them off the way you did your shirt."

"No. I don't wear tear-aways like I'm about to get put into an NBA game."

Maisy unbuckled his belt. Contemplated whipping it off dramatically fast but figured the chance of it then whipping her in the face and cutting her cheek was quite high. So she just let it dangle and finished undoing the pants. With very little room to maneuver due to the sizable erection.

Slim hips and that gorgeous vee shape that his waist whittled down to had them sliding to the floor. Maisy lightly clawed her nails down the front of the navy boxer briefs. And even though it seemed unimaginable, his penis grew even larger, poking out the top.

"Are you sure it won't grow wings?" She brushed her thumb back and forth across the tip of the velvety head.

"Maisy." His voice rasped as if he'd just done a shot of pure gravel. "No teasing. I'm begging you."

Never before had she felt more powerful. "Give me a reason to stop."

Rhys pulled her legs over his shoulders and knelt on the floor. His hands shredded her panties, but Maisy didn't feel so much as a tug. All she felt was the blast of heat as he exhaled deeply right over her cleft. Then his thumbs held her open for his tongue to delicately slide along each edge.

Payback wasn't a bitch—it was *torture*. The very best kind. The light strokes made her tremble, head to toe, with need. It created the simultaneous wish to have it last and to race to the finish line.

Maisy lost track of exactly what motion, which rhythms Rhys employed with his tongue. Because her brain shut down.

There was only sensation.

Pleasure.

Overwhelming pleasure. Her knees locked around his head. And when he inserted two fingers without so much as a hesitation in the licking, Maisy screamed.

"Are you ready for me, sunshine?"

Desire squashed all her sass. She simply said, "Yes."

By the time she managed to prop herself up on her elbows, Rhys was naked.

The condom was on.

Maisy barely had time to admire the line of dark hair bisecting his abdomen—one of the absolute sexiest parts of a man—or even fully take in the...well...*magnificence* of his erection. He nestled the tip right at her opening.

"Watch me join you," Rhys commanded in the stern tone that had always annoyed her until right now.

"Believe me, I am."

Rhys used one hand to help spread her wider to accommodate his girth, but the touch of the pads of his long, deft fingers just added one more layer to her shuddering enjoyment. Maisy convulsed around him repeatedly. Every time she did, the vein along the top of his penis throbbed in response. It was *mesmerizing.*

Once he'd worked his way all the way in, Rhys lifted hooded midnight eyes to meet hers. "Hang on tight. We're about to fly."

Did he mean it literally? Just in case, Maisy hooked her wrists behind his neck instead of around his shoulders. Even then, her entire body jolted when he began to pound into her. Long, measured strokes that didn't have any break between the in and the out. Simply a constant barrage of *filling* her.

It was perfect.

Fast. Hard. Continuous perfection.

Watching the war between steely determination and slack-jawed lust morph back and forth across Rhys's face almost made her laugh. His sense of responsibility of *course* spurred him to make certain that Maisy climaxed. Which she appreciated. But it was obvious that he was right on the edge and fighting to hold off.

Good thing she was, too. All that pent-up desire just needed to explode.

Maisy curved her hands around his skull. Locked her ankles around his hips in an effort to pull him closer. "Rhys. Can we please finish this?"

"Absofuckinglutely."

Again, she wanted to laugh—but couldn't. Because he shifted his angle, fanned a thumb across her nipple, and kissed her.

Right as searing heat spread out in every direction from where they were one. Maisy arched her back, moaning her delight past the seal of his lips. And as his entire body shuddered, his wings flared into visibility, the soft underfeathers brushing the back of her hands and sending yet another quake of satisfaction to her core.

Maisy slid her hands down his lats through the aftershocks that kept rippling through her. It gave her more contact with his feathers, which seemed to be doing good things for Rhys, too. Even the most minute movement on her part caused him to pulse deep inside her.

She wouldn't mind doing that for the rest of the day...

But first, there was the awkward *after* to get through. Impossible to cuddle on a lab table. If *Nephilim* even liked to cuddle. If Rhys would want to with her. Or would that ever-present responsibility have him dressed and ready to keep hunting before Maisy even stopped panting?

After was hard enough with an average man.

It was a million times worse with a different...species? Version of man? Half angel? Were their protocols different? Or was she spiraling into mental self-babble to avoid opening her eyes and simply talking to him?

Sex changed everything.

Intimacy changed everything even more.

It sure felt as if they'd leaped both of those hurdles. But

now what?

"Maisy." His deep voice was almost a purr in her ear.

"Hmm?"

"Thank you."

That popped her eyes open. "Are you mocking me?"

"No." Rhys gently brushed an errant strand or six of hair off her cheek. Which turned into a slow sweep of a caress. "I'm quite sincere."

"You just gave me an orgasm for the record books. You did all the work."

"Nowhere close. Touching you, tasting you, feeling your responses—that all amplified my pleasure tenfold. I didn't want to jack off. I wanted to be with *you*, Maisy. So thank you."

"Right back at ya."

"Thank you for trusting me." His caress moved down her neck, whispered along the curve of her breast.

"Glad we've got that established."

"Would you extend that trust a little more? Back in the bedroom? So we don't have any surprise interruptions?"

Maisy realized that his wings were moving. Not the entire wings in the powerful waves that propelled them across the chasm. No, this was just the outer edge, articulating in such a small motion that they hovered just below the light fixtures. They were slowly floating backward out of the lab area and toward the hallway.

And Rhys was still deeply seated inside her.

That show of strength and control—not to mention the amazing novelty of it—surged fresh desire to every inch of her body.

"Are you saying you're up for a second round?"

Rhys tipped back his head and *howled* with laughter. It was another first for Maisy—hearing him let go like that.

It was another revelation of a wholly new layer of sexiness and appeal.

And a teensy bit of the habitual annoyance. Why wasn't she in on the joke? Hopefully this wasn't an "oh, the human doesn't know something" laugh?

"What's so funny?"

"You think we'll be done at two rounds? Sunshine, I've got the equipment of a man, but I have the staying power of an angel. You'll run out of fingers to count today's orgasms."

Oh.

Ooooooh.

Fine by her.

CHAPTER SEVENTEEN

This was a first for Rhys.

He was in bed, with a woman, *talking.*

Not having sex, not gearing up to have more sex. Simply talking. And holding each other. Cuddling.

After eighty-seven years, he didn't expect many more firsts. Nor did he expect to have a connection that went beyond the physical.

It was...different.

Uncomfortable in that he didn't know what to expect or what to do next.

But lying with Maisy, snuggled up against him in his bedroom, lazily stroking her hair while they talked, was turning out to be...

...well...

Fantastic. It didn't matter that he was unsure of what was supposed to happen. Being with her felt natural. Easy. Comfortable.

Rhys simply knew that he didn't want to ever stop. Which he knew to be a problem. But that was for later.

Her fingers trailed up and down the forearm he had tucked across her breasts. That small motion might be one of the most soothing luxuries he'd ever experienced. How was it possible?

"What's your life like? As a *Nephilim*?"

Funny question, but he'd answer anything as long as her ass

stayed nestled right on his dick. "You've been living it with me for a week now. You've seen it. Business meetings. Battles with supernatural evil. Training with the guys. That's about it."

That answer netted him a playful pinch. "I've seen a focused hunt to find my Key. It doesn't strike me as business as usual."

Ah. Maisy thought he was glossing over details again. Only sharing what she absolutely needed to know. Rhys understood why it pissed her off, so he pressed a kiss to the side of her head before elaborating.

"It is, to an extent. When we're hired to, ah, troubleshoot, we drop everything else and devote all our time to the job. Because whatever time we waste not working on it? Means more people injured or killed. I know you're sick of hearing it, but each mission really is a matter of life or death. Sometimes humans." He hesitated. Swallowed hard, thinking back to an incident he worked very hard not to remember. "Sometimes our own."

Her hand stilled. Squeezed gently. "Did you lose a friend?"

"Yeah."

"Do you want to tell me about it?"

Strangely enough, Rhys *did*.

It was an off-limits subject. The guys didn't revisit the tough decision they'd made once it was final. Definitely taboo to discuss with the rest of the paranormal world. He just wanted to off-load.

"I might go into lecture mode again," Rhys warned. "I know you hate that."

"It's more, ah, palatable when you're naked." Maisy ran the arch of her foot up his shin playfully. "I want to learn. To understand you."

That'd be a tall order, but he'd try. Even though it was uncomfortable as fuck sharing anything personal. *Nephilim* didn't do that. Revealing yourself revealed vulnerability. No warrior wanted to make that mistake.

And living with humans meant constantly being on guard against letting anything slip about his true nature. *Not* sharing was as automatic as going for the extra point after a touchdown. Or women going to the bathroom in pairs.

For Maisy, though, he'd give it a shot.

"Being only half angelic means that we're shunned: banned from Heaven and occasionally hunted by full angels as an abomination. *Nephilim* are born of the union of humans and fallen angels. Some see us as mongrels. Tainted."

She flipped around on the gray satin sheets. Even in the dimmed light, her eyes burned. "That's bigotry."

"Turns out a lot of angels can be prejudiced assholes," he teased. "Just like humans."

"None of the perks? No access to Heaven? That's rough."

Indeed.

Although, looking at her sweep of flaming hair cascading over her shoulder, Rhys felt quite overflowing with perks at the moment.

"*Nephilim* are taken at birth—or as soon as they're discovered— and brought to a training center for the *Right and Holy Seraphic Order of the Nephilim*. Heaven doesn't approve of us, but they do want to use us. Figure it's safer to put our powers to use on the side of right. So we're trained as soldiers."

Her eyes no longer burned. Moisture gathered, sitting in fat, unshed drops that trembled on her lower lashes. "You're taken away from your mothers? How can that possibly be the side of right? To have no family? That's monstrous!"

Rhys couldn't bear to see her pain, even when it was for him. He pushed up against the pile of pillows to sit, then pulled Maisy close to lay across his chest. "It is the way of it. Gideon and Zavier became my family. We were raised together, trained together; we fought together. I can't imagine brothers by blood being any closer."

"I'm so glad you have them."

Rhys looked across the room to the painting of their sigil: a black three-headed lion, charging fiercely forward with wings fully unfurled. "I wouldn't be alive today without them."

"I take it that's literal, not figurative?"

She was catching on. "What we do is dangerous. *Nephilim* are sent out without regard for the chances of success in a mission. Because the ultimate end goal—destruction of a demon—must occur. Period. No matter how many *Nephilim* are killed in the process."

"It sounds as if you're treated like fighting machines, not people."

See? She did understand. "Correct. Easy to have little regard for the life of something that's considered an abomination. We're expendable."

"Nobody is expendable," she said with unexpected fervor.

That was his Maisy. So sure that there was good harbored in every being.

Her certainty was even starting to rub off on him. "That viewpoint is what makes you so special, Maisy. You have no idea how rare it is."

"I rather think I like being called rare. Especially when you do it in that dark, dreamy voice." She feathered her hands across his chest.

Rhys captured one, nibbling from the translucent skin at the underside of her wrist up to the crook of her elbow. "I call you many things. Beautiful. Tenacious. Annoying in an…invigorating way."

"Stop." She canted her head back to look at him. "I mean, stop for now. I want to hear the rest of it."

Fine. He'd rather get it all done at once. "As you said, there was no choice. This was the life we were given—to be the protectors of humankind. It is literally our job to look out for the bad to crop up in every situation, on any given day, *because it does*. We learn to trust almost no one. Believe the worst of almost everyone. It's the only way to stay safe."

Maisy leaned her cheek back against his chest. "I'm so sorry."

Those three words destroyed him.

Or, rather, they destroyed the chains around his heart.

No one, not a soul celestial or mortal or demonic, had ever expressed sorrow—or empathy—for his lot in life.

Not until Maisy Norgate. And Rhys hadn't known that he'd needed to hear it.

Until today.

What did the kids on his loading crew say? "I feel seen." That summed it up. Rhys felt *seen* for the first time.

And he never wanted to give that—or her—up.

He laid his head atop hers. "The only exceptions are Z and Gid. They always have my back as we constantly put our lives on the line as troubleshooters for the supernatural world. Six decades of trying to help and safeguard humans means we've saved the world from complete destruction dozens of times."

"For no thanks, I'd imagine. All the risk, none of the reward."

Wasn't she adorable? Not dying was enough of a reward. Pushing back at evil was the even bigger reward. "I don't want a medal."

"Really?" Her lips trailed soft, open-mouthed kisses from his nipple to the middle of his sternum. "It'd look so good, nestled right here over your dark hair."

"I thought you wanted to hear the rest of it?"

"Sorry. Your physique is very distracting."

"As is yours, my sweet." The feel of her lithe body tucked along his was the only thing enabling him to open up. It was a necessary distraction from the thick mental walls he'd buried all this behind. "We're given considerable room and board, but we're expected to go on every mission without question. That didn't sit well with us. When two other *Nephilim* were killed due to—"

Rhys cut off, swamped by the still-strong memories of that horrible week. They'd told Kerr and Dimitris not to go. That more time was needed to work on counter spells, arrange more backup. But the orders were given, and their friends had obeyed.

Good soldiers—and they'd died for it.

Died for nothing.

"If you're at a ballpark and your napkin flies away in the wind, you don't chase after it. Not worth it. You just get a new one. We're like pennies. The change you drop on the street and don't bother to pick up. That's how *Nephilim* are treated. So the three of us quit."

Maisy sat up. Gaped at him. "You can quit on Heaven?"

They certainly weren't the first to do so. Lucifer Morningstar and his group of fallen angels had paved the way.

Didn't go well for them.

But the difference was that Rhys and his friends weren't breaking any celestial rules. Merely...opting out of the game.

"It was a calculated risk. Turns out they valued us enough as their top soldiers to let us go, as long as we agreed to maintain contact and work for them on a contract basis. And staff the Watchtower."

"You mean the rest of them aren't fighting for the plum assignment of living in Canada in the winter?" she teased.

"That's an understatement. Usually, the Watchtowers are assigned to injured or old *Nephilim*, of which there aren't many. They were happy to pawn it off on us. So we feed Master Caraxis info on our missions, on intel that could be useful to all. And we choose what jobs to accept when they desperately need our help. We call the shots ourselves now."

Looking around the large room with its light gray walls, black leather bench at the foot of the bed, and its matching squat chesterfield chair, Maisy asked, "So this is not a part of the official *Nephilim* dorm facility?"

Rhys bit back a laugh. "We live as humans. That's why we founded Metafora Enterprises. To support ourselves, to give us the autonomy to still offer assistance when sought out."

"For a price."

"Yes. For missions that we believe we can execute successfully and safely. And when—you know—the world is in danger of being overrun by evil."

She twisted onto her knees, sadly tugging the sheet up to her neck. With a ferocity that hit Rhys hard, Maisy said, "There's nothing wrong or weak about wanting to live to fight another day."

"You'd think so, wouldn't you? Take the long view—better that we successfully fight twenty battles than lose one and die."

"I'm so sorry. It must make you bitter—being reviled for an accident of birth that's no fault of yours."

That was it in a nutshell. Which they'd realized long ago could either be the thing that burned in their belly or the thing they pushed to the side to concentrate on the work instead. And when that work was destroying demons? You chose to fight evil, every time.

"Yes, but that can't be the overriding emotion of every day. We had to accept it. We have the strength and the power to keep humans safe. So that's what we do."

"It strikes me as a solitary, lonely existence. Never being able to share with people what you're truly doing."

Maisy was saying things he'd never bothered to acknowledge himself. And they were certainly striking a chord. As if she were peeling off layers of a scab Rhys didn't know existed.

"There are some *Nephilim* we still talk to. Obviously a whole network within the paranormal world. But yes, you don't indulge in close connections. People die. Humans, fairies, demons, jinn, witches, you name it. We do our duty. We have one another. That has to be enough."

"Duty." She seemed to mull over the word. "That's an interesting way to put it."

What else could it be? Heaven-given powers gave you the duty to use them. "How do you mean?"

"Well, you and the others act like you don't really care much about humans. That you're just doing your duty to keep the world in balance. But you have this company that sustains you.

There's no *actual* reason you keep fighting the good fight. Every time you risk your life, you're making a choice to put humans first. So you must still care a lot and have faith in their goodness."

Was it true?

They'd been fighting on autopilot for so long. You used your talents—anything less was selfish—but perhaps she was right. "Maybe so. Maybe I needed a beautiful, soft-hearted redhead to remind me."

"Isn't that a coincidence?" Maisy laughed. The sound made his heart lurch. Like an engine finally turning over after the tenth try.

But before Rhys could tumble her backward onto the mattress, his watch beeped. "It's Gideon. He's found a witch for us to shake down. We've got to meet him."

"Now?"

"An hour."

"I don't know about you, but I can pull on my clothes and pop a ponytail in about three minutes. That means we've still got plenty of time for…well…" Instead of finishing the sentence, Maisy simply put her lips around his cock and began to suck.

Rhys closed his eyes. Crossed his arms behind his head. "I'll follow your lead, Keeper."

"You want to accost a woman in a deserted parking lot at night? No." Maisy shook her finger at Gideon like he was a dog who'd peed on her purse. Rhys particularly enjoyed when she focused her ire on someone *other* than him. "That's cruel. Scary. That's how the bad guys do it. We're supposed to be the good guys."

Gid gave a yank at the open collar of his white dress shirt. Guess he didn't like defending himself against Maisy's righteous wrath any more than Rhys did. "I want to coerce a powerful witch into cooperating with us. The leader of her coven. In a place where she isn't surrounded by protection spells and the ability to call for help."

The streetlight shone down on Maisy as if she was the one out of the four of them with a halo. Before she could do more than glower at him, Liss got out of the car and jumped into the fray. "Your attempt to restate it in a better light doesn't remove the misogynistic, patriarchal heavy-handedness of this plan."

"Okay, then. Mark me down as someone who doesn't give a fuck."

His unrepentant attitude didn't even make Maisy flinch. Which tickled Rhys even more. His woman had moxie. She *also* had a point. "Gideon. Be better than that. As a gentleman and as a *Nephilim*."

"I've been plenty good to her already. The whole reason I know where to ambush Aradia is because I'm sleeping with her."

Liss gasped. "That's....that's—"

"Convenient," Rhys said.

"More like who *isn't* he sleeping with," Zavier muttered.

"I do it for our mutual benefit," Gideon said with a beatific smile that practically had moonlight bending to sparkle off of him.

The man was so damned sure of his own charm. And, frankly, it was good for all of them when he wielded it as a weapon. Rhys tossed him a lazy salute. "Thanks for the sacrifice and the intel, Gid."

"Believe me, it was entirely my pleasure."

"Ew. Ewwww." Maisy blindly reached out to grab Liss, then scrunched up her face. "You sexed her schedule out of her? Have you no shame?"

"No," Gideon said with a simple shrug. "Maisy, this is war. The ultimate war. Good against evil. We do what we have to. And I'm sorry, but there's no time to coax you into coming around to seeing that."

"Because you gave the Key away," Zavier helpfully piled on.

"Reasons, ignorance, extenuating circumstances—all excuses. We're under the gun now due to *your* actions."

Good to have them heavy-hand the truth to Maisy. Rhys slow-clapped. "Couldn't have said it better myself."

"Why didn't you? Isn't it your role to be the heavy?" Gideon wrinkled his nose, sniffed at himself. "It doesn't suit me."

"You were on a roll."

Maisy tightened her ponytail. "Enough already. I get it."

"Aren't you supposed to be half angels? Brimming over with goodness?" Liss yanked the holder off her messy ponytail. They'd picked her up from her bartending shift on the way. "Can't they at least start out politely?"

"Great compromise. If it goes poorly, you three can bring the hammer. Or just send Liss." Maisy beamed at her best friend. "She's never lost a girl fight. She's fierce."

There she went again. Comparing a powerless human to a witch strong enough to lead a coven. Maisy still believed humanity had its own indomitable strength. Which was true— but not enough to stand up to—let alone best—a supernatural.

"Go for it." Gideon held a hand out to Maisy. "When you change your mind, know that you'll owe me five dollars." They shook. "Aradia's always the last one out. Long black hair, green eyes. Figure for days."

"Does she use a glamour?" Z asked.

Gideon slid him sharp enough side-eye that it should've come with warning blinkers and a beep. "She's the head of the coven. What do you think?"

That earned him another finger shake from his feisty redhead. "Stop it. You can't try to suss out if a woman's used plastic surgery, magical or otherwise. Geez. You've really got it in for her. What's the deal there?"

"Witches are…tricky. They play both sides. Whichever suits them at the time. They can't be trusted."

After a dramatic wince, Liss asked, "This is who you sleep

with in your spare time?"

"Why not?" A smirk lifted one side of Gideon's lips. "Believe me, she's on my side when we're together."

Liss covered her eyes, turning away with a groan. Maisy just shot out her upraised palm in the direction of Gideon's mouth. "Stop talking. Seriously. I can't *even* with you right now." A dark-haired woman pushed through the office-building door into the parking lot. "Is that her?" At Gideon's nod, Maisy hustled across the street.

Rhys knew he should yell at her for not waiting for him. He also knew that *she* knew that he'd keep up—while keeping a discreet distance. Plus, he was enjoying the hell out of her pushing around Gideon and taking point.

"Aradia? Hi. I'm Maisy. Could I talk to you for a few minutes? Buy you a coffee—or a glass of wine?"

The woman's eyes closed to slits. Her hand slid into her oversize bag, probably seeking charms and potions against whatever danger she thought Maisy posed. "Why do you presume you know me?"

"A mutual friend. I'm hoping, in the spirit of friendship, you'd be willing to help me with a small favor."

No way would the head of a coven that used dark magic as often as light bend over to a request that didn't pack a punch. Even though Maisy looked as innocent as a fawn wrapped in a blanket of four-leaf clovers. Rhys and the others hung back, behind an SUV in the lot. It was better than watching WWE.

"I'll take some of that action," Zavier said abruptly. "Fifty says the Keeper begs for our help in two minutes or less."

No way. "What's one of Maisy's most notable traits?" When the other two didn't answer, Rhys gave a feral grin. "Stubbornness. I'll double your bet. She won't ask for help at all."

"Deal." Gideon and Zavier nodded at him.

Which led to Liss elbowing both of them. "You two know nothing. I don't have any spare money, but this one's so easy

I'm doubling down with Rhys. I'd like my winnings in two crisp Grants, please."

Aradia had relaxed her pose a bit, but the sharp brackets bisecting her forehead proved she hadn't succumbed to Maisy's charm. "I don't grant favors. I'm a witch, not a jinn."

Maisy shifted to tap the toe of her rainbow sneaker against the pocked asphalt. "What if I told you the fate of the world was at stake?"

"I'd say it must be that time of the month."

Gideon snickered. "Aradia's got attitude; I'll give her that. And an ass that Botticelli would cream himself to paint if he was still alive."

That didn't come anywhere close to being relevant. "Will she let us use her?" Rhys asked.

"Eventually. With the right pressure. Wouldn't have dragged you all down here if I didn't think she could be controlled. Just didn't expect that Maisy would insist on taking point."

"Maybe now you'll stop underestimating my bestie."

"Maybe, if you don't stop busting our balls, we'll make you wait in the car." Zavier stroked his chin, thick with dark stubble. "Nope, wait. That's a *definitely.*"

Aradia had made it to her car. Put her bag in the back seat. Guess she really didn't see Maisy as a threat.

Maisy, however, clearly *did* see that she'd been dismissed. She braced a palm on the driver's-side door. "I respect a hard-working woman. Clearly, I made a mistake in undervaluing your services. What if I offered you ten dollars?"

"I won't talk to you for less than a Hamilton. And the fact hasn't changed that I don't do favors for strangers."

"My bad! I put the cart before the horse. I'm not a stranger. I'm a part of, ah, your special community."

Aradia glanced back toward the studio. "You're a belly dancer?"

"No. My coordination—let's just say the one time I tried a hula hoop, I ended up trapped in it and had to be rescued. I meant the, um, paranormal community. I'm the Keeper."

"Yeah. You're *keeping* me from getting into my car." She made a shooing gesture with one arm.

Maisy didn't budge. Which Rhys had fully expected. She wasn't just stubborn—the woman puffed up with a righteous passion for whatever she believed in. Her human tenaciousness was more than a match for a snooty, cantankerous witch.

She crossed her arms, and her scowl broadcast her disappointment even without much light from the moon. "You know, I tried to be nice. Appeal to your better nature, woman to woman. You could've at least heard me out."

"And then do you a favor?" Aradia huffed out a laugh. "I'm a working witch, not a charity. If I granted favors to every rando that asked, I'd be broke and exhausted and out of potent spell ingredients."

"Forget the favor." She spread her feet wider. Fisted her hands at her hips. A power pose, Rhys believed it was called. "Consider this a demand. A *command*. Your chance to right a wrong. Because this little problem of mine is your fault."

"I don't even know you."

"Like I said, I'm the new Keeper. Keeper of the Key to the Gates of Hell's worst prison. That oughtta strike a little fear into your heart. If it doesn't? Know that I've already been the cause of two demon deaths this week. Summoned a third *to do my bidding*. If I don't get your assistance, things will get real bad, real fast. For everyone."

Holy hell, the woman was magnificent.

Out of the corner of his eye, he noticed Liss give a fist pump.

Rhys couldn't see Aradia's face any more at this angle, but her response was swift and a little shaky. "What did I do?"

"One of the witches in your coven has my Key. It won't do her any good. I'm the only one who can wield its power. If I don't start wielding that power in exactly six days, shit will substantially hit the fan. Do you want that on your conscience? Worse yet, do you want to die?"

Zavier whistled, low and long. "She's really blasting the fear cannons. Didn't know the Keeper had it in her."

Rhys would've agreed with him on day one, but by now he was well aware of Maisy's depth and strength. And that, for a guy who purportedly had never known her, the dead uncle had evidently known exactly what he was doing when he chose her.

Gideon clamped his palm over Liss's mouth. "I'll give you an extra fifty if you don't say *I told you so*."

"Of course not. I'll help you." Aradia thrust her phone at Maisy. "Put in your contact info."

As Maisy's thumbs raced across the screen, she said, "Get your people under control. Find out which of them has the Key. Make it happen fast." She handed the phone back, then added, "Oh, and you missed out on your shot at a finder's fee by being a bitch. Don't make that mistake again."

Maisy sauntered across the lot, past the *Nephilim*, and across the street to their SUV.

Rhys held out his hand. "Pay up."

"Don't be an old-fashioned ass," Z snarled. "I'll Venmo you."

Liss crossed her arms and let ooze the smuggest smile he'd ever seen. The men waited until Aradia had backed out of her spot and faced them. Then they flared their wings, just to prove that Maisy had the wherewithal to make things get even uglier.

As they crossed the street, Aradia peeled out, leaving black marks on the road as she swerved to avoid a motorcycle. That was when Rhys broke into a jog. Because he couldn't wait another second to get his hands on his Keeper.

He planted his hands on her luscious butt and lifted, twirling her in a circle. "You did great!"

"I did, didn't I?" And her smile, as usual, was as bright as the sun.

She was back with both feet on the sidewalk by the time the

others made it around the side of the car. Liss shoved Rhys out of the way—well, he *let* her—to envelop Maisy in a quick hug. Then she pointedly moved to the side and used both arms to present Maisy to the men.

Gideon clapped, hands raised high. "Maisy, you really held her feet to the fire. That was impressive."

"Especially after you started out so nice." Zavier offered a high five. "Well done. I thought you'd give up."

"Please. I taught high school, remember? Worse yet, I did my student teaching semester with seventh-grade boys." She shuddered, sending her hair rippling over her chest. Which made Rhys remember how that looked without clothes on. "Talk about a hellscape. There comes a point where being nice and friendly and understanding stops working. Then you bring down the hammer."

"I thought we were your hammer," Gideon protested.

"You're my last line of defense." Maisy jammed her thumb just above the low vee of her hot pink tee. "*I'm* the front line."

Rhys had never been so proud.

Or more turned on.

Too bad they couldn't do anything about that. There were more things left to do, all of them best done in the dead of night.

Dangerous and possibly deadly things.

CHAPTER EIGHTEEN

Maisy leaned over the back porch railing, looking into the midnight darkness of the yard. Then she whirled back to Rhys. "Are you seriously breaking into my dead uncle's house?"

"No."

"Good." She hadn't yet reconciled her feelings toward the dead man, but she knew he deserved better than a B and E.

"I already did." He turned the knob, and the door swung inward.

What the— He'd just committed a misdemeanor. "You can't just go around picking locks."

"I can, and I do." Rhys gave her one of those patronizing smiles that had set her teeth on edge since day one. Sleeping with him hadn't changed that one bit. "Would you have preferred I throw a rock through the window? How did you think we were getting in?"

"I didn't think that far ahead. I'm new to this action-packed lifestyle, remember?" Maisy *had* thought ahead far enough to change into a sleek black jumpsuit she'd borrowed from Liss. Her own wardrobe was far too colorful for sneaking around in the middle of the night.

Rhys had downgraded from his standard suit coat. Tonight he wore black jeans, a black knit shirt, and a black jacket that looked like he normally wore it over workout gear. It was tight…

and Maisy was now wondering if that was to help him wriggle through windows.

"He died what, ten days ago? No way has the estate closed. Especially with the lawyer for it dead-slash-disappeared. This is the safest break-in I've ever executed."

She understood how Rhys took the demons in stride. That was his world, but breaking-in was a human thing to do. No powers required. Maybe that's why it was hard for her to swallow?

"Hang back a second." He tucked something that looked like an overdeveloped paper clip back into his wallet. Maybe she should ask him for lessons on how to use it. Evidently lock picking now fell under necessary skills for her? "Let me make sure it's empty."

"Nope. Mrs. Rathbone said the house was being watched, remember? So standing on a shadowy porch by myself? That's not safe." It wasn't *not* scary was more to the point.

"Fine." Rhys toed the door open farther, but then Maisy grabbed his arm.

"Wait!"

"Now what?"

"What if he's got protection?"

"No visible alarm panel when I looked in the side windows by the front door. None back here, either." And *another* one of his patented, patronizing smiles. She could almost see the words "this isn't my first rodeo" in a thought bubble over his head.

Which Maisy intended to burst. "No, I mean *supernatural* protection. A spell or something with a magical tripwire. I don't want you to get hurt."

"I'm your bodyguard. That's literally my job."

"Let's say your job is avoiding *either* of us getting hurt with your finesse and know-how."

"Maisy, I'm touched—genuinely—at your concern, but your uncle was a Keeper. With the Key sent off to the lawyer, he wouldn't have had anything worth protecting."

She followed Rhys inside. The place looked normal enough. Wood accents around every window and doorframe, wood paneling in the kitchen made kitschy with cartoon moose and maple leaves. "Guess he enjoyed crossing the border. And bringing the entire gift shop back with him."

Rhys snorted. "We should check his pantry for a maple syrup stash. That stuff is too good to be left behind."

Maisy bit back a grin. It was fun seeing the human side of him. She liked the wings, sure, and the angelic perfection of his abs, but she liked the *man*, too.

When they got to the hallway, Maisy stopped. It was covered with pictures of *her*. Every official school photo. Her college IDs. Candid shots from around town. The gallery climbed both walls. Each one was beautifully framed and matted.

And there wasn't a single photo of the mysterious not-the-Keeper son.

"I...I guess Mrs. Rathbone was right. He really did care about me."

Rhys's arm locked around her shoulders a split second before Maisy registered that her knees were wobbly. "This is good, right?"

"Yeah. Yes. Absolutely." She steadied herself by covering his hand with her own. "It just makes me sad for everything we missed."

At the front entryway, stairs led up, and rooms branched off. Rhys canted sideways to peer into a living room. "There's a reason your teacher sent us here. Look for an office. Maybe he left instructions for the new Keeper."

"Wouldn't he have left those with the Key? The manual traditionally comes with the equipment."

"Safer to split them up. If you made it this far, you'd survive the testing to become Keeper."

She sank onto the dark wood of the stairs. Hugged her knees to her chest, taking a few seconds to absorb a reality so dangerous that you couldn't attach the freaking instructions. "I hate how you keep reminding me that something big and bad—or equally big and good bent on doing something bad to me—could leap out at any second."

"Sorry, Maisy." Rhys bent to drop a kiss on the top of her head. "But complacency is deadly. I'd rather piss you off than risk losing you."

"That's good to hear." The mellow tenor voice came from… the ceiling?

Maisy and Rhys both looked up.

Nothing.

Rhys instantly crouched over her, wings curled around to form a protective cage. "Who are you?"

"Drat. Hang on."

She couldn't see anything but the beautiful blue ombre shading of the wings. "What's going on?" Maisy whispered.

"I don't know. Which is never good," he muttered back.

Maybe. But the invisible thing at least sounded friendly.

"How's that?" the voice asked.

"Being able to see you just means I've got a target to throw my knife at now." A whisper-soft snick at his wrist sent his dagger into his palm. Maisy had to admit it was cool seeing it happen. Behind-the-scenes, as it were. "I repeat, who are you?"

"Oh, dear. I put the cart before the horse. I'm Harold Sasson."

"Nice try. He's dead."

"Precisely why I was invisibly hovering at the ceiling. Managing ghostly energies is not an easy trick to master."

This protective cage no longer suited her. If that really was some ethereal vestige of her uncle, Maisy needed to see him. "Rhys, let me look. There was a photo of him at the funeral. I'll be able to tell."

"Not if he's a shapeshifter," Rhys grumbled, but he did open his wings enough for her to peer through.

The semi-transparent man at the top of the stairs was average height. Slender build. A face you wouldn't look twice at in a crowd...except for the bright red hair that perfectly matched the shade of Maisy's. And that of her mom's. And her grandmother's.

For the first time since that fatal car ride, she could talk to a family member. Her throat thickened with tears threatening to erupt.

"It's him."

"It *looks* like him," Rhys corrected. "Maisy, move behind my legs."

"How's this for proof? Chazaqiel was my *Nephilim* Watcher. He had what I'm guessing is now your job. Guarding the Keeper of the Key. Who is now my niece."

"For goodness' sake, Rhys. Enough already." Maisy pulled at his wing. Which wouldn't have accomplished anything, truthfully, if he hadn't immediately folded them away. "Uncle Harold?"

The man beamed like it was Christmas *and* his birthday. "My darling Maisy. I've waited so long to see you. No hugs, I'm afraid." He let his hands flap against his sides, and they just... went through.

It wasn't disgusting like a demon exploding, but it was extremely off-putting.

"I can fix that." Rhys plucked out a feather. A single droplet of something wet and translucent beaded at the tip. He took the stairs two at a time, then pressed it onto the blurred shape of Harold's shoulder.

Suddenly, the man was in HD. And 3D.

"It won't last," Rhys warned.

"That's all right. You two can't stay long. Thank you." He gripped Rhys's arm. Then Harold flew down the stairs to pull Maisy into a long, tight hug.

It was like coming home.

To a complete stranger—and yet still familiar, somehow. It was a wonderful gift.

"Come upstairs." He kept hold of her hand as they walked.

"No windows in the hallway. It's the safest place for us to be."

Right. Because this average house in the Buffalo suburbs was suddenly the Alamo, about to be stormed by vengeful demons. It just didn't compute. "You sound as paranoid as Rhys."

"That's your name, *Nephilim*?"

"Rhys Boyce." They shook hands. Rhys stalked to the end of the hall, poking his head in every room and doing a quick scan. "How about you enlighten your niece as to how *not* paranoid I am? Especially since she's barely survived three demon attacks and one angel trial in little more than a week?"

Harold tut-tutted, clicking his tongue. "Maisy. I'm sorry the transition's been so difficult." He shook his head. "Where to even begin about how sorry I am about so many things? Not just the big ones, like graduations, but everyday things like family dinners on Sunday and not being able to help out when you broke your wrist."

Oh, wow. She'd broken it three years ago. On a regrettable first date horseback riding—or, rather, falling off the horse. Sure, she'd whined about it on TikTok, but still. "You really *did* keep track of me."

Her uncle winked. His open eye was identical to hers—brown but with a ring of green around it. "Much more easily with the incognito tab on my browser. You are my dear niece. I've loved you fiercely since the day you were born. I visited you in the hospital. Paid a nurse handsomely to infuse you with a protection charm when she did the heel stick for blood."

Maisy wriggled her eyebrows at Rhys. "Looks like you're out of a job."

He didn't rise to the bait. Just leaned against the wall, facing down to the front door, and crossed his arms. "Hardly."

"That only kept you safe until you hit puberty." Harold patted her forearm. Squeezed her hand. Like he couldn't believe he was really touching her and had to keep proving it. "My oh my, the things hormones do to a body scare off even the strongest of potions."

While, sure, grateful for any protection, still... "So you had people spy on me and report back? Couldn't we have, oh, met up at a park like CIA agents? Back-to-back on opposite benches?"

"We could have—once. And once only. It didn't seem fair to drop all of this on your shoulders and then disappear. Far safer, as well, for you to stay off the supernatural world's radar completely until necessary. I couldn't be selfish and sacrifice your safety simply to assuage my desire to spend time with you."

Oh.

Suddenly, her pain at being alone didn't seem so bad. Maisy hadn't known any different. Poor Harold, however, had to make the choice on a daily basis not to reach out. Self-inflicted loneliness had to be the worst.

"I understand. It must've been so hard for you."

"Indeed. To circle back to Rhys's point, however? It *is* dangerous. There's no nicer way to put it. Nothing is easy when Hell is involved. Aside from getting there." He snort-laughed.

Hopefully *that* wasn't genetic.

"Let me get this straight. You love me. You want to keep me safe. And yet you gave me the Key. Set me on the path—unwittingly—to become Keeper. Maybe it's cowardly to ask, but isn't there anyone else who can do it? Because it turns out I'd very much like to keep myself safe."

"There's not a cowardly bone in your body, my dear. Exploring your options makes you strategic, not scared. Could someone else be Keeper? Possibly. But not like you will do it. Not as well as you'll do it."

That was cryptic. It gave her wiggle room—and yet didn't.

Why wasn't anything straightforward in this mystical world?

Well, then she'd have to straighten it out. "What about your son?"

"Ah. Mrs. Rathbone filled you in. Dennis was a youthful mistake. Chazaqiel tried to talk me out of it, but I was overzealous in my attempt to be a good Keeper. I'm not the, ah, type of man who would procreate with the opposite sex, but it felt like my duty. I got a potion from the local coven to enable me to, ah, do the deed with a willing surrogate."

"It backfired?" Rhys asked.

"I believe so. Dennis is…not right. Definitely not good. Or he wasn't. Last I heard from him was a good twenty years ago. He was spending his days in an ayahuasca haze in Peru."

"So you chose me instead."

"You have more goodness in your pinkie than Dennis has in his entire body. Yes, I'm afraid he wasn't suitable to hold fast against Volac. But you, my dear, are more than enough."

So much for the escape route of dumping this onto someone else.

Maisy stared into his kind face. Chances were good she'd never see it again, so she wanted it burned into her memory. Kind of wanted to take a selfie with him, too, but was afraid to ask. She didn't want Rhys to launch into a stern lecture about how her phone could be hacked and any proof of this meeting was dangerous, blah blah blah.

"I'm sorry Mom never even mentioned you. Even just in old stories so I could've known some little part of who you were."

"Well, your mother didn't know about me."

Maisy blinked. Soap opera–esque family drama? This was *huge*. She couldn't wait to drop this bomb on Liss. It also made her want to take out a free trial subscription to Ancestry.com to dig for more dirt.

"You're a secret love child?"

From behind, she heard Rhys try—unsuccessfully—to cover a laugh with a cough. The guy was an expert at so many things, and yet he hadn't mastered a trick the average high school junior could do?

Uncle Harold guffawed. "I'm a secret; that's true." Then the smile crinkles around his eyes and mouth morphed into something equally crinkled but more somber. "I'm actually your great-uncle, Maisy. Your grandmother and I decided to keep my existence a secret from her family once I became Keeper."

Again, the loneliness walloped at her heart. Similar to the loneliness Rhys went through. Maisy threw her arms around him tightly. "I'm so very sorry. And I'm so glad I get the chance to hug you finally."

"Me, too, but we've so little time." He stepped back. Stretched out his arms. "This house is yours. Paid off, too. Fully furnished, although I'm sure not quite to your taste."

There went her knees turning to jelly again. Shock had Maisy reaching out—and Rhys's hand was right there, laced through hers and squeezing tightly.

She hadn't opened all the doors or anything, but from the outside it looked like a three- or four-bedroom house. Free and clear? No more rent and living in a run-down, drafty duplex across from a cemetery? "That's too generous."

"Nonsense. You take the good with the bad. This house and all my money—that's the good to offset the, ah, travails of being Keeper. I've left the will with a separate attorney for safety. As soon as you finish transitioning, there won't be any danger in your being seen here. He'll contact you as soon as the two weeks are up."

What was the appropriate response when you got a free ride to life? When someone snapped their fingers and poofed away your burdens? Eyes welling, Maisy smiled and hoped it showed the depth of her gratitude. "Thank you."

"I know it's been a struggle for you, financially. There's a trust that'll pay off your student loans as well. Again, it all triggers right after you become Keeper."

"Guess I'd better make it through the Testing, then." The hollow laugh in no way disguised Maisy's apprehension.

The worry that he'd been oh-so-wrong to pass the role on to her.

That she wouldn't be *enough*.

"You can't doubt yourself, my dear. Believe in what you can do, and you will be able to do it."

Aww. A motivational pep talk from her uncle. Or, rather, great-uncle. Sadly, it proved how little he knew her to think that she *wouldn't* doubt herself. "I need that on a poster. Below a pic of a jaguar about to leap across a canyon or something."

"I can't provide a poster, but there is a gift that can't wait until you officially own the house."

This hallway with its dated wood paneling and oil paintings of ducks was like Aladdin's Cave of Wonders. "Uncle Harold, you've given me so much already. You just made up for thirty missed Christmases and birthdays in one fell swoop."

"You'll need this to finish the transition." He led her back downstairs to a study. A glass-and-wood curio cabinet was stuffed with curiosities that a quick glance showed to be from all over the world. Jade carvings. Intricately painted scarab beetles. Hammered gold bowls that reminded her of the traveling Mayan exhibit at the museum.

"Is this all"—she circled her hand, not knowing what to say— "um, souvenirs? Or powerful supernatural objects that could possibly explode or curse me?"

"Yes." Another avuncular chuckle.

Uncle Harold would've been fun to hang out with if he was alive. But then she wouldn't *know* he was alive. Maisy again keenly felt the loss of their non-relationship.

"To all of the above," he continued. "There's a full accounting in the ledger behind the desk. I liked to travel and pick up things that might be useful in battles against evil."

Rhys shouldered in next to her. "This is an impressive collection." He pointed at a long tube with holes made from a… reed? "Is that a dryad's flute?"

"It is. And it will still call the dryad who fashioned it. Trillis. She's quite friendly, but if you call her, be prepared with a vanilla bean pod for payment. They're her favorite."

"Noted," Rhys said.

Her head was spinning.

Dryads were real? From the Greek myths she'd adored as a preteen? Guess it shouldn't come as a surprise after the whole boyfriend-with-wings thing, but still, it made Maisy triple-blink as a preventative against gasping out loud in shock.

"This is yours now, Maisy." Harold drew out a blown-glass bracelet. It was a stunning string of bright blue evil eye beads. "It's from the first century BC. Made by the ancient Etruscans."

Sure. Prank the niece you only got to see once in a lifetime about a museum-quality antique. Still, it was beautiful, so she slid it on. "It doesn't look more than fifty years old."

"It's a protection amulet. If it has enough oomph to protect you, it can certainly protect itself from the passage of time." Harold wore the same *oh, you poor naive human* look that Rhys had leveled at her for the first two days straight that they'd known each other. It could also be an elder scoffing at the foibles of a youngster, but it smarted nonetheless. Thirty was a full-blown adult by anyone's measure. Even by the surprisingly old *Nephilim* and—

—hang on. Uncle Harold was her *great*-uncle? She'd have to go back and check family tree rules to be certain, but if that was true, he should be close to eighty. He barely had wrinkles. Maisy would've put him at a solid forty. How could that be?

"It's a powerful piece," Rhys said as he ran a finger a hair-breadth above the actual beads.

She put aside the age issue for examination later and studied the bracelet. "But how will it protect me? Is it like the ruby slippers of Oz? Or Wonder Woman's cuffs? Will it shoot sparks at anyone who tries to touch me?"

"You'll see." And then Harold…shimmered into translucence for a few seconds.

Oh. Great. More ambiguity.

He solidified with a blink. "It has been imbued with centuries of protection, as it was worn by all Keepers and boosted by their energies. I wish I could remember why it didn't work on…" His voice trailed off as he shimmered to ghostliness again.

"Keeper?" The diamond-edged sword Zavier had proudly shown her in the armory wasn't half as sharp as Rhys's tone. "Are you saying you were murdered?"

Trust a suspicious-of-everything *Nephilim* to leap to an over-the-top conclusion.

Frowning, Harold rubbed at his temples. "It was too soon. I still had much to make ready to prepare Maisy for her role. It wasn't close to my time yet. I would've reached out to her before the end. I wish it wasn't so hazy, that final day…"

"Don't expend what little energy you have left trying to remember. It won't do any good," Rhys said gently.

Harold patted Maisy's cheeks. "I hung on to see my Maisy girl, just once, in person. Know that I have loved you every moment of your life. You brought me joy."

"I love you, uncle." It didn't matter how little she knew him. Maisy *did* know that he'd sacrificed to keep her safe. That alone was reason enough to love him and be grateful.

"Remember, above all else, to trust your heart." He shimmered again. Then, instead of becoming even more translucent, he brightened. Sun-sharp radiance started at the center of his body before expanding through every limb.

It was so bright that Maisy had to shield her eyes. So bright that Rhys curled a wing around her again, blocking the light.

And then there were only two of them in the room.

"Do you think he's really gone now?"

"After that display? No doubt. Ghosts are stuck here for a reason. Once he saw you, nothing tethered him to this plane."

That wasn't the answer she wanted. "But I still need him. I was hoping he'd be like the ghosts in movies. Popping in whenever I needed advice or someone to laugh with at the end of a hard day."

"I can assure you that very little in Hollywood gets our world right. There are threads that reveal a hint of truth. Not many, though. Your uncle won't be coming back." Rhys looked around the room. "Neither will we, until you've finished the Transition. It's not safe."

"You believe he was murdered?"

"I believe that if there's even a chance, that's too much to risk." He ran a hand along the bookshelves behind the desk. Grabbed a thick, leather-bound green journal. "This looks like his ledger. We'll take this along to see what useful knickknacks he's amassed."

Maisy put a hand on top of her bracelet. "It was worth it. Meeting him. Hearing why he stayed away. It makes all the difference."

Rhys tucked the book under his arm and nudged the small of her back. "We can talk about it in the car. We'll be in it for a while, making sure nobody's tailing us."

"Will it freak you out if I cry a little?"

"Aww, Maisy. You care so easily and so well. Don't ever stop."

That was an odd thing to say. Who could stop caring? Being touched by simple acts, big and small? Had Rhys truly hardened himself to the point where crying for a dead relative was *noteworthy*?

Maybe she'd spare a few of her sobs for him, too.

But if her uncle—who'd been doing this way longer than her, who knew the ropes and the tricks of the trade—was *murdered*? What chance did she stand? How soon would the next attack come? At the rate they'd happened so far? It could be as soon as tomorrow.

Would a pretty bracelet really keep her alive?

CHAPTER NINETEEN

"I should've let Zavier come along when I tracked you down. *He* should've been your bodyguard. Then *he* could be the one suffering at the crack of ass." Rhys eyeballed the patisserie's espresso machine. It looked complicated. Easy to screw up, with all of those handles and dials and a single mysterious lever.

He didn't mind bruises and cuts from sparring. He *did* mind the idea of a steam burn from wrestling to get a dose of caffeine after only getting four hours of sleep. Yeah, due to taking his time licking Maisy from head to toe—and letting her return the favor—but the cause in no way lessened the effect.

"Not a morning person?" Maisy inquired with more sweetness than the entire rack of cupcakes behind her.

"Not unless you count morning sex." She'd rushed him out of the Watchtower, intent on getting her belongings, leaving her keys, and getting out of the patisserie before any staff arrived. He hadn't been able to inveigle more than a single distracted peck out of her. He jerked his chin toward the big metal table in the center of the kitchen. "I could get on board with that."

"That would be a breach of the health code." Her voice was as prim as if he'd suggested going down on him in the middle of the Sistine Chapel. "For goodness' sake, if you want coffee, just ask. Stop poking at the machine. We've got a solid half hour before anyone should arrive."

"Really?" He leaned against the doorway between the front of the shop and the kitchen. "Because I 'just asked' you not to come in here today, and you blew me off."

"Are you intent on picking another fight simply because you're intimidated by the espresso machine?" Maisy slammed down the box she'd been filling with her aprons and an envelope that no doubt held her final check. Because she had such a big heart, she tied on an apron and stepped right up to the gleaming contraption and built him a latte, *despite* the fact that they were bickering.

"I don't want to fight." Well, Rhys sort of did, but they'd had a half-hearted fight about it in the car to no avail, so obviously he needed to take a different approach. "I want you to listen to me."

"The ground rules were clear. If something red and scaly with horns charges toward us?" Maisy threw up her hands, palms out, in surrender. "I will do exactly as you say without question or hesitation. Otherwise, I retain my free will to think and argue and decide for myself."

"There's an inherent danger to being in a public place."

"At four thirty in the morning? The only living things around are the rats in the alley."

"If you're attacked, innocent people could be hurt." That ought to do the trick. Maisy's bleeding heart would kick in, and they'd be out of here before his coffee was cool enough to drink.

But...she didn't whirl around in alarm. Didn't rip off the brown apron with pink lettering that cinched tight over her hips right where he'd like to rest his hands.

Instead, she chuckled. "An assassin demon is going to postpone its objective of killing me to randomly attack a guy who needs caffeine and an éclair to start the day...two hours from now? Riiiight. That's not strategic."

"We're talking about demons, Maisy. They enjoy wreaking havoc. Some would rather start their day with a pastry—and some would prefer to start with steaming intestines, freshly harvested. You never know which it'll be."

"Well, then, you'll just have to be on your game. This ought to help." She passed over a thick white mug.

"Thanks." Maisy had topped it with whipped cream, a drizzle of caramel, and chocolate shavings. She might be mad at him, but she still clearly cared.

Would that still be the case if they kept fighting?

Rhys didn't know.

He had zero experience in...well...relationships.

Nephilim didn't do those. It'd leave them vulnerable. It'd be a distraction. Yeah, he watched movies. TV. He knew how the fantasy versions of relationships worked—under the careful tutelage of a script-writing team.

The same geniuses who thought angels couldn't lie or steal or kill.

Or that the right aftershave made you irresistible to super-models if you were a ninety-pound weakling with an overbite and zero personality.

Rhys didn't have a lot of faith in taking his lead from shows, but he didn't have any other examples to follow. All he could do was be himself and hope for the best.

Which, in Hollywood, almost never worked.

"You told me to quit. I did. Left my boss in the lurch. I feel like a jerk. So drink your coffee and give me ten minutes of quiet while I finish decorating that tray of cookies for the gender reveal party. They begged me to do this *one* order. It'll take me an eighth of the time it would take anyone else. And then we'll be gone, without endangering *anyone*." Maisy brushed past him with such a cold shoulder it made him wince.

The weird thing was that he enjoyed arguing with her. Verbal sparring, every bit as invigorating as a good boxing match with Zavier. *Everything* about the woman invigorated him. Awakened a depth of feeling he'd either forgotten possible, or simply never bothered to activate.

Yes, a part of him admired her for abiding by her commitments.

Just not the part of him that was in charge of maintaining her safety through the Transition and Testing.

Strategy was about making the best decision. The simplest path to your objective. Maisy being in lockdown in the *Nephilim*'s ultra-fortified Watchtower would be so much simpler.

Years of experience had proven to Rhys that the best way to come out as winner in a fight with evil was to avoid the fight altogether.

"You've got your inheritance now—or will in a few days. A place to live. No worries about paying bills. You must focus solely on being the Keeper."

"Now you really are spoiling for a fight. You have to stop thinking of me as 'The Keeper.'" Maisy even made finger quotes around the words. "That will simply be one of my jobs. If I make it—not that I have any clue yet what it'll entail on a daily basis. I still want to teach, if I can find another position."

He didn't actually know the daily duties involved, either. Hopefully Harold's instructions would come with the will. Regardless, she still wasn't grasping the enormity of it.

Rhys made sure not to crowd her, staying in the doorway with a glance at the predawn blackness outside the wall of windows at the front of the shop, but he didn't even try to keep the stern lecture tone out of his voice.

"Keeper is your most vital job. It will forevermore be who you are. You have to stop clinging to the life you knew. You have to sacrifice that version of yourself, who you were. For the greater good."

"I won't, Rhys." Her hand clenched around the pastry bag. A thin ribbon of blue frosting squirted through the air. "I keep saying that, and you keep ignoring me. I don't want to shut down who I am. You've sacrificed a family and meaningful connections, and it's turned you into a closed-off shell of a man. Half man. Whatever."

It was impossible to refute her statement. And Rhys had been content that way, too, until Maisy upended his life. He speared his fingers through his hair. "I envy the way you want to tackle this role. I don't know how to balance my two halves. The angel part has always driven what I do. Who I am. My service in the name of good has defined me wholly. I won't say it is what I was born for, because I wasn't supposed to *be* born. So I do as I'm told."

She shook her head. "No. You *did*. Until you quit. Because, deep down, the three of you understood that who you were as individuals mattered. That you weren't automaton soldiers. You chose yourselves over blind sacrifice. That's exactly what I'm doing."

Rhys cupped both hands around the mug. Took a long, slow sip to buy time before responding. Because Maisy had just taken the wind out of his argument's sails. She'd flipped the thing around one-eighty degrees on him.

There was a strong chance she was—well, if not right, then at least with a hefty dose of rightness on her side.

He had been dismissive of her choices simply due to her humanity. Due to assuming she didn't "get" the scope of the battlefront the *Nephilim* skirmished on daily.

Hell. He'd been wrong. Worse, he'd been a stubborn fool. Precisely what he'd accused Maisy of...

"You've, ah, given me something to think about."

The fire in her bicolor eyes banked immediately. She dropped the bag and came around the worktable to loosely clasp her arms around his waist. "You're all astonished by my light and warmth and humanity. I like it, too. I won't give up what makes me *me*, which are the things and people I care about. Including you."

"Glad to be included," he deadpanned. He didn't want to get her hopes up that it would work between them. Rhys didn't know what he was doing, but he was utterly dazzled by every last bit of her. "If I stop hounding you, will you promise to take something else under serious consideration?"

"Seems fair. After all, you're not a trickster *jinn*. If those exist." Her eyes went wide, and she clasped her hands in front of her chest. "Omigosh, I was just kidding, but do they? Do they live in lamps?"

"Maisy. Focus." Sighing, he gave in to the anticipatory lift of her lips. "Yes. They're real, but they don't hang out in lamps. Now, you've got to be less trusting. Your belief in the basic goodness of all? That naïveté could be your undoing. You never should've been out on that ledge with your suicidal ex-student."

"You're wrong. I saved lives, so I was *meant* to be out there. Plus, it was a test I needed to pass as part of the Transition. I was doubly meant to be out there."

"This is what I'm talking about. Your belief in her could've gotten you killed."

"Didn't."

It infuriated Rhys beyond all words how attractive he found her persistence. But then a rattle at the front door put him on alert. "When's the staff supposed to arrive?"

"Half an hour at the earliest. We don't open for another two hours. There's a problem with the oven, so Kim is doing all the baking at a shop a few miles away."

"Stay here." He closed the swinging door to the kitchen and flipped off the lights to the front of the shop. No body-shaped shadows lingered at the door. Rhys edged along the far wall, making his way to the display window. Maisy would've written off the noise as a gust of wind.

Good thing *he* was the bodyguard.

The faint noise in the alley caught Maisy's attention. She hoped it wasn't an oversize raccoon upsetting the trash cans. Then there was a screech of spinning tires. And a scream. No, a wail—a baby's wail. Loud and unceasing.

Maisy rushed to the door. She did *think* about alerting Rhys, but he was out front chasing what could be dangerous shadows. A baby wasn't dangerous; it'd just need her help. So she unlocked the door and turned the handle. Still holding the piping bag *sort* of for protection (thanks to all of Rhys's warnings), which was admittedly not her finest choice, she eased through the doorway.

There was a car seat in the middle of the alley, tipped on its side. In it was a skinny baby, only wearing a diaper against the chill. Its scrawny foot rested on the rough gravel. It looked as though it had been dumped out the window of whatever car had sped away.

Lucky she'd come in so early. The garbage trucks would roll through in an hour and might've run right over the poor little thing in the dark.

She took the precaution of glancing at the dumpsters, at the shadowed fire escapes and doorways on the other side. Nothing stirred in the darkness.

The car seat was heavy as it banged against her knee. The baby in no way seemed calmed by her presence, and who could blame it? She'd cover it with kitchen towels, and they'd take it right to the hospital.

Oh! This had to be another angelic test. To see if she'd move past her self-centered fear of attack to rescue an innocent. Maybe she'd get another dimensional-shift chat with an angel.

Maisy set down the car seat to lock the door. Heard a fleshy slap. Had it toppled over and the baby fallen out?

Then she screamed. Not for long but very loud.

The fleshy-sounding slap hadn't been the baby hitting the floor. No, the baby was gone. In its place was the body of an eight-foot-tall black snake. Well, mostly a snake. Clawed paws raked at the air between them. And it had an owl's head with a curved, pointed beak that looked as dangerous as a scimitar. Yellow, pupilless eyes frightened Maisy to her core.

"Keeper."

The voice that somehow rasped out of the animal's throat was high, verging on the squawk of a bird. And while it didn't matter in the greater scheme of being confronted by a demon, coming off her argument with Rhys about being more a person than a title, it annoyed Maisy to be greeted that way.

"You want to do formal introductions?" Ridiculous. Who knew Hell spawn had such good manners? "Fine. I'm Maisy. And you are?"

"Keeper," it rasped again. "Volac warned you."

Volac. Her evil counterpart. The thing that blew up Milton Turk. He'd warned her to stop searching for the Key.

Geez. She hadn't found it yet. And how dare it pretend to be a helpless infant? That was unsporting, even for a demon.

Maisy tried to back up a few steps without looking obvious about it because they were conversing. No attack. She certainly didn't want to insult the big scary demon by letting on how completely snakes made her queasy.

So far, in her dealings with the supernatural, continuing the conversation had kept her alive. Maisy lobbed the pastry bag underhand into the sink. Eyeballed how many steps it would take to get to the knife block.

Oh, and she plucked at the maple leaf–printed leggings she'd put on in honor of her uncle's apparent love of either the tree, the syrup, or its country. Because attitude was everything. "Yes. I remember Volac. He of the super specific 'or else' warning. Are you here to elaborate?"

And what the heck was taking Rhys so long? Was he fighting another demon in the front?

A shrill screech emanated from the beak. Much more like nails down a chalkboard than a kindly owl's hoot. The snake dropped down into a few coils so it fit just beneath the doorframe.

Then it shot *lightning bolts* from its yellow eyes.

The bolts hissed by her with the noise of a live wire on a street. They struck the wheels of the worktable behind her.

Meaning they missed her ankles by, oh, maybe an inch. Did it have bad aim? Did it have a limit on how far the bolts could be thrown? Should she run into the walk-in or upend a table and use it as a shield like in a Wild West bar fight?

Really, screaming again was the only thing that landed as a solid decision. Obviously it wasn't as half-assed a demon as the *Aldokriz*, possible to be distracted by chitchat. It was a snake of action, not words.

"Maisy!" Rhys bellowed her name just in time for her to scuttle out of the way...because he took a running leap and *vaulted* over the worktable one-handed. Even in the midst of her deep terror, Maisy couldn't help but catalog the breathtaking, superhero sexiness of the move.

As he landed, he aimed both feet at the owl head.

And missed. That was the advantage to having the body of a skinny snake. It popped up from its coils and made a hairpin bend in its body to avoid the kicks.

The paws had looked a bit T-Rex ridiculous, barely sticking out from the snake. Except, again, the way the snake part could slither through the air and contort meant that the paws were as good as attached to a garden hose.

The snake body just corkscrewed its way forward close enough to Rhys for the paws to slash across his torso.

No tactical vest or body armor for him, since they'd been headed into Metafora next. The French blue dress shirt shredded like tissue paper. Blood immediately welled up in the slashes. An alarming amount, really. At least, Maisy assumed that the deep silver—almost like mercury—liquid was his blood.

Rhys threw two daggers at it. Simultaneously. And that was when Maisy learned that an eight-foot-long snake could actually put *multiple* bends in its body. With demonically quick speed. The paws easily batted away the daggers.

To Maisy's admittedly untrained eye, it looked like the only way to defeat the demon would be to attack the head. If Rhys could fly, it'd be easy to dive-bomb the thing, but the ceilings weren't high enough to allow that tactic.

"Get it outside," she said. Maisy made a flapping motion with her arms, hoping he'd take the hint.

"No. In here it's contained."

Aww. He was protecting random innocent humans from being caught up in the fight. That was thoughtful.

Aside from how the two of *them* were still stuck in a room with a demon thing.

He fired off three throwing stars in a row. The demon managed to slither and bend out of the way of the first two.

She'd never seen anything move that quickly that wasn't computer generated. It saw and reacted to every move as soon as Rhys made them. The third star struck its beak—and rebounded back toward Maisy.

Rhys let out a hoarse, sharp yell and dove to cover her. It felt… very different than when he covered her with his body during sex. It was like being hit by a wall. The combination of Rhys landing on her and being pushed into the concrete of the floor knocked the wind out of her.

Despite trying desperately to kick-start her diaphragm back into action, Maisy noticed that Rhys had been successful in keeping her from being hit. Every inch of her ached from the dual impact. Her ankle throbbed from being twisted beneath her, but her skin was intact.

The silver fluid now dripping down from his hairline told her that Rhys's head had intercepted the star instead.

Then he… Maybe it was the oxygen deprivation, because it *looked* like Rhys spiraled off of her. As if his body had been lifted by wires and spun sideways. Without the space to unfurl his wings, she couldn't tell how he managed it without a special effects team.

The spin landed him on the bottom coil of the snake. His body pinned it to the ground.

That *did* keep it from getting away from the dagger he was pulling from his ankle sheath. However, it also allowed for the demon to fold in half and slash at him with its claws.

Worse yet, the beak was trying to rip pieces out of his arm. Luckily, Rhys's sport coat was sturdy enough to repel the first few snaps. It wouldn't protect him from many more, though.

Maisy butt-scooted toward the knife block. With Rhys pinning it down and the demon distracted by trying to peck him to death, maybe she could stab it? Her succeeding at skewering it where Rhys had failed multiple times...well, the odds weren't strong. But she had to try.

The other option was scooting right on out of the kitchen. Running outside and calling Zavier and Gideon for help. It seemed unlikely they'd arrive in time to save Rhys. There wasn't a waterfall a block over for them to instantly transport through.

More to the point? She couldn't, *wouldn't* leave him.

Rhys was being attacked because of her. That made her responsible. For the man she cared...a lot...about. She'd stick by his side, no matter what.

Maisy grabbed a cookie sheet to use as a shield. Then she stood to reach the knives. Wobbled on her bad ankle.

"Brûlée torch," Rhys yelled.

It didn't make sense to her. If the snake could dodge daggers, it could certainly bend out of the way of fire. But she'd *promised* him—in life-and-death situations, she'd follow his instructions without question or hesitation.

A marble rolling pin crashed to the floor as she scrabbled for the torch. When they were safe, she'd laugh about the mental image of using the pin on the snake portion of the demon. Tempting but unworkable.

An entire spring semester spent tossing a Frisbee to try and get the attention of a boy (didn't work) meant Maisy had solid aim. She had no doubt that Rhys had a better-than-average ability to catch, even while being torn at by a demonic beak and holding down a writhing snake tail. He was just that good. So she hurled it at him after flicking off the safety catch.

Of course he caught it. Instead of wielding it on the demon, though, he aimed it up. Then he reached in his pocket and threw something at it. Instead of just fire, sparks burst out. The demon cringed, and its yellow owl eyes shut.

And Rhys slashed the snake in half.

He kept going. Severed the paws. Decapitated it. Then, with several bloody armfuls, he quickly dumped the pieces in the sink and set it all on fire. Rhys braced both hands on the counter and watched intently as though the danger might not be entirely over yet.

The smell was...

Maisy had never smelled anything similar. It was eight miles past nauseating and rotten and bad. Was that what Hell smelled like? The feathers on the head smoked for a few seconds. The sink was full of nothing more than ashes in less than a minute.

"Okay." Rhys let go of the sink, but his hands remained fisted tight. His shoulders were slumped, too. "You're safe now."

"*We're* safe now," she corrected.

"Will you grab a mop? I've got to get this cleaned up before anyone else arrives." He sprayed the ashes down the drain. "Is there something you can do to mask the scent?"

"Sure. But can we take a minute first?" Maisy didn't know where it was safe to touch, how deep the wounds were under his clothing. So she just reached out her hand, palm up. She needed the comfort of feeling him, alive and mostly whole.

To her surprise, Rhys ignored it. Instead, he sucked in a deep breath. Let his chin sag all the way to his chest.

Then he spun around. Crushed her to him tightly. Which was *perfect*.

Rhys lifted her so he could bury his face in her neck. First, he just breathed with her until their racing pulses had slowed and synced. Despite everything they'd just gone through? It was one of the most intimate moments she'd ever shared with anyone. Then he kissed a line up her neck, across her forehead, and down her cheek.

"I killed a demonic panther on the sidewalk. Never expected to find you being attacked when I got back here." Lips a breath away from hers, he murmured, "I wasn't sure I could hold it off. Didn't know if I could protect you."

She stared back into his magnificent indigo eyes that matched his wings. "I never doubted that for a moment."

"I couldn't have done it without your help. You should've run away, though."

"Then why didn't you order me to?" Maisy sassed.

"Knew you wouldn't."

"That's right," she lobbed at him in her primmest teacher voice. "So…ah…what was it?"

"An *eye-killer*. A Native American demon. As long as it can see you, it'll be able to evade the attack. Blinding it is the only way to win. Burning it, too. Or else it'll reform."

He set her down. Putting weight back on her ankle made her hiss at the sharp shock. Rhys glanced down, then immediately circled her ankle with one hand and closed his eyes.

In the next instant, her pain vanished. At the ankle, anyway. Her other aches and pains still annoyingly throbbed. "That's amazing. What did you do?"

"I redirected the pain." Then he took a few steps away— limping—to look at the condition of the floor. "It's not safe to leave my blood where anyone else can touch it. I'll take care of it."

"No." Guilt poured through her as she looked at the line of droplets, the silver pool of it on the floor. Not to mention the guilt from realizing he'd transferred her ankle pain to *himself*. "You're bleeding because I didn't take to heart what you tried to hammer into my head. I was too darned trusting. That ends now." Maisy opened the back door and chucked the car seat into the dumpster. Relocked it.

"Little late for that," he said drily. "An *eye-killer*'s the big guns. Don't expect another attack anytime soon. Volac will wait to hear back from it. We're safe for a bit."

Pulling out her phone, she shot off a quick text. "Regardless, I'm leaving the cookies undone. I won't risk anyone else getting injured because of my stubborn insistence on not changing my life." Maisy thought about how close she'd come to losing that life, to losing Rhys, and had to swallow the tears choking her throat. "I'll clean up—*not* you, because you'll just bleed more—and then I'll take you to Zavier and Gideon."

"You think you're driving my car? I'm not in danger of dying in the next ten minutes, Maisy. So that'd be a *no*."

Hard to tell how seriously he was hurt. The attitude was a positive sign, however. Maisy popped open the step stool, since it was at hand. Pushed Rhys down onto it. Handed him a roll of paper towels.

"Staunch what you can. It's too risky to drive across the border with you all sliced up. Then I *will* drive you to Metafora. Can you get us through the waterfall to the Watchtower in this condition?"

There was too much silence before he mumbled, "Doubtful." Rhys pressed harder on a wound and straightened up. All the color leached out of his face. "But—but we have a house here in town. More protected than the office."

"Good. I'll drive you straight there. You can be safe while you heal, and I'll apologize to you about my carelessness the entire way there. That ought to make the drive more endurable."

Rhys would no doubt give her a line about how he'd been doing his job.

But Maisy wasn't sure she'd ever forgive herself for his spilled blood.

Which was the *best*-case scenario.

Because...what if he died? Because of her carelessness?

What if she lost him? Forever?

CHAPTER TWENTY

The black marble of the shower ledge was icy under Rhys's ass. Even *with* his boxer briefs still on. The early morning sun streaming in the window on his back wasn't doing anything to warm him.

"I told you we should've installed steam showers," he grumbled.

Zavier just cocked an eyebrow. "You really want me stitching you up with sweat dripping into my eyes and steam clouding my vision?"

"No. But I *really* don't want to be freezing my ass off in my shower." He'd lost more than a little blood. Had to be compounding the chill. It'd be all kinds of painful if he was shivering when Zavier started poking him with a needle.

"Would you rather bleed all over the bed and have to change it? I'll sew up your cuts, but I'm not providing maid service."

"Yeah, yeah." He hissed out a breath as Zavier kept "exploring" the severity of his wounds. *Aka* picking shreds of his shirt out of them with tweezers. "I know *why* we're doing this in the shower. I'm just not thrilled about it."

"This is your fault. Your choice. Your human brought you to this state."

"It's Maisy. Not 'the human,'" he snarled. She deserved the respect of a name, damn it.

"I know." His top lip quivered the millimeter that, for Zavier, was a full-on smirk. "Don't I get to have a little fun while I'm wrist deep in your blood?"

"Annoying me is your idea of fun?"

"Just for the last eighty years or so, yeah."

Rhys was well aware that he was being a pain in the ass, but he'd almost failed in his mission. Almost *lost* Maisy. And, yes, came far too close to dying himself. He deserved to be out of sorts.

Just like Zavier deserved whatever he wanted after being rousted from bed to tend to him. "Then go for it. As long as you don't leave me with a scar in the shape of a whale for 'fun.'"

His friend's hand froze in midair. "Man. Already having to go to plan B. Fine."

"And it wasn't her fault. It was a trap. Even *you* would've picked up that baby and brought it inside."

"Did you tell Maisy that?" Gideon paused on the pattern of black-and-white tile that bordered the shower. He was in pajama bottoms just like Z. And equally displeased at this pre-breakfast interruption to the day. "Is that why I just left her on the upstairs porch looking like she'd run over a kitten with a lawnmower?"

Rhys elbowed Z away so he could lean forward. It made more blood trickle down his stomach—okay, *more* than trickle—but he had to know how Maisy was doing. "Is she okay?"

"Did my masterful simile not work for you? The woman's a mess. Guilt-stricken. That you got hurt, that it was her fault, that it was her stubbornness and her refusal to be as distrustful as you that allowed the attack to happen—do I need to go on? Because *she* did. On and on and on."

"Then why'd you leave her alone?" Rhys erupted, half standing. That only lasted a second. His thighs gave out and plopped him right back on his ass. Those claws must've stuck some venom in him. The dust motes in the sunlight looked three times their size. The mirror over the sink undulated in waves.

It was why he'd insisted Maisy wait elsewhere. He didn't want to scare her with whatever might happen next.

Gideon waggled the three potion bottles in between his fingers. "Because my job is to get you healed. Not to soothe a spoiled child."

"She's not spoiled. She's sure as hell not a child."

A deep, bitter laugh rumbled out of Zavier. "All the humans are spoiled. They don't have any idea about all this. About how the balance could shift in the blink of an eye. About just how scared they should be."

"Maybe we concentrate on the bad too much." If they only looked for the bad, the evil, the about-to-wreak-havoc? What was left to live for?

Their motivation had dwindled down to not wanting to die and doing their duty to save humanity...so as not to die. That wasn't enough.

It was like being stuck in a black-and-white movie. Then Maisy came along, flipped a switch, and showed him what Technicolor looked like. Wasn't it better to appreciate the goodness in humans? Fight to save that, and not just fight because they were supposed to?

Gideon took the curved needle. Dipped it in a deep red potion, then stuffed the thread in, too. "And she's a baby compared to us."

Rhys remembered that thick red liquid. It was going to burn like a motherfucker. "About that. When we talked to her uncle—he was the wrong age. Harold was actually her *great*-uncle. So he should've been her grandparents' age. But he looked...I dunno, maybe fifty, tops? On top of that, he said he'd died way too soon."

"They all say that," Z muttered.

Concentrating on the mystery surrounding Maisy's dead uncle might distract him from the pain. On the other hand, the probably poison in his system made his thoughts feel as if they were on a carousel. Going in circles without getting anywhere.

"Harold gave me the impression that Keepers get elongated lives. Just like us. Do you remember hearing that?"

Gideon thrust the needle back at Zavier. Motioned for him to start sewing. "We don't remember *anything* about the extremely little we learned about Keepers. That became clear eight days ago."

Which wasn't that long when you were a being that lived for two centuries. But when said celestial being *knew* they only had fourteen days to prevent Hell spilling up onto Earth? Keeping them in the dark didn't make sense. It *did* feel deliberate.

Rhys bit back a moan as Z's needle started weaving in and out of his flesh. "Still nothing from Caraxis?"

"He's gone dark. At this point, it's obvious that he's purposefully ducking us." Zavier raised a single eyebrow. "Which I'm sure you already guessed."

"Did you try reaching out to any of the *Nephilim* at the training center?"

"They assured me they gave our many messages to Caraxis. He's 'unavailable.' That new kid? Leo? With the green spotted wings?"

Gideon crouched, using a washcloth to clean up the silver streaks of blood that Rhys had dripped across the floor. "The one who came out to spar with us a few months ago? He had real potential with his sword skills. He thinks we're the best there is."

"He's not wrong," Z deadpanned.

"The hero-worship translated to him trying to keep a channel open with us. He offered up that even if we flew through the waterfall, Caraxis wouldn't meet with us. No communication until after our Keeper's installed."

That was bullshit. After all the intel they fed Caraxis, he owed them reciprocity. And he owed the world any help he could give to make sure the Gates stayed locked.

"Z, make sure to give him another sparring session for that info. So we're supposed to figure…*something* out all by ourselves.

But why? Doesn't that put us, and the Keeper, and the world at greater risk?"

"You'd think," Gideon said succinctly. He tossed the washcloth down by the drain. Handed over the second bottle that glowed a putrid green. "Drink this. Then cover your mouth. The belch it's going to cause will get out the poison. We don't want any part of that."

"We've got a human with an elongated life span, maybe murdered. Some other secret about Keepers that we aren't supposed to know. And we're not even getting paid for this mission." Zavier backed out of the shower. Then he shut the door as if to contain a blast zone. "Did you leave the woman crying, Gid? Even I'm not that heartless."

"For fuck's sake, no. She's not crying; I'll hand that to her. Pale. Shaking. Self-flagellating, but no tears. Maisy's strong."

"She's stubborn." Rhys chugged the potion shot. It didn't burn going down. Had a matcha flavor to it. But as soon as it cleared his gullet? Each of his wounds—the ones inflicted by the claws, not the beak—felt like they'd been hit by a blowtorch. "Uh, definitely poisoned over here, if anyone was curious."

"I gave her coffee," Gideon continued, not even acknowledging his poison announcement. "Spiked with whiskey. Offered to bring her roommate over from the Watchtower if she wanted, to keep her company. She asked to let Liss sleep for now and bring her over later, but only once I promised this house was every bit as secure as the Watchtower."

"Guess this finally scared some sense into her."

Rhys let out the foulest belch of his life. Like vomiting toxic air. Then he sagged back against the tiles. "She's got plenty of sense. She just balances it with optimism."

"You've been trying since day one to lecture that out of her. You should be pleased this latest attack finally did the trick."

Not so much.

The thoroughly chastened version of Maisy that had driven

them home had been painfully quiet aside from apologizing every time the wheels jostled over a pothole. Which, spring in Buffalo, was about every six feet.

A subdued Maisy didn't sit right with Rhys.

"Did you two notice that the Keeper isn't an immortal? The Keeper on Hell's side is a child of Lucifer, but not our Keeper. The descendents of earthbound angels are still pure, vulnerable humans. I think it's because immortals get inured to the wonders of life. You take for granted what's always there. Humans *feel* that clock ticking to their end. Makes them appreciate more. Maybe you need that human optimism and joy to perfectly balance the Gates."

Zavier jerked his head to look at Gideon so fast that his neck cracked. "What in the living hell did you put in that potion?"

"Nothing that should've turned him into a reincarnation of Plato." Gideon plastered his face against the glass door. "Rhys? Buddy? Are you still in there?"

"Don't be a dick. I can have thoughts, can't I?" And Rhys was certain that his were rolling in the right direction now. "If my job is to help the next Keeper assume their role, shouldn't I try to understand all that that encompasses? Stop trying to tamp down the very attributes that make her stand out?"

"I see. You're sleeping with her," Zavier stated flatly. "With the Keeper." He pushed past Gideon to wrench open the door and step back inside. Moving on to stitch the next oozing gash, he asked, "Why didn't you tell us?"

Uh, because he barely wanted to admit it to himself?

Because he *knew* better and had done it anyway?

Because it was another layer of complexity they didn't need— and he didn't need to have his friends remind him of that?

Rhys wiped at a trickle of blood slowly wending its way from his hairline. "Is that a new rule? If Gid tells us every time he sleeps with a woman, we'll have maybe four and a half minutes left in each day to do work."

After the requisite scowl, and then letting out a low whistle of surprise, Gideon said, "You're screwing the Keeper? I'm impressed. I figured she was too perky for you. Too bright. Too happy. Too...everything. Too human, that's for sure."

"She was." It was a perfect list of all the reasons Maisy had bothered Rhys from the start. Except... He lifted his hands, then let them fall back on his lap. "And then she wasn't."

Did it make sense? No. Had he tried to resist the attraction? Of course. Was it possibly the aftereffects of the poison?

No.

He wouldn't take the coward's way and blame it on the *eye-killer*'s poison. Rhys had known how much he cared about Maisy days ago. Knew that with every passing day, that caring and attraction grew exponentially stronger.

Trying to explain it to his friends was about as painful as the needle and its burning thread going in and out of his flesh. "I pushed back against Maisy's hopefulness because I was scared that she might be right. That there's more good out there in the world that we need to open ourselves up to."

"Which equally opens us up to the potential of getting hurt. Hasn't that happened enough?" Zavier said in a tone so dry it made it clear he wasn't at *all* open to the conjecture.

Rhys really didn't want to piss off the guy in the middle of sewing him back together, but his subconscious had been chewing on this nonstop. It'd finally settled on this answer. Agree or disagree? He had to let them know where his head was.

"Being *Nephilim* means that we've been hunted and attacked and reviled our entire lives. We closed off hope of things ever being different."

"Yeah. Lesson learned. No thanks from Heaven for all our near-death saves of this planet. No thanks from humans. Just a metric shit ton of people, demons, *and* angels trying to kill us." Zavier poured the final potion bottle Gideon had brought in onto a square of gauze. Began dabbing it over the stitched-up wounds.

And when he met Rhys's gaze, those tawny eyes reflected all those decades of pain and bitterness. "Where's the good in that?"

"I don't know, Z. This theory's a work in progress."

"Sounds to me like you've been sneaking in too many daytime talk shows. Getting in touch with your inner butterfly yearning to break free." Gid's mockery was delivered in a breathy, pseudo-supermodel voice. "Get real, Rhys. That doesn't work on *Nephilim*." By the time he finished, his voice had sharpened to an ice shard piercing Rhys's skull.

It didn't change his mind.

At least, it didn't change his feelings about her. "All I know is that Maisy is absolutely different from anyone we've met in almost a century. She makes me realize that just staying alive isn't nearly as good as truly *living*. The humans aren't as miserable as we are. And being with her? It makes me happy."

"We'll see how long that lasts. Trust me—I've cycled through more women than I can count. Whatever happiness you're looking for isn't wrapped up in red hair and a winsome smile."

It wasn't a numbers game. That's where Gideon was wrong.

Unless...he turned out to be right...

"Don't drink anything," Gideon cautioned. "No booze for twenty-four hours after that de-poisoning potion."

Rhys dropped onto a stool. Swallowed a smile at watching the far shorter Maisy working to hitch herself up onto another one and keep her purse on her shoulder. A purse loaded down with a dagger, gauze pads and surgical tape in case he ripped his stitches, an actual rock she'd picked up in the parking lot "the right size to clock something in the head," and an extra shirt. In case more toxic demon blood splattered across any of them.

He'd told her it was all unnecessary with three *Nephilim* escorting her. And Maisy had just looked at him with big, sorrowful eyes and said she wasn't taking any chances.

He hated how broken her ebullient spirit was after this last attack. Ironic, since that's what he'd been trying to do at the start of this mission.

"But we're at a brewpub." With some of his favorites written on the chalkboard behind the Big Ditch bar as being on tap today. "And I'm in pain, Gid."

"You'll be in a lot more pain if you mix alcohol and the residue of that potion. Trust me."

Maisy shook a finger at Gideon. Tipped with nails painted blue and swirled with gold like the Van Gogh masterpiece. "Ah. I can listen between the words. You tried it once, didn't you? Pushed your luck?"

"We're out in public with you, Keeper," Zavier said with a frown. "We're all pushing our luck."

Oh, for fuck's sake. They'd both liked Maisy until he'd told them about his feelings for her. Now they were picking sides? Mid-mission? To, what—protect him from the allure of the petite redhead?

They didn't have time for throwing any attitude at one another. "Hey," Rhys barked. Which tensed his abs and made him extremely...*aware* of the forty-one stitches Z had put in him. "Enough. It made sense to acquiesce to Aradia's request to meet here. This isn't on Maisy."

"Why would she want to meet here, though?" Liss craned her neck to look around the high-ceilinged space with its glass walls. They were up on the second-floor balcony, and it was still elbow-to-elbow people, upstairs and down. She'd been glued to Maisy's side since hearing about the attack while Rhys slept the day—and the poison—away.

Gideon stood, dropped his bomber jacket over the stool. "Aside from the awesome coffee stout? It's run by werewolves. They hate witches and *Nephilim* equally."

"They hate all non-werewolves equally," Zavier corrected.

"Totally neutral location."

Gideon started to head for the bar. Rhys snagged his wrist. "Order me a beer anyway. If I don't have one sitting in front of me, Aradia could figure out I'm injured. We can't risk a hint of weakness."

With a shrug, Gid said, "As long as I get to drink yours before we leave."

Maisy stroked two fingers across the back of his hand. "You really don't trust her, do you?"

Funny question.

Seeing as how Rhys didn't trust *anyone*. Which he'd told her over and over. "I trust her a little more since you scared her shitless the other night, but no. We work together when we have to, but it's always a tenuous truce at best."

Zavier snorted. "I don't know why Gideon risks screwing the witch."

Maisy and Liss both jumped as Aradia slid in between them to rest her hands on the table. "Because I'm a very enthusiastic and inventive partner." Aradia slo-mo licked her lips while keeping her gaze locked on Z.

Like Zavier would fall for that.

Or go anywhere near a woman Gideon had been with.

Or go anywhere near a *witch*.

With her position next to Maisy, the contrast between the two women was notable. Aradia was dressed for a night of choosing her next bedroom toy—leather bustier, leather pants, and a silver Celtic shield knot dangling between her breasts. Guess she thought she needed its protection after her last encounter with Maisy.

The Keeper, however, wore a blue-and-white shirt patterned with a leaf design, a blue sweater, and jeans with her rainbow sneakers. Rhys knew she was thirty—and knew the bouncer had carded her at the door after a single head-to-toe. She looked fresh and bright.

Until you looked at her subdued expression.

"Gideon went to get us all drinks." Rhys stroked his chin. Glared. Good to remind Aradia that Maisy wasn't the only one at the table she should fear. "If you can skip your usual blood-of-a-newborn-infant shooter."

"Very funny. We don't do blood sacrifices."

Z hopped right in. "*Some* of you do."

Aradia's thick lashes dipped down for more than a few seconds. When she looked back up, it was as if her fighting stance had been stripped away. "That's true. And extremely regrettable. None in my coven; I give you my word. None in our region. We've done everything possible to excise witches who still practice the darker magics."

Rhys jolted at her words...and then held his breath as pain spiked through him at the motion. Her honesty was a surprise.

"That is good to know, High Priestess. We're honored that you trust us with that knowledge. If you ever need our help with it, we would do what we can."

Gideon caught the tail end of Zavier's oddly formal response as he rejoined them. Aside from shooting a *what the fuck* look at Rhys, he let it pass. "Drinks will be here soon. How about we get right to it? You asked to meet, so you'd better have the answer we're looking for."

Aradia inclined her head slightly. Then she turned all her attention to Maisy. "I was able to learn who holds your Key now. Please know that it is beyond my ability to influence the one who has it."

"Leading off with an excuse." Maisy raised an eyebrow and looked cool and disinterested. It was adorable. "That doesn't bode well."

"Your demon did *not* give the Key to a member of my coven."

"Don't you have territory rules? Like the mob?" Liss, who'd been so visibly shaken by the demon sightings, seemed perfectly comfortable poking the powerful head of a witch coven. She actually leaned in closer, twisting a piece of dark hair around her finger. "Does this mean you've got to go to the mattresses with the infiltrator?"

Rhys bit back a laugh. Saw Z and Gideon doing the same. Because they knew that Aradia could swat Liss like a gnat with a single flick of her eyelids but would probably treat her with the tolerance given to a puppy with the *Nephilim* at the table.

To his surprise, she did neither. Instead, the witch gave a slow, appreciative once-over that seemed to get stuck in the deep vee of considerable cleavage revealed by Liss's clingy black top.

"Oh, if it were that simple, you can be assured I would. I protect what is mine." And then she gave a repeat slo-mo lip-lick while staring at Liss.

Hell. Rhys was barely holding himself together as the potions battled to heal him. He didn't have any time to waste watching Aradia pull her *witches are a sensual sisterhood* act on a human.

He rapped his knuckles on the table. "Who has the Key?"

"The demon you so unwisely dispatched gave the Key to Lilith."

Holy. Fuckballs.

Could nothing be easy about this Transition? Rhys was tempted to bang his head against the table. The only thing holding him back was the wicked headache that already had his temples in a vise grip from the poison.

"Lilith *who*?" Maisy asked. "Didn't you get her last name?"

Aradia squinted at Gideon. "Where'd you find this one? Under a rock? With no more sense than a child?"

"Didn't think I'd have to remind *you* that the Keeper is human," he said placidly. "She's still getting up to speed on the major players of our world."

"But you've got no more sense than a child to intentionally insult *her*. To her face." Zavier leaned forward, baring his teeth in what was absolutely *not* a smile.

Okay. So the guys might not be on board with Rhys's new

outlook on humanity—or his sleeping with Maisy—but, as always, they were presenting a united front to everyone else.

That was reassuring.

He still wanted to pitch Aradia over the balcony for talking about Maisy like that. They needed her help today, but next time the situation was reversed? He'd remember the witch's patronizing words and not be in any hurry to aid her.

Or raise their rates by 30 percent. Call it a rudeness tax.

Maisy shook back her red waves from her face. "You can get back in my good graces by explaining what it is that I'm supposed to know about this apparently famous Lilith."

The High Priestess wasn't stupid. She read the room and knew she'd overstepped. With only patience in her tone, she said, "Think one name. Like Beyoncé. *The* Lilith—Adam's first wife, who refused to submit to him and then left the Garden of Eden and became the Mother of Demons."

Liss hurriedly lifted a napkin to her mouth. Rhys was pretty sure it was to cover her jaw literally dropping, but the only hint of Maisy being bowled over by the eons-old gossip was visible as she worked her throat in a hard swallow. "Guess my Sunday school taught a censored version. We only learned about Eve being in the Garden."

"Well, Lilith's found most of all in Jewish folklore." The witch twirled a ring set with amethyst and black obsidian—protection crystals. "Who wrote it down doesn't change the facts, though."

"Right. History isn't open to interpretation. It just *is*."

Aradia set her elbows on the table and clasped her hands. It sent the myriad of silver bracelets—some undoubtedly charms—cascading down her arms. "Some modern witches revere her as a goddess, as our mother. I personally do not. My coven doesn't practice dark magic. At all. There's no blurring the lines for us since I took charge. And Lilith, well, she's constantly played on both sides of the fence in the immortal war between good and evil."

Maisy rubbed at the back of her neck as the waitress set down their beers. "So someone who sells out to the highest or most interesting bidder has my Key? That's not good."

Waggling her hand back and forth, Aradia said, "It *could* be. It could definitely be worse. Lilith, unlike pure demons, doesn't really answer to anyone. She makes up her own mind. The good news is that I've already contacted her on your behalf."

"Great. Thanks. My, ah, contacts haven't been updated for all these new people I'm learning about," Maisy blustered.

Rhys, however, knew *exactly* how much of a gesture it was that Aradia had worked a spell to entreat Lilith. Damn it. He was going to have to be nice to her. He lifted a mug in a toast. "We appreciate you being proactive, High Priestess. This expression of goodwill will not go unrewarded."

With a toss of her long, black hair, Aradia toasted back and took a sip. Must've liked the compliment, because she directed her next remarks straight at Rhys. "She's agreed to listen to your request to return the Key to your Keeper. The bad news? She's insisting it happen *at* the actual Gates. If she doesn't like what she hears from *your* Keeper, she can turn the Key over immediately to Volac. For a price, of course."

Hell? He was supposed to take her *into* Hell?

That hadn't occurred to any of them as being the next step. Rhys had been there, as part of his training, but he only knew the basics—getting in and getting out—and he certainly couldn't picture Maisy down there.

Maisy picked up the closest mug. Took a big swig. Then just kept swallowing, with no break, until the entire thing was empty. Slamming it down, eyes watering and narrowed, she said, "I am *not* okay with going to Hell. Nobody ever mentioned that was a part of this gig."

"You're the Keeper. Of *course* you have to go. Many times." Cocking her head, Aradia simpered at Gideon. "Were you not in charge of teaching her?"

"We've been working on a need-to-know basis so as not to overwhelm her. It's a lot to absorb all at once."

Gideon's answer was believable. Smooth as a twenty-year-old whiskey. His delivery dead-on. It in no way revealed to Aradia that they'd had *zero* idea that a trip to Hell was a requirement. Due to Master Caraxis holding back on them about just about everything Keeper-related.

When Caraxis did finally agree to meet with them, it wouldn't happen over the phone. Rhys wanted his enraged spit to dot Caraxis's face as he yelled at the man in a righteous fury.

"That is the voice of the patriarchy, right there. Men in charge holding back the advancement and knowledge of women. I'm disappointed in you, Gideon. In *all* of you." Aradia dug in her miniscule scrap of a purse, then handed a business card to Maisy. "When you have questions, call me. I'll be straight with you. Good luck, Keeper."

"Um…thanks?" As Aradia strutted away, Maisy pulled over Liss's beer and began to guzzle.

Rhys put a gentle hand on her arm. "Hey, take it slower. At least until we order some food. You don't want to be hungover in Hell."

Her usually bright smile was strained. Forced. "Don't I? Seems fitting. Why not be miserable in the most miserable place ever?"

"You're coming back," Zavier muttered.

"What?"

He looked up from his half-drunk beer. "Look, I know it still doesn't sound great, but you won't go into the depths of Hell. Just the outskirts. You won't be staying. Once your business with Lilith is done, you'll come back."

Liss spread her hands, palms up, in a gesture of utter futility. "How, exactly? I mean, I know people talk trash about budget airlines, but even Frontier won't fly her to the Gates of Hell."

Gideon waved off her question. "That's the easy part. And

it explains why we're paired up with every Keeper. As *Nephilim*, we can get to Purgatory and the Gates. Angels can't enter Hell, but half angels—or, more to the point, half men—can."

Maisy shifted to fully face Rhys at her right. "Why didn't you warn me that my itinerary for two weeks—chock full of fun, near-death attacks—included a hopefully round trip to Hell?"

That question skewered him to the wall, didn't it? The pain across his stomach and chest was nothing compared to meeting her infuriated, betrayed, accusing glare. "We didn't know," Rhys mumbled.

"I'm sorry, what was that?" Maisy flattened her hands on the sticky wooden table and leaned over it. "You all-knowing, been-there-and-done-damn-near-everything, long-lived, know-it-all, pretentious jerks didn't know that I was signing on to *go to actual fucking Hell*?"

Zavier put a single finger to his lips, a reminder not to be so loud about the reality of Hell.

Half under his breath, Rhys said, "There's been a bit of a communication gap."

"I'll say!"

"We honestly had no idea this would be required, but you can handle it." He'd better share what little he did know, right now. "I'll be your guide. In order for you to accompany me, you'll take an herb that renders you comatose and near death."

"That's your definition of handling the situation?"

"It is." Gideon reached across to put a hand over hers. "Because we swear we can reverse the effects as soon as Rhys brings you back."

"That's hardly comforting." Liss grabbed for her friend's other hand and interlaced her fingers tightly. With a ferocity Rhys had never seen in her before, she stared them down with blazing eyes that practically gave off sparks. "How many times have you pulled that off?"

The three men looked at one another. Nobody spoke. Why

wouldn't Gid or Z help him out here?

Liss glared at them. "*Never?* Is that the grand total you're looking for and don't have the balls to admit?"

Maisy caught the edge of her upper lip with her teeth. "I'm just supposed to put all my trust in Rhys to keep me alive?"

She'd made him promise not to sugarcoat things any more. "Yes."

Her always pale complexion seemed to drain even more bloodless. Maisy closed her eyes for a few seconds. After a deep, slow breath, she looked up. "Yesterday, I wouldn't have agreed to it, but your injury has driven home the seriousness of my assuming this mantle of responsibility. I'll do it."

Rhys was simultaneously relieved—and still worried. This was so far outside their comfort zone. Hell was…tricky. And, of course, evil. He flicked his gaze at Z and Gid. "I don't like it," he muttered.

Maisy threw her napkin at him. "A, I can hear you, and B, join the freaking club!"

How was being poisoned and almost killed the least shitty thing to happen today? Rhys had trained. Knew he could get in and out of Hell.

Didn't mean he wanted to.

Volac had put considerable effort into stopping her Transition to Keeper so far. Rhys did *not* expect him to scale back once they got to his turf. Whatever happened down there would undoubtedly go sideways at some point.

And yeah, it was Hell. So bad things were *very* fucking bad.

CHAPTER TWENTY-ONE

Maisy stared out over the treetops. "I should figure out some final goodbye thing to say to Liss."

Rhys followed her gaze but knew she wasn't seeing anything. It was pitch dark. Plus, he had a strong feeling that what she was *truly* straining to see was her future. He joined her at the balcony railing. Put an arm around her waist. "No need. You'll be back tomorrow night."

"Will I?"

He smoothed a hand down her hair. It was tousled from all the tugging and twirling she'd nervously done all evening. "Yes."

"C'mon. You can't guarantee that."

It figured that Maisy would push back just as hard at him being reassuring as when he was trying to make her worried about danger. The woman never simply accepted his words, which was now a lot less annoying and a lot more intriguing. Alluring, actually.

Drawing her over to the porch's rattan sofa, he said, "There are no guarantees. About anything. Ever. But I have faith in Gideon and Zavier's abilities with potions. And when we're in Hell, I have even more faith in myself to keep you safe."

"How often have you been there?"

"Twice."

Rhys would always know the exact number of times. Hell

was not an experience that you forgot. Or that even blurred with the passing of decades. Not because the part he'd been to was so terrible but because of the niggling, underlying fear that he'd be stuck there. *Forever.*

So he understood what had Maisy all knotted up.

She looked down her nose at him as she tucked her feet under her. At the opposite end of the green-and-white striped cushions, because she still acted as though a single touch from her would reopen each and every one of his wounds. "Frequent flyer, huh?"

Her sarcasm sounded half-hearted.

"Once with my trainer, and once solo to prove I could do it. No, it's not a fun-filled vacation destination."

"What would be, for you?"

"Is this a magazine quiz?"

She pushed yet another bottle of water at him. Gideon's insistence that he hydrate to help the potion metabolize had been taken far too seriously by Maisy. At this rate, as soon as they got to Hell, he'd be looking for a bathroom.

"I'm genuinely curious. For a man who can fly between countries and continents with a few wing pumps, what makes for an ideal vacation spot?"

He'd already survived a poisoning today. How much worse could being honest with her be? "I have two answers. One has been true for decades. The other is, well, new."

"If you were one of my students, I'd never allow this blatant fence-straddling." She wrinkled her nose. "But since you've promised to keep me safe in Hell? Yes, you may have two answers."

"Salina. A quiet island just off the coast of Sicily. There's a resort where every room has a view of the ocean or the vineyards. It reminds me of where I grew up. It feels...serene. Like nothing bad has ever so much as touched it. Like I can let down my guard there." It was the most restful place he'd ever been. It made Rhys wonder if that was what Heaven felt like.

"It sounds beautiful. I can't imagine why you'd need a second choice, but what's the other one?"

He locked his gaze on her mysterious brown-and-green eyes. "Anywhere you want to go."

Maisy became inordinately focused on tracing the ribbing on the pillow she yanked onto her lap. "Don't tease."

"I'm not." Leaning over, he stroked the backs of his knuckles down her cheek. "I want to watch your eyes light up when you look at Monet's gardens in Giverny. Or float in the waters off Bali. Watching your joy *is* a vacation for me."

"That's the most romantic thing you've said to me." Maisy hugged her knees to her chest. Burrowed into the corner of the sofa. "Oh, God. I *am* going to die tomorrow, aren't I?"

"Shit." Talk about blowing it. Guess he sucked at romance. And Rhys was unaccustomed to being bad at anything he set his mind to.

"I really am?" Her voice squeaked up on every word.

"No. I, *fuck*, I didn't mean to scare you. I'm not good at this."

"Clearly." But she did let her arms drop back to her sides. Although she still wasn't looking at him.

Rhys had lost on that gamble. This conversation was clearly far worse than the poison and the oozing wounds he'd suffered earlier. He'd scared the crap out of her. The complete opposite of what he was *trying* to do.

He got up to crouch right next to her. To sandwich her delicate hand in between his own.

"On my honor, it was nothing to do with our odds of escaping Hell tomorrow. I was trying to say the right thing. A...sweet thing. To let you know how I feel about you. Be like a regular man."

Maisy went very, very still.

If their house didn't have seven layers of protection, Rhys might wonder if Volac had sent a *Gorgon* to deal with her.

Then she finally blinked. And when she looked up, all her signature sassy sweetness had returned. The Edison-style string lights overhead picked up the sparkle in her eyes, the wry tease in the twist of her lips, and the flutter of her lashes that made him want to rip off her clothes right then and there.

"Meh. Regular men are only okay. I'd rather have a *half* man. The mix of angelic goodness and human messiness really works for me."

He blinked. "That sounds like a compliment wrapped around a dig."

"Well, you made me certain I was about to die, so that's what you get."

He'd take it. In response? Rhys decided to go against her wishes and sugarcoat their chances. Maisy needed a pep talk—not a cold hard dash of reality.

Because it was dangerous.

There *were* no guarantees. Aside from being positive that they had no idea what would happen down there and it'd be worse than expected. And yeah, it was Hell. So bad things were *very* fucking bad.

Again, not what his Keeper needed to hear. Rhys infused his voice with slow, deep certainty. "I don't think you'll die. Or be stuck in Hell."

"*That's* a possibility? Oh, geez." She worried at her upper lip with her teeth. "Let me just get this out, and then I promise I'll be all positivity and confidence. If something goes wrong, I want you to make sure Liss isn't stuck paying the rent by herself. Use Uncle Harold's money. Heck, move her into his house. For as long as she wants."

"I'll tell the guys."

"I'm making my official last request here. It's kind of a big deal, Rhys." Pique had her snatching her hand back and layering her words with snark. "Why can't *you* do it?"

Did she truly not understand the depth of his commitment to her safety? Not simply because he was her official bodyguard. *Simply* because of how much she mattered to him.

Bracing his hands on his thighs, Rhys pushed up enough to resettle on the sofa. Then he let his arms dangle off his knees.

Open.

Vulnerable. Unguarded. Unknowing of what the future held for them.

"Maisy, the only way something goes wrong and *you* don't come back is if *I'm* gone."

The only sound on the porch for the space of several breaths was the rustle of the vine against the side of the house. And maybe a few early cicadas.

It was quiet for long enough that Rhys was certain he'd gone the wrong way by hammering home the simple truth in the hopes that she'd see it as a promise of the only kind of devotion he knew how to show.

Finally, Maisy scratched at the side of her nose. "Oh. Ah. I don't like the sound of that."

"Then make sure it doesn't happen. Do whatever it takes to get that Key. You can't out-trick Hell, but you can do what you do best. Be you."

"That sounds like a motivational speech for a seventh-grade, seventh-place flag football team. Will you give me a trophy just for trying my best, too, Mr. Boyce?"

Her analogy was hilarious, but it also meant she'd missed his *actual* advice. "I'm serious. You don't see how special you are. With your humanity. With your trust. Believing the best exists in all people. Focus on that. It's where agents of Hell won't be able to match you."

"I feel like I'd have to be in the middle of an example in order to see it, but thank you." Maisy cracked her neck side to side, then spread her arms across the top of the cushions. "Any advice that might get me back here, on this peaceful porch in twenty-four hours is welcome."

Twenty-four hours. *After* getting the Key back. *After* her full transition to Keeper.

After...

Except that they weren't supposed to have an *after*. Rhys didn't want her to assume again that she wouldn't survive the transition. He also didn't want to lie to her, even by omission. Going to Hell with a lie on his conscience felt like a shitty strategy.

Not to mention that Maisy didn't deserve anything less than the full truth from him.

Rhys had gone very still. And too silent for too long. Whatever weird, circuitous path his brain had just taken couldn't bode well. He'd been so sweet just moments before. Now his brow was furrowing, and those kissable lips had tightened to a thin line.

Finally, he clasped his hands in his lap. "Maisy. I don't do relationships. Falling in love's a vulnerability for a warrior. Which is all I am."

Here she'd thought Rhys's attempt at a pep talk was as bad as it could get. At least his sharp features were contorted in a grimace that proved he felt...awkward? About doing it?

Good.

"Are you actually breaking up with me? Hours before taking me to Hell? And you expect me to feel safe with you after this?"

"Fuck."

She sprang up, vibrating from head to toe with anger. The hurt would come later. "Your timing is what's fucked."

"No." Now his expression melted, like Munch's famous *The Scream* painting, into abject misery. And...was that a flicker of his wings showing? Wasn't that only supposed to happen if he lost control? "God, no. Maisy, I don't want to be without you. I just don't know how to say it."

"You just did?" She was so confused. In a new habit, her hand went to the security of her evil eye bracelet. If Rhys *wasn't* breaking up, why did his statement sound so dire? Final? Crushing?

"Please, sit down. Hear me out." He waited while she sat. Gingerly. As far away as possible in the cozy seating grouping.

Maisy didn't want to waste any of her suddenly precious time. If this was the precursor to a breakup, she wanted it done as soon as possible. Then she could get on with spending what might be her last night ever with ice cream drizzled with Baileys and her best friend. Liss was downstairs playing pool with Zavier, but she'd give that up in a heartbeat for ice cream.

"What can't you say?"

"I'm going to put this badly, so please, don't react until I get it all out. Hopefully by the end, I'll have made sense."

This was ridiculous. "I thought Zavier said that angels speak every language on earth?"

"Half angel, remember?" He'd barely started to quirk one side of his mouth before he—thankfully—read her stiff body language. "Okay, I get that this is no time to joke. Yes. We can."

"But you can't speak the language of love?"

Rhys arched a single dark eyebrow. "Now who's joking?"

"I'm *really* not."

"Well, then, evidently not. We'll call it unnecessary. Love is a weakness. The need to protect a loved one trumps strategy, practicality. It gives others a way in, to hit at my very heart. That's how it's a vulnerability. That...and wanting to be with someone more than you want to stay and fight another battle."

His summation made her so sad. This was how all the *Nephilim* lived? "Love makes you...lesser?"

"We've always *thought* so," he said cautiously. "Trained under that precept. So there was no possible future for you and me, together. I'd be torn. Half warrior. Half boyfriend. Not doing well enough at either."

"I think you'd excel at that," she said with as much acerbity as a kumquat. Because right now, stitched together like

Frankenstein's creature, he was sucking at both being a warrior *and* a boyfriend. Maisy wasn't content with this watered-down version of him. "You've certainly learned how to balance the whole half-man, half-angel thing. You're uniquely qualified to skate that line."

Rhys rolled his wrist in a "there's more" gesture. "There's also the whole age gap."

Omigosh. Was Rhys worried that *he* was the one dying tomorrow? He sure seemed to be doing his creative best to push her away. If he wasn't so injured, Maisy would beat him with a pillow until his sense returned. "You mean because you're technically old enough to be my grandfather?"

"Yes, but not quite. More that you'll live your life—and then end it sooner than I will mine."

Talk about cutting off your nose to spite your face. Who would've known that angels were as clueless as human men when it came to relationships? "Maybe. Maybe not. Depends on if what Uncle Harold alluded to is true. Perhaps the Keeper gets a certain amount of added longevity." Maisy shook her head. "Still not a reason to *not* be together. So you only get X number of happy years with me. With any significant other. Uh, that's far, far more happy years being loved than you've had up to this point."

The silhouette of his wings flared again. Still just a shadow, but visible. "I asked you to just listen. I'm laying out why this has felt so impossible from the start."

"Okay. Thanks for the recap." Maisy wasn't feeling very charitable toward Rhys or empathizing and stroking his feelings down from being ruffled. His laundry list of why they shouldn't be together was not anywhere on her list of How To Spend Her Possible Last Few Hours.

Rhys scrubbed both hands up and down his face. Huffed out a breath. "The bigger problem is that every day, it feels more and more impossible to *not* be with you."

Her irritation washed away with one gigantic pulse of her

heart. Because his one sentence had just changed everything.

"This is your extraordinarily roundabout way of saying you do want to be with me?" Maisy kept going. There was no room for anything but the utmost clarification at this point. "To have an *after*? Together?"

"Yes." He stood, pacing along the edge of the railing. And for once, the stylish, always put-together man looked a wreck. Only a soft robe topped his navy pajama bottoms. The exertion of going to meet Aradia at the bar had upped his pain levels. His black hair stood in spikes from how often he'd raked his hand through it as his wounds pulsed with healing. Which had been more than a little disgusting as she watched the lines of stitches *actually* quiver and pulse. "I don't know how we'd manage it. I can't promise anything—"

Maisy silenced him with a finger across his lips. "We don't have to know how. Heck, some couples don't figure that out for years. We simply have to know that we *want* to be together."

"Really?"

"Really. I'm not looking for promises, Rhys." Especially since she didn't feel certain that there would be an "after" tomorrow. The intent was enough. "I wasn't looking for any of this. We'll go day by day. Figure this out as partners."

He put a flattened palm right over her heart. As though he needed to feel the rapid beating of it to believe her. "You want it, too?"

Well, that was just too adorable. The big, brawny, lethal half angel needed reassurance that she liked him.

Maisy decided to go with simplicity. Rhys probably couldn't handle, in his relationship-newbie state, a big declaration of her feelings. So she simply echoed him. "Yes."

That was all it took. His wings flared to solidity. The stunning ombre fade of indigo to ice blue ruffled slightly in the spring breeze. Maisy had always been cautious about touching his wings. Always asked first.

Not anymore.

She stepped forward into what could be an embrace, except that she extended her arms in a looser circle to skim her fingers along the curve right where the wings met his spine. Back and forth, luxuriating in that unreal softness on the backs of her hands.

And Rhys? He *wobbled*.

At first, Maisy attributed it to her stellar stroking. Then she remembered that the man had almost died earlier in the day. She jerked back, careful not to touch any part of him. "Am I hurting you?"

"No. I'm fine." With a boyish grin she hadn't seen before, Rhys shook out his limbs like a drunk puppet. "I mean, I'm *actually* fine. The potion's got a powerful kick to it at the end. Kind of an all-clear for your body. Look." He opened the robe. The stitches were still visible, but the wounds weren't even red. The black *X*s of thread looked like someone had taped them onto healthy skin as a special effect for Halloween.

It was Maisy's first real glimpse of the power of magic. Yes, she'd drunk the potions and seen the true demon forms, but it didn't make you *feel* different. Didn't give you the ability to, oh, shoot fire out of your fingertips.

Seeing the healing transformation on Rhys was mind-boggling. Even more so than seeing the demons and her dead uncle's spirit. She could "accept" demons as just another species, like dinosaurs or pangolins. His healing, though—it should've taken weeks.

This new world she lived in scared the pants off of her, but it was also incredible.

"I'm glad you're feeling better." Maisy paused. Took note of the thick trees effectively screening them from any prying eyes. Then she pulled off her tee and pushed his robe the rest of the way off his shoulders. "Because I'd really like to show you how *I* feel. Since, you know, we're sharing and opening up."

"Are you sure?" Rhys had both hands lifted, already brushing the bottom of her jaw, but he stopped. "There is more I could say, Maisy." Then he gave a wry grimace. "No doubt I'd bungle it as badly as I did the first part. I could try, though. Listing your attributes. Your beauty. Your maddening, argumentative side that inflames me. You deserve more."

What more could there be in a man than one who'd put his life on the line for her? Who held her when she cried and rightfully poked at her for not trying hard enough? "You said that you want to be with me. *After.* That's all I need to know."

His fingertips caressed up the back of her skull through her hair. "I'm certain that you're letting me off the hook. Being selfless to keep me from humiliating myself with another attempt at romance. I'm discovering, however, that I'm selfish enough to let you. It's a new feeling, being taken care of. It's...addicting."

"Then I'll continue to do so." Maisy dropped to her knees. Untied his pajama bottoms until they sagged low around his hips. And then, with her palm underneath, guided his heavy weight into her mouth.

His knees wobbled again. This time, she was *certain* it wasn't the potion, because his cock was pulsing on her tongue.

She wrapped one hand around the shaft; the other lightly squeezed his balls. That caused another, stronger twitch, combined with a surge of his hips forward. If she'd been crouching, it might've knocked her off balance. Her *Nephilim* was gratifyingly responsive to her every swirl.

Which made it that much more fun. His fingertips pressed into her scalp when she carefully scraped her teeth around the bulbous tip. The salty taste on her tongue just made Maisy suck harder.

The crisp hair of his thighs rubbed against her bare arms. She couldn't wait to feel it on her legs. Couldn't wait to feel all of him spread across her, so she bobbed her head even faster. Heard a thick, guttural moan break free of his throat...which made her lose her rhythm, because Maisy just had to smile at that.

Yes, she *very* much enjoyed "taking care" of Rhys.

"Maisy. Stop."

"Not yet."

"Right now." He gave an insistent tug backward on her hair. "It is life-and-death. I'll die if I don't get inside you."

Adorable. Totally transparent, but adorable. She leaned back on her heels. "That only works once. You hear me? You can't abuse the *do whatever I say in a life-and-death situation* rule like that. Sex is not that important."

"It is," he insisted. And the urgency in his tone, along with the way his eyes darkened in intensity, told Maisy that he truly was not kidding. "With you, it is. Never before."

Rhys really didn't think he was romantic? Sheesh. Her panties had just melted right off. "You're right. Sex with you is that important to me, too."

The wings disappeared first. Then he slid down until his back was against the railing, legs wide on the floor. "Then climb on."

"That potion really knocked you for a loop. No condom?" She scooted back to the couch, where she'd stashed her bag. Pulled out the long blue strip. "Good thing I loaded up. In, you know, the impossible hope that Zavier was telling the truth when he said you'd be healed by tonight."

Rhys kicked off his bottoms while she rolled the condom on. "Zavier doesn't lie about magic. Gideon, by the way, doesn't lie about sex—but usually sounds as if he's lying."

She straddled his legs and crossed her ankles behind him. "Here's a truth for you. I want more of you, Rhys. More days with you. More nights with you. More laughs, more fights, more kisses, more dinners. More of everything."

He splayed one of his big hands over her heart. "Hang on to that. Looking forward to goodness will be a shield against whatever Hell throws your way."

"But I've already got *you* as my shield." Maisy put her own hand over his heart. "You hold on to it. Think of the promise of getting to have all of that. However we want it. Whatever we make of this. Let it be your strength."

With their hands still connecting their hearts, Maisy impaled herself on Rhys. She rode him slowly. They stared at each other, soaking each other and the moment in. Rhys used his other hand to anchor her hip as she lifted up and down. Her nipples chafed pleasurably against his chest hair with every motion.

And it wasn't until she felt his legs turn to iron under her as he ground out, "My sunshine," that Maisy let her hand drop so she could press as close as possible. As the first quakes of her orgasm overtook her, she held her breath.

It was the only way to feel like the moment wouldn't end.

Even though she knew that it was very possible *everything* was about to end.

CHAPTER TWENTY-TWO

What's the dress code for visiting Hell?

That thought had kept Maisy tossing and turning overnight. Okay, probably a liberal sprinkling of fear of death and accidental everlasting incarceration in Hell also kept her up, but her conscious mind had target-locked on the fashion issue.

She'd thought of classical togas, like Orpheus wore to go after Eurydice in the Underworld. Then layers of khakis and cargo pants and knapsacks like archaeologists digging into the pyramids. A hazmat suit had seemed like a stellar idea around three a.m.—who knew what sort of toxic/noxious gasses were swirling around down there?

In the end? A woman wanted to feel confident as she walked to possible death. Maisy had used her mousse. Flat iron. Liss helped her choose black leggings patterned with bright tropical flowers and a teal tee.

Of course, her lucky rainbow Converse.

Live or die, she was going to do it in the most Maisy way possible.

But now, sitting in a leather chair in the Watchtower's armory, it felt like she'd gone the wrong way. The men wore their fighting gear. All black. Sleek. Weaponed up everywhere she could see and probably several places that she couldn't.

And then, of course, there was Liss, set up at a long table

with all the gift basket contents she'd insisted Zavier lay out for her. She was still in her black bathrobe, since it was still early. Nobody knew how long this trip would last, so she intended to stay busy while waiting for Maisy to return—and make the other two *Nephilim* help her finish stuffing the stress-relief baskets.

Maisy could smell the lavender from across the room. She pointed at Zavier. "Do I need a Kevlar vest, too?"

"No."

Quick shutdown. Like he didn't think it merited discussion. Maisy disagreed. His scowl, crossed arms, and overall IDGAF vibe in no way deterred her from pushing, though, because that was Zavier's vibe twenty-four seven.

"How is that fair?"

"We strategize for a mission that goes well—and for one that goes south. We're dressed for the worst-case scenario." He patted the holsters on both hips. "Volac gets the Key. Gates to Hell's worst prison open. Unimaginable horror suddenly is free on Earth. If that happens, we're ready for battle."

Maisy didn't know any hand-to-hand combat unless you counted the one all women knew—the knee-to-groin move. Who knew if that worked on demons, though? Or what if there was a whole troop of female demons?

Nope, she needed weaponry.

"So...should I take a big purse? Maybe stuffed with a gun and a knife and a snazzy exploding potion?"

"No." This time, it was all three men who'd shut her down, in unison.

"Again, how is that fair?"

Rhys rubbed a hand up and down her forearm. "You don't need it. You're unprepared to fight anything that lives in Hell. You wouldn't survive round one of a hair-pulling contest with a demon."

"Good pep talk," Liss said, tongue in cheek as she joined the group.

Gideon double thumped his sternum. "*We're* planning for the worst because that's our job. To protect humanity at all costs. But we believe in you, Maisy. Sorry—we should've said it sooner. We plan on you getting the Key. Then we can strip out of this gear and celebrate."

"Promise? Everyone strips down—to trunks, of course—and we party in that giant hot tub I spotted on your patio?"

"Yes."

Maisy held up her index finger. "And you promise you can bring me back from my coma?"

This time, there was a slight hesitation before Zavier said, "Yes."

Uh-oh.

Sure, she was committed to this now, but her question had been rote. Like NASA asking if all systems were green before launch, even though they could all see the readouts that everything was good.

"That was less convincing. What's that about?"

Zavier straddled a stool, feet behind him. Then he held up his right hand—adorned in spiked brass knuckles—and ticked off each point of the plan. "You drink the potion that renders you comatose. Rhys flies your soul through the waterfall portal to Hell. You get the Key. He flies you back. We administer the counter potion. That's the plan."

"So why the hesitation? Don't lie," Maisy hurriedly added. "I noticed it."

Liss nodded. "High school teacher, remember? Maisy can spot an obfuscating male at twenty paces."

Gideon crouched next to her. "Our plan is solid, I promise you, but we don't know what your Test will be. Whatever is done to you down there could affect the outcome. Hell is a wild card, to say the least."

"But...this should work, right? *Nephilim* and Keepers have been doing it for centuries. Solid track record of success." Maisy knew she was trying to convince herself as much as the men.

Zavier shrugged one shoulder. "The Transition, sure, but remember, you aren't the direct descendent of the earthbound angel. Your Keeper qualities aren't automatic or full-fledged, for all we know. Your uncle *hoped* choosing you would work. And Keepers haven't had to do it *in* Hell, necessarily."

Why, *why* had she ever asked them not to sugarcoat things? Ignorance really would've been bliss compared to the fear-induced reflux now burbling up her throat.

Rhys slapped his fingerless gloves against his leather pants with a loud snap. "There's no point what if-ing it. There's no other option. Lilith will only hand over the Key—if she's so inclined—in Hell. So let's get going."

"You're right." Taking action helped to quell anxiety. She could either sit here all morning fretting or just go do the thing, which was what she'd tell her students. Don't worry about what you can't control. Simply do what you can. Turned out that talking the talk was *far* easier than walking the walk. His matter-of-factness was just the kick-start she needed. "I'm sorry. I'm, well, nervous."

Rhys was suddenly next to her with his super speed. He braceleted her wrists on the armrests with his hands. "*Use* that. Think about how nervous you are. How knotted your belly is. That your throat's closed. Your heart's racing. Think about how shitty you feel. Then remember that *you* can make it end. You just have to get the Key and then get through the Test."

Checklists were good. She could do this. But she really did need one little smidgen of reassurance. "You won't leave me alone down there?"

"Not intentionally, but if we do get separated, believe that I won't stop until I'm back with you."

"I believe you." She leaned over to tighten her laces. Then she cinched her ponytail tighter. Sure, it was just her soul that was making the trek. Her physical body would stay right here, but Maisy's soul needed to feel locked and loaded, as it were.

Liss gave her a hug that was almost over before it started. "No big goodbyes. Or good luck. You don't need it. The Keeper's supposed to be strong and hopeful. You're annoyingly optimistic, so clearly you're going to do great. And you *will* get a whopper of a hug once you're back."

No goodbyes. Well, that made it easier. Pressure enough to defeat the wily machinations of demons and witches and children of Lucifer. Coming up with a succinct yet heartfelt speech on the fly would've been almost impossible.

After a final, reassuring clasp of her Keeper bracelet, she nodded. "I'm ready."

"No, you're not."

Rhys bracketed her knees with his, then leaned forward. Gave her a devastatingly slow and thorough kiss.

Huh. That was even better than a pep talk.

Gideon handed her a shot glass with Niagara Falls etched across it. Sure, a kitschy souvenir seemed appropriate for a drink to send her to Hell. It contained a pale blue liquid that matched the tips of Rhys's wings. "Good luck, Maisy."

"Kick some ass," Zavier added.

Fearful of its flavor, she downed it like a shot.

Felt…nothing.

Blinked.

When Maisy opened her eyes, she was in Rhys's arms as he approached the powerful cascade of Niagara Falls. She felt like normal. Looked normal. But she'd definitely lost minutes of unconsciousness, if he'd picked her up, walked through the rooms, and launched.

"Am I…"

"At least a hundred pounds lighter? Yes."

"Rude." But she appreciated his teasing jab. It was what they did. It was habitual—

Without feeling a drop of moisture, they were through the

waterfall. She knew that the portal on the other side fed into the River Styx. No clue where the water originated that tumbled over a cliff.

This side of it was gray. All of it. Looking over Rhys's shoulder, she saw that the waterfall itself was gray, as were the rocks on the edges of it. As was the river. As were the cavernous walls that climbed up to an uneven, pockmarked ceiling.

It was hard to see much, though. The gray landscape kept being obscured with random billows of smoke. Almost like tiny geysers going off.

Hellfire smoke? Official, spoken of in myth and lore and legend through all of history, smoke from the ever-burning pits of fire in Hell?

That was sobering.

It made her wish she'd gone with the hazmat suit.

Rhys set her down. It was beyond tempting to jump right back into the safety of his arms, but this was one of the times in life that called for officially donning the (metaphorical) big-girl panties. Her actual panties were black satin. With tiny bows that would hopefully drive Rhys wild. Just in case there was a celebration later tonight.

Maisy didn't even hold his hand. From here on out, she knew everything rested solely on her shoulders. She was prepared for whatever.

Except...the random smoke billows had ramped up. She could barely see two steps ahead as the gray smoke gusted, thicker and thicker. Hollow echoes of wind that she couldn't feel whipped against the rocks.

No more gawking. Get in, get out, get un-coma-fied.

"Where do I go? Did you take us through the right portal exit? Shouldn't we be able to see the Gates? Or is this one of those things where they're actually the size of an atom and I just have to intuit where they are?"

Rhys scowled—as she knew he would from her dig at his

directional choice. "We're in the right place. There are only two entrances *Nephilim* can use. Think of this as the lobby to Hell's prison. It reforms for each who comes. When the smoke clears, it'll be the prison you need to see."

"Great. Maybe the whole cast of *Orange Is the New Black* will greet me. That's something I need to see."

The smoke vanished. All at once. The river, the waterfall, and the rocky cavern were also gone. As was the constant *whoosh* of the wind.

They were in a hallway. Institutional. Narrow. Low-ceilinged with, yep, gray walls and gray linoleum. And an annoying but barely discernible hum, like off fluorescent lights.

But the walls on both sides were lined with very colorful paintings.

Paintings that looked a lot like what she'd done in school. Not just stylistically similar. No, these were *her* paintings. Years' worth.

How could that be?

Maisy had no idea how they'd gotten there. Hell hadn't cheaped out on the framing, either. Each frame was the perfect accompaniment to the image. Some stark black glass. Some were wide and ornate rococo gold that looked museum worthy.

She turned in a slow circle, her sneakers squeaking. "How... what..."

"The lobby presents as a prison of the mind. I couldn't tell you. You'd start thinking about your greatest fears and end up in a pit full of poisonous snakes or something. Plus, the prison only forms for one person in the group. I'd hoped it would target my angelic blood and choose me as the greater danger."

Whatever.

Her paintings were far more interesting than Rhys's excuses.

Maybe that was a little harsh. She'd been counting on the comfort of having Rhys by her side in Hell.

As Maisy kept walking down the hallway, she didn't see a

door at the end of it. Or a turn. But she *did* see paintings on the walls now that she'd only imagined over the years.

Ones she'd dismissed as being too big an undertaking. Too time-consuming. Too far beyond her talent. Colorful splashes that would haunt her on the nights when sleep wouldn't come. Vibrant landscapes of places she'd never been and wasn't sure even existed.

They were everything she could paint in the course of her life. *If* she had the time. *If* she could stop working other jobs and focus purely on making art. *If* she had just a bit more talent.

If she stopped having sex with the *Nephilim* and applied herself.

Maisy shook her head. Why were these thoughts popping into her brain? She'd had issues with painting long before meeting Rhys. It wasn't his fault.

It was very much her own stupid fault.

Maisy's hands fisted at her sides. Seeing her old paintings had been nice. Like discovering a shirt in the back of a drawer you hadn't worn in a while. But seeing the paintings she'd wanted to paint and hadn't?

That wasn't nice.

It was, in fact, torture. The torture of what *could* be. All the images that tortured her with undoable possibilities when she was drifting off to sleep were a million times worse lined up in front of her.

"Maisy? Maisy, we should keep going. Hell's not a place that rewards loitering."

Classic Rhys. Trying to order her around. Insistent that his plan was the only plan. Not bothering to take the time to appreciate life.

Wait. She clenched her fists, digging her fingernails into her skin. That wasn't how she felt about Rhys. Was Hell itself poisoning her against him?

Maisy shook out her hands. The hands that now itched with

the need to hold a brush. Well, this was *her* journey to become Keeper. They were on *her* timetable now. And that included time to soak in all this amazing artwork.

It wasn't like she planned to come back to Hell anytime soon to be able to see them again...

An easel appeared, right in front of her. Good-quality stretched canvas on it. A stool. A table full of tubes of paint, her three favorite brushes, and a palette. A damp rag hung over the side, anchored by the palette knife. Even a sweating glass of iced tea.

It was precisely how Maisy set up her own station at home. This was a gift. Here she was, surrounded by inspiration. She could see how spectacularly they'd turn out, but it wasn't enough that they already hung on the walls.

No.

She needed the pleasure of *creating* them. It didn't even matter which one she started with. She could hang out here and do all of them. And the one she hadn't even seen.

The most important one.

Maisy grabbed for the brush. It fit in the crook of her thumb and index finger with such ease. She lifted the palette. Inhaled deeply the sharp scent of the oil paint. Took note of the colors already daubed on. Turquoise. Teal. Seafoam green. Viridian. Ultramarine. Yellow ocher.

Ah. She knew where to start.

This was an image that she'd dreamed all her life. Over and over and over again. At least once a week? It was one of those maddening dreams that was completely familiar when she was in it, but when Maisy woke up, the only thing that stuck with her was a hint of color and the deep certainty that she'd repeated the same dream before.

Now she remembered.

A great key, burnished to a soft antique gold. It was the centerpiece of the image. It hovered in air—or underwater; the colors were too similar to differentiate. Beautiful swirls of all the colors currently on her palette.

Kelp? Trees? Stood tall around it. The bottom of the key rooted into the ground, spreading thick and wide and strong.

It had always seemed impossible to capture the mystic vibrancy of the colors. Now, though, Maisy didn't have to guess or hope she got it right. She *knew* the exact proportions of each shade to mix and swirl and dab.

She started painting. The sensation of the soft brush bristles sweeping against the taut canvas sent goose bumps of pleasure up her arms. Oh, and the light overhead adjusted to be both warm and bright without casting any shadows from her hand.

"Maisy. There's no time for this. You can paint later. Lilith's waiting to meet us. We should keep moving." Rhys's voice had that annoying, stuffy professorial edge to it. Happily, it wasn't as loud as usual. Much easier to ignore. Thankfully, he was halfway down the hall from her now.

The walls full of her other, imagined artwork faded away. That was fine.

Maisy didn't need to see those paintings anymore. They'd reminded her of what was important. Of the myriad tempting possibilities. It didn't matter that the barren Hellscape was back, surrounding her. There was light on her canvas. Fresh paint on her palette. It was all she needed.

She finished the Key. It was so beautiful. One of the best things she'd ever painted—in perspective and color palette and artistry. It'd been a warm-up, a way to see if her ability really was greater.

Now, she could finally paint a portrait of her parents that would do them justice. One that she could remember them by *forever.*

"Remember the mission," Rhys insisted. "That horrific demons will be let free to unleash literal Hell on Earth if you don't get the Key back from Lilith."

Couldn't he stop telling her what to do for five damn minutes? "I can paint and get the Key back. There's time enough for everything." He worried too much. Overthought everything. Talk about someone who needed to lose himself in a great work of art.

Good thing she was making one right now.

"Then get the Key *first*!" Rhys shouted. "You can keep painting after."

Omigosh. There was no point in arguing with the stubborn *Nephilim*. Far easier to ignore him. Just like she was ignoring the screaming, agonized souls that paraded by on the edges of her periphery.

But he was just trying, in his heavy-handed way, to look out for her. That was sweet. So she'd throw him a bone. Explain what should be excruciatingly obvious.

Maisy tucked her brush behind her ear. Gave him her most winsome smile. "I'm not doing this for me, Rhys. These paintings I'm making? They'll be magnificent. And it *feels* so good. Knowing that they'll bring people joy. Better than ever before. *I'm* painting better than ever. I could paint like this forever." Except for this painting of her parents. It was just for her. If it turned out as well as she planned, she might just spend a solid month staring at it down here, feeling almost like they were back with her.

His wings, which he'd tucked away as soon as they'd landed, unfurled with an audible pop and a whoosh. His arms flew wide as well. "That's the danger, Maisy. You've fallen into your own prison. Of ego and lust. Feeling successful doesn't mean that you are. It doesn't mean it'll make you happy, either. You could be stuck, right here, forever. Stuck with that single emotion."

Paging Mr. Worst-Case Scenario. Oh, wait—he was already here. "There are worse things. I could be stuck on a broken roller coaster teetering at the top of a hill. Or stuck working the counter at a discount shoe store. Or—have sympathy for me, because this one actually happened to me—stuck at a rock concert next to a guy who puked up all his beer."

Their forms had taken no time to whip out, and now their faces were really taking shape. By the amount that was filled in and the Key painting, she'd say at least an hour should've passed. Funny how it only felt like five minutes. Her arm wasn't even tired. She could keep going like this for *ages*.

But when she twisted the brush around in her grip, a splinter snagged her thumb. Blood dripped onto the canvas.

When she blinked again, her parents were there, standing just off to the side of the easel.

"Maisy, my darling. We've missed you so." Her mom's voice was so *right*. It was her. From her red hair to the silly red-and-green taffeta skirt she wore every Christmas to the wedding rings Maisy had cried about when she'd realized they'd been buried.

It was wonderful to see them, but it was *wrong*. They weren't damned souls. They weren't evil or bad. Nothing about their appearance made sense.

"Mom? Dad? Why are you here? Stuck in Hell? It has to be a mistake. I'll work it out and get you released. I promise."

Her dad held up a hand. Old habits kicked in, and she stayed seated at the easel. "You already did. *You* released us from the prison of death, Maisy. You brought us back to life with the power of your painting."

Rhys pushed his way into her field of vision. Again. His hands were fisted at his sides. Veins corded down the length. Mmm. When she was ready to take a break, once this painting was done...and maybe two or three more...he'd be a good distraction.

"Maisy!"

"Don't yell at me." Insufferable man. "You should come around and look at the Key I painted. See how beautifully the colors are melding together." That was obviously the problem. He hadn't seen the scope of what she was doing, but couldn't he see her parents? The man was being *rude*.

Maisy started to get up. Discovered that she seemed to be

glued to the seat. Which was fine. She'd only been going for a hug from her mom. Staying in place, in front of the canvas, felt right, too. Especially with her thumb still pressed to it, blood seeping into the fabric and slowly mirroring the shape of her parents.

"I'm sorry. Rhys has a one-track mind. I think you'll like him, though. I mean, he's an angel, even if an imperfect one. That's got to rank higher than bagging a doctor or a lawyer for a boyfriend, right?"

The warmth of her mom's smile was like a rainbow chasing away damp after a storm. Especially since she'd gotten so much colder on the inside. "We just want you to be happy, Maisy. You don't need a man to make you happy. You have us."

"I know. But you and Dad had such a great marriage. That's what I want. Someday."

Her mother shifted, blocking her view of Rhys. "You don't need him. We're a family again. The three of us. We love you. We're happy right here, with you. We can be this happy forever."

Rhys's voice carried over her mom's. "Remember how hard you fought to not give up your crappy gift-basket job for the past few weeks? The *actual* fate of the world rests on your shoulders, and you refused to shirk and skip a day. So let's continue with today's job. Getting the Key."

Her poor parents. Being ignored by him. "That was the old me. Consider that I've now taken your exhortations to heart. I'm going to stay right here until I'm done."

"With what? With one painting? Ten? Fifty?"

His question scratched at Maisy's brain like a mosquito bite. Worse than that, it made her set her brush on the lip of the easel to consider. It was such a hard question. Pain lanced at both temples the more she considered it.

Her parents shifted to black-and-white images rather than the full color she'd painted them.

"If you stop, Maisy, we'll be gone again. For good, this time." Her dad's voice hardened. Bludgeoned. "And it will be *your* fault."

"Maisy," Rhys barked. "This is taking too long. Lilith won't wait. If she gets antsy, she may give the Key to Volac. You need to be done!"

"I'm not. I don't know when I will be. I just have to paint." There. That made the pain dissipate. And her parents shot back through into bright reds and pinks and blacks.

"Wrong again. Focus on that overcharged sense of responsibility of yours and do your job as Keeper. Forget the 'what if' in favor of the 'what now.'"

"You're not listening to me, Rhys. As usual. What now? I'm painting now; that's what." She was keeping her parents alive. Couldn't he *see* that?

"Choose us, Maisy. That *Nephilim* doesn't matter. Only us." Her mom rested her head against her husband's shoulder. It was a gesture Maisy had witnessed countless times. It was comforting. It was grounding.

But...she still didn't understand why they were in Hell. It was like adding five and seven and insisting the answer was ten. And things were *really* confusing when Maisy resorted to math comparisons.

She turned, just a bit, on the stool. She might want to look around her mother to Rhys. Just to explain things. Her mother suddenly had a gray haze around the edges.

"You can paint later, too, but there are other things you like. If you stay down here, just painting, you'll miss so much." The sharp break in Rhys's voice had her looking at him for the first time. Looking *away* from the painting for the first time. He was so much brighter than her parents. "You'll be giving up on so much goodness. And you're the one who searches out the goodness in every person, in every situation. Don't give that up, sunshine. I'm begging you."

Rhys flew at her—literally *flew*—knocking the canvas to the floor. With a cry, Maisy stood. And that's when he grabbed her shoulders and kissed her.

She leaned into him, soaking up the length and strength of his body even as she melded to his mouth. It was a good kiss.

Rhys knew his way around a pair of lips.

But it wasn't the physical that struck her so much as the *feeling* he poured into the kiss. The sensation reminded Maisy of the potion she'd taken to give her the ability to see auras. Down here, she *knew* every emotion Rhys was feeling in the moment. The raw panic, the lust, the desperation, the want, the need, the uncertainty.

Most of all, though? The happiness. The warmth that pulsed out of his heart every second they were together.

And she felt cold, dark nothingness emanating from the... things that were her parents. Well, the things masquerading as her parents. Even though she knew there was no way the people she'd loved were in front of her, it ripped at her heart saying goodbye to their faces.

She didn't know if words would send them away.

She did know that she couldn't let them vanish without saying it, for herself. For the tween version of herself who'd been in the hospital and unable to say goodbye at their funeral.

With a tight grip on Rhys's hand, Maisy said, "I'm sorry. I love you. I'll cherish your memories forever, but I have to keep the world safe."

That snapped her out of what she suddenly realized had been a kind of trance. The floor undulated, breaking them apart. Rhys flared his wings to return to her side.

"You came back to me." His hair was rumpled and his face sweaty. And the relief smoothing out the wrinkles on his forehead was as soothing to her as icy lemonade on a summer day.

Belated panic knotted her stomach as Maisy realized how close she'd come to being stuck in that hallway, painting forever. How close she'd come to never seeing Rhys again. "Well, I wouldn't want to be the only black mark on your successful mission stats."

With another undulation of the earth, the easel vanished. There was only grayness and rocks for as far as the eye could see.

Until she turned around.

The Gates shimmered in front of her—two sets. The ones closest to her were shiny silver. The next set were pure flame. A tall figure that surely had to be Volac stood just beyond them.

Guess this was it.

Maisy just hoped those admittedly beautiful gates weren't the last things she'd ever see.

CHAPTER TWENTY-THREE

Rhys needed a time-out.

He'd never felt the urge to ask for a break in the middle of a mission before, but standing there, helpless to get through to Maisy for three long hours had almost broken him. He was sweating. His muscles ached from tensing them nonstop.

Her not wanting to be interrupted had created a force field around her that had snapped into place the moment she saw her paintings.

He'd been terrified.

That was new.

Rhys hadn't felt that level of uncontrollable fear in more than half a century. In every battle, he knew his abilities—and those of Gideon and Zavier—would either see him through to fight another day, or they wouldn't.

Today, that hadn't been an acceptable scenario.

He'd fought with all his strength. Nothing had worked. He'd worked so hard to ignore the parental demons she'd blood-summoned. Any attention he'd given them would've made them more real. But how did you fight against something without recognizing it at all?

He'd been tempted to go back and get Zavier to help, but Rhys wasn't certain he'd be able to find her again.

His strength hadn't made a difference.

It was his one *weakness*—how much he cared for Maisy—that had reached her.

He.

Was.

Exhausted.

Rhys wanted to do nothing more than hold Maisy close and breathe her in. And she had to be twice as drained. There were still tear tracks down her face from her encounter.

Instead?

There was *this* guy. Volac. A few extra folds on his saggy gray face, but it was a little hard to discern much beneath the ubiquitous black hooded robe. He held a staff, which was never good. It could just be window dressing to intimidate the human. Or it could be a supremely effective way to boost his power.

"*Nephilim*," he intoned in a deep, hollow voice that still conveyed a world of insult in the single word.

Rhys never bothered to get insulted by whatever one of Hell's minions said. "Volac." He angled toward Maisy and gave a half bow. "This is Maisy Norgate, the new Keeper. In case you missed that part when you inhabited that lawyer."

"We shall see," he said in a monotone that also made it clear he didn't believe it would come to pass. "From what I hear, she's the *second* choice—the backup Keeper. Not enough to worry me."

A woman appeared in the no-man's-land between the two sets of Gates. "Don't start, you two. I've sat through plenty of dick-measuring contests in my day, and they were all a waste of time."

Lilith.

Whether or not it was her true form, she looked a lot like the nineteen-forties actress Rita Hayworth. Long, wavy red hair. Generous lips. A va-va-voom figure poured into a floor-length, see-through black robe and tiny scalloped bra and panties. Seemed about right for a woman whose many titles included demon of chaos and sexual seduction.

Most importantly, she waved what had to be the Key overhead.

Maisy straightened next to him. Tightened her ponytail. "This isn't about the men. The Key is rightfully mine."

"Ah, the little human." She sashayed right up to the silver gates. "Aradia told me you had moxie. That you might actually be worthy. I'm certainly impressed that you were brave enough to accept the challenge of meeting me in Hell."

"Well, I haven't had much of a chance to travel. Thought I'd cross a new destination off my list."

Rhys bit back a snort. That was his woman, all right. Sassing in the face of danger and demons. He'd even call it her signature move.

Lilith gave an approving nod. Waited for her hair to finish artfully cascading in actual slow motion to drape across her breast before saying, "I might like you very much."

"Then we're all good?" Maisy dusted off her hands. "You'll give me the Key?"

"Not yet." She swished away to go back to the dead center between the Gates.

Maisy walked right up to the Gates. Raised her hands to grab on but then dropped them. Probably afraid the things would burn her. Honestly? Rhys had no idea if they were safe for her, even on this side. He wanted to edge up next to her, just in case.

But he *also* didn't want Volac or Lilith to think that Maisy *needed* protecting. Posturing in front of demons was complicated.

With a patient half smile that no doubt had been practiced on her students, Maisy said, "I really hate to be one of those annoying people who repeat themselves, but it *is* rightfully mine."

"I really don't care. At this moment, it is *mine*." Lilith waggled it again overhead. Gave another hip pop. Rhys wasn't sure if it was for his benefit or Volac's, or simply centuries of ingrained habit.

"Volac already has his Key." The patience had evaporated from Maisy's tone. It'd been replaced by righteous indignation.

Seriously, there should be popcorn for this show. The way she stood up to one of the oldest creatures alive, with an evil child of Lucifer just beyond... Watching Maisy go at it energized Rhys and was simply flat-out fun.

"I want yours." It came out just as hollow and monotone as everything else Volac had said. His arms were tucked into the bell sleeves. And...*things* were starting to crawl out from beneath the hem of his robe. Fat and wide like slugs, but with fast-moving centipede-esque legs and flaming red.

Definitely spooky.

Fortunately, Maisy seemed to be far more on the side of pissed off than spooked by him.

"Omigosh. Even a toddler is aware that you can't always get what you want. A sentiment so true that one of the most iconic rock bands ever wrote a song about it. We both know you don't need a second Key. How about you try acting your age? A little maturity, hmm?"

This time, Rhys didn't hold back his snort. It wasn't every day a child of Lucifer got put in his place by a thirty-year-old human female in rainbow sneakers. He was beginning to think they'd get out of here unscathed. Successful.

Of course, that feeling was usually followed by mere seconds before everything about a mission went to shit...

Maisy held out both hands, beseechingly, to Lilith. "The Key you're holding belongs to the side of good. To the human world. To *protect* the world. A world full of witches who worship you. A world full of innocents."

Lilith tucked the Key in her cleavage. "I'm far less interested in hearing your plea, and much more interested in hearing what each of you will offer me for it."

Oh, for fuck's sake. Rhys couldn't stop himself from interrupting. "You want to be *bribed*?"

"I want to be...rewarded. A finder's fee, for keeping something so valuable quite safe." And she patted where it nestled between her breasts.

Safe? Hardly. That spot had seen more traffic than the road to Mecca, the I-95 corridor, and the Silk Road combined.

"Oh." Maisy scratched at her temple. "I thought this was like a debate—the most fervently proposed request wins. I wish you'd been clearer about that to Aradia. I would've prepared a list. I definitely would've brought you a stellar gift basket."

Rhys knew better.

Unless it was something under lock and key, like the Hope Diamond or the long-missing Amber Room from Russia's Catherine Palace, Lilith would've gotten it herself already. No, she'd want something impossible—or impossibly daunting.

Good thing he was there to conduct a negotiation. One far outside Maisy's experience. Under no condition would they accede to her first request. Or even her tenth. Rhys would bargain Lilith down, no matter how long it took.

When the witch smiled, it was easy to see how she'd seduced men since the dawn of time. Rhys noted that the humanity in him was enticed by her. To an uncomfortable extent. Good thing his angelic blood would keep him impervious to her tricks.

"I would have been charmed by a gift basket. I would have appreciated the effort, but beyond that, it would not sway me. What I want from you, Maisy Norgate, is a sacrifice. If you demur, then I make the same offer to Volac." She gestured behind her with a twist of the wrist at the hooded figure.

Maisy audibly cracked her jaw, flexing it from side to side. "That's...disturbing. A human sacrifice?" Scuttling backward, she asked Rhys in a stage whisper, "Does she mean a pinkie toe or something?"

Again, he wished he knew. "Probably not. What would she do with it?"

But if she did? It'd damn well be *his* toe, not hers, that got chopped off. No discussion on that front.

Lilith appeared amused. Or her seductive half smirk was just how her face fell after so long. "What I desire is of far greater value. No riches; no physical sacrifice. It must be something that matters—quite a lot—to she who gives it. And willingly."

Maisy's bluster evaporated. Her shoulders hunched forward. "I...I don't have anything that matters that much. I don't have very much at all."

Steepling her hands, Lilith brought them to her lips as if about to share a profound concept. "It is not *things* that stay with a person to their deathbed. It is experiences. Feelings. Joy and love and laughter. What I would like is for you to give up all the memories of your parents. To give them to me."

Rhys was ready to shoot out an arm to steady Maisy, but she didn't sway backward in shock as he'd anticipated. He could at least buy her some time to process the absurd request. "Why?" he bit out.

"They will provide me a buzz—a charge from the stored-up love. What humans would equate to the high brought about by doing drugs. This would be far stronger and last much longer, though." This time, her smile bared her teeth in a way that made obvious the demonic underpinnings beneath that pretty facade. "Knowing the pain that giving them up causes her will sweeten the gift all the more."

Good thing those Gates stood between him and Lilith, or else Rhys would've charged her right then and there.

Nephilim didn't generally pick fights with the creatures of Hell. They had their hands full when called on to play defense against them.

He'd be willing to make an exception, however. No matter how this exchange turned out, Lilith had just made an enemy. A dangerous, vengeful one.

Three, actually. Gideon and Zavier would absolutely get on board. Her downfall was no longer a question of *if*, merely *when*. Rhys would make sure of it.

He turned to the resolute, brave woman at his side. This

woman who'd initially tried to slough off any and all responsibility to her inheritance of the role. Now here she was, her first trip to Hell, already being forced into an unfathomable sacrifice. She astounded him.

That wasn't just a sacrifice. Hell, giving up an entire foot would be easier. It was the worst possible thing to demand of Maisy.

And Rhys couldn't let her even entertain the thought of going through with it. It was too much. It couldn't be part of the usual Transition and Testing. After all, they'd fallen ass-backward into this situation. They'd regroup and come up with another way to get the Key.

Or...

Fuck.

Was it part of the Testing? That all of this had been fated from the start? Was Maisy's test more challenging because she wasn't the direct descendent of the Keeper? That significantly lowered the odds of them finding an alternative.

Still, Rhys grabbed her wrist and said, "Maisy, you don't have to do this."

"Of course you don't," Lilith agreed with a flutter of her lashes. "Free will and all that jazz. Who knows? Perhaps Volac won't accede to my request, either. Then we'll go around again. And again. But eventually? One of you will agree to my terms. I will wait as long as it takes for my reward."

Volac's arm lifted...and then disintegrated. As the shreds of it fell, it reformed into more of those many-legged slugs. The same happened to his other arm. Now he was a single column, surrounded by a moat of the disgusting things. "I don't like to wait."

Almost under her breath, Maisy said, "He's stuck in Hell. Isn't waiting forever sort of the name of the game in these parts?"

The echoes of wind careening off the rocky cliffs had been a steady background ever since the art-laden hallway melted away.

But now, another layer of sound added on.

A growl.

One so menacing that the tiniest feathers by Rhys's spine raised like goose bumps.

It was low. Wet. Rough. And somehow it sounded like three growls sandwiched unevenly on top of one another.

From the swirling smoke behind the fiery Gates, a shadow charged.

It was a hellhound. Bigger than a lion on steroids. Mangy, matted gray fur. Triple rows of razor-sharp teeth. Rhys had fought hellhounds a few times. They weren't easy to bring down. He flicked his wrists to bring his daggers down from their arm sheaths into his palms.

Hopefully the silver Gates would prevent the escape of any Hell creatures.

Trusting in "hopefully" hadn't kept him alive for this long, though. Especially as the hound charged right through the set of fiery Gates. Its fur smoked and sizzled, but it continued for its now obvious target—*Lilith*.

Maisy shrieked. "Do something!"

He didn't want to let her down. She trusted him to do the bodyguard thing.

Hell had rules, though. Lines he could and could not cross due to his angelic and human construct. So Rhys didn't move a muscle. "I can't. She's in a space that exists between good and evil. There's nothing I can do while she's in there."

"You and your rules. Good thing I don't know 'em all—and I don't see it that way."

The beast stopped, its drooling, gaping jaws an inch from Lilith. Then it looked back at Volac for a command. Volac, who had now disintegrated into an entire writhing column of the slugs. Lilith let out an unending and definitely inhuman high scream and pressed herself against the silver Gates.

Maisy grabbed her under her arms. She tried to pull the

demoness through the bars. The thing about well-made prison Gates, though, was that the bars were close enough together to prevent a body from just sidling through.

"Get back," he cautioned. "You don't need to be that close to the hound."

"I really think I do."

Simultaneously, Volac's semblance of a face reformed into a ghoulish smile. He waved his arm appendage in a go-ahead gesture to the beast. About half of the slugs on the ground broke off and rushed through the fiery Gates.

Fuck.

When in another form, Volac was able somehow to subvert the rules. Those slugs were headed right for them. For *Maisy*. Rhys didn't know what they were, but he was damned sure they were venomous, if not fatal to a human. Maybe a venom that could keep her down in Hell for the rest of her life.

He had no idea how to save her. At the rate they were covering ground, they'd be through the silver Gates in seconds. Rhys couldn't attack them until they breached, but they'd probably swarm Maisy first.

And then Maisy stuck her ridiculous rainbow sneaker through the Gates and gave a mighty kick.

Rhys leaped into action. He encircled her waist with his arm to drag her out of danger.

But he was too late.

When her foot connected with the hound's body, a stream of light erupted. The golden burst disintegrated the hellhound in the blink of an eye. The burst also obliterated all the slugs in the no-man's-land.

"No!" Volac yelled. He partially became a human-type body again, but with gaping holes that revealed where his slugs were now missing. It was even more disgusting. He wrapped his hands around the fiery rods of the Gates, his sagging face twisted in pain.

Lilith slid to the ground, her back still pressed against the silver Gates. He didn't see any blood—or whatever could be dripping out of her—so Rhys assumed she was simply in shock.

She wasn't the only one.

Momentum and training carried Rhys and his armful of Maisy several yards away before stopping and returning to the gates. He wasn't at all eager to let go of her, but he did. Because down here, she was the Keeper. She had to present as the one in charge. As being wholly capable.

Which he no longer doubted.

Quietly, he asked, "Are you okay?"

Maisy's head was all the way down. Pointed right at her shoe. "I think so. My foot feels normal. It looks normal, aside from the gray smudges from all this dirt, but...you saw what happened, right? I didn't hallucinate it or go into another trance like in the hallway?"

"Not a trance. Saw the whole thing. Will be replaying it in my head for the rest of my life as one of my top five favorite battle moments. When Maisy Norgate came into her power—without even realizing it."

She circled her foot a few times in each direction. "I don't know what I did, what that was, or how to do it again. Why didn't that happen when the *Aldokriz* demon attacked and I thought it'd kill me?"

"I can explain." Lilith pulled herself up on the bars. Dusted off her dress. Then patted her cleavage to make sure the Key was still secured.

"Why should we believe you? After how cruel you're being with your demand?"

Good for Maisy. Even stunned, she wasn't letting Lilith use any of her tricks.

"You saved me." She folded her hands over her heart and gave a small bow. "I'm very grateful, child. I've been around a long time. I have knowledge that you, obviously, are lacking. It will be the truth."

"All right. So what was that shooting out of my foot?"

"Keepers are imbued with a shard of the First Light. Any demon they touch will be destroyed."

Rhys had been along to protect her this whole time, but he'd had no idea that she could protect *herself*. The First Light was the purest brightness. It was what shone from angels' halos. To say it was a powerful weapon was like calling Lake Erie a puddle.

Maisy clicked her heels together. Waited. Of course, nothing happened. "I've been attacked more than a few times since I got that Key. Why didn't it work until now?"

"You were unaware of this power?"

Maisy opened her mouth, closed it, and then nodded. "Let's just say the Key didn't come with a user's manual."

Rhys didn't love that she'd admitted that. On the other hand, he did believe in the depth of Lilith's gratitude. She wasn't known for lying—only switching sides as it suited her best. Clearly, they were on her good side.

For the moment.

Lilith looked back at Volac, then at the stirred-up dust where the hellhound had disappeared. "You weren't trying to save yourself just now. You were defending someone else. That's what triggered your power. Your selfless intent."

"Is that the only way I can use it?"

"No. You can defend yourself now. Or, soon. You'll have to train to get control of it. I'd recommend using your hands rather than your feet next time. With time and practice, you'll be able to wield it as neatly as your *Nephilim* does his daggers."

Maisy walked right up to her. Extended a hand but kept it an inch away from Lilith's skin. "Did I hurt you?"

"No, child." She patted Maisy on the forearm. There was no scheming behind her black eyes. Only kindness. "Your intent focused the power on the hound, but I'm touched that you'd ask."

"Then this is one heck of a kick-butt ability." She aimed

a cocky smile at Rhys. "What've you got that I can practice evaporating? A few dozen empty shipping containers?"

Lilith grabbed at her wrist. And the openness on her face hardened into a mask. "Not so fast. There's still a transaction at stake."

Maisy's jaw dropped. Rhys heard it snap, even though Lilith's lightning-fast switch didn't surprise him one bit. "You won't give me the Key for saving your life? Even after Volac tried to kill you to get it?"

"The information about your power was my thanks. Volac's heavy-handed attempt was merely a typical temper tantrum. If the hound had killed me, he wouldn't have gotten the Key." She waggled an admonishing finger at the evil angel. "It must be given willingly, remember?"

"I would have found a way." Volac's holes hadn't filled in. It made his speech mushy. Rhys wondered if he'd eventually heal or be stuck in this incomplete form forever. That'd no doubt make him more inclined to seek out vengeance on Maisy.

Lilith laughed with genuine humor, like Volac had told a fart joke. "Nobody has since the dawn of time. Do you really believe you're smarter than all those who came before you?"

"It matters not. If the human gives you her memories, I'll win because she'll no longer be *worthy* of being Keeper—she won't have enough love left in her heart."

Maisy's hand flew to her chest, double patting right on top of her heart. "That's a thing? My love tank has to be topped off to Transition fully to become the Keeper?"

"It is the balance, you see," Lilith said. "Hell's Keeper is full of hate. In opposition to that, Heaven's Keeper is full of love. All kinds of love. Love of the beauty of a spring morning. The love given to you by a friend. As well as more physical sorts of love." Lilith swung her hips in a circle. Shimmied. Winked.

Yeah, they got it.

No matter what she offered, he wasn't buying.

"We need a minute." Rhys tugged at Maisy until she left the Gates and stepped back into the swirling gray smoke with him. "You can't trust Lilith. I know you hate it when I tell you what to do, but for once, please listen to me."

She rolled her eyes as if they were back in his apartment instead of facing down pure evil in Hell. "I always *listen* to you. I just don't always react the way you're hoping."

That attitude killed him. Combined with the eyes that...holy shit, her eyes were glowing. The green ring around the brown looked lit up from behind. Must be a residual from her burst of power.

God, he wanted her. He wanted the *after* they'd promised each other. But that would only happen if she turned Lilith down. Rhys didn't know who she'd be without the grounding love of her parents to fall back on.

Yes, he needed her to step up and fully be the Keeper.

But he needed her to fully be Maisy *more*.

"Those memories are all you have left of your parents. Those memories are what helped shape you. They continue to shape the person you are to this day. They mean too much to give away. Don't do it," he said, even though he knew deep down it wouldn't do a lick of good. Maisy would do what she believed was right.

Saving the entire world from demons? Yeah, she'd choose that.

And he'd lose her—the intrinsic caring, wonderful pieces that made her the woman he was falling in love with—forever.

CHAPTER TWENTY-FOUR

Maisy couldn't believe that Rhys was *encouraging* her to walk away from this deal. He'd never so much as blinked away from his single-minded goal of getting her fully installed as Keeper before. But now?

He was worried about her.

Talk about a romantic gesture!

Sure, the smoky, dusty, terror-filled surroundings weren't romantic, but her heart swelled nonetheless. This man *got* her.

Except for the part where he was wholly wrong.

She gripped her hands together tightly. "Look, I swear I'm not arguing just for the fun of it. However...I don't believe you."

"Why am I not surprised?" Rhys shook her arms. A deep scowl creased his forehead. His eyes burned with frantic energy. "Maisy, I'm trying to *save* you."

"I can tell. And I'm very appreciative. I just don't need saving right now. Yes, it's a sacrifice. Especially after just seeing them, talking to them."

"You know those were demons, right? Manifestations, but definitely not even a little bit your parents."

"I figured it out. Eventually. I can't imagine living without those *real* memories."

"Then don't. We'll fly out of here."

The desperation in his tone choked her up. Didn't change her resolve, though. Maisy triple blinked to clear the tears welling up along her lower lids.

"I want them, Rhys. I don't want to give up a single memory of a pancake breakfast or bedtime hugs or the pride in their faces when they saw my sketches. Where I disagree with you is that I don't *need* them. My parents' love was wonderful, but it's a drop in the bucket. There's love and goodness overflowing in the world if you just look for it. I happen to be excellent at looking. Visual acuity's my thing—I'm an artist, remember?"

At least, she was semi-sure that she wouldn't change. Mostly positive that the abundant love all around would keep her personality from shifting. Most of all, she had to try. This was her job. Her mission. Rhys ought to understand that.

"Fine. *I* don't want you to be without them." He carefully placed his big, warm hand across her chest. "In your heart."

"Neither do I. It pains me more than I can say to give up their memory, but, after all, the fate of the world depends on it." Maisy cocked her head. Mustered a wan smile. "Sound familiar to you?"

Without waiting for a response, she spun on one heel and returned to the Gates. "I agree to your terms. All memories of my parents in exchange for the Key."

Lilith slowly licked her lips. Lifted her chin and tilted her head the tiniest bit to the side. "My, you are a brave one. I was right. I *do* like you."

The nerve! Maisy didn't want approbation from the torturer about to inflict such pain on her—even if she would never remember it. Mustering as much ice to her tone as was possible surrounded by the fiery pits of Hell, she said, "Forgive me for not reciprocating the compliment. My parents are the ones who taught me to be polite, so I'm just skipping ahead sixty seconds."

Lilith extended her hand through the Gates. "Clasp my hand, and the memory exchange will be done."

"Hang on." Maisy took a deep breath. Frantically tried to cycle through to her favorite memory. Christmas? Birthdays?

Trips to the zoo? Then it came to her. Being tucked in at night. The feeling of pure safety and love as her mom and dad kissed her cheek.

Swallowing hard, she reached out with her left hand.

"Don't try to pull anything, witch," Rhys growled. Just before she touched Lilith, he lunged to grab her wrist *and* Lilith's.

In the blink of an eye, Lilith disappeared.

Maisy was holding the Key.

The Gates solidified, stretching as far as she could see on both sides. Volac howled his displeasure in a haunting shriek that echoed off the walls.

And in the next blink, she was awake. Back in the chair in the Watchtower. Staring at Zavier and Gideon, with the Key still clutched tight in her right hand. Gideon had his hand on her open mouth, an empty vial in his other hand.

She swallowed. "Tastes like chocolate."

"Seemed like the best flavor incentive to pull you out of a coma. Zavier argued for chili cheese fries-flavored, but I stuck with gender lines and chocolate."

The taciturn-but-sweet dark-haired man sniffed. "I did no such thing." And as he removed it, Maisy realized his hand had been gently cradling the back of her head. Guess bringing her back had been a team effort.

"I'm really here? Awake? Out of Hell?" Searching for reassurance, her gaze pinged around the room. There were at least two hundred completed gift baskets lined up on the tables. Ah. There was her *Nephilim*. Sprawled on the floor, weirdly enough. With a head-shaped dent in the wall behind him. Liss knelt at his side, helping him sit up.

Zavier tracked her gaze. "I pushed him out of the way so Gideon could administer the counter potion. He was...hovering."

"Literally, I'll bet."

Rhys stiffly pushed up to his feet. "You're really back, sunshine. You did it."

But before he could close in on her with the kiss she could practically taste and definitely deserved, a fifth figure moved out of the opposite corner.

Older, with a sort of dad vibe about him. Longish silver hair that made her think of a surfer, just as tall as the others, but with eyes that shone like sunlight from his pupils. And—super weirdly—dressed in a belted tunic and breeches combo that made her think of Jedi Knights.

"Congratulations, Gate Keeper."

Oh, geez. "If this is another surprise test, I'm going to kick someone in the balls. It's been a *day*."

"This is Master Caraxis. The angel in charge of training *Nephilim*." Gideon's voice was so tight that the words almost came out with a clipped British accent. "He showed up right after you two lit out."

Rhys crossed his arms. Jutted his chin. "We've been trying to contact you for ten days, and you wait until we're completely out of touch, in Hell, to respond?"

"If you imagine that to be a coincidence, you've lost your touch," the older man said drily. "Ask your questions. I've come to provide answers. It is time."

Maisy had *many* questions. Rhys beat her to the punch, though. Which was fine, because Gideon had called the man an *actual* angel. Like Elohiala, but without the halo and the full-body glow. She was probably too worked up to be as polite as one should be when conversing with a heavenly being.

"Why did you keep us in the dark about the Keeper transition?" Rhys's voice thundered through the room.

His volume didn't seem to bother Caraxis. "It is the way it must unfold."

Rhys slapped a hand against the counter. "Why'd you bother to wing here if you're just going to mouth such useless bullshit?"

Hmm. Guess you didn't have to be super respectful to celestial beings after all...

Caraxis spread his hands, palms up, gesturing first to Maisy and then Rhys. "The bond between a Keeper and their *Nephilim* can't be forced. If it was explained, at least one of you would no doubt have pushed against it. It must unfold naturally. Facing unknown challenges together helps that process. Helps you bring out the best in each other. Helps you to discover the best about each other."

Maisy thought about how much Rhys had irritated her the first time they met. *And* the second. *And* the time after that. Yeah, if she'd been told they "had" to like each other to save the world? She would've walked away. Given up right then and there at the impossibility of it all.

Zavier looked back and forth between them. A sharp chortle burst from his lips. "You mean Rhys and Maisy had to fall for each other in order for her to fully become Keeper?"

"Yes."

Gideon bent down to stage-whisper in her ear. "Good thing Rhys volunteered that first day. Zavier's got about seven dark sides too many to have a woman go head over heels for him."

The black glare Zavier aimed at his friend would've sent any human man into the fetal position. "I wouldn't want it. Or agree to it."

"It was never meant as a role for Zavier Carranza. Only Rhys Boyce felt the energy in his wrist to find the Keeper once she was blood activated." Caraxis lifted an eyebrow. "Am I right?"

Gideon casually slid his hand over her wrist. Not so casually that she couldn't tell he was checking her pulse. "Anytime he asks that, he already knows he's right. He's just rubbing it in. Yeah, Rhys was the only one with the energy blip in his wrist." He squeezed her shoulder. "You okay, Keeper?"

Maisy felt...mostly fine. Coming down from a massive adrenaline surge, to be sure. But no residual coma hangover or anything. And she could do with about a solid week of peace, quiet, and naked cuddling with Rhys.

He, however, had his legs spread wide and fists balled, apparently on the brink of beating up an angel. "You're saying we have no choice?"

"Not at all. Free will is sacrosanct. You know that." Caraxis clasped his hands at his waist. Stared down at them. "There have been pairings between a Keeper and their *Nephilim* that did not work out. With regrettable consequences."

Zavier's head jerked up. "The Gates *opened*?"

"Yes. More than once. We have always managed to close them, but not without great loss."

"How have we never heard of that?"

"Many secrets are kept above, below, and here on Earth," he said with...omigosh, was that a know-it-all smirk? Angel or not, Caraxis had to realize that Rhys was a lit fuse about to go off. Liss had her arm around his shoulders, but it was a futile gesture if her *Nephilim* decided to attack the angel.

All that wishy-washy mumbo-jumbo that Maisy had expected from a supernatural creature really wasn't worth wasting their time. So she'd take over.

Maisy stood. Both Zavier and Gideon instantly provided support under her elbows. Sweet, but not who she wanted. And ooh, those first few steps were as wobbly as if she'd just run a marathon. Luckily, Rhys sprang to her side. Which was all she'd wanted.

Hand firmly clasped in his, she faced off with the angel. "Is my lifespan extended now that I'm Keeper?"

"Yes."

Nice. That went into the *this could work* column for her and Rhys staying together. "Is there someone who can teach me to use my power?"

"The previous Keeper will have left you instructions. Explanations. If not, you may have Rhys contact me. I will answer with alacrity next time, I promise." Another smirk.

Maisy did *not* like this angel. Or at least didn't like his attitude. No wonder the guys had ditched the Order. She wanted to wrap this up quickly and get him out of here.

Squaring her shoulders—this was the hard one—she asked, "Was my uncle murdered?"

His silver hair swooshed forward to hide his face as Caraxis nodded. "We believe it probable. His *Nephilim* Watcher, Chazaqiel, as well."

His oddly formal speech pattern didn't blunt the sting of his words. Damn it. Anger fired through her at the unfairness of it. Just as quickly followed by the equally burning need for justice. "Do you know by whom?"

"No."

Ah, a little elaboration? The man worked for the good guys. Shouldn't they be figuring out why and how his life was cut short? "Do you plan to do anything about it?"

"No. The *Right and Holy Seraphic Order of the Nephilim* is not a detective agency." Caraxis waved languidly at the others. "You are welcome to investigate. We would be most…interested in your findings."

"Yeah." Gideon spun what had been Maisy's chair around and straddled it backward. "We're aware you prefer us doing the dirty work and sending you the write-ups."

The outline of Caraxis's wings became visible. Not a color so much as a shadow of an outline. "You are compensated for your work, Gideon Durand. Do not forget this was the choice you made when you left us."

"A choice I've never regretted. Don't *you* forget it."

A simmering tension filled the room. Maisy realized there were decades of history between them that no doubt complicated every exchange.

She didn't care.

She'd survived Hell today. She didn't want any more trouble. And her *Nephilim*, all with furrowed brows, looked more than ready to start some with their former trainer. Probably for very good reasons.

"You know what? I think we're good for now. If more questions come to mind, we'll make a list. Email it over."

"Congratulations on your ascension, Gate Keeper. We were... concerned when the previous Keeper made the unusual choice to promote you rather than his son. There was no certainty that you would have the strength and goodness of heart to ascend. We are pleased that all has fallen into place with you and Rhys Boyce." Caraxis bowed to her. Pretty much cold-shouldered the others as he walked to the edge of Niagara and launched into the air.

She let her entire body sag against Rhys. "I hope he doesn't get an auto-invite to your parties."

"More like an automatic blackball from parties."

"*If* we threw them. Which we don't," Zavier said decisively. Like it was an argument he'd won. Repeatedly.

She could see how men without a circle of friends wouldn't realize what a stress reliever a party could be. Well, she'd fix that. They had a nice yard. Maybe ease in with a barbecue to thank everyone who'd helped them on this quest. What did a *mandragora* eat, anyway?

Liss rushed over and gave her, as promised, an epic hug. "I always believed you could do it."

"I know."

"But I was pretty terrified, anyway. The Tripadvisor ratings for Hell are horrific."

"Are there really—"

Liss nodded vociferously. "Yes. I kid you not. You should add one. Later. When you're rested."

Maisy threw her arms around Zavier, then bent and did the same to Gideon. "Thank you for bringing me back."

"Not much of a choice." Gideon kissed both of her cheeks in a very European way that almost made her giggle at its sweetness. "Rhys would've killed us otherwise. Had to be a guaranteed round trip."

"Aww, I didn't even bring you a souvenir."

Rhys put his arm around her, not-so-subtly pulling her away from Gideon. "Trust me, the tale we'll tell will entertain them far more than a *Wish You Were In Hell* T-shirt."

"I do have this." Maisy waved the Key. It matched the one in her recurring dreams, the one that she'd painted. Which was different from the toned-down version she'd originally touched in the lawyer's office. This Key was a little *more* of everything: heft, length, curlicues, sheen, and color. It was as if it'd needed its power and its Keeper restored before it could show its true form.

Zavier took it from her. "Heavy. A little warm."

"That's probably from being down Lilith's cleavage."

Gideon crossed his arms over the back of the chair and leaned his chin on his wrists. "Go on..."

Rhys kicked at the chair's leg. "Not now. Give Maisy some time to recover. A few hours, at least. Then we'll fill you in."

It was like he'd read her mind. She knew the guys deserved the full story. She just wasn't up to it quite yet. "I *would* very much like a shower. Rinse all this Hell smoke and dust off, even if it's only on the soul version of me."

"I've got a better idea." Rhys pointed at Zavier. "Z, will you lock up that Key? Now that the Transition's complete, I don't expect anyone to come after it, but..."

"Yeah. Better not to take the chance. I'm on it."

"We'll be back." He lifted Maisy in his arms—that'd never get old—and flew straight at the waterfall.

"For the record, I don't care where we go, as long as it isn't back to Hell."

"How's Italy?"

"Very funny." And then they were through the waterfall. A lush green forest surrounded it on three sides. Rhys stayed close enough that mist from the falls dotted their skin. "Where are we?"

"Italy. Marmore Falls." He tilted his head quizzically. "I don't know why you find it funny. I took you to Greece a few days ago."

"That's right. It's kind of a blur, to be honest. Italy, really? Wow." They were up at the top of the waterfall now. A long serpentine stretch of green river below. Above, the sky was barely beginning to purple. A crescent moon hung just above the horizon. "Aren't you worried about being seen?"

"No. The park closes at dusk."

They'd left for Hell right after breakfast. It didn't seem as if they'd been gone for more than an hour. Even with the six-hour time difference… "How is it dusk already?"

"Time is more of a fluid concept in the Underworld. You never know how much has elapsed until you get back. Plus, you were painting in that hallway a lot longer than you realized."

"Oh."

"Hang on tight," he warned with a wicked grin. Then Rhys folded his wings and dove straight down the face of the waterfall.

It was drenching and exhilarating and exactly what Maisy needed. They landed in a little grotto full of ferns and moss. To the side was a narrow, offshoot trickle of a falls. Laughing, she asked, "Can we do that again?"

"Of course. As often as you like. I just want to tell you something first."

Since when did her strong, silent type of a boyfriend want to *talk* first? "Uh-oh. Gotta say, I've had my limit of surprises for the day."

"It can wait." With an unexpectedly boyish grin, Rhys stroked her cheekbone. "It's a good one, though."

"Okay." Honestly, she didn't care. They were in *Italy*. The world was safe. Maisy leaned back, sinking her fingertips into the spongy moss. "I'm ready."

"I think I'm in love with you."

Her fingers slid on the dampness, and she would've fallen onto her back if Rhys hadn't grabbed her.

Or, you know, she'd almost fallen over because he'd shocked all basic reflexes out of her with his statement. Maisy blinked up at him. "You *think*?"

"I don't have any experience one way or the other to be certain. The fact that it feels different than anything else is a huge clue. I wanted to tell you last night, but I didn't want to stir up anything too..." He trailed off, then rubbed at his forehead. "We barely talked about *after*. I couldn't weigh you down with something more until after you finished the Transition."

"Love isn't a burden. It's more like a hot-air balloon for your heart. Or—to put it in terms you're familiar with—wings." She reached around to stroke his silky feathers. "It gives your heart wings."

Rhys nodded sharply. "Then I'm certain. That's what it feels like." He resettled her, propping her against the craggy rock wall. "It's important that you know I felt that way *before*. Because seeing what you did—making that sacrifice—that would've made any man or woman watching lose their heart to you."

Nope. She wouldn't let him think that for a second. "You get the credit, actually."

"I tried to talk you out of it. I was selfish. I didn't want to see you hurt."

Which was unselfishness, but she'd explain the finer points of love to him later. It'd be a learning process. "You gave me the strength to make the decision. To make the deal with Lilith that I can't remember."

"How did I—" He circled his hands in the air, those perfectly sculpted lips hanging agape.

"You talked, from the start, as though you'd given up on humans. But your repeated actions to save them, to save me, prove that you still have hope in your heart. Despite all the evil you've seen and battled. You think we're worth the effort. So I leaned on that to make my own leap of faith."

He sat back on his heels, his wings puddling across the dirt. "That's humbling. I'm grateful to hear that I helped you when I felt so damn help*less* standing next to you."

It was time to ask the question that had her holding her breath. "What did I sacrifice?"

"You agreed to give up the memories of your parents."

Maisy blinked. Thought hard. Came up with...nothing. Obviously she had a mother and father, but that biological fact was all she had. "If that was enough of a sacrifice for Lilith, they must've been great memories. Oh—*memories*. They must be dead, too. I should be sad, shouldn't I?"

"No." And even in the shadowy cave, she could see the glint in his blue eyes. "Because I tricked her."

"You tricked a Hell creature...*in* Hell? Will your wings get taken away for being that devious?"

He mimed locking her lips and tossing away the key. "Not if you keep the secret."

"What did you do?"

"Right before you touched her, I grabbed both your wrists. That allowed me to link into the memory transfer that Lilith did. I redirected some of the energy from it, like a faint copy of the memories, into your evil eye protection bracelet."

"Like when you redirected my pain after the *eye-killer* attack?"

He wavered a hand back and forth. "Close enough."

Even without knowing how any of it worked, it seemed brilliant. "Because what could be stronger protection than love? It'll charge it up even more."

"The memories won't be as vivid as your original ones," he warned. "And we'll need to figure out how to unlock them. I knew it was possible, but I can't remember how to undo them. It may take a little while, or it could take decades, but—"

"But that's what you and I do. We find things. Together. Thank you so much, Rhys." Maisy crawled forward, uncaring of the rocks biting through her leggings. She tapped a finger right over his heart. "This all proves that you've got faith in love. That you believe it makes a difference." She grinned. "That you finally listened to me."

"I'm still listening," he said pointedly. Drummed his fingers on his thighs.

"What...oh!" She gasped with a dramatic clutch of her chest. This would be *fun*. "Did you want to know if *I'm* in love with *you*?"

"Were you possessed by a demon while we were down there? Because my sunshine would never make me wait to hear something good."

"Hmm. They do say that couples grow to be like each other." She scowled. Scrunched up her face so tight that it hurt. "Maybe I've picked up your disgruntled reticence."

"You *are* possessed." Rhys yanked her to his chest. Walked to the edge of the grotto. "Guess I'm going to have to go old-school. Dunk you in the river to drown the demon out."

"Yikes. You're too new at this to be teased, clearly. Message received."

The sway of his wings stilled. His expression hardened. He didn't even blink. "Not the message I want."

So serious. Well, it was probably a good thing that he was now as serious about love as he was about battles and demons.

Maisy couldn't keep him in suspense any longer. Not when she'd been bursting with the possibility of the idea ever since he took her to bed the first time. "I think I love you, too, Rhys. I think, in fact, that I'm fairly certain about it."

"So will you not just keep the Key but keep me, too?"

No wonder Uncle Harold had told her to trust her heart. Logic and common sense would say that this hardened warrior was all wrong for her.

Maisy, however, knew that Rhys was *perfect* for her. "Yes."

She wanted to say more, but he was kissing her. The whole picture-is-worth-a-thousand-words thing (which, as an artist, she highly endorsed)? Rhys's kisses said a hundred thousand words.

They'd get to the actual words later. Because it turned out they had time. The world, actually, was *not* going to end.

At least not for the rest of this week.

ACKNOWLEDGMENTS

I spent a solid ten years pleading with agents and editors to let me write a paranormal romance. Every time, I was told that the market was dead. Until the wonderful Liz Pelletier let me pursue my dream and I'm ever so grateful. Getting this series out into the world is extraordinarily satisfying to me, having spent so many years devouring PNR romances by Karen Marie Moning, Kelley Armstrong, P.C. Cast, Richelle Mead, Chloe Neill, MaryJanice Davidson and Jessica Andersen (and if you haven't read them, I'm spreading the love and telling you to go check them out!). I suppose I should credit my fascination with the subject going all the way back to the *D'Aulaires' Book of Greek Myths* I read and re-read a zillion times (more to come in that vein in the next book HELL OF AN ANGEL #spoiler).

Thanks to Heather Howland for her patience and persistence in editing this book. Thanks to M.C. Vaughan for reading it to make sure I had the right balance of paranormal and romance– an author worries! Please know that I do not and can not so much as doodle, so any painting-related-mistakes Maisy might have made are wholly mine. I'm beyond thrilled that all of you wonderful readers took a chance on this book and my *Nephilim*— thank you!

ENTANGLED
BRINGS THE
Laughs

THE HOOKUP DILEMMA

Rashida and Elliott's lives get turned upside down when they find themselves on opposite sides of an ongoing fight.

BACK IN THE BURBS

Two powerhouse authors bring you a hilarious tale of one woman's journey to find herself again, and remind us - when life gives you lemons...add vodka.

APRIL MAY FALL

April is a social influencer who shows moms how to stay calm and collected with yoga. But then a live video of the "always calm" mom -being anything but- goes viral...

ENTANGLED
BRINGS THE
Heat

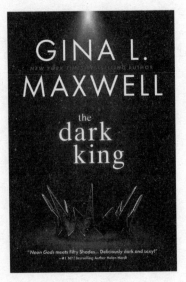

THE DARK KING

NY Times bestselling author Gina L. Maxwell is back with the first in the Deviant Kings series set in a modern world but with a dark, erotic fantasy twist perfect for fans of *Neon Gods*.

FOLLOW ME DARKLY

One chance encounter is all it took for Skye to find herself in the middle of a Cinderella story... but self-made billionaire Braden Black is no Prince Charming, and his dark desires are far from his only secret.

FETISH

Step into a world of secret appetites with this enticing collection. From achingly tender to utterly carnal, these stories will stir—and thoroughly satisfy—every dark, hungry craving...

ENTANGLED
BRINGS THE
Heart

CONFESSIONS IN B-FLAT

Essence bestselling author Donna Hill brings us an emotional love story set against the powerful backdrop of the civil rights movement that gripped a nation—a story as timely as it is timeless...

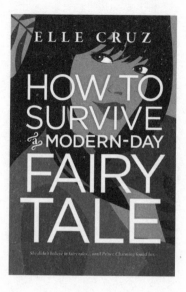

How to Survive a Modern-Day Fairy Tale

Bookworm Clarie may wish she had a fairy godmother, but in the twenty-first century she knows the only way to get her happily ever after is by letting her heart be her guide...

The Things We Leave Unfinished

Told in alternating timelines, *The Things We Leave Unfinished* examines the risks we take for love, the scars too deep to heal, and the endings we can't bring ourselves to see coming.